Peter May was born and raised in Scotland. He was an award-winning journalist at the age of twenty-one and a published novelist at twenty-six. When his first book was adapted as a major drama series for the BBC, he quit journalism and during the high-octane fifteen years that followed, became one of Scotland's most successful television dramatists. He created three prime-time drama series, presided over two of the highest-rated serials in his homeland as script editor and producer, and worked on more than 1,000 episodes of ratings-topping drama before deciding to leave television to return to his first love, writing novels.

His passion for detailed research for his books has taken him behind the closed doors of the Chinese Police force, to the kitchen of a three-star Michelin chef, and down the Paris catacombs; he has worked as an online private detective, was inducted as a Chevalier of the Grand Order of Gaillac wines and earned honorary membership of the Chinese Crime Writers' Association.

He has won several literature awards in France and received the USA's Barry Award for *The Blackhouse*, the first in his internationally bestselling Lewis Trilogy, and the ITV Crime Thriller Awards Book Club Best Read for *Entry Island*.

He now lives in south-west France with his wife, writer Janice Hally.

BY PETER MAY

The Enzo Files

Extraordinary People
The Critic
Blacklight Blue
Freeze Frame
Blowback

The China Thrillers

The Firemaker
The Fourth Sacrifice
The Killing Room
Snakehead
The Runner
Chinese Whispers

The Lewis Trilogy

The Blackhouse
The Lewis Man
The Chessmen

Standalone Novels

Entry Island
Runaway
Coffin Road

Non-fiction

Hebrides with David Wilson

PETER MAY

THE
FOURTH
SACRIFICE

riverrun

First published in Great Britain in 2000 by Coronet Books
This paperback edition published in 2016 by

riverrun
an imprint of
Quercus Editions Ltd
Carmelite House
50 Victoria Embankment
London EC4Y 0DZ

An Hachette UK company

A CIP catalogue record for this book is available
from the British Library

ISBN 978 1 78429 269 0
EBOOK ISBN 978 1 78087 957 4

10 9 8 7 6 5

Typeset by CC Book Production

Printed and bound in Great Britain by Clays Ltd, St Ives plc

For Carol

PROLOGUE

By now he knows he is going to die. And he feels something like relief. No more long, lonely nights and tortured dreams. He can release all those dark feelings that he has carried through life like some great weight strapped to his back, causing him to stoop and stagger and bend at the knees. Still this knowledge, that death is close enough almost to touch, is not without fear. But the fear has retreated with the effects of the drug, and lurks somewhere just beyond consciousness.

He is only vaguely aware of those things around him that have been so familiar these last months: the scarred and naked walls, the rusted window frames, the washing hanging out to dry in the glassed-in balcony beyond the screen door. There is still a smell of stale cooking in the air, and sometimes the occasional hint of raw sewage that rises from the drains in the street four floors below, especially when it rains, like now. He hears the rain pattering on the windowpanes, blurring the lights of the apartment block opposite, like the tears that he can feel, warm and salty, on his cheeks. Only now does he succumb to an overwhelming sense of sadness. What futility! His life, the lives of his parents, and of their parents before them. What did any of them mean? What point had there been?

Now he feels rough hands forcing him to his knees, and a cord is passed over his head, a flash of red characters on white card as it drops to hang around his neck. Now his hands are drawn behind his back, and he feels the soft, familiar texture of silk as it tightens around his wrists, grazing and bruising. He would have been gentler with it. Despite the best efforts of the drug, his fear is re-emerging now, rising in his throat like bile. He sees a flash of light on dark, dull metal and a hand pushes his head forward and down. No point in resistance. No point in anything, not even regret. And yet it is there, big and scary and casting a shadow in his consciousness, fighting for space alongside his fear.

He is aware of the figure on his right, and he sees the shadow of the rising blade trace its pattern across the pale linoleum. He swallows and wonders if he will feel any pain. How good is his executioner? And then, fleetingly, he wonders if the brain ceases the instant the head is severed. He hears the swish of the blade and has a sharp intake of breath.

No, there is no pain, he realises, as for a moment, before blackness, the room spins crazily and he sees the twin jets of blood spewing from the strange apparition of his own headless body as it topples forward. But he will never be able to tell anyone. So many things he will never be able to tell.

CHAPTER ONE

I

The rain fell like tears from a leaden Beijing sky. Ironic, Margaret thought, for hers had long since dried up. From the shelter of her balcony on the sixth floor she could see, across the treetops in the park opposite, the dull reflection of a tiny pavilion in the rain-spotted lake. Above the rumble of traffic, and the mournful banter of furriers in the street below, she could hear the wail of a single-stringed violin and the sad cadences of a woman's voice breathing passion into a song from the Peking Opera.

Margaret moved back into her hotel room and slipped a light coat over her blouse and jeans. She had told herself she had chosen this hotel because of its proximity to the American Embassy. It was nothing to do with the park across the road. That's what she had told herself. But Ritan Park was her last connection to him. A place where the death of a man had first brought them together and, in the end, forced them apart. Just one more failure in a life that seemed destined always to let her down. She lifted her umbrella and closed the door firmly behind her, resolved finally to act on a decision she had delayed for too long.

On the fourth floor, an elderly woman with brassy lacquered hair and too much make-up stepped on to the elevator. Margaret saw that she was wearing a name badge on the lapel of her blue suit jacket. Dot McKinlay, it read. Margaret registered some surprise. Mostly the Ritan Hotel was filled with the wealthy but unsophisticated wives of Russian traders, desperate to spend their roubles before the exchange rate fell any further. The woman drew painted lips back across long, slightly yellowed teeth in what she clearly imagined was a smile.

'Where y'awl from?' she drawled.

Margaret's heart sank. 'The sixth floor,' she said, keeping her eyes firmly fixed on the illuminated numbers above the door, willing them to descend more quickly.

But Dot just laughed, heartily, as if she had enjoyed the joke. 'Ah do like a sense of humour,' she said. 'Y'awl from the north, that's for sure. We're from the south. Louisiana. Only thing further south than us is the Gulf of Mexico.' She laughed again, as if demonstrating that southerners could be just as amusing as northerners. 'Ol' Dot's Travellin' Grannies, that's what they call us. We been all over. Just our luck to choose China during the rice crisis. Don't you just get sick of those noodles?' She leaned in confidentially. 'And if Ah'd known this hotel was gonna be so full of goddamn Ruskies, Ah'd 'a booked us in somewheres else.' She nodded emphatically. 'But it's great to know there's a fellow American on board. Even if ya do come from the sixth floor.' She grinned. 'Why don't y'awl join us for a drink tonight?'

Margaret glanced at her. 'I'm afraid that won't be possible,' she said. 'I'm leaving tomorrow.'

The doors opened on the ground floor as Dot was about to express her disappointment, and Margaret hurried away past a group of a dozen or so elderly ladies all sporting name badges. She heard Dot greeting them with, 'Hey, you'll never guess who that was . . .'

No, Margaret thought as she pushed through glass doors and out into the sticky, warm rain, they never would. Not in a million years. The two security men at the gate glowered at her as she opened her umbrella on the way out. It was only in the last couple of weeks that Western newsmen had stopped hanging about the gate in the hope of getting photographs or an interview. The security guards in their brown uniforms, privately hired by the hotel, had been forced to take their duties seriously, instead of sitting around all day smoking and looking important. They didn't much like Margaret.

She ran the gauntlet of some half-hearted stall owners who thought she might be Russian and interested in the furs that hung row upon row under dripping canopies. But most of them knew her by now and didn't give her a second glance, sitting folded up on tiny stools, nursing jars of cold green tea, smoking acrid-smelling cigarettes and spitting noisily on the sidewalk. Everywhere you looked here, the names of shops and restaurants were written in the distinctive Cyrillic Russian alphabet. You could almost believe you were in some seedy corner of Moscow, if it wasn't for the Chinese faces. Someone had lit a brazier, in preparation for an early lunch, and smoke mingled with the mist and rain. Margaret almost stepped into the path of several bicycles, alerted only at the last moment by a flurry of bells. Oriental faces glared at her from glistening hooded capes. She grasped the railing at the edge of the pavement and held tightly, overcome by a moment of giddiness. She breathed deeply and steadied herself. She had not realised until now just how stressful this was going to be.

To delay the moment, she took the route through the park, although she would have denied, if asked, that she was procrastinating. But she knew immediately it was a mistake. The place was too full of memories and regrets. She hurried past small damp groups of people practising *tai ch'i* under the trees, and out through the south gate. Again she took a circuitous route, along Guanghua Road and down Silk Street, past the new visa block in the Bruce Compound of the American Embassy. Women in white masks and blue smocks swept wet leaves from the gutters with old-fashioned brooms. Dismal marketeers sat under the shelter of trees opposite their empty stalls, tourists kept away by the rain.

A young woman with cropped hair approached Margaret hopefully. 'CD lom?' she said. 'CD music? Looka, looka, I have new ones.'

Margaret shook her head and hurried by. A very thin young man in a dark suit and white shirt with no tie approached. 'Shanja dollah?'

'No!' Margaret snapped at him, and stepped briskly away

along Xiushuibie Street. There was no point in delaying any further. Past the Consular Section of the Bulgarian Embassy, the US Commercial Section, she stopped outside the gate of *San Ban*, No. 3 Building of the American Embassy. The Chancery. She pushed open the door of the gatehouse and found herself facing a scowling Chinese security guard.

'Margaret Campbell,' she said. 'I have an appointment with the ambassador.'

An unsmiling marine in dress uniform watched her from behind the glass booth just inside the front door of the Chancery. A young Asian woman appeared at the door to her left and it clicked open to the accompaniment of a long electronic buzz. She smiled at Margaret. 'Come on through,' she said. Margaret entered and heard the door shut behind her as the woman held out her hand. 'Hi. I'm Sophie Daum. I'll be looking after you for the next while.'

'Will you?' Margaret looked at her suspiciously. Small, short dark hair, beautifully slanted eyes, sharp but not unattractive features, she barely looked old enough to be out of high school. 'What happened to the Regional Security Officer?'

'Oh, Jon Dakers is pretty well tied up these days. I'm the new assistant RSO.'

'You don't have a very oriental name for a Chinese-American.'

'Vietnamese-American,' Sophie corrected her. 'And I was adopted by a very old-fashioned, old-money family from California.' She led Margaret up a flight of stairs lined with pictures of previous ambassadors to China. 'I guess you probably think I look too young for the job. Everybody does.' She was trying to sound bright, but Margaret detected more than a hint of weariness in her voice.

'Not at all,' she said. 'You look at least old enough to be in the second grade.' She glanced across at the girl and saw that her smile had frozen on her face, and she immediately regretted the jibe. 'I'm sorry. You caught me on a bad day.'

Sophie stopped and turned on the stair. 'Look, Dr Campbell,' she said, the smile gone, the eyes suddenly cold and hard. 'I'm being polite here. But I'm twenty-three years old. I got a degree in criminology, and I'm straight off the security staff of the Secretary for Defense. I got a black belt in *tai kwondo*, and I could kick your ass all the way down the stairs. I don't need your bad days, I got enough of my own.'

'Hey,' Margaret held up her hands. 'I believe you. Sounds like you've got enough bad days to make up a whole week. PMS can be a real bitch.'

And to her surprise, Sophie's face broke into a reluctant grin. 'Yeah, OK, maybe I got that coming. But it's PCS I'm suffering from, not PMS. Post China stress. You know? I've been here a month and all I've heard is I don't look old enough to be out of high school. It's bad enough when I get it from the guys without the women turning on me, too.'

'And how many of the guys have you threatened to kick down the stairs?'

'Oh, just you,' Sophie said breezily.

'I'll take that as a compliment.'

Sophie grinned, a rapport established, and opened French

doors into the ambassador's outer office. To their right, the secretary to the Deputy Chief of Mission was talking on the telephone. To their left, the ambassador's secretary's desk was empty. She was just emerging from the inner sanctum.

'Oh, hi.' She held the door open. 'Go straight on through. The ambassador's expecting you.'

Margaret followed Sophie into the carpeted hush of the ambassador's office. It was a big room – high ceilings, tall windows, a large polished desk facing the door, the US flag hanging limply from a pole behind it. Margaret had been in here several times, but it still intrigued her. The walls were lined with photographs of the ambassador with the president and his family. It was said they were close friends whose friendship predated politics. There was a picture of the president at his inauguration, smiling to the heavens, an appetite whetted by the prospect of supreme power. Something to be savoured and enjoyed.

To the left was a sofa and several armchairs around a coffee table, pictures loaned from some US art gallery on the walls, Chinese chests lined up as filing cabinets. The ambassador, in shirtsleeves, and another, younger, man wearing an immaculately tailored dark blue suit, rose to greet them.

'Margaret,' the ambassador nodded curtly. He was an attractive, dark-haired man. A senator for nearly twenty years, he clearly felt more at home in the rarefied atmosphere of high politics than at this, more mundane, level of real life. 'I think you know First Secretary Stan Palmer.'

'Sure,' Margaret said, and they all shook hands and sat

down. The First Secretary poured them coffee from a tray that had just been brought in.

The ambassador sat back and cast his eye curiously over Margaret. She looked tired, older than her thirty-one years, her pale blue eyes strained and dull, fair hair falling listlessly over her shoulders in big sad waves. 'So,' he said. 'You've reached a decision.'

Margaret nodded. 'I want to go home, Mr Ambassador.'

'When?'

'Tomorrow.'

'That's very sudden, isn't it?'

'It's been on my mind for some time.'

The First Secretary leaned forward. 'Have you told the Chinese?' His tone was sniffy, almost superior.

Margaret hesitated. 'I was hoping you would do that.'

The ambassador frowned. 'Why? Is there a problem?'

Margaret shook her head. 'No, I . . . I've just had enough. I just want to go home.'

'You could have gone home ten weeks ago. You know that.' The ambassador's tone was faintly accusatory. 'After we secured your release.'

'Sure.' Margaret nodded. 'It was my decision to stay on and co-operate with them. I thought it was the right thing to do at the time. I still do. But I spend night after night sitting alone in a hotel room watching CNN, and day after day being debriefed on the same old stuff. I'm tired of it. I didn't think it would go on this long.' She paused, a horrible thought occurring to her for the first time. 'I *am* free to go, aren't I?'

'As far as I'm concerned, you are.' The ambassador leaned over and put a reassuring hand on her arm. 'You've done more than your fair share, Margaret. More than they had any right to expect.' He turned to the First Secretary. 'Stan'll tell the Chinese, won't you, Stan?'

'Of course, Mr Ambassador.'

But Stan was none too pleased, a fact betrayed by his demeanour as they descended the stairs. He didn't like playing messenger boy. He ignored Sophie as if she wasn't there – she was clearly an irrelevance – and addressed himself to Margaret. 'So . . .' he said, 'the charges have been dropped against your Chinese policeman.' He ran a hand back through thinning but perfectly groomed blond hair.

'Have they?' Margaret feigned indifference.

'Didn't you know?' Stan feigned surprise.

'For a start,' Margaret said, tetchily, 'he's not *my* Chinese policeman. And the authorities have told me nothing.'

'So you haven't had any contact with him?'

'No, I haven't. Nor do I intend to.' In spite of herself she couldn't keep the hurt and anger out of her voice.

Stan was quick to capitalise. 'Really? You surprise me.' He smiled. 'I'd heard that you and he were . . . well, how shall I put it? Close.'

'Had you? I'm surprised that a man in your position would waste his time listening to gossip like that – never mind give it credence.'

'Ah, well, that's where you're wrong, Margaret.' Stan was

so smooth he positively shone. 'Gossip is the lifeblood of the embassy. I mean, without it how else would we know what was going on? After all, diplomats and politicians never tell one another the truth, now, do they?' He shook her hand. 'Have a good trip home.' And he disappeared into the hushed interior of the building.

'Prick,' Sophie muttered.

'Oh, you noticed?' Margaret grinned ruefully. 'If I'd had your talent for kicking ass I'd have practised it on him.'

'Yeah, well he's pretty high up my list of ass-kicking priorities, too.' And they shared a moment of juvenile amusement – for Margaret a brief release, a breath of fresh air after weeks, months, of relentless intensity.

The marine pressed a button and the door clicked open. Sophie followed Margaret out on to the steps. 'Listen,' she said. 'What are you doing tonight?'

'You mean apart from packing and watching CNN?'

'Yeah, apart from that.'

'Not much. But you know, I'd probably have to consult my social calendar to know for sure. Why?'

'There's a reception on at the ambassador's residence for Michael Zimmerman.'

'Who?'

Sophie pulled a face. 'Aw, come on, you're kidding, right?' Margaret shook her head. Sophie said, 'You don't know who Michael Zimmerman is?'

Margaret continued shaking her head. 'Keeping asking won't change that.'

'Where have you been for the last five years? Don't you ever watch television I mean, other than the news?'

'Not in a very long time, Sophie.' And Margaret couldn't remember the last time she had watched anything but CNN in a Chinese hotel room. 'So who is he?'

'Only the most sexy man alive – at least, according to a poll of *Cosmopolitan* readers.'

'I thought that was George Clooney.'

Sophie shook her head. 'You *are* out of date.' The rain had stopped and they walked slowly to the gatehouse. 'Michael Zimmerman's an archaeologist.'

'An archaeologist?' Margaret was taken aback. 'That doesn't sound very sexy to me. What is he, real life's answer to Indiana Jones?'

Sophie smiled dreamily. 'Well, not far off it. He's made a whole bunch of documentary series for NBC on great arch-aeological finds around the world. He gets better ratings than the top cop shows.'

Margaret looked sceptical. 'The great American public finally discovers culture. So, what's his secret?'

Sophie shrugged. 'There's something about him . . . I don't know, he just brings the whole thing to life.' She paused, giving it serious thought for a moment. 'Plus, he's got a great ass.'

Margaret nodded seriously. 'Well, when it comes to cul-ture, that definitely helps.' She went into the guardhouse and retrieved her purse and umbrella and stepped out on to the sidewalk. Sophie walked out after her. Margaret said, 'So why's the ambassador holding a reception for him?'

'It's a pre-production party. Shooting starts tomorrow at the Ming Tombs outside Beijing. Some new documentary series on one of China's most revered archaeologists. Some guy I never heard of. But it's a big deal here. The Chinese have been bending over backwards to facilitate the shoot, so the ambassador's just doing his bit.'

'And Zimmerman's fronting the series?'

'Yes. It's his production company that's making it.' Sophie paused. 'So do you want to come? I can get an invitation sent round to your hotel.'

Margaret thought about it for a moment. It wouldn't take her long to pack, and it wouldn't break her heart to give room service and CNN a final miss. 'Sure,' she said. 'Why not? I can run a rule over Mr Zimmerman's ass and see if it measures up.'

Margaret left Sophie at the consular section on the corner of Silk Street, grateful that the assistant RSO had had the sensitivity not to ask her the questions that everyone else she had met over the last ten weeks had asked. She pushed her way down through the narrow market lane, past great bolts of silk and racks of dressing gowns and shirts and dresses, to the six-lane Jianguomenwei Avenue that cut through the east-central city like an open wound. Here, twenty-first-century towers of glass and marble rose above the roar of traffic into the pall of pollution that hung low over the capital, and from their upturned Chinese eaves looked down on the crumbling remains of a disappearing city: the *hutongs* and *siheyuans* where street and family life bled one into the other; the real

Beijing that was in danger of being swept away on the tide of financial success generated by a new devotion to the free-market economy.

She had no plan, no real notion of where she was going or what she wanted to do, other than the certain knowledge that she did not want to return to her hotel room. There was some desire in her, some need, to drink in this city for the last time, to let it wash over her, to feel its vital, vibrant life. She realised, with a dreadful ache, that she would miss it, with all its noise and pollution and traffic, its shouting, spitting, staring people, its sights and sounds and sometimes awful smells. But then she knew, too, that none of it meant anything without the man who had steered her through it, taught her to love it.

Why had he never been in touch? There was as much anger as hurt raging inside her. Not a call, not a letter. Nothing. Despite what she had led the First Secretary to believe, she had heard about Li's release. They had told her, during one of those countless debriefings, that he had been reinstated. She had expected him to contact her. It was one of the reasons she had made no attempt to integrate with the social life of the embassy, despite umpteen invitations. Instead she had waited night after night by the phone in her hotel room for a call that never came. Once, she had phoned the offices of Section One of the Criminal Investigation Department in Dongzhimen and asked, in English, for Deputy Section Chief Li Yan. The request had caused some consternation at the other end of the line. Finally, someone speaking halting English had asked who she was, then told her that Deputy Section Chief Li was unavailable.

The No. 4 bus appeared out of the haze, and Margaret jostled with the Chinese in the queue to climb aboard and hand her five fen to the bus conductress, who scowled at her suspiciously. *Yangguizi*, foreign devils, never travelled by bus. Margaret ignored the faces turned towards her in unabashed curiosity as she clung to the overhead rail, squeezed in among all these bodies. It was extraordinary, she thought, how it was possible to feel so alone in a city of eleven million people.

She battled her way to the door and got off just past the Beijing Hotel, from where Western journalists had watched the tanks heading for their confrontation with demonstrating students in Tiananmen Square eleven years before. She crossed to the other side of East Chang'an Avenue via an underpass. This was foolish, she knew, a needless, self-inflicted pain. But still her feet carried her to the corner of Zhengyi Road, and she turned down into its tree-lined seclusion, away from the thunder of traffic on the main avenue. On her right, the compound of the Ministry of Public Security was hidden away behind a high stone wall, occupying the former home of the British Embassy. Further down, the apartment blocks provided for senior police officers rose above the still-lush green trees of early fall.

She felt sick now, and there was a lump in her throat as if something she had swallowed was stuck there. She had no difficulty identifying Li's apartment on the second floor, the three rooms he had shared with his uncle. She smiled, remembering the night they had spent there, when they might have made love but hadn't because she had drunk too much. And she remembered a cold, damp railway carriage in some anonymous siding in the north of the country where she had finally lain in his arms and they had declared their love. When they had returned to Beijing to reveal why three men had been murdered, and to clear Li of the accusations levelled against him by frightened men, he had told her to wait for him. He had told her he loved her. And she had waited. And waited.

She wiped the tears from her face and became aware of the security guard at the gate watching her curiously, this strange blonde-haired, blue-eyed *yangguizi*, standing weeping on the sidewalk, staring up at an anonymous apartment building. She turned quickly away. This was futile, stupid. It was history, and she was leaving in the morning. Her life was too full of pain for there to be any pleasure in looking back. She could only go forward.

A small, red taxi cruised slowly up the other side of the street. She called, and waved, and ran across the road. The taxi stopped and she jumped in. '*Ritan fandian*,' she told the driver, and for a moment marvelled that he knew immediately what she meant. And then straight away felt saddened. China, its language, its people, had taken a long time getting into her soul and under her skin. And now that it had, she had no further use for it.

As the taxi headed back up towards East Chang'an Avenue, a tall broad-built Chinese man with close-cropped hair wheeled a bicycle out from the apartment compound. He was wearing an open-necked white shirt tucked into dark trousers at a narrow waist. He stopped for a moment, feeling in his pockets. Then he turned to the security guard. 'You got any cigarettes, Feng?'

The security guard was uncomfortable. None of the other officers in the compound even spoke to him, never mind knew his name.

'Sure, Deputy Section Chief,' he said, taking an almost full pack from his pocket. 'Here, have it. I've got plenty.'

Li took it and smiled. 'I'll bring you a replacement on the way back tonight.'

'No need,' the guard said.

Li grinned. 'Yes there is. My uncle always told me a man with a debt is a man with a burden. See you tonight.' And he lit a cigarette and pushed off on his bike following, oblivious, in the wake of Margaret's taxi.

II

It was almost dark when Margaret passed through the security gate of *Yi Ban*, No. 1 building of the American Embassy on Guanghua Road, west of Ritan Park. On the right was the main administration block housing the Press Office and the Department of Cultural Affairs, a huge satellite dish oriented south-west on the lower roof. Straight ahead was the ambassador's residence, a plain two-storey building with a brown tile roof. It stood at the end of a paved drive bordered by immaculately kept flowerbeds and silently weeping willows.

On a tall flagpole the Stars and Stripes fluttered listlessly in the gentle evening breeze. From the street Margaret had heard the sounds of traditional Chinese music drifting languidly from the direction of the residence. Now, as she approached the double red doors at the front, she could see, through a latticed wall off to her right, the musicians – three men and two women – playing on an illuminated terrace.

The ambassador himself met her at the door, accompanied by his wife, an attractive, statuesque woman in her middle-fifties. Margaret hadn't met her before, and the ambassador made the introductions.

'Oh, yes,' his wife said, regarding Margaret with curiosity. 'You're the rice lady. I've heard so much about you.'

Sensing Margaret's embarrassment, and perhaps knowing something of her unpredictability, the ambassador ushered her quickly inside to the cool of a dark marble-floored hallway. At the far end, a green-carpeted staircase curled up to the second floor where the ambassador's family had their private apartments. Off to the left was a cloakroom and a guest bedroom. Through a square arch to the right, came the sound of voices lubricated by alcohol, early inhibitions already washed away. Margaret had not come early.

From the cloakroom, she saw the ambassador having a quick word with his wife. Perhaps he was telling her that for a diplomat's wife she had just been very undiplomatic. Whatever he said, she did not seem impressed and strode away into the main lounge to rejoin her guests. He, however, remained unflappable, and took Margaret by the arm and steered her across thick-piled Chinese rugs through a passage towards a long lounge crowded with people. They passed a square room on their right, opulent classical Chinese furniture facing in to an ornately carved low table inlaid with mother of pearl. 'Our little reception room, specially for the Chinese,' he said. 'They do like us to make a little fuss. Makes 'em feel like *honoured* guests.'

The lounge was a subtly lit oblong space with full-length windows down one side, sofas and armchairs neatly arranged in ordered groups. White walls were hung with pastel-coloured silk and paper collages, different coloured discs representing ancient seals dangling from each like pendulums. The ambassador followed Margaret's eyes to the pictures. 'Produced on paper handmade by master papermakers in Annhui Province. The works of Robert Rauschenberg.' He smiled his regret. 'Just on loan, sadly. Like most of the pieces in the house. Part of the State Department's Art in Embassies Program. Great idea. Just a pity we've got to give 'em back.' He signalled a waiter with a drinks tray. 'What'll you have?'

'Vodka tonic with ice and lemon,' she told the waiter. He nodded and melted away.

Meantime, the ambassador had contrived some hidden signal, and Sophie emerged smiling from the crowd. 'Hi, glad you could make it.'

'I'll leave Sophie to introduce you to folk,' the ambassador said. 'Got to keep mixing.' And with a smile and a wave he was gone. Margaret was relieved. There was something about him that always made her slightly uncomfortable – her sense that somehow he felt uncomfortable with her.

'You hungry?' Sophie asked, steering her towards the top of the room and through another square arch to a dining room which made a T with the lounge. Beneath a regimented array of photographs of vases and artefacts, a very long table groaned with salads and cold meats, and hot trays with bubbling Chinese dishes. Everything looked delicious, but Margaret had little appetite.

'Maybe later,' she said, looking around for the waiter and her drink. A group of guests had spilled out through open French windows on to the terrace where the quintet was playing. 'Who is everyone?' She was beginning to wonder why she had come. There was no one here who looked remotely as interesting as Sophie's description of Michael Zimmerman, and she wasn't really in the mood for making small talk.

'Oh, there's some senior members of the production team, representatives of the companies who're sponsoring the series. That bunch of Chinese over there . . .' she nodded towards a group of men standing uncomfortably in suits and holding glasses of wine like they didn't know what to do with them, 'they represent the various government departments that have facilitated the shoot.'

'Excuse me, I think this is yours.'

Margaret turned to find a young man in a dark suit holding her vodka tonic. 'Oh, thanks,' she said, taking it from him.

'My pleasure,' he said and leaned across her to Sophie. 'Sophie, I think the ambassador's looking for you.'

Sophie jumped. 'Oh. Is he?' She raised her eyebrows to Margaret in apology. 'Be right back.' And she hurried off.

Margaret took a long pull at her vodka and was slightly disconcerted to find that the young man was still there.

'Don't you just hate these things?' he said, tugging uncomfortably at his collar.

'Sure,' said Margaret, a little surprised. 'But in my case it's self-inflicted. At least you're getting paid to be here.'

He gave her a very odd look. 'I'm sorry?'

A sudden cloud of apprehension descended on her. She waved her glass at him. 'Well, aren't you . . . ? Didn't you . . . ?' She didn't have the courage to finish, and he laughed suddenly.

'You thought I was the waiter?' And his face lit up with amusement, dark warm eyes twinkling at her.

'Oh, my God.' Margaret couldn't bring herself to look at him. 'I am so sorry.' But when she did sneak a glance, it was clear he had not taken offence.

'I'm afraid I'm a self-inflicted guest, just like you.' He had dimples either side of a wide smile, strong eyebrows below shiny auburn hair swept back from his temples. He was older than Margaret had first supposed, she saw now. Mid, perhaps even late, thirties. There was just the hint of grey streaked through his hair. 'The waiter was looking for you down the other end of the room. He said you were with Sophie, so I took the drink off him and figured if I could find Sophie I'd find you. And I did.'

Margaret was still overcome with the embarrassment of her *faux pas*. 'I'm so sorry,' she said again, at a loss for anything else to say.

'Don't be. It's my own fault really. I was so keen to meet the woman who wanted to . . .' he paused for effect, 'run the rule over my ass, that I completely forgot to introduce myself.'

Margaret felt her face flush with embarrassment.

He held out his hand. 'Michael Zimmerman.'

It was one of those few times in her life when Margaret was at a complete loss for words. She shook his hand, feeling like a total idiot. How could he possibly know about her conversation with Sophie? How could she possibly mistake him for a waiter? She didn't know which was more embarrassing. And those smiling eyes of his continued to hold her relentlessly in their gaze. She might have sunk without trace, but recovered just in time. 'Actually, the only way I'd measure anything of yours would be on an autopsy table.'

'Ah, yes,' he said, 'Sophie told me. We both deal in death, you and I.'

'Do we?'

'You cut them up, I dig them up.'

Margaret fixed him with a steely glare. 'And I've been *set* up, haven't I? Sophie hadn't even appeared when I ordered my drink. Who is she anyway, your little sister?'

'Close,' Michael said. 'She went to school with my little sister. Had a crush on me since she was three and I was fifteen.' He lifted a glass of red wine from the table and took a sip. 'She thought you needed cheering up.'

'Oh, did she?' Margaret wasn't sure she liked being an object of pity.

'Hey, don't be hard on her. She's a good kid. Smart, too.'

He took another sip of wine. 'She just couldn't believe you didn't know who I was.'

'And neither, presumably, could you. Must be a bit of a blow to the celebrity ego to find that not everyone in the world knows who you are.'

'Hey . . .' Michael grinned. 'Now don't start getting chippy on me. I said I would only participate in this childish prank if you turned out to be drop-dead gorgeous.'

In spite of herself, Margaret couldn't resist a smile. 'Oh, did you?'

'So I watched for you coming in, and . . .'

'And . . . ?'

'Well, I just figured anybody that ugly sure as hell needs cheering up.'

Margaret laughed, and was surprised to find herself attracted to him. Which was disturbing. Was she really drawn to the same stereotypical male that appealed to the readership of *Cosmopolitan*? The thought filled her with horror. But then, she consoled herself, the readership of *Cosmopolitan* had never met him in the flesh. It wasn't the image she found attractive, but the man. And she had no preconceived perception of him as a media personality. She'd thought he was a waiter, for God's sake! Anyway, it was a long time since she had indulged in a little harmless flirting. 'I should have realised,' she said. 'A real waiter would have had more class.'

'I'm sure he would,' Michael said. 'It's what my critics accuse me of. A lack of class. You know, the kind of snobbish élitism that would normally consign a documentary on archaeology to some obscure cable channel watched by a handful of people.'

'Ouch,' said Margaret. 'Did I touch a nasty contusion just beneath the skin?'

'No,' Michael grinned. 'A great big open wound. I just got mauled by the TV critic of the *New York Times*, who thinks I reduce history to the level of soap opera.'

'And do you?'

'Well, yes, actually I probably do,' Michael nodded. 'But, you know, what that guy missed is that good soap opera is just good storytelling, and history is bursting with good stories to be told. I mean, you're a forensic pathologist, right?' Margaret nodded. 'So nobody knows better than you. Every crime has its story, motivated by any number of things – greed, lust, jealousy ... And it's your job to peel away the layers that obscure that story, to piece together, bit by bit, the trail of evidence that will lead eventually to the truth.'

Margaret laughed. 'You make it sound almost exciting. I can assure you, most of the time it's pretty dull.'

He had become quite intense, focused, as if holding something in his mind's eye that required absolute concentration to describe. 'Of course it is. It's a painful, painstaking process that requires endless patience and a clear vision of where it's leading. But the truth is never dull – that extraordinary mix of human passion and frailty, maybe darkness, that leads to the commission of the crime. Do you see what I mean?'

Margaret shook her head. She had no idea where he was leading her. 'I'm afraid not.'

'It's what *I* do,' he said. 'The same thing as you. It's what archaeology is all about. Peeling back the layers – usually of time – to uncover the evidence, all the little clues left us by history, that will lead eventually to the truth. And how extraordinary that truth can be. How compelling and emotive, and filled with the same human passion and frailty and darkness that motivates the crimes that you investigate. Why shouldn't I bring those stories to people? They're good stories. A good story is always worth telling. And if you tell it well you'll get an audience.' He stopped suddenly, as if surprised by his own outburst and uncertain as to where it had led him.

Margaret shrugged. 'So . . . the TV critic of the *New York Times* can stick it up his ass?'

There was just a moment before Michael burst out laughing, an uninhibited, infectious laugh. 'Now why didn't I think of that? I could have saved myself a lot of hot air.'

But in that 'hot air', Margaret had caught, perhaps, a glimpse of what it was that had made him so successful on the small screen: the passion and personality that compelled you to listen, to hear his story, an intensity that in life, she thought, could become wearing. Although in Michael's case, she considered, his sense of humour might just be a mitigating factor. That, and a great ass.

He drained his glass and lifted another, nodding towards the terrace. 'You want to step outside? It's getting a bit airless in here.'

They followed the dark marble tiles out from the dining room through the French windows on to the terrace. It was immediately cooler, a light breeze stirring the hanging fronds of the willow that in daytime would provide much needed shade from the sun.

'Two moons out tonight,' Michael said, and Margaret immediately looked up, but could see nothing through the dark haze of pollution and cloud. He smiled at her consternation and nodded towards the quintet playing intently, lost in their own world, at the far side of the terrace. He leaned towards her, confidentially. 'The two guitar-like instruments with the circular sound boxes – they're called *ruans*, or sometimes "moon guitars". You can see why.' And Margaret could, particularly out here on the terrace, the pale wood of the perfectly round sound boxes flashing in the reflected light of discreet overhead lamps, for all the world like two moons dancing in time to the music. She liked the analogy. There was something pleasing about it. She finished her vodka.

'Shall I get you another?' Michael asked.

'No. It would only encourage me to get drunk.' She paused self-consciously, then added quickly, 'And, besides, the waiters in here aren't up to much.'

He smiled, but had sensed in her the melancholy she had immediately tried to disguise. He said, 'You've had a rough few months.'

She flashed him a look, more defensive than hostile. 'And you'd know all about that.'

He shrugged. 'No. All I really know is that you're the lady who put out those scare stories on the Net about genetically contaminated rice.'

'They weren't scare stories,' she almost snapped.

'Hey,' he said, and raised his palms protectively. 'I don't know about you, but I figure that claims that half the population of the world is at risk are pretty scary.'

She relented a little and forced a half-hearted smile. 'We feared the worst. You should just be glad it didn't turn out that way in the end. But don't underestimate it. OK, so the virus wasn't there in all the rice, and thank God a lot of people turned out to have a natural immunity, but there are still millions of people at risk.'

'I read they think there's a cure just around the corner.'

'Well, let's hope they're right.'

There was an awkward pause. Then Michael said, 'So, I suppose it's you to blame for us having to eat all these goddamn noodles. Boy, that must have made you popular with the Chinese.'

She grinned sheepishly. 'Another few weeks and the first new crop'll be in. They just went back to the old, natural seed. And they can harvest three crops a year, so they'll get their precious rice back soon enough.'

They stood in silence then, listening to the strange cadences of the traditional Chinese music, the wail of the two-stringed *erh hu* violin, the haunting breath of the purple bamboo flute, the two moons dancing, and the twang of the dulcimer. Margaret had no idea what to say. She had just dismissed the last three months of her life in a sentence, and made light of it, as if none of it had ever really mattered. She was aware of Michael's sheer physicality as he stood silently at her shoulder.

How was it possible, she wondered, that she could be attracted to this man when her relationship with Li had left her so raw? The thought scared her a little. And she remembered what it was most people usually forgot – that there was no such thing as harmless flirting.

'I'd better go,' she said.

'You've only just arrived.'

'Yeah, but it's your party. I don't want to monopolise you.'

'You can monopolise me any time.'

She glanced at him, looking for the smile, but he wasn't smiling, and she felt a flutter of fear in her breast, like a butterfly trapped just beneath the skin. But, then, suddenly she felt him relax again.

'Look, why don't you come out to location tomorrow? We're setting up some dramatic recreations at the Ming Tombs. It's only an hour out of Beijing.'

'I'm sorry, I can't,' she said. 'I have a flight to catch in the morning.'

He frowned. 'Where are you going?'

'Home,' she said simply.

He seemed confused. 'Home being where?'

'Chicago.'

'When'll you be back?'

'Never,' she said, and the finality of the word struck her like a blow, bringing her to her senses. 'I really do have to go.'

'Hi, how are you two getting on?' They both turned at the sound of Sophie's voice as she stepped on to the terrace.

'You didn't tell me she was leaving tomorrow,' Michael said, almost a hint of accusation in his voice. He turned to Margaret. 'And we haven't even been properly introduced.'

'Probably better that way,' Margaret said. 'If you never say hello, you never have to say goodbye.' She turned to Sophie. 'Thanks for the invite. I've enjoyed it. But I still have my packing to do.' She forced a smile and nodded, and pushed off through the dining room, bumping shoulders with guests down the length of the long lounge. She retrieved her things from the cloakroom and hurried through the big red doors and down the steps into the cool evening.

In the street she stopped for a breath. The sound of the music had receded to a distant tinkle. She put a hand on the wall to steady herself. It had been her first encounter with real life, with normality, for far too long. And it had been much too heady. Like the first draw on a cigarette after years of abstinence. She would have to break herself in more gently.

III

He heard Margaret calling for help. Long, insistent cries. But he couldn't see her – only a flickering glimmer of light somewhere beyond this darkness that enveloped him like a web, entrapping him in its blind, sticky mesh. But the plaintiveness of her voice was gut-wrenching, and he knew he could not reach her, could not help. He sat bolt upright, suddenly awake, lathered in sweat, entangled in the bed sheet. And the long, single ring of the telephone in the living room pierced his consciousness. He leaped quickly out of bed and was halfway down the hall, intent on reaching the phone so it wouldn't waken his uncle, before he remembered that Yifu was dead. And the memory came like a blow in the solar plexus, painful, sickening. He almost cried out from the pain. He clattered breathlessly into the living room, and in the darkness knocked over the tiny telephone table. The phone rattled away across the linoleum, the receiver tumbling from its cradle. He could hear a strange and disembodied voice in the dark. '*Wei* . . . *wei* . . .' Scrambling naked across the floor, struggling to see in the reflected glow of the streetlight outside, he finally found the receiver. 'Li Yan.'

'Deputy Section Chief, this is the duty officer at Beixinqiao Santiao. There's been another murder.'

Li had retrieved the rest of the phone by now and turned on a lamp beside the sofa. He sat down and glanced at his watch. It was 4 a.m. 'Another beheading?'

'Yes, boss.'

'Where?'

'An apartment on the fourth floor at No. 7 Tuan Jie Hu Dongli in Chaoyang District.'

'Who's out there?'

'Detective Qian left a few minutes ago. Do you want me to send a car?'

'No, it'll be as quick by bike. I'm on my way.'

Li hung up and sat for a moment, heart pounding, breathing hard. Another murder. He felt sick. Then he wondered if he would ever get used to his uncle not being there. That quiet voice so full of calm and reason, a wisdom and intelligence that Li knew he could never aspire to. He rubbed his face vigorously to try to banish the final vestiges of sleep, and the cloud of depression that hung over him whenever he thought about Yifu. He wished he believed in ghosts. He wished that Yifu would come back and haunt him, not just be there in his mind, in his memories. And yet he knew that a part of his uncle lived on in him. He still had a responsibility to him, and a hell of a lot to live up to. It had never been easy to walk in the footsteps of one of the most revered police officers in Beijing while he was alive. It was even harder now that he was gone.

Li went back to his bedroom and pulled on his jeans, a pair of trainers and a white tee shirt. He took his black leather jacket from the wardrobe and checked that he had cigarettes and his maroon Public Security ID wallet. He lit a cigarette and screwed up his face at the foul taste of it. He paused for a moment, then on an impulse he went into his uncle's bedroom. He'd left it just as the old man kept it when he was alive. Personal things laid out neatly on the dresser, pictures on the wall; a photograph of Yifu as a young police officer setting off for Tibet in 1950; a picture of Yifu and his wife – the aunt Li had never met; a photograph of Yifu at his retirement banquet, his round face beaming broadly below a mop of curling black hair, a glaze over his normally bright eyes – he had drunk far too much beer. Li smiled and touched the picture, as if in touching the image of his uncle he could somehow reach him again in some other life. But it was just glass beneath his fingers, cold and lifeless. He turned quickly and switched out the light, and hurried from the apartment.

The night-shift security guard nodded as Li wheeled his bike out into Zhengyi Road and headed north up to East Chang'an Avenue. There was very little traffic about at this time, the odd private car, the occasional convoy of great rumbling trucks hauling coal south from the pits north of the city. There were virtually no other cyclists, and Li had the cycle lane to himself. He pedalled hard through the dappled light of streetlamps shining through the trees. Most of the neon and coloured arc lights that illuminated so many of the new buildings at night were turned off at this time. It was the darkest hour of the night. And Li fought to keep the darkest thoughts from his mind.

This was the fourth beheading in what were, as far as anyone knew, the first ever serial killings in Beijing. Four murders in as many weeks. Bloody, execution-style killings, each following the same bizarre ritual, chilling in their cold, calculated and entirely premeditated nature. He tried to shut out of his mind the scene that he knew would confront him. He had seen many murder victims in his time, and victims of all manner of accidental death, but never had he seen so much blood. It was hard to believe the body held so much. And when it was such a vibrant, freshly oxygenated red, the effect was shocking.

Li passed under the flyover of the second ring road and continued east, past the CITIC building and the China World Trade Centre, before turning north again on the third ring road. In a couple of hours, the city would be waking, bleary-eyed cyclists jamming the cycle lanes heading for work. The traffic would start to build, so that by eight almost all the main arteries would have ground to a halt, and row upon row of frustrated motorists would peep their horns and rev their engines, belching filthy, unregulated fumes into the already toxic atmosphere. Cycling in Beijing had long since ceased to be a pleasure.

But as yet the third ring road was still deserted, not a single vehicle or cyclist along its length as far as Li could see. He could almost believe he was alone in the city. Until he turned east into Tuan Jie Hu Dongli and saw, about two hundred yards along this normally secluded, tree-lined street, a crowd of several hundred people gathered around a phalanx of police and forensic vehicles drawn into the sidewalk at Building No. 7. These were people from up and down the street, woken from their sleep by the sirens of police and ambulance. Hastily dressed figures, some still in slippers, pressed around the official vehicles, puffy faces below tousled hair straining for a sight of what was going on. Several dozen uniformed officers assigned to crowd control were already erecting temporary barriers. More people were emerging all the time from tenement closes. Li had to force his way through to the barriers, and a po-faced young uniformed officer would not let him through until he had flashed his Ministry ID. Another officer, this time one Li recognised, stood sentry by the entrance to the close.

'Where's Detective Qian?' Li asked.

The officer jerked his thumb over his shoulder. 'Up the stairs. Fourth floor.'

The walls of the close were scarred and dirty. They had probably never been painted since the apartments were first built in the seventies. There was a damp, airless smell in the stairwell, a faint whiff of urine. Rusted old bicycles jostled for space on each landing, doors to apartments shuttered behind steel grilles. Li climbed the stairs two at a time. A number of uniformed officers stood smoking on the fourth landing, a couple of forensics men, wearing tell-tale white gloves, leaned on the rail and watched him come up. Bright light spilled out from the apartment.

Li nodded grimly and squeezed in the door, past a tiny kitchen on his left, a toilet on the right. There were a couple of flimsy flip-flop sandals by a cabinet just past the kitchen door – a change of footwear for the interior in more fastidious times. Beyond was a narrow room with built-in cupboards at the far end, and a table littered with the detritus of everyday life: newspapers, cigarettes, an overflowing ashtray, dirty dinner plates waiting to be cleared away. To the left, interior windows gave on to a bedroom filled with light from the streetlamps outside. To the right, a tiny living room with a sofa and TV, and a screen door opening on to a glassed balcony. There was a smell of stale cigarettes and cooking, and the merest hint of something strangely sharp, almost sweet, that Li could not identify.

The body was in the living room. Li smelled the blood before he saw the crouched shape of the fallen decapitated figure, the head two feet further away, lying on its side, eyes staring back towards him. The flash of the police photographer's camera unexpectedly burned the image into Li's brain, the great pool of red made more vivid in the sudden blinding light.

Detective Qian's gaunt face swam into view. He nodded grimly. 'Just the same as the others, boss.'

Qian was nearly ten years older than Li, considerably more experienced. But he didn't have Li's flair or imagination, which is why Li, at the age of thirty-three, had been promoted ahead of him. But Qian had had no ill feelings. He knew what his limitations were, and he was a good judge of others' abilities. He was absolutely dependable, and Li leaned on him heavily. Besides which, he was as straight as they come. There was no side to Qian. What you saw was what you got, and Li knew there was never any danger of their misunderstanding each other.

'When the photographer's finished let's clear this place,' Li said. 'There's too many people in here.'

'Sure. I think he's just about done. The doc's looking at the body now.' Qian immediately started moving people out.

Dr Wang Xing, the duty pathologist from the Centre of Criminal Technological Determination in Pao Jü Hutong, was crouched over the body. He had an unlit cigarette clamped between pursed lips and blood on his white gloves. He stood up and slowly peeled them off, stepping carefully over an area of floor where the linoleum had been pulled back and floorboards lifted. Avoiding the great pool of blood that had drained into the hole, and the characteristic spatter patterns left by the jets of blood that had shot from the carotid arteries, he picked his way out into the hall. The cigarette had stuck to his lips and he peeled it carefully away and grinned. '"If you can keep your head when all about you are losing theirs and blaming it on you" . . .'

'Rudyard Kipling,' Li said.

'Ah,' said Pathologist Wang. 'A man of letters.'

'My uncle had a book of his poetry.'

'Well, of course . . . He would, wouldn't he?' The pathologist dropped his soiled gloves into a plastic bag and almost sang, 'You're going to have to catch this guy, Li. Or it'll be *your* head.' He pulled a lighter from his pocket.

'Don't light that in here,' Li said. 'I don't suppose there's any need to ask you about the cause of death?'

Pathologist Wang shrugged and put his lighter away. 'Well, it's pretty obvious that someone cut his head off. Not quite as cleanly as the previous victims – but it might just be that his blade's starting to get a little blunt.' Li ignored the jibe. 'From the amount of blood I think you could safely say that his heart was still beating when the blow came. So, yes, I'd happily put money on decapitation being the cause of death.'

'But only,' said Li, 'if the government ever decides to legalise gambling.'

Pathologist Wang smiled. His addiction to cards and *mah jong* was well known. 'I was speaking figuratively, of course.'

'Of course,' said Li. He would not have been surprised if money changed hands at Pao Jü Hutong on the outcome of autopsies. 'What about time of death.'

'Ah,' said Wang. 'Now that really is a lottery.'

'Your best guess, then.'

The pathologist scratched his chin thoughtfully. 'It takes about twelve hours for rigor mortis to reach its stiffest. He's not quite there yet.' Wang looked at his watch. 'About nine hours, maybe. Say ... eight, eight-thirty last night, give or take two or three hours.' He waved his cigarette at Li. 'I'm going outside for a smoke if you need me for anything else.' He pushed out on to the landing.

Li stepped carefully into the sitting room and surveyed the scene. Qian followed at his shoulder.

The body had toppled forward from a kneeling position, and then fallen on to its side, so there was something oddly foetal about its final resting position. Except for the fact that the arms were pinned behind the back, tied at the wrist. Li crouched to have a closer look. Silk cord. Just like all the others. As he stood up and moved carefully round the body, he saw the eyes of the disembodied head watching him. They gave the disconcerting impression of following him as he stepped across the room. He looked away, and his eyes fell on a once-white placard lying partially in the main pool of blood. The cord with which it had hung around the neck of the victim had been severed and was stained dark red. Carefully, Li lifted an unbloodied corner of the placard to reveal characters daubed in red ink on the other side. A nickname, Digger, was written upside down and crossed through. Above it, three single, horizontal strokes. The number 3. All so familiar.

Li stood up and looked around the room and realised that

something wasn't right. There was a sofa, a table with a lamp, a TV cabinet with a small set on top. The sofa was old, but it didn't look sat in. There were no knick-knacks, personal belongings of any sort, papers, mail. Li picked his way carefully around the body and saw that a wastebasket by the TV cabinet was empty. He opened the cabinet. Nothing.

'What is it, boss?' Qian asked.

Li went out into the dining area and opened the built-in cupboards against the back wall. There were a couple of jackets, a pair of trousers, a couple of pairs of shoes. They were big cupboards, but they seemed very empty. 'Do we know who he is yet?' Li asked, and he went through to the kitchen.

'Still working on it, boss,' Qian said. 'It's a privately owned apartment. The guy had been renting for about three months, but none of the neighbours knew who he was. They hardly ever saw him.'

'What about the street committee?'

'They don't know either. Since the apartment wasn't provided by his *danwei* . . .'

Li cursed the move to privatise housing. It might be desirable for people to own their own homes, but it was breaking down the traditional structure of Chinese society. The opposite ends of the new economic spectrum, home ownership and unemployment, were creating a large, unregistered, floating population that was almost impossible to keep track of. It was proving a breeding ground for crime. He threw open the kitchen cupboards. Apart from a few cans, and some prepackaged dried noodles, they were empty, too.

'Who raised the alarm?'

'Couple in the flat below.' Qian wrinkled his face 'The guy woke up to find the top sheet of their bed soaking wet. He thought for a minute he'd pissed himself during the night. Till he got the light on. The sheet's bright red. He starts screaming, thinking it's his own blood. His wife wakes up and she starts screaming, too. Then she sees the big red patch on the ceiling, and the blood dripping through. They were both pretty shaken up.'

He followed Li through to the bedroom and watched him as he carefully pulled back the top covers and examined the sheets, then checked inside the bedside cabinet before getting on his knees to look under the bed. 'What is it you're looking for, boss?'

Li stood up and was thoughtful for a moment. 'No one's been living here, Qian,' he said. 'Someone's been using the place, cooking the odd meal, staying over the odd night. But it's not been lived in. There are no clothes or personal stuff, no food . . .'

Qian shrugged. 'There's washing hanging out there on the balcony.'

'Let's take a look.'

They moved with great care back through the living room and out the screen door on to the glassed balcony. A circular drying rack was suspended from the ceiling, and hanging from it were a shirt and two pairs of socks. Li put out his arm to stop Qian from touching it. He rummaged in his pockets and brought out a small pocket flashlight. He shone it towards the ceiling above the drying rack, and in its light they saw the complex silver traces of an elaborate cobweb. A big, fat, black spider scurried away from the light. Li switched it off. 'There was certainly a washing done here. But it was some time ago.' He looked thoughtfully at Qian. 'Let's talk to the folk downstairs.'

The officer who'd been sitting with old Hua seemed glad to get away. As he passed Qian on the way out he put his hand up to his chest and made a mouth with it that opened and closed, and he raised his eyes to the heavens. The apartment was the same layout as the one above, but old Hua and his wife used it differently. They dined in the same central room, shelves of crockery hidden behind a checked drape, but slept in the smaller back room, and lived in the front room that looked down on to the street. The contrast with the apartment above could not have been greater. Here was a place that was lived in, every corner crammed with furniture, every surface cluttered and piled with the stuff of daily living. There were family photographs pinned to the wall, a calendar, some old posters from the twenties and thirties advertising soap and cigarettes. The place smelled of soiled clothes and body sweat and cooking. It smelled of life.

'Have some tea.' The old man waved his hand at the table. 'The water's still hot.' But Li and Qian declined. From the bathroom they heard the sound of running water. 'That's her third shower,' old Hua said. 'Silly old bitch thinks she's still got blood on her. I told her she was clean. But she won't listen.'

The old man was almost completely bald. What little hair remained he had shaved into his scalp. He was wearing blue cotton trousers and a grubby-looking white shirt that hung open, exposing a buddha-like belly and breasts. He had nothing on his feet and was smoking a hand-rolled cigarette.

'I mean, it's not as if I'm not used to death,' he said. 'I was only scared when I thought it was my blood. Other people's blood doesn't bother me.'

Li pulled up a chair. 'How is it that you're used to death?' he asked. He had encountered death himself, many times, and had never got used to it.

Old Hua grinned. 'I work for the Public Utilities Bureau,' he said. 'Have done for thirty years. It's not unlike your Public Security Bureau. We're both in charge of people. Only with you it's the living. With me it's the dead.'

Qian frowned. 'Public Utilities ... You work at a crematorium?'

'I don't just work there,' Hua corrected him. 'I'm a mortician,' he said proudly. 'It's a long time since I went round with the wagon fetching corpses from their homes. I dress up the bodies now – for the benefit of the living, of course. Taught myself from books on cosmetics and barbering. Mind you, it's not so easy with some of these accident victims. You know, when the face is all smashed up and you've got to use cotton wool, and paper pulp, and plaster and the like to re-make it—'

'Yes, well right now,' Li interrupted him, 'we're all dealing with the dead.'

Old Hua jerked his head toward the ceiling. 'Him up there?'

'How well did you know him?'

'I didn't. I passed him on the stairs, maybe twice. Didn't look like he had that much blood in him. A washed-out sort of face he had, pasty and pale. What did they do to him to make him bleed like that?'

'They?'

'Well, whoever did it.'

'So you didn't see anyone coming or going last night?'

'Not a soul.'

'And you didn't hear anything?'

'Not a thing. The wife's half deaf, you know. We have to have the television up at a terrible volume. We never hear anything from above or below.'

'When did you go to bed?'

'That would be about nine o'clock. I'm normally at my work by six.' He scratched his belly and stubbed out his cigarette.

So there was no sign of the blood at nine. Li guessed that beneath the floorboards there wouldn't be much of substance between floor and ceiling. That amount of blood would have soaked through fairly quickly. Which would put the killing perhaps a couple of hours later than the doctor's estimate.

'When did you wake up?'

Old Hua started rolling another cigarette. 'I don't know for sure. About three, half-three maybe.' Which narrowed the time of the murder to a six-hour window.

Li said, 'How long do you think the blood had been dripping on you?'

Hua shrugged. 'Who knows. Usually I sleep like a baby. And

the wife takes pills, so it takes a bomb to wake her. But it was pretty sticky, so it couldn't have been that fresh.'

Maybe around midnight, then, Li thought. When the street would be deserted and most people in their beds. He jerked his thumb towards the bedroom. 'Do you mind if we take a look?'

'Go ahead.' Hua finished rolling and lit his cigarette.

Li and Qian went to the bedroom door and surveyed the dark stain on the ceiling, the blood drying brown on the crumpled bed sheet below.

'Just who's going to clean up all that mess?' the old man shouted through. 'That's what I want to know.'

Li turned back into the hall and was startled by the apparition of old Hua's wife, stark naked, emerging from the bathroom clutching a towel. She let out a tiny scream of fright and with a judder of old and sagging breasts, hurried back into the bathroom and slammed the door.

Old Hua just laughed. 'Not a pretty sight, eh?'

Li and Qian exchanged glances and suppressed smiles.

'Thank you, Mr Hua,' Li said. 'We'll take full statements from you and your wife later.' He paused at the door. 'One more thing. Do you have any idea who owns the apartment upstairs?'

'Nope. The guy who had it died about a year ago and left it to some relative who's been renting it out. Just like the old landlords, eh? We had a revolution to get rid of these types. Seems like we've just come full circle.'

As Li and Qian re-entered the victim's apartment on the fourth floor, two assistants were manoeuvring the corpse into a body bag for removal to Pao Jü Hutong, where the autopsy would be carried out in a few hours' time.

'Once forensics are finished, I want the apartment sealed off,' Li said. 'No one gets in here without referring to me first. And I want to know who the hell owns this place. If anyone knows who our John Doe is, it's got to be the guy who rented him the apartment.'

A sudden commotion in the back room distracted him. One of the assistants called out, 'Is Deputy Section Chief Li still around?'

'Here,' Li said, and crossed quickly to the room.

The assistant stood up and handed him what appeared to be a small, dark blue notebook. 'It was hanging out his back pocket.'

Li held the corner of it between thumb and forefinger, and his heart skipped a beat as he recognised the silver crest on the front. It wasn't a notebook. It was a passport. He eased it open and looked at the photograph inside, then at the head still staring back at him from the floor. His eyes flickered down the page to the name, Yuan Tao.

'Shit,' he whispered, realising the implications.

'What is it?' Qian asked anxiously over his shoulder.

'This might be the same as the other murders in almost every other detail. But there's one very big difference.' He held up the passport and Qian immediately recognised the eagle crest. 'This guy's an American.'

IV

'This had better be good.' Margaret strode across the floor of the lobby in the Ritan Hotel, glancing at her watch, Sophie hurrying in her wake. 'I've got exactly two hours to finish packing and get to the airport.' She stopped at the glass doors and turned to Sophie. 'Anyway, how can you *not* know what it's about?'

'Because they haven't told me anything. Honest, Margaret. All I know is the RSO's been in with the ambassador for the last two hours and all engagements for the rest of the morning have been cancelled.'

They ran down the steps to where a sleek black embassy limousine idled quietly in the damp morning air.

'And they didn't need to send a car, for God's sake!' said Margaret. 'It's just a couple of streets away.'

'They said it was urgent.' Sophie opened the door for Margaret and then slid in after her.

'This isn't one of your little jokes, is it?' Margaret said, suddenly suspicious. The car drew away from the steps and swung out of the gate, past the glowering security guards.

'Of course not,' Sophie said. Her tone was defensive, even hurt. 'I'm sorry if my little bit of fun backfired last night.'

'It didn't,' Margaret said quickly, but she avoided meeting Sophie's eye. 'Bit of a coincidence, though, you being his little sister's best friend.'

'Not really. Michael was out here most of last year shooting the series that starts back home next month. It was he who encouraged me to apply for the posting. China sounded, well . . . a bit exotic. And so here I am.'

'And so is he – for the next few months if he's just starting filming. I don't suppose that had anything to do with your decision to apply for the job?'

Sophie turned and smiled. 'I can always dream, can't I? But I'm sure he'd much rather spend time with you than me. He was disappointed that you left so early last night.'

Margaret checked her watch again and changed the subject. 'I hope this isn't going to take too long, Sophie, or the American government will be picking up the tab for me missing my flight.'

Sophie shrugged. 'Who knows – maybe the Chinese have refused you an exit visa.'

Margaret turned, genuinely shocked. 'They couldn't do that, could they?'

The ambassador's secretary led them straight into his office. The ambassador, in his customary shirtsleeves – rolled up this time – was standing with hands on hips looking out of the window. Stan Palmer sat at the coffee table sipping black coffee, papers spread in front of him. His normally smooth façade seemed a little ruffled.

Jon Dakers, the Regional Security Officer, was perched on a corner of the ambassador's desk, talking into the telephone. He sounded agitated. 'Well, get them to give me a call as soon as they've got it. And fax it direct to the embassy.'

The ambassador turned as Margaret and Sophie entered. 'Thank you for coming so promptly, Margaret.'

'What's this all about, Mr Ambassador? I need to be at the airport in less than two hours.'

'And I need a favour, Margaret.' He crossed the room and indicated that she should take a seat. She did so, reluctantly. The ambassador remained standing. He paused for a moment. Then, 'A member of the embassy staff, a Chinese-American called Yuan Tao, was murdered last night,' he said. 'Someone decapitated him.'

'Jesus,' Margaret said.

'And it gets worse,' Stan said, raising what looked suspiciously like a plucked eyebrow.

'Really?' said Margaret. 'I can't think of anything much worse than decapitation.'

'For us, not for him,' Dakers said, crossing the room to stand beside the ambassador. The RSO was a solid, square man, an ex-cop, bald and aggressive, with a close-cropped silver-grey beard. 'He was murdered in an apartment he'd been renting in the Chaoyang District.' He paused, as if this should mean something to Margaret.

'So?' she asked.

Stan said, 'Embassy staff are allocated apartments in special embassy compounds. In Yuan Tao's case, a two-room affair in a block just behind the Friendship Store.'

'Technically,' Jon Dakers said, 'he was breaking the law.'

'Yeah, I know,' Margaret said. She had bitter experience. 'You got to register where you're staying with Public Security, and they get pretty pissed if you spend even one night some-where else.'

'And the Chinese are, indeed, pretty pissed,' said the ambassador.

'They're embarrassed,' Dakers corrected him. 'An American citizen's been murdered on their patch. They're looking for any way to pass the buck.'

A sudden worm of suspicion worked its way into Margaret's mind. 'Wait a minute. When you say this guy was "a member of the embassy staff", is this some kind of euphemism?'

The ambassador chuckled grimly. 'He wasn't a spy, if that's what you mean.'

'And, of course, you'd tell me if he was.'

'No,' the ambassador said, 'but I'm telling you he wasn't. He was a low-level official. Only been out here about six months, working on the visa line.'

'Which probably gives a few thousand people a motive for doing him in,' Stan said.

'We're waiting on the State Department sending his file,' Dakers said.

There was a pause, then, that no one seemed anxious to fill. Margaret glanced around the faces looking expectantly at her.

'So what's any of this got to do with me?' she asked.

The ambassador rounded the sofa and sat down. 'The Chinese police believe they have a serial killer on their hands. They think Yuan Tao is victim number four. The other three were Chinese nationals. But this guy's an American citizen. And we'd like you to carry out the autopsy.'

'What?' Margaret was stunned.

'You've worked with them before,' Dakers said.

'Look,' Margaret said, 'I came here last spring to lecture for six weeks at the University of Public Security. I did one autopsy as a favour – and spent the next three months regretting it. I do not want to get involved again.'

'Margaret, I understand perfectly.' The ambassador leaned forward earnestly. He was drawing on all his powers of diplomacy. 'But there's no way we can get anyone else out here fast enough. Besides which, the Chinese trust you.'

'Do they?' Margaret was amazed.

'Well, they've agreed to let you do the autopsy – or, at least to assist.'

'And if I refuse?'

'We all have certain obligations to our country, Margaret.' The ambassador sat back, playing his trump card – the appeal to her patriotism.

Margaret had always wondered what all that swearing allegiance to the flag and singing the national anthem at school was about. Now she knew. She sighed. 'I'll have to rearrange my flight.'

'Already taken care of,' Stan said smugly.

'Oh, is it?' Margaret threw him a hostile glance and stood up.

'Oh, and one other thing,' Stan said, and she saw a strange look of anticipation brighten his eyes. 'The officer in charge of the case is Deputy Section Chief Li Yan of the Beijing Municipal Police.' He beamed at her. 'I think you know him.'

CHAPTER TWO

I

The half-dozen detectives freshly drafted in from CID head-quarters at Qianmen had been sitting smoking and talking animatedly for nearly half an hour. Their cigarette smoke hung like a cloud over the top floor meeting room at Beixinqiao Santiao, reflecting the mood of their Section One colleagues, who joined them now around the big table to sift through the evidence which had been collected over the past month. The detectives of the serious crime squad were depressed by their failure to achieve any significant progress, and embarrassed by the need for reinforcements.

Li sat brooding in his seat with his back to the window. He had been reinstated as Deputy Section Chief shortly after the first murder, and he was frustrated by the lack of a single substantial lead. He had even begun to question his own previously unshakable faith in himself, and wonder if the death of his uncle and the events of the past three months had taken a greater toll on him that he had realised. There were times, he knew, when his concentration was not what it should be.

He had found himself sitting in meetings, his mind wandering to thoughts of Yifu. And Margaret.

Simply bringing her name to mind was painful, accompanied as it was by a host of memories, bittersweet and full of hurt. He thought back to the only time they had made love, the sun streaming in through the dirt-streaked windows of a neglected railway sleeper on a siding near Datong.

'Boss . . .'

He became aware of an insistent voice forcing its way into his thoughts.

'Boss, are you still with us?'

Li looked up suddenly and saw Detective Wu, sunglasses pushed back on his forehead, eyeing him oddly from across the table. He glanced around at the other detectives, almost twenty of them now, and saw that they were all looking at him.

'Yeah, sure. Sorry . . .' Li shuffled the papers on the desk in front of him. 'Just following a train of thought.'

'Perhaps you'd like to share it with us, then?' Li looked towards the door, startled to see that Section Chief Chen Anming had come in without his even noticing.

'Not worth it, Chief,' Li said quickly. 'It wasn't going anywhere.'

'A bit like this investigation,' Chen said. He pulled up a chair and sat down, folding his arms across his chest and surveying his detectives with a stony gaze. Chen was a lean, sinewy man in his late fifties, a thick head of prematurely silver hair streaked with nicotine. He was renowned for his apparent inability to make the muscles of his face form a smile, although the twinkle in his eyes frequently betrayed the very human person that concealed itself behind the hardman image. But there was no twinkle there now. 'Four victims,' he said. 'And we've got nothing. Nothing!' He raised his voice, and then sat silently for several seconds. 'And now that this latest victim turns out to be an American, the whole thing is turning political.' He leaned forward, placing his palms carefully on the table in front of him. 'I just took a call in my office from the Deputy Minister of Public Security.' He paused. 'I have *never* had a call from a Deputy Minister of Public Security. And it's not an experience I want to repeat.' He sat back again. The room was absolutely still. 'So let me make this quite clear. However many more officers we have to draft in, however many hours of overtime we have to work, we are going get a result.' He waited for maximum dramatic effect before adding, 'There are careers on the line here.'

'You mean heads will roll?' Wu said, grinning, and there was a gasp of smothered laughter around the table.

Chen turned a steely glare on him. 'Be assured, Detective Wu, yours will be the very first.'

Wu's grin faded. 'Just trying to lighten things up, Chief.'

'OK,' Li stepped in before 'things' went any further. 'Let's go over what we've got for the benefit of the guys from HQ. And then we'll have a look at last night's killing. Wu, you kick us off.'

Wu lifted his file from the desk, tipped his chair backwards and pushed his sunglasses further back on his head. With

Wu image was everything, from his faded jeans to his denim jacket and sunglasses. Even the gum he chewed, which must have long since lost its flavour. He was putting on a show for the newcomers.

'OK,' he said. 'Number one. August twenty. Tian Jingfu, aged fifty-one, a projectionist in a movie theatre in Xicheng District. Fails to turn up for work. His wife's away visiting relatives in the south, so his work unit connects with his street committee, who go to his door. No one answers, but they can hear the television going. So they call the census cop and he comes and bursts the door down. The place is filled with twenty million flies. The guy's lying in the front room with his head cut off. Pathologist reckons he's been there for two days. There's no sign of forced entry. But the guy's been drinking red wine. Unusual. And the autopsy shows its been spiked, a drug called flunitrazepam. His hands have been tied behind his back with a silk cord, and a white card hung around his neck. It's got the name Pigsy written on it upside down in red ink and then scored through. Pigsy, I think we're all agreed, is some kind of nickname. The card also has the number 6 written on it. From the position of the body, it looks like he's been made to kneel, head bowed, and a bronze sword or similar bladed weapon used to decapitate him. Hell of a lot of blood. Other than that, the place is clean, no rogue footprints, fingerprints. Forensics came up with zip.'

He dropped his file on the desk, tipped his chair forward and held his hands out, palms up. 'I talked to just about everyone who ever knew him. Workmates, neighbours, friends, family.

Parents are dead, an aunt still living in Qianmen. Everyone says he was a nice guy, lived quietly. No one knew why anyone would want to kill him. No one saw anything unusual the day he was murdered.' He shrugged. 'Zip.' And with finger and thumb he smoothed out the sparse growth on his upper lip that he liked to think of as a moustache.

Li turned towards Qian Yi. 'Detective Qian.'

Qian took a breath. 'OK. Number two. Bai Qiyu, fifty-one, same age as victim number one. Married, with two kids at college. He's a businessman, manager of a small import-export company in Xuanwu District. August thirty-first, the staff arrive at work in the morning to find him lying in his office. Decapitated. Same thing. Silk cord tying his wrists behind his back – and forensics tell us it's cut from the same length as the killer used on the first victim. An identical piece of white card round the neck, the same colour ink. Only this time the nickname is Zero and the number is 5. So now we assume we're counting down the victims. A tape lift from the severed vertebra during autopsy tells us it is a similar, or the same, bronze-bladed weapon. Bai Qiyu has also been drinking red wine, also spiked with flunitrazepam. Like Tian Jingfu, his wife was away visiting relatives. His kids were still there, but not particularly concerned when he didn't come home before they went to bed. The crime scene is clean, except for one smudged, but printable, bloody fingerprint found on the edge of the desk. But it doesn't match with anything we've got in the AFIS computer.'

Qian took a deep breath and concluded, 'I personally

interviewed nearly fifty people. Same as victim number one. No one knows why anyone would want to kill him. He had no appointments marked down in his diary for that night. He was alone in his office when the last person left the building.'

The detectives from CID headquarters were scribbling furiously, making copious notes, and referring frequently to the files with which they had been supplied. The others watched them apprehensively and with mixed feelings. While each was keen to achieve a break in the case, none of them wanted some smart-ass from HQ to pick up something they'd missed.

Li was aware of the additional tension. He turned to Zhao, at twenty-five the youngest in the section, still lacking a little in self-confidence, but sharp and diligent and shaping up as a prospect for future promotion. 'Tell us about number three, Detective Zhao.'

Zhao flushed a little as he spoke. 'September fifteen. Yue Shi, a professor of archaeology at Beijing University, has an arrangement to play chess and drink a few beers with his uncle. His uncle arrives at his apartment in Haidan District near the university campus and finds his nephew lying dead in the sitting room. He has been beheaded, hands tied behind his back, again with the same silk cord. A placard, half-soaked with blood, is lying beside the body. It bears the number 4 and the nickname Monkey. It's written in red ink, upside down and crossed through.' He paused for a moment. 'I'll stick with the parallels first. He has red wine with flunitrazepam in his stomach and blood specimens, just like the others. Tape lift again shows that the weapon used was bronze, suggesting it is probably the same one. But this is where it starts to get a bit different. There is hardly any blood at the scene, but the body is virtually drained of it.'

'So he was killed somewhere else, then taken to his apartment.' This from one of the newcomers.

'Yeah, very clever,' said Wu. 'Like we never spotted that one.'

The detective blushed.

'On you go, Zhao,' Li said.

Zhao glanced nervously around his listeners. 'Like the man said, the body had been moved. Fibres recovered from it show that it had been wrapped in a grey woollen blanket of some sort. He had a fine, blue-black, powdery dust in the treads of his shoes and on his trousers. Forensics tell us they are particles of fired clay, some kind of ceramic. But the clay's not of a type found around Beijing. Apparently it's a soil type found more commonly in Shaanxi Province.' He shrugged. 'We don't know what that tells us.' Then he went on, 'There were smudges and traces of blood in the hall, but no readable footprints or fingerprints anywhere. And the pathologist thinks he'd been killed about twenty-four hours before the body was discovered.'

'What about the university?' one of the other detectives from HQ asked.

'We were all over the place,' Zhao said. 'His office, his classrooms, the laboratories. If he'd been murdered in any of these places we'd have found traces. You just can't clean up that much blood without leaving something behind. His colleagues in the department were stunned. Again, no one could think of a single reason why anyone would want to kill him. He wasn't married, he didn't have many friends. He lived for his work, and spent ninety per cent of his waking day absorbed in it.'

'What age was he?' The same detective from HQ again.

'Fifty-two – just a few months older than the others.'

The detective turned to Li. 'What about the latest victim? What age was he?'

'Date of birth on his passport was March 1949, which makes him fifty-one. I'm sorry, detective, I don't know your name.'

'Sang,' the detective said. 'Sang Chunlin.'

'OK, Sang,' Li said, 'it's a thought worth holding on to. But let's look at the fourth victim first.' And he glanced around all the expectant faces. 'Yuan Tao,' he said, 'was a Chinese-American working in the visa department of the US Embassy.' And he took them through the murder scene, step by step, as he and Qian had done in reality five hours earlier. He told them that Yuan had been illegally renting the apartment at No. 7 Tuan Jie Hu Dongli where the body was found, but not necessarily living there, at least not full time. 'Apparently,' Li said, 'the US Embassy had no idea. They had provided him with accommodation in an embassy compound behind the Friendship Store.' He paused. 'They have kindly allowed our forensics people access to the apartment.' There was just the hint of a tone in this. 'They have also promised us full access to their file on him – just as soon as Washington can find it and fax it to us.' There were a few laughs around the table. 'So until we get that, and until we have the results of the autopsy later this morning, there's not a lot more I can tell you at this stage.'

He got up and opened a window behind him before lighting another cigarette. The room was almost blue with smoke and his eyes were starting to sting. 'So what do we know?' He looked around the assembled faces. 'We know the killer used a bronze-bladed weapon of some sort – probably a sword. We know that the victims probably knew him. They were drinking wine with him, and as far as they knew had no reason to be on their guard. After all, he managed to spike all their drinks. He knew them well enough to know their nicknames.

'Red ink on white card – an ancient Chinese symbol for the end of a relationship. I think that underlines the fact that he was well known to his victims. All the names written upside down and scored through – well, we all know the significance of that image. And the numbering of the victims. Starting with six and counting down. Which would lead us to believe that there are another two victims out there somewhere.'

It was a sobering thought, and helped refocus minds around the table.

'I keep coming back to this age thing.' It was Sang again.

'Go on,' Li said.

Sang scratched his head. He was a good-looking young man, probably not yet thirty, and almost the only detective around the table not smoking. 'Well, if they're all the same age, and this guy knows all their nicknames, wouldn't it be reasonable to assume that at some time they'd all been in the same organisation, or institution, or work unit together?'

'The first three were at the same school,' Zhao said, and reduced the room to a stunned silence. He blushed fiercely as all eyes turned on him.

'What?' Li asked. His voice was steady and very level.

Zhao said, 'I figured you usually get your nickname at school. So I spent yesterday checking it out.'

'Why the hell did no one think of this before?' Chen thundered.

It was a reasonable question. But Li had no answer to it.

'It's more than thirty years since any of them were at school,' Zhao said, almost apologetically. 'I guess that's why it wasn't the first thing we were looking at.'

'And you didn't think to share your thoughts with us before now?' Chen asked pointedly.

'I only got confirmation this morning, chief,' Zhao said.

'In the name of the sky, Zhao,' Li said, 'this is a team effort. We share information, we share thoughts, we talk to one another. That's why we have these meetings.' But how could he blame Zhao when he was the only one who had had the thought?

The detectives from Headquarters sat silent, happy that they shared no responsibility here. Sang, however, was riffling through his file.

'What school was it?' he asked. 'I can't find it here.'

'It's not in there,' Zhao said. He cleared his throat, embarrassed. 'It took me some time to track it down. It was the No. 29 Middle School at Qianmen.'

There was a brief hiatus, and they could hear the scratch of Sang's pencil in his notebook. Then Li moved away from the window. 'Right,' he said decisively. He sat down and pulled his notebook towards him, taking notes as he spoke. 'We'll divide up into four groups of five. Group leaders will be Wu, Qian, Zhao, and – Sang.' Sang positively glowed. 'I want each group to review the evidence from all four murders and bring their thoughts back to this table. Additionally, each group will take responsibility for specific areas of the investigation. Zhao, we need to talk to the victims' old teachers. Qian, we need to interview fellow pupils, all their old classmates. It may be that somewhere among them are the next two victims. And we want to get to them before the killer.'

Sang interrupted. 'Aren't we jumping the gun a bit here, boss? I mean, OK, so the first three went to the same school. But obviously the American didn't.'

'Fair point,' Li said. 'But the fact that the others did is too big a coincidence not to be significant. And it's the first chink of light we've had in this case. There's every possibility it could illuminate a great deal more.' He paused. 'Sang, I want your group to try to identify the weapon used. And Wu, I want your people to look at all the forensic evidence again. There's got to be something we're missing. We'll meet again when we've got more information on Yuan Tao.'

The meeting broke up amid a hubbub of speculation on new developments, and as a pink-faced Zhao got to his feet, Li caught his eye and nodded. 'Well done,' he said. Zhao blushed more deeply.

Clouds of cigarette smoke wafted out into the corridor with the detectives.

Chen wandered round the table to where Li was collecting his papers. 'I'm glad you finally seem to have learned the importance of working as a team, Deputy Section Chief Li,' he said with a tone.

'Just when they're talking about introducing the concept of one-officer cases, too.' Li's tone echoed that of his boss, to Chen's annoyance.

'You know I don't agree with that,' he said.

'Which is just about the only thing you and my uncle would have agreed on.'

'But you don't?'

'I think the old way has its virtues, Chief. But we're living in a changing world.' Li glanced at his watch. 'I'm sorry, I've got to go. The autopsy starts at ten.'

'I'm afraid it doesn't,' Chen said, stopping Li in his tracks. 'That's why the Deputy Minister of Public Security was on the phone. The autopsy's been delayed until this afternoon. And the Commissioner wants to see you at headquarters right away.'

II

The first blink of sunshine for days dappled the sidewalk beneath the locust trees in Dong Jiaominxiang Lane. The haze of pollution, as it sometimes did, had lifted inexplicably and the sky was breaking up. The city's spirits seemed raised by it. Even the normally dour bicycle repairmen opposite the rear entrance to the municipal police headquarters were chatting enthusiastically, hawking and spitting in the gutter with renewed vigour. Li cycled past the Supreme Court on his right and turned left into the compound behind police headquarters. He alone, it seemed, was not uplifted by the autumn sunshine that still fell warm on the skin. As he passed an armed police officer standing to attention, and free-wheeled under the arch through open gates, he recalled his first encounter here with Margaret. Her official car in collision with his bicycle . . . his grazed arm . . . her insolence . . .

His smile at the memory was glazed over with melancholy.

He parked and locked his bicycle and walked apprehensively into the redbrick building that housed the headquarters of the criminal investigation department. He had stopped off at his apartment on the way to change into his uniform – dark green trousers, neatly pressed, pale green short-sleeve shirt with epaulettes and Public Security arm badge, dark green peaked cap with its red piping and loop of gold braid. He removed his hat as he stepped inside, ran his hand back across the dark stubble of his flat-top crewcut and took a deep breath.

The divisional head of the CID, Commissioner Hu Yisheng, was standing by the window when Li entered his office. The blinds were lowered, and the slats adjusted to allow thin lines of sunlight to zigzag across the contours of his desk. They fell in bright burned-out bands across the red of the Chinese flag that hung behind it. Li stood stiffly to attention as the Commissioner turned a steely gaze in his direction. He was a handsome man, somewhere in his early sixties, with a full head of iron-grey hair. He held Li in his gaze for what seemed an interminably long time. At first Li felt just uncomfortable, and then he began physically to wilt. It was worse, somehow, than any reprimand that words could have delivered.

Finally the Commissioner said, 'I was sorry to hear about your uncle.' And his words carried with them the weight of an accusation, as if Li had been personally responsible. His uncle was still casting a shadow over him, even from the grave. The Commissioner walked round behind his desk and sat down, leaving Li standing. 'He wouldn't have been very proud of the way you're conducting this investigation, would he?'

'I think he would have offered me good advice, Commissioner Hu,' Li said.

Hu bridled at the implication. 'Well, I'll give you my advice, Li,' he said. 'You'd better break this case. And quickly. And let's stick to conventional Chinese police methods, shall we? "Where the tiller is tireless, the earth is fertile," your uncle used to say.'

'Yes, he did, Commissioner,' Li said. 'But he also used to say, "The ox is slow, but the earth is patient."'

Hu frowned. 'Meaning what, exactly?'

'Oh, I think my uncle meant that if you use an ox to plough a field you must expect it to take a long time.'

The Commissioner glared at him. 'You've always been an advocate of assigning cases to individual officers, haven't you?'

'As the crime rate rises we have to find more efficient ways of fighting it,' Li said.

'Well, I'm not going to get into that argument here,' the Commissioner responded tetchily. 'Decisions on that will be taken well above our heads.' He paused. 'Like the decision to let the Americans carry out the autopsy on the latest victim.'

'What?' Li was stunned.

'It has been agreed to let one of their pathologists assist. Which means, in practice, that they will conduct it.'

'But that's ridiculous, Commissioner,' Li said. 'Their pathologist hasn't been involved in any of the previous autopsies. It doesn't make sense.'

'You want to tell that to the Minister?'

Li pressed his lips firmly together and refrained from responding.

Hu put his elbows on the desk in front of him and placed his palms together, regarding Li speculatively. 'So,' he said. 'I understand you have taken on board your section chief's admonitions regarding the American, Margaret Campbell?'

Li nodded grimly. 'I have.'

'Good.' Hu sat back and took a deep breath. 'Because she will be conducting the autopsy.'

Li looked at him in disbelief.

He emerged into the glare of the compound in a trance. He took off his hat, turning his face up to the sky, and let the warm sunshine cascade over him like rain. He closed his eyes and tried to empty his mind of its confusion, hoping beyond hope that when he opened them again the world might have turned in a different direction and all his troubles would be washed away. But he knew it would not be so. He had tried so hard to banish her from his thoughts, from his very soul. How could he face her again now? What could she believe but that he had somehow betrayed her? And in a way, he knew, he had.

He opened his eyes and they fell upon the place he had parked his bicycle. It was not there. He frowned, momentarily confused, and glanced along the row of bicycles parked up against the redbrick building. His was not among them. He glanced in the direction of the armed officer at the gate who was staring steadfastly into the street. Then he looked again for his bicycle. He must have put it somewhere else, or someone had moved it. The parked bicycles stretched all the way round the building to a long line beneath a row of trees. His bicycle was not anywhere to be seen. He could not believe this was happening, and he approached the armed officer angrily.

'I parked my bicycle just there,' he said, and he pointed along the inside wall. 'Just there. Half an hour ago. You saw me come in.'

The officer shrugged. 'People come and go all the time. I don't remember.'

'You don't remember me parking my bike there, and someone else taking it?' Li snapped.

'No, I don't,' the officer snapped back. 'I'm not a parking attendant.'

Li cursed. It was unbelievable. Someone had had the audacity to steal his bicycle from inside the municipal police compound. And who would think to question someone taking a bicycle from outside CID headquarters? He shook his head and could not resist the tiniest of ironic smiles at the barefaced cheek. There was not even any point in reporting it. Bike theft in Beijing was endemic. And with twenty million bicycles out there, he knew he would never see his again.

He pulled his hat firmly down on his head and walked the three hundred yards around the corner to his apartment block in Zhengyi Road. He picked up his mail and climbed the stairs to the second floor two at a time, and stormed into the apartment, throwing his mail on the table and his hat across the room into an armchair. 'Fuck!' he shouted at the walls, and the release of tension made him feel a little better. He went into the bedroom and stripped off his uniform and caught sight of himself in the mirror. He was tall. A little over six feet, with a good frame and a lean, fit body. He looked at his face and tried to see himself as Margaret would see him a few hours from now. He looked into his own eyes and saw nothing there but guilt. He didn't want to see her. He didn't want to see the accusation he knew would be there in her eyes. The anger, the hurt. He had thought he had put the worst of that behind him. And now fate had conspired to contrive this unhappy reunion.

To his annoyance, he found himself choosing his clothes with a little more care than usual, and ended up throwing on his old jeans and a short-sleeved white shirt, angry with himself for even thinking about it. He stuffed his wallet and ID into his back pocket, his cigarettes and lighter into the breast pocket of his shirt, and grabbed Old Yifu's bike from the hall and carried it down the stairs on his shoulder. He did not notice the letter with the Sichuan postcode that he had dropped on the table, delivered an hour earlier, only three days late.

He cycled east along East Chang'an Avenue, and then turned north, moving with a furious concentration, ringing his bell at errant pedestrians and growling at motorists who seemed to think they had the right of way. The sweat was beading across his brow and sticking his shirt to his back. He still felt like shouting, or throwing something, or kicking someone. Here he was being made to face the two demons he had been trying to exorcise from his life – forced to ride his dead uncle's bicycle to a meeting with the woman he had been ordered to give up. If he could have brought his uncle back, and fallen into the arms of the woman he loved, he would. But neither of these things was possible, and there was nothing for it but to move forward and face the demons head-on.

Great woks of broth steamed and bubbled on braziers as preparations all along the sidewalk began for lunch. Li smelled dumplings frying in oil and saw women rolling out noodles on flat boards. Charcoal burned and smoked in metal troughs as skewers of spicy lamb and chicken were prepared for barbecue. People ate early on the streets, and for an hour beforehand there was a frenzied activity both by those preparing the food, and those preparing to eat it. Children spilled out of schoolyards in blue tracksuits and yellow baseball caps, and factories spewed their workers out into the sunshine. For a time, Li had been stuck behind a tousled youth toiling over the pedals of his tricycle cart, hauling a huge load of the round coal briquettes that fuelled the winter fires of Beijing. Finally he got past him, squeezing between the cart and an on-coming bus at the Dongsi Shitiao junction. Then he left the sights and smells of food behind as he free-wheeled along the final shaded stretch of road before the corner of Dongzhimennei Street, where he hoped his own lunch would await him in the form of a *jian bing*.

Mei Yuan was busy preparing two *jian bings* for a couple of schoolgirls as Li drew up his bike. It gave him the chance to watch her as she worked the hotplate inside the small glass house with its pitched red roof that perched on the rear of her extended tricycle. Her dark hair was drawn back in its customary bun, her smooth-skinned face a little more lined and showing more strain than usual. She grinned when she saw him, cheeks dimpling, and the life immediately returned to her lovely, dark, slanted eyes. She had, he knew, a soft spot for him. There was an unspoken empathy between them. In some very small way he filled the space left by the son she had lost, and she the hole in his life left by the death of his mother – both victims of the Cultural Revolution. Neither made demands on the other. It was just something that had grown quietly.

She poured some pancake mix on to her hotplate and watched it sizzle and bubble before breaking an egg on to it. He could barely resist the temptation to give her a hug. The previous week she had been missing from her corner for a few days, and finally he had gone to her home to find out why. He had found her in bed, sick and alone. One of the new breed of self-employed, she had no work unit to look after her welfare.

He had cooked her a meal himself that night, and paid for a girl to go in every day to feed her and keep the house clean. The previous evening she had told him she would be back at her usual corner today, even although he felt she was not completely recovered. And here she was, pale and strained, and fighting to kick-start her life again.

She flipped the pancake over, smeared it with hoisin and chilli, and sprinkled it with chopped spring onion and coriander, before breaking a square of deep-fried whipped egg white into its centre, folding it in half and in half again, and then handing it, wrapped in brown paper, to the second schoolgirl. 'Two yuan,' she said, then turned beaming to Li. 'Have you eaten?'

'Yes, I have eaten.' He made the traditional response to the Beijing greeting, then added, 'I'm sorry I missed breakfast. Work.'

'That's no excuse,' she chided him. 'A big lad like you needs feeding.' She began another *jian bing*. 'I'm beginning to think you're avoiding me.'

'Why would I do that?'

'Because you don't have an answer to the last riddle I set you?'

He frowned. 'When did you set me a riddle?'

'Before I got sick.'

'Oh,' he said sheepishly. 'I don't remember it.'

'How very convenient,' she said. 'I'll remind you.'

'I thought you might.'

She grinned. 'If a man walks in a straight line without

turning his head, how can he continue to see everything he has walked past? And there are no mirrors involved.'

'Oh, yes,' Li said. 'I remember now. It was too easy.'

'Oh? So tell me.'

Li shrugged. 'He's walking backwards, of course.'

She narrowed her eyes. 'Yes, it *was* too easy, wasn't it?' She finished the *jian bing* and handed it to him. He bit into its spicy, savoury softness and drew out a two-yuan note. She pushed his hand away. 'Don't be silly,' she said.

'I'm not being silly,' he insisted, and reached beyond her to drop the note in her tin. 'If your house was burgled and I was sent to investigate, would you phone my bosses and say, "It's all right, you don't need to pay him for this investigation, I know him"?'

She couldn't resist a smile. 'Is this a riddle for me?'

'No, it's not. I don't have one today. You didn't give me enough time to prepare.'

'OK,' she said, 'I've got another one for you, then. Much harder this time.' He nodded, and continued stuffing *jian bing* into his mouth. 'Three men check into a hotel. They want to share a room, and the receptionist charges them thirty yuan.'

'That's a cheap hotel room,' he cut in.

'Depends what kind of hotel,' she said. 'Anyway, for the purposes of the riddle it's thirty yuan and they pay ten yuan each.'

'OK.'

'So, after they've gone up to their room she realises she should only have charged them twenty-five yuan.'

'This hotel gets cheaper and cheaper.'

She ignored him. 'She calls the bellboy, explains the situation, and gives him five yuan to take up to the room to pay them back. On the way up, the bellboy figures it's going to be hard for these guys to split five yuan three ways. So he decides to give them only three – one each – and keep the remaining two for himself.'

'Dishonesty,' said Li, shaking his head sadly. 'This is what I have to deal with every day.'

'The question is,' she ignored him again. 'If each of the three men got one yuan back, that means they only paid nine yuan each. A total of twenty-seven yuan. The bellboy kept two to himself. That makes twenty-nine yuan. What happened to the other yuan?'

Li stopped chewing for a moment as he did a quick calculation. Then he frowned. 'Twenty-nine,' he said. Then, 'But that's not possible.'

She raised her eyebrows. 'Therein lies the riddle.'

He did the calculation again and shook his head. 'I'm going to have to think about this. Obviously it's something really simple.'

'Obviously.' She delved into the bag hanging from her bicycle. 'Oh, and I nearly forgot. I brought you this. I thought you might be interested to read it.' She took out a battered, dark blue, hardcover book. '*Redgauntlet* by Sir Walter Scott.'

'I know the name. I think my uncle might have had some of his books. Who is he?'

'Was. He was a very famous Scottish writer. I saw the movie

Braveheart recently, about the Scottish freedom fighter William Wallace. It made me interested in the country. So I've been reading Sir Walter Scott. I think you might enjoy him.'

Li took the book. 'Thanks, Mei Yuan. It might be a while before I can get it back to you. I'm pretty much up to the neck in a case just now.'

'That's all right. Whenever,' she said. 'What a friend has is never lost.'

Some people came for *jian bings* and she turned to cook them, and Li stood silently watching the traffic, reflecting on the tragedy of a dozen years of madness that had stolen the life of a clever, educated woman, and cast her eventually on to the streets to make a living cooking savoury pancakes. But by the time Mei Yuan had finished and turned back, his mind had drifted again to Margaret and the encounter he could not avoid. He came out of his reverie to find her watching him.

'What's on your mind, Li Yan?' she asked.

How could he explain it to her? How could he even begin to explain it? He said, 'What would you do if your heart said one thing and your superiors another?'

'Is this a riddle?'

'No, it's a question.'

She thought about it for a moment. 'This is a conflict between . . . what . . . love and loyalty?'

'I suppose it's something like that, though not quite that simple.'

'If only everything in life was as simple as the solution to a riddle,' she said, and touched his arm. 'Is there no way to accommodate both? It is better to walk on two legs.'

He shook his head sadly. 'I'm afraid there isn't.'

III

Li walked past the games court, cracked concrete baking behind a chickenwire fence. A group of students was playing volleyball, shouting and laughing. Li felt envious of their youth, free from the concerns of the real world that lay beyond the campus. He had been a student here himself once. He knew how it felt, and he experienced a sense of loss at an innocence long gone.

He had been angered, on his return to Section One, to discover that the Americans had insisted on carrying out the autopsy at the Centre of Material Evidence Determination on the campus of the University of Public Security in south-west Beijing. Dr Campbell, apparently, had complained that facilities at Pao Jü Hutong were not good enough. He remembered just how much she had irritated him when they first met. She was having the same effect on him now.

He saw the limousine with its big red *shi* character, meaning *envoy*, followed by 224, identifying it as a US Embassy car. It was parked outside the Centre, and for a moment all his anger and irritation was displaced by a huge sense of apprehension. He felt his pulse quicken, and his mouth became dry.

Detective Qian was already there, and he glanced anxiously at Li as he entered the autopsy room. There was a very young-looking Asian woman with short, dark hair standing at the back of the room. Her face was very pale and she looked as if she wished she were somewhere else. Pathologist Wang had brought his two assistants from Pao Jü Hutong. With Margaret he had been examining photographs of the crime scene laid out on a white covered table, along with the placard that had been hung around the victim's neck. The room almost crackled with an unspoken tension.

Li's first sight of Margaret put him at a distinct disadvantage. Preparations for the autopsy were almost complete, and she was dressed ready to begin, almost unrecognisable beneath layers of professional clothing: surgeon's green pyjamas, a plastic apron, a long-sleeved cotton gown. Her hair was piled beneath a shower cap, and her face hidden behind her surgeon's mask and goggles. The soft, freckled skin of her forearms was concealed by plastic sleeve covers, and her long, elegant fingers, by latex gloves. All these layers were like a barrier between them, concealing and protecting her from his gaze. He, on the other hand, in jeans and open-necked shirt, felt exposed and vulnerable to the eyes he sensed piercing him from behind the anonymity of the goggles. She looked long and hard in his direction, then the voice he knew so well said, 'Late as usual, Deputy Section Chief.' And he felt himself blush.

'For the record,' he said. 'I would like it to be known that I object to this autopsy being carried out by anyone other than our own pathologist, who has conducted the previous three autopsies in this case.'

'Really?' That familiar acid tone. 'Perhaps if you had called in a professional sooner, there wouldn't be the need for a *fourth* autopsy.'

Li heard the Asian girl gasp. It was like a slap in the face. A calculated insult. He glanced at Wang, uncertain as to whether his English had been good enough to follow this quick-fire exchange. But if the Chinese pathologist had understood, he gave no indication of it. His loss of *mianzi*, face, like Margaret's hurt, was hidden behind mask and goggles.

Margaret nodded to the two assistants. 'Now that the boss has finally arrived, I suppose we'd better begin.'

They glanced at Pathologist Wang, who made some imperceptible gesture of consent, and they went out and wheeled in the body, still fully clothed, on a gurney, and positioned it beneath a microphone hanging from the ceiling.

It was a bizarre sight, lying on its back, arched over the arms which were pulled behind to where they were still tied at the wrist. The head, propped on a blood-soaked towel, was placed approximately at the neck, but lying at a very odd angle and staring, open-eyed and open-mouthed, off to one side.

Margaret used the moment, when all attention was focused on the corpse, to sneak a proper look at Li. He was thinner than when she had seen him last, the strain showing in shadows beneath his eyes. She was shocked by how Chinese he looked. When she had been with him almost every waking hour, she had ceased completely to see him as Chinese. He was just Li Yan, who touched her with a gentleness she had not known before in a man, whose eyes were soft and dark and full of humour and life, drawing her unaccountably to him. Now all that familiarity was gone. He seemed almost like a stranger, and she succumbed to an odd sense of disappointment. All she really felt towards him now was anger.

She turned her attention quickly back to the body and switched on the overhead microphone, escaping into a professional world where death took precedence over life. But she paused for a moment, struck by the strange posture of the body, flexed against the hands behind its back, the odd position of the disembodied head. It somehow reinforced the sense of a man forced to his death, much more than a simple stabbing or shooting. There was something in his demeanour that hinted at the terror he had experienced in the anticipation of his own beheading. It was unimaginable. She quickly began the preliminary examination, recording for later transcription, what she saw as she went.

'The body is that of a well-nourished Asian man, appearing to be in his early fifties. The decedent is the victim of decapitation that will be described further below. The decedent is clothed in charcoal grey pants, white socks and black leather shoes, and is wearing a white shirt that is blood-soaked about the anterior and lateral aspects of the collar, and about the chest area.'

The assistants turned the corpse over, creating the macabre illusion of the body rotating around a fixed head. The ensemble now resembled something far more difficult to see as human than as some unrelated waxwork body parts. Margaret examined the white silk cord binding the wrists, raised the ring-flash camera offered by one of the assistants, and took several photographs. The other assistant handed Margaret an eighteen-inch length of twine. She tied its two ends to the silk cord, a couple of inches apart, and about three inches from the knot, and then cut the cord between the two twine knots, preserving the cord knot intact. Pathologist Wang laid it out on the adjoining table. Margaret photographed the wrists again.

'On removal of the cord, the wrists are seen to bear faint pink contusions that will be described further below.'

Pathologist Wang's assistants then carefully removed Yuan Tao's clothes and laid them out on the table next to the silk cord. They checked and found nothing in the pockets of the trousers. They turned the body again to lie on its back, and Margaret began to examine it in detail.

'The body has been refrigerated and is cold to the touch. Rigor mortis is present in the jaw and extremities, but is not observed in the neck, due to the decapitation. Fixed post-mortem lividity is only faintly observed in the posterior dependent parts.'

Li interrupted. 'Can you give me any idea of the time of death?'

She sighed and switched off the microphone. 'Why do policemen always insist on asking a question they know cannot be answered with any degree of accuracy?'

Li thought he could detect a smile somewhere beneath Pathologist Wang's surgical mask. But Margaret pressed on. Her question had been rhetorical.

'Since the body has been refrigerated, there is no point in my taking liver temperature. I'd say rigor mortis has been set for a few hours, so I would guess perhaps he died somewhere between twelve and sixteen hours ago.'

That would put time of death between 10 p.m. and 2 a.m. the previous night, Li thought. A little later than Wang's estimate, but it fitted better with the movements of the people in the apartment below.

'May I proceed?' Margaret asked. Li nodded.

She examined the head, turning it freely this way and that, at one stage lifting it up by its hair, leaving soft, currant-red clots of blood on the table. She described the dark, staring eyes that remained fixed as she turned the head, the mouth held open by rigor, as if frozen in the act of screaming.

'*There is a two-to-two-and-a-half by four-centimetre area of pink contusion with golden, parchment-like abrasion over the malar area of the right cheek and the lateral orbital rim.*'

Injuries sustained as the head hit the floor and rolled. Now she moved to a description of the trauma, scrutinising the neck wound in detail.

'*There has been complete decapitation as mentioned above. The posterior edge is three centimetres inferior to the anterior edge and the wound edge is sharpest on the left posterolateral aspect. There is a thin rim of abrasion at this posterolateral edge, and its anterior aspect bears a one-by-two-and-a-half-centimetre flap of skin. This flap of skin rests against the anterior, exterior aspects of the neck. There is vital reaction at the wound's edge. The wound crosses the spinal column at the fifth-sixth intervertebral space. There is complete transection of all*' *soft tissue structures of the neck: the trachea at the level of the third tracheal ring; the carotids inferior to their bifurcations. The soft tissue edges indicate a forward direction of the instrument.'*

'Meaning what exactly?' Li asked.

She threw him a withering look. 'That I've seen a cleaner cut,' she said.

She proceeded to photograph the neck from various angles, before examining the grey-green discolouration on the pale tan cut surface of the spinal column. She indicated that she wanted a tape lift. Pathologist Wang cut a length, several inches long, of broad, clear, sticky tape. Holding it by the ends, he placed it over the cut surface of the tough, fibro-cartilaginous tissue between the fifth and sixth vertebrae, and Margaret pressed it home. Wang then peeled it away, taking with it some of the microscopic metal or mineral particles left by the blade of the murder weapon, and preserved them by sticking the tape across the rim of a glass petri dish.

Margaret looked up at Li. 'I take it you've followed similar procedures on the previous victims?'

'We have.'

'And?'

'The particles were subjected to analysis under a scanning electron microscope. The primary elements detected were copper and tin.'

'Bronze,' she said. 'Some kind of ceremonial or ornamental sword? Perhaps even a genuine artefact?'

'Perhaps,' Li conceded.

'Well, it must be one of the three,' she said. 'No one's made bronze swords for serious use since they discovered iron.' She paused for thought. 'What about the signature?'

Li frowned. 'I don't understand.'

Margaret was impatient, and addressed him as if talking to a child. 'Even the smoothest blade has nicks and imperfections that leave microscopic striations on the cut bone – a signature. I assume you have taken sections of vertebrae from the previous victims?'

Li glanced at Wang who nodded.

'Good,' said Margaret. 'Then there's an outside chance that if you examine the cut surface of the bone or disc, using a comparison microscope, you can match up the striations and tell if the same murder weapon was used in each case. An experienced swordsman would normally strike with the same part of the blade each time, what you might call a sweet spot. So it might have left the same signature each time. And, of course, if you ever recover it, you will certainly be able to match the sword to the murders – a little like a ballistic comparison. It's called toolmark examination.'

'This is not ... mm ... a procedure we have previously employed,' Pathologist Wang said, and Li was surprised at the fluency of his English.

'Well, I'd like you to employ it now,' Margaret said. 'It could be important. If your criminalist needs advice on the procedure I'll be happy to help.' She gave the nod to one of the assistants to cut a section of the spinal column. Using the same oscillating saw he would later employ to remove the top of the skull, he cut through the spinal column a few inches below the wound and put the severed chunk of vertebra into a formalin-filled storage jar held by his colleague.

The sound of the saw had been sharp and mournful, for all the world like some unearthly creature wailing for its dead. Sophie, who had been standing at the back of the room, sweat gathering across her scalp, her complexion like putty, put a hand over her mouth. But she caught Margaret's eye and knew that one way or another she had to stick this out. She swallowed hard, breathed deeply, and tried to think herself somewhere else.

Margaret stood back to let the assistants collect blood and vitreous samples for toxicology. Again she took the opportunity to steal another look at Li, who kept his eyes steadfastly on the procedure. She wanted to grab him and shake him and ask him why. But she felt the tears start to fill her eyes and she looked quickly away again, as the needle inserted by one of the assistants to draw fluid from the right eye of the decedent caused the eyeball to collapse. She refocused on the job in hand. The rest of the autopsy was largely routine and would take around forty-five minutes. Just forty-five more minutes.

The assistants placed a block of wood under the body, mid-chest, to help expose the chest cavity when she made the initial 'Y' shaped incision, starting at each shoulder, meeting at the bottom of the breast bone, then continuing on down past the umbilicus to the pubic bone.

Once the ribcage had been cut away, providing easy access to the organs, Margaret worked her way systematically through the heart and lungs, finding nothing abnormal, until she came to the stomach. She clamped and transected the oesophagus, freeing the stomach from its fatty connections, then cut it from the duodenum. Everyone was hit by the smell of alcohol. Margaret sniffed two or three times and raised an eyebrow.

'Smells like vodka to me. A man after my own heart.'

She held up the stomach and, making a small incision, drained its contents into a measuring jug. The stink of it filled the room. She opened the stomach up for inspection.

'*The oesophagus is lined by grey-pink mucosa. There are no diverticula or varices. The stomach contains four hundred and seventy-five cubic centimetres of thin, blue-brown liquid containing multiple tiny, pale blue particles resembling medication residue. No recognisable food is identified. An ethanol-like odour is noted. The gastric mucosa is stained pale blue, apparently by the gastric contents, and the rugal pattern is normal.*'

She switched off the microphone again. 'Roofies,' she said. 'Classic date rape drug. Two or three 2 mg tablets and the recipient becomes looped, spacy, sleepy . . . Even more effective when taken with alcohol. Explains why he submitted so placidly to his execution. Except for the minor bruising around the wrist ligature, there is absolutely no sign of trauma to indicate that he put up any kind of a fight.'

'It was a drug called flunitrazepam that was identified in the stomachs of the other . . . mm . . . victims,' Pathologist Wang said.

'Same thing,' said Margaret. 'Roofies is the street name. Rohypnol is the trade name. Made by the Roche Company. Very popular in the wrong hands when it was first marketed because it was colourless, odourless and tasteless when dissolved in drink. So Roche changed the formula to make it turn blue. Kind of hard to slip into someone's drink without them noticing.'

Wang said, 'In the other three it was mixed with red wine.'

Margaret thought about it for a moment. 'Hm. I guess that would probably do it. Might make it a bit turbid, though if you weren't a practised wine drinker you might not know the difference. But in this case,' she indicated the open carcass on the autopsy table, 'it would sure as hell have turned bright blue in vodka.'

Li frowned. 'Then why would he have drunk it?'

Margaret shrugged. 'Who knows? It's amazing what most people will do with a gun pointed at their head.' She nodded towards the blood-stained placard lying on the adjacent table. 'I guess they hung that placard around his neck before they gave him the chop.'

'That's our assumption,' Li confirmed.

She waited, but he volunteered nothing further. 'So what does it mean?' she asked.

He returned her gaze and spoke evenly. 'The top character represents the number three.'

Margaret furrowed her brows. 'But I thought Yuan Tao was the fourth victim?'

'He is. The killer started at six and seems to be counting down.'

'So there are another two victims on his list?'

'That's how it looks.' Li paused for a moment, then carried

on, 'The character scored through is a nickname. They all had nicknames – Zero, Monkey, Pigsy. They were all at the same middle school together.'

Margaret raised an eyebrow and thought about it for a moment. 'But not Yuan Tao?'

'Until we get the file from your embassy, we don't know anything about him. But given that he's an American, that would seem unlikely. His nickname, apparently, was Digger. The name character for it, as with all the others, is upside down'

Margaret was intrigued. 'Why? Does that have any special significance?'

'During the Cultural Revolution,' Li said, 'people who were held up to ridicule as "revisionists" or "counter-revolution-aries" were sometimes publicly paraded with such nameplates hung around their necks, their names written upside down and crossed through. It was to signify that they were consid-ered "non-people".'

She wondered what it must have been like to be a "non-person". During these last months she had learned enough about the Cultural Revolution to know that almost everyone in this room would have been a target for such persecution. The humiliation, degradation, and sometimes death inflicted on intellectuals, educated or professional people, during those dark years was unimaginable. And it was only just over twenty years since it had all come to an end. Still too close for comfort.

She switched on the mike and returned to the rest of the autopsy. Liver, spleen, pancreas, kidney, guts, bladder. The only problem arose when the assistants had difficulty preventing the head from slipping away across the table while cutting through the skull with the oscillating saw. Finally, they achieved their aim, one holding the head steady with two hands, the other cutting, and then delivering the brain into Margaret's hands for weighing.

With sections taken from each of the organs, and the autopsy virtually over, the assistants sewed up the carcass and roughly stitched the head back on to the neck. It was a grotesque parody of a human being that they then hosed down. They scrubbed off the blood and blotted it dry with paper, before slipping it into a body bag and wheeling it away for return to the refrigerator.

Margaret peeled off her latex gloves, removing the steel-mesh glove from her non-cutting hand, and untied the gown and apron, letting them fall away. Despite the coldness of the autopsy room she was perspiring freely. She snapped off her goggles and mask and pulled away the shower cap to shake her hair out over her shoulders.

Li saw her properly for the first time – her pale, freckled skin, the slightly full lips, her well-defined brows, the ice-chip blue eyes – and his heart flipped over. All he wanted to do was take her face in his hands and kiss her. But he did not move. She turned to find him looking at her, and she had an overwhelming desire to slap his face as hard as she could. But instead, she moved to the adjoining table to look at the items that had been removed from the body, and the photographs taken at the crime scene.

Li, and Doctor Wang, and a very pale-looking Sophie gathered around. Margaret glanced at Sophie and saw that her hands were trembling. At least she had stuck it out. Not many people made it through their first autopsy without throwing up. Then she turned her attention to the photographs.

'What's this hole in the floor?' she asked Li, picking up a print that clearly showed where the floorboards had been lifted.

'We don't know,' Li said. 'The linoleum had been pulled back and the boards removed. Most of the blood drained into the hole and dripped through the ceiling of the apartment below.'

'Were the boards nailed down or loose?'

'They had been nailed down at one time, but it appears that the nails had been removed some time ago. The boards must have fitted very loosely. They would have creaked or rattled underfoot.'

'Some kind of hiding place?'

'Possibly.'

Margaret examined the picture some more. 'Had the linoleum been lifted, or was it torn?'

'It appeared to have been torn.'

She nodded thoughtfully and dropped the picture back on the table. 'Pathologist Wang says the other victims had red wine in their stomachs.'

This was a sudden leap that left Li more than a little puzzled. 'That's right,' he said. 'I don't see the connection.'

'Of course not,' she responded curtly, and clearly had no

intention of explaining. 'So we can assume that the killer was known to them. They're having a drink with him.'

'Yes, we have already made that assumption.' Li's response came with a tone. But she appeared not to notice.

'And he endeavoured to disguise the fact that he was drugging them by dropping the Roofies in red wine,' she said pensively. 'So why did he hand Yuan Tao a bright blue vodka? And why, as you asked yourself, did Yuan drink it?'

'Coercion,' said Li. 'You suggested as much.'

'Yes,' said Margaret, 'but it's a change of pattern. Serial killers are usually very predictable. Once they have established a pattern, they normally stick to it. Religiously.'

She began scrutinising the other photographs taken at the death scene: the body taken from several different angles, the main pool of blood draining into the space left by the removal of the floorboards; the arterial blood spatter patterns from the two carotid arteries from which blood had spurted at approximately two and ten o'clock directions from the neck, travelling between one and two metres from the body. It was a bloody event. The main pool had formed once the body had collapsed and blood continued to drain from the carotids. Margaret became very interested in a less dramatic scatter of blood, following a line at right angles to the body on its right side. She put the photograph down and gazed at the white-tiled wall in front of her. 'So our killer was left-handed,' she said finally.

'How can you possibly know that?' It was the first time that Sophie had spoken and everyone looked up at her in surprise.

She became suddenly self-conscious. 'I mean, everything I've read says it's almost impossible to tell the handedness of a killer in a blade attack.' She felt she had to explain.

'True,' Margaret said. 'But I'm not looking at the angle of a blade entering a body here. I'm looking at the cast-off pattern left by the sword. Look, see . . .' She pointed out the line of tiny blood droplets that she had been studying. 'When the blade goes through the neck in a downward slicing motion, it collects a certain amount of blood en route. And as the swordsman follows through with the downward arc of his sword, a certain amount of blood is cast off by the momentum. That's what this line of droplets is here, on the right side of the body.'

'How does that tell you the handedness of the killer?' Sophie had forgotten, for the moment, about her squeamishness.

'You ever heard of Tameshi Giri?' She looked around the blank faces. No one had. 'It's a Japanese martial art,' she explained. 'The art of cutting things with swords. Its exponents practise on tightly bound bundles of straw. I believe it might even be Chinese in origin.' Li and Wang still looked blank. Margaret smiled. 'I did an autopsy on an assisted Hara Kiri suicide, where once the victim had disembowelled himself, his Tameshi Giri assistant beheaded him.'

'Eugh!' Sophie shivered. 'You mean people actually choose to die by having their heads cut off?'

Margaret nodded. 'It saves you from too much suffering once you've slit your belly open. It's not exactly common, but there have been several cases. I had to make a small study of them for mine.' She turned to Li. 'The cutter stands behind the victim and to his left if he is right-handed. And on the right if he is left-handed.' She passed him the photograph. 'As you can see, the cast-off pattern is on Yuan Tao's right. So his killer was left-handed.'

Li looked at the picture for a long time. 'Are you saying this killer is some kind of Tameshi Giri expert?'

'No. I'd say he wasn't a novice. He certainly knows how to handle a sword. But the cut is not very clean. There was a marked abrasion at the entry edge, and quite a large, irregular flap of skin at the exit edge. So he wasn't an expert.'

'Pathologist Wang thought perhaps the blade was getting blunt,' Li said drily, and Margaret smiled at the pathologist's implied criticism of the investigation.

'All the more reason to think this was no expert,' she said. 'An expert would keep his blade well honed.'

'The first three . . . mm . . . victims were much more cleanly cut,' Wang offered.

'Were they?' Margaret frowned, computing several possibilities in her mind. At length she asked, 'Are the photographs from the other crime scenes available?' Wang nodded and sent one of his assistants to get them. 'I'd also like copies of the autopsy reports on the other victims. Translated, please. And access to all the other evidence.'

Li bridled. 'This is a Chinese police investigation,' he said.

'Of an American citizen,' Margaret fired back. 'And we don't have two years to wait for a result.'

'Two years?' Sophie said. 'What do you mean?'

Margaret turned a syrupy smile on her. 'Deputy Section Chief Li once told me that it took him two years to clear up a murder here. Par for the course for the Chinese police, I think.'

'That was one case,' Li retorted, barely containing his fury. 'And at least we broke it. If it had been in America, it would still be languishing in an unsolved cases file.'

The assistant returned with three large brown envelopes, and Margaret held them for a moment. 'And am I allowed to look?' she asked Li pointedly. He kept his lips pressed together in a grim line and nodded curtly. She smiled sweetly. 'Thank you.' And she spread the photographs from each envelope out on the table. Immediately she gasped with frustration. 'I thought you said this was a serial killer?'

'It's what we believe,' Li said more confidently than he felt.

'Well, victim number three's been moved from the murder scene. There's not nearly enough blood here.'

'We *are* aware of that.' There were echoes in this for Li of that morning's meeting. Fresh eyes casting a sceptical look at the evidence.

'Another break in the pattern,' Margaret said. And she started examining the blood spatter patterns in the photographs of the first two murders. 'And yet another.' She dropped the photographs back on the table. 'Victims one and two were killed by a right-handed bladesman. You can see for yourself. The cast-off patterns are on the left side of the bodies.'

Li examined the photographs. 'Well, there's no way of making that comparison with victim number three. And, anyway, it's perfectly possible that the killer is equally good with left or right hand.' He was getting defensive now.

But Margaret was dismissive. 'Unlikely.' She picked up and began studying the photographs of the bound wrists of each of the victims in the order of their killing. 'Pass me the silk cord we took from the decedent,' she asked Sophie.

Sophie blanched at the prospect, and very gingerly lifted the cord between thumb and forefinger and passed it across the table. Margaret took it and looked at it very closely.

Li said, 'We have already established that the cord used to bind the first three victims was all cut from the same length. I am sure we will find the same with that one.'

Margaret shrugged, clearly unconvinced. 'Then why', she asked, 'when he was tying the wrists of Yuan Tao, did he use a different knot than the one used on the other three?'

Li frowned and took the cord, looking at the knot closely, then examining the photographs. 'They all look the same to me,' he said.

'They all *look* like reef knots,' Margaret said. 'But the first three were tied by a right-handed person. Right over left and under, left over right and under. The fourth is exactly the reverse. Tied by a left-hander.' Li looked at her, trying to absorb the implications. 'The point is,' Margaret went on, 'Yuan Tao was clearly killed by someone else. It's a copycat murder.'

CHAPTER THREE

I

The warmth of the sunshine seemed somehow surprising after the chill of the autopsy room. Margaret fished in her purse for her sunglasses and put them on. Li followed her out on to the step and lit a cigarette. They had left Sophie in the office phoning her boss to arrange protocol clearance for the handing over of autopsy reports and photographic evidence. They stood for some minutes in silence. On the games court, beyond the fence, students were still playing volleyball, their catcalls and laughter echoing back off the walls of the Evidence Centre. Somehow the simple pleasure they took in their game made the contrast with the act of dissecting the dead all the more bleak.

Finally Li said, 'It cannot be a copycat murder.'

She shrugged her indifference. 'The evidence speaks for itself. You can think what you like.'

'It is impossible,' said Li. 'This is not America. Accounts of crimes are not splashed all over the newspapers or on television. The details of these crimes can be known only by the killer himself, and by my investigating team.'

'Then maybe you should have a look at your investigating team.'

Her flippancy angered him, but she clearly was not in a mood to be reasoned with. He bit back a retort.

After a moment she turned and looked at him levelly. 'Are we finished?' She paused and added, 'Professionally speaking.'

'I guess so.'

'Good,' she said, and hit him as hard as she could across the side of his face with her open palm.

He was shocked. He had been taking a draw of his cigarette, and it was knocked from his mouth by the force of the blow. His face stung from the slap, and his eyes blurred as they filled involuntarily with tears. He blinked at her furiously. 'What was that for?'

'What do you think?' And he wondered why he had even asked. 'Why, Li Yan?' she said. 'Why?' He couldn't meet her eye. 'Ten weeks. You never once tried to get in touch, never once tried to see me. You've avoided every attempt I've made to see you.' She fought to hold back the tears and control her voice.

At the sound of raised voices, the driver of her embassy car, parked no more than ten feet away, turned to look out the rear windscreen. Li turned his back to the car and kept his voice down. 'They told me that under no circumstances was I to see you, or contact you.'

She looked at him in disbelief. 'So you're happy to let *them*, whoever *they* are, tell you who you can and cannot see?'

'I'm an employee of the state, Margaret. It is a privileged and trusted position that cannot be compromised by a relationship with a foreigner.'

'Oh, I see. So your job's more important than the woman you love, or the woman I thought you loved. Good thing I found out you didn't. Otherwise I might have made a fool of myself by doing something stupid like falling in love with you.' She turned away in disgust.

He got angry in his own defence. 'You have no idea, have you?' He found his breath coming in short bursts. 'With my uncle dead, my job is the only life I have. And if I go against my superiors I will lose that job. And what would I do then? An ex-cop! Sell CD roms to tourists in the street? Get myself a market stall and pass off junk with phoney designer labels as genuine? If I want to be with you, Margaret, I have no future in China. We would have to go to the United States. And what future would I have there?' He tugged her arm and pulled her round to face him. 'You tell me.' His eyes appealed to her desperately for understanding.

But she could not think of anything to say. She tried to imagine how it would be to leave everything in the States behind – her home, her family, her job – to come and live in China. But no picture of it would come to her mind.

'This is my home,' he said. 'This is who I am. And no matter how painful it has been for me to accept it, I know there is no future for you and me.'

She saw the pain in his eyes and knew that it was real. But it did nothing to diminish her own. She said, 'I was right, then. I gave up on you, Li Yan. Finally. I was supposed to catch a plane home this morning. Then they asked me to do the autopsy.'

'And now you have done it,' he said, 'there is no reason for you to stay. This is a Chinese police investigation. There is no point in either of us putting ourselves through more pain.'

And it was as simple as that, she thought. Get on a plane, fly away and don't look back. She had come here in the first place to escape the failures of her personal life back home. She would be returning home to escape the failures of her personal life here. Everything she touched, it seemed, turned to dust. Including Li. She reached out and ran her fingers lightly over his cheek where the imprint of her hand was raised and red.

'I'm sorry I hit you,' she said.

He reached up and put his hand over hers and squeezed it gently. He had an overpowering desire to bend his head and kiss her. But he didn't.

She slowly withdrew her hand. For a moment she had thought he was going to kiss her. She had wanted him to, with all her heart. And when he didn't she had felt a terrible aching emptiness with the realisation that there was no way back, and no way forward.

'Well, that's that fixed.' Sophie pushed through the swing doors and down the steps. 'It's been agreed that translation of the autopsy reports and copies of the photographic evidence in all four murders will be delivered to the embassy as soon as possible.' She stopped, realising immediately that she had walked in on something, and saw the unmistakable shape of a raised handprint on Li's face. 'I'll wait in the car,' she said hastily, and turned towards the limousine.

'It's all right. We've finished,' Margaret said, suddenly businesslike, and she brushed past Li and followed Sophie to the car.

'Jesus,' Sophie said, as they slipped into the back seat. 'You hit him!' And then she saw the tears rolling slowly down Margaret's cheek, and she quickly turned to face forward. 'Sorry.'

Li watched the car pull away from the kerb, and felt as if some invisible umbilical cord was dragging the inside out of him as it went.

II

They drove in silence for nearly fifteen minutes before Sophie sneaked a look at Margaret. The tears had either dried up or been brushed away. They had both been staring out of their respective windows at the traffic on the second ring road, tower blocks rising up all around them and casting lengthening shadows from west to east. 'That was my first autopsy,' Sophie said.

'I'd never have guessed.' Margaret kept her eyes fixed on the traffic.

Sophie smiled and blushed. 'That obvious?'

Margaret relented and drew her a wan smile. 'I've seen worse. At least we weren't forced to inspect the contents of *your* stomach as well.' Sophie grinned, and Margaret added, 'But you'd better get used to it. It certainly won't be your last.'

'How do you ever get used to something like that?' Sophie asked. 'I mean, you must be affected by it. Surely. All these poor, dead people laid out like . . . like meat. Like they never had a life.'

'You should try dealing with the living,' Margaret said. 'Personally I find it's a lot less stressful working with the dead. They have no expectation that you're going to make them better.'

And she wondered if that's what was wrong with her. That she could be so at home with the dead: breadloafing their organs, dissecting their brains, examining the contents of their intestines, all with a detached expertise and self-confidence. And yet when it came to the living she was ill at ease, protective, defensive, aggressive. It had always been easy to blame her failed relationships on someone else. It had always been clear to her that she was not at fault. But what if she was? After all, wasn't she the misfit, the one happier to spend time with corpses? Had all those years spent dissecting the dead stolen away her ability to relate to the living? The thought left her feeling empty and depressed. Because what lay ahead on her return to the States but more years spent in autopsy rooms? An endless conveyer belt of tragedy. A bleak, white-tiled future with nothing more to stimulate her senses than the touch of refrigerated flesh.

Sophie's mobile phone rang, a silly electronic melody that Margaret took a moment or two to identify as 'Scotland the Brave'. Sophie fumbled to find it in her purse.

'Sophie Daum,' she answered, when finally she got it to

her ear. 'Oh, hi, Jonathan. Sure. We're just on the way back to her hotel now.' She glanced at Margaret. 'Well, I guess . . . Sure. OK, see you.' She switched off and leaned forward to the driver. 'Change of plan. We're going straight to the embassy.' She turned to Margaret. 'The ambassador wants to see you.'

'Well, fuck the ambassador,' Margaret said, and Sophie's eyes widened with shock. Margaret told the driver, 'Go to the Ritan Hotel.' Then to Sophie, 'First thing I'm going to do is take a shower. Strange as it may seem, I prefer the scent of Fabergé to formaldehyde. Then I'm going to change into some fresh clothes. And if he still wants to talk, *then* I will see the ambassador.'

The driver glanced back at Sophie for clarification. She hesitated a moment, then nodded. 'I'm going to get bawled out for this,' she told Margaret.

'Well, bawl right back. It's not your fault if this cranky pathologist won't do what she's told.' She grinned. 'Tell them I was scared I'd get blood on the ambassador's nice new carpet.'

Their car cruised past the Moskva restaurant on the south-west corner of Ritan Park, a stone's throw away from the ambassador's residence, past the rows of traders in Ritan Lu and the dull gaze of the furriers squatting beside the pelts that hung on long rails opposite Margaret's hotel. Their enthusiasm had waned in almost direct correlation to the decline of the Russian economy and a drastic drop in business. Long gone were the days when Russian traders would measure the furs they bought by how many they could squeeze into a baggage car on the night train to Moscow. Even the Russian mafia, dealing exclusively in dollars, was feeling the pinch.

Margaret stepped out of the car at the door of the hotel and leaned back in to Sophie. 'Come for me in an hour.' She looked at her watch. 'Say five thirty.' Sophie nodded, but did not look happy.

In her room, Margaret stripped off her clothes and dumped them in a laundry bag for collection by room service. The shower felt good. Hot and stimulating. She tipped her head back, eyes closed, and let the water hit her face, pouring down between her breasts in a small stream cascading from the end of her chin. She tried to banish from her mind all thoughts of the autopsy, of her last encounter with Li. The two seemed inextricably linked, a single unhappy experience. She knew, of course, that she would have to wait for the results from toxicology on the samples she had prepared before she could write her autopsy report. Twenty-four hours, forty-eight at the most, and then she could go. No looking back. The trouble was she didn't want to look forward either.

She stepped on to the bathmat and dried herself vigorously with a big soft towel, before collecting her wet hair in a hand towel and wrapping it around her head. From the wardrobe she took the black silk dressing gown embroidered with gold and red dragons that she had bought on an idle afternoon in Silk Street. It felt wonderful as she wrapped it around her nakedness, sheer and sensuous on her skin. She caught a glimpse of herself in the mirror, the skin of her face fresh and pink. But she was shocked by how tired and lined her eyes were, shadowed, and sunk back in her skull. And, unaccountably, they were filled suddenly by tears that ran hot and salty on her cheeks. She looked quickly away from her reflection. There was little less edifying, she thought, than the sight of one's own self-pity.

She was startled by a knock at the door, and she quickly wiped away the tears. 'Just a minute,' she called, and she took a couple of deep breaths.

A bellboy stood in the corridor holding an expansive bouquet of flowers. He thrust them at her. 'For you, lady,' he said, and hurried away before she could even think about a tip.

She carried the flowers back into the bedroom, kicking the door shut behind her. She had always been scornful of those women who were suckers for flowers. Men knew exactly how to use a bouquet, or a single rose, to manipulate them. And, as far as Margaret was concerned, no one was going to manipulate her. Still, she felt an unexpected rush of pleasure. They *were* beautiful, a host of wonderful scents mingled in a dazzle of colour. She laid them carefully on the bed and saw the card tucked into the wrapping. For a moment she hesitated. She was not sure she wanted to know who it was from, or what it said. But curiosity quickly got the better of her and she ripped open the envelope and pulled out a small, simple card with a floral design on the front. She opened it up and, inside, in a hand she did not recognise, were the words, 'Glad you're still around. Pick you up at eight.' It was signed simply, 'Michael'.

She felt the blood physically drain from her face, and for a moment felt dizzy, and had to put a hand on the wall to steady herself. Michael was dead. How could he possibly— She stopped herself, mid-thought. Of course it wasn't him. Her mind raced for a few seconds before she realised. Michael Zimmerman. He was the only other Michael she knew, and certainly the only Michael she knew in China. She had forgotten about his very existence. She smiled, but it was a grim smile, because she was reminded that the man she had married and lived with for seven years could still reach out and touch her, even from the grave, even now. She shivered at the thought, and then just as quickly pushed him from her mind.

Michael Zimmerman. She remembered his smiling eyes, and how she had been attracted to him. Was that only last night? Already it seemed like a lifetime ago. *Pick you up at eight.* She felt a tiny thrill of pleasure like the faintest glimmer of light in a very dark place.

'The ambassador was furious,' Sophie said. She seemed very agitated.

Margaret was unimpressed. 'Was he?' She slipped into the back seat beside her, and the limo purred quietly out into the street.

'He couldn't wait. He had some engagement he couldn't get out of.'

'That's a pity,' Margaret said. 'So why are we still going to the embassy?'

'To see Stan and Jonathan.' Sophie flicked her a look. 'Jonathan gave me a hell of a dressing down for not bringing you straight back.'

'Jesus!' Margaret felt her hackles rising. 'Who the hell do these people think they are? I don't work for the US government. I'm doing them a favour, for Chrissake. We may be in the People's Republic, but I am a citizen of the United States, a free person, and I will do what the hell I like.' She breathed hard for a few moments, then took a long, deep breath and let the tension slip away as she exhaled.

They sat in silence for a couple of minutes, then Margaret said, 'So how come Michael Zimmerman knew I was still in Beijing?'

Sophie was caught off guard. 'What?'

'He sent me a bunch of flowers and a card saying he's going to pick me up at eight tonight.'

'Lucky you.' There was just a hint of pique in Sophie's voice. 'He called before lunch. I guess I must have mentioned you'd postponed your departure to do this autopsy.'

'And just happened to mention where I was staying, too?'

She shrugged. 'He asked.' She paused. 'So where's he taking you?'

'I've no idea.'

They were kept waiting for ten minutes in the security foyer of the Chancery, under the implacable gaze of the marine behind the window. Then a harsh electronic buzz and the dull click of a lock announced the arrival of the First Secretary. He was brusque and businesslike and came through the door without so much as an acknowledgement. 'Follow me,' he said, and hurried out and down the steps. Margaret and Sophie exchanged looks and went after him.

'Want to tell me where we're going, Stan?' Margaret asked as they walked round the side of the building. The late evening sun washed yellow across the compound.

'To get a bite to eat. I don't know about you, but it's more than five hours since I ate, and I'm hungry.'

'Well, you know, that's funny,' but Margaret wasn't smiling. 'I haven't eaten either. Not since before I did the autopsy. You remember? The autopsy I did as a favour for you guys? By the way, thanks for the acknowledgement. It's nice to know how much your country appreciates you.'

Stan stopped in his tracks, looked skyward for a moment, then turned, pursing his lips. 'You are a real pain in the ass, Margaret, you know that?'

'You bet,' she said, and Stan found himself smiling, albeit reluctantly. Margaret added, 'After two hours hacking about a dead body, a girl's entitled to a shower, Stan.'

'OK.' He raised his hands in self-defence. 'Point taken. And the ambassador appreciates your efforts, Margaret. He really does. But we need to talk. This whole thing's in danger of turning nasty. Political.'

He turned and they carried on past a long blue canopy set among a grove of trees. Embassy staff sat at tables chatting animatedly, taking their evening meals al fresco. Immediately opposite, was the canteen – a long, single-storey building. Stan headed for the door.

'Political in what way?' Margaret wanted to know.

'You'll see when you look at Yuan Tao's file,' Stan said, and they followed him inside, past long rows of bookshelves, to a large white board with an extensive menu scrawled up in blue felt pen. There was a clatter of crockery from the kitchens behind it. 'Turns out the guy was born here. Didn't go to the States till he was seventeen, just before the Cultural Revolution. Never came back. Eventually applied for and got US citizenship.' He lifted a piece of paper and a pencil from a table in front of the menu board and thrust it at her. 'Here. You write the number of dishes you want, the number of the dish – they're up on the board – and the price.' He rapidly filled out his own slip. 'And don't forget to put your name on it.'

Margaret glanced across at an opening leading to the bar. 'I'd much rather have a drink,' she said.

Stan followed her eyes and smiled. 'Sorry, Margaret. It's only open Friday afternoons for an extended happy hour. You can get a soft drink from the cold cabinet.'

Margaret sighed and scrutinised the board and chose sweet-and-sour pork, fried noodles and a Coca-Cola. 'So he was born here,' she said. 'How does that make it political?'

'There are folk back home who would like to think that the Chinese are capable of storing up their revenge for as long as it takes.'

'Revenge for what?'

'Someone like Yuan Tao might have been seen as having jumped ship,' Stan said, 'and then betrayed his country by going native in the States.'

Margaret was incredulous. 'So they wait thirty-odd years for him to come back and then bump him off? You don't really believe that, do you?'

'Not for a minute.' Stan shook his head. 'But you've got to remember, Margaret, the right wing back in the States has been scratching about looking for another bogeyman ever since the Soviet Union turned turtle. And China's it. The press is full of anti-China propaganda. Some of it's pretty gross. But some of it's pretty subtle, too. Sometimes it's all in the tone. And then they make movies like *Seven Years in Tibet* or *Red Corner* which get the folks back home all in a rage about Chinese injustice. I mean, *Red Corner*'s an entertaining story if you like that kind of thing, but its portrayal of the Chinese justice system was just ludicrous. Laughable. Except that the Chinese authorities weren't laughing. They banned it, and then got accused of censorship.'

Margaret followed him to a desk where a woman sat at a cash register. 'I didn't know you were such a champion of the Chinese, Stan.'

'I'm not,' he snapped. 'But people back home who don't know anything about this country should keep their ignorance to themselves. All it does is make our job more difficult.'

He passed in his order, paid for it and collected a bottle of water from the cold cabinet before heading for a table where Jon Dakers was waiting for them. Margaret realised she was expected to pay for herself. She took a few yuan from her purse, grabbed a Coke and joined them. Sophie sat down beside Dakers and folded her hands on the glass top that covered a garish floral print tablecloth. She hadn't ordered anything to eat. Dakers had already eaten. He grunted some kind of acknowledgement across the table to Margaret and passed her a buff-coloured folder. 'The Yuan Tao file,' he said. 'Sophie tells us you don't believe he was murdered by the same person who killed the other three.'

'That's right.'

'But you think it's a copycat job?'

'That's how it looks.'

Stan and Dakers exchanged glances. Dakers said, 'So what about this cop who's leading the investigation?'

'What about him?' Margaret looked suspiciously at Stan.

'You trust him?' Dakers asked.

'Trust doesn't enter into it. He's a good cop. As straight as they come.'

They all sat back as a Chinese waitress came to the table with their orders. Margaret flipped open Yuan Tao's file and glanced down the photocopied pages. A few dates and paragraphs, reports and statistics. A man's life in black and white. As easy to scrumple up and throw in the trash as it had been to cut off his head. She wondered if he had gone to the same middle school as the other victims but couldn't immediately see where to find it.

'The thing is, Margaret,' Stan leaned in confidentially when the waitress had gone, 'this is already making headlines back home. Chinese-American murdered on return to ancestral homeland. You know the kind of thing. But a lot more lurid. The anti-China brigade are jumping on it, rubbing their hands with glee. And with the Chinese president due to visit Washington next month we'd like this cleared up as soon as possible.'

'I don't see what that's got to do with me.'

Dakers said, 'We want you to stick with the investigation.'

Margaret laughed. 'When I finish my autopsy report, I'm out of here. Why don't you investigate it yourself, Jon? You used to be a cop.'

'The Chinese wouldn't contemplate taking an American cop on board. Even an ex-cop like me. You're an expert in a specific field, one they acknowledge we know more about. That's quite different. And besides, you've worked with them before.'

Margaret shook her head. 'I figure you'll find that after what happened last time, they wouldn't consider involving me again.'

'I reckon you could be wrong there, Margaret,' Stan said.

Margaret shook her head, smiling at his ignorance. 'What makes you think that, Stan?'

'Because we already asked them,' said Dakers.

III

It was dusk outside Li's top-floor office window. Streetlights had gone on all over the city. People were eating at streetside stalls, or were hurrying home to cook meals for themselves. The barber shops were doing brisk business. Traffic had ground to a standstill on the ring roads and on the tree-lined avenues and boulevards, and arc lights had snapped on high above those construction sites where work would go on all night, bare-chested workers scrambling over bamboo scaffolding twenty storeys up.

The trees in Beixinqiao Santiao below cast deep shadows and darkened the street. The staff of the All China Federation of Returned Overseas Chinese opposite had all gone home. Police vehicles, some blue-and-whites, some unmarked, were parked bumper to bumper on the sidewalk. Officers going off duty greeted officers coming on for the night shift.

Li stood at the window, smoking, engulfed by a deep inertia. He heard a couple of kids laughing as they kicked a ball along the street. Other people had real lives out there. Hopes, aspirations, a future. Life went on. There was a purpose to it. He wondered if he had just lost all purpose to his. For as long as Margaret had existed in his mind, just as he remembered her before they were parted, he could not really believe that he would never see her again. Somewhere deep inside him was buried a small seed of hope. Now that he had confronted her, felt her anger and hurt, and told her they had no future, that seed had withered and died. It was finally over.

There was a knock at the door and Qian appeared with a folder in his hand, fluorescent light flooding in from the detectives' office outside. 'You not want a light on in here, boss?' he said. 'Can't see a thing.'

Li shook his head. 'I like it that way.'

Qian shrugged. 'That's the file on Yuan Tao in from the American embassy.'

'Leave it on my desk.'

Qian dropped the file on the desk and went out.

Li ran his fingers lightly down his cheek, still tender where Margaret had slapped him with such force. When he had arrived back at Section One, the detectives had all looked at him very oddly. But no one had said anything. As he had gone into his office he had been aware of some stifled laughter, and each time he emerged the room had fallen silent. Finally he had demanded to know what was going on. There had been a moment's embarrassed silence before Wu said, 'The boys were just speculating, boss, about your new technique for collecting handprints from crime scenes.' There was laughter around the detectives' room. Li had frowned at first, not understanding. Wu went on, 'So, you just press your face against the print and lift it off – is that how it works?'

Li had put his hand immediately to his face and felt the weals that ran diagonally across it, left by Margaret's fingers. His embarrassment was acute, but he daren't show it or he would lose face. He must wear his slap like a trophy. After all, it was not so uncommon in China for men to be assaulted by women. A large percentage of the 'domestics' that the police were called out to involved husbands being battered by their wives. Li had grinned ruefully and said, 'Come here, Wu, and I'll show you how it's done.' He held his hand out, palm open, towards the detective.

Wu had backed off, grinning like an idiot. 'Hey, boss, if you hit me half as hard as she hit you I'll not get up again.'

'Damn right you won't,' Li said, to roars of laughter.

Later, in the washroom, he had examined his face in the mirror, shocked to see how clearly the shape of her hand was left on his cheek, red and raised. And as he touched it again now, it made a kind of connection between them, like touching her.

He finished his cigarette and flicked it out of the open window, watching a shower of orange sparks fly up from it briefly as it hit the ground below. He turned and looked at the file Qian had left on his desk. Here was an enigma. All the evidence pointed to Yuan being the fourth victim of the same serial killer. And yet Margaret had concluded that it was a copycat killing, that Yuan had been murdered by someone else. How could he doubt her assessment? She was a practised professional with enormous experience. But still he knew that no one other than his own detectives and the killer himself could possibly know enough to duplicate all the tiny details.

He had made a preliminary report on the findings of the autopsy to a packed meeting of the detectives working on the case. A number had been dismissive of Margaret's conclusions. Left-handed, right-handed, they said, was a minor detail. As was the change from wine to vodka as a carrier for the fluni-trazepam. Li pointed out that the severing of the head had also been less cleanly performed. Sang had suggested that perhaps the killer had deliberately made changes to his *modus operandi* in order to confuse the investigation, and a switch from right hand to left would explain why the cut had been less clean. No one believed these details to be of much importance compared to the number of identical features. But Li knew that Margaret believed them to be important, and his uncle had always said that the answer invariably lay in the detail.

Now he sat down at his desk and switched on an anglepoise lamp which spilled light across its surface. He looked at the buff folder in front of him. A man's life lay within. Perhaps, also, a reason for his death. He opened it. Inside were duplicates of official documents: medical reports; education history in the United States; Yuan's own curriculum vitae; his application for citizenship; an official report collated by some government agency on his political background; the assessment of his oral examination on application to join the State Department; the results of the State Department's own security checks and medical examination. Li shuffled back and forwards through the documents, piecing together Yuan's history.

Yuan Tao was born in 1949, the year of the birth of the People's Republic. The year of the Ox. The same year as all the other victims. They were, all of them, children of the Revolution, progeny of the Liberation.

He had left China at the age of seventeen, in May of 1966, just under a month before the start of the Cultural Revolution, whose beginning was marked, in most people's minds, by the suspension of classes at schools and universities across the country on 13 June. He had got out just in time, granted an exit visa to go to Egypt to study physics at the University of Cairo. But that had been a subterfuge, for he had spent less than a month in Cairo before flying on to the United States, where he had been accepted on a degree course to study political science. His sponsor was an uncle who had fled from China to San Francisco in 1948. Yuan had spent the summer working in his uncle's restaurant in the city's Chinatown to help pay his tuition fees when he started at the University of California, Berkeley, in the fall.

These had been turbulent years at Berkeley, with student civil rights demonstrations, and protests over the Vietnam War. Li shuffled in vain through the papers in the file searching for the report the FBI would surely have compiled on Yuan Tao at that time. He had known, of course, it would not be there. Just as there was no report of the CIA's certain attempt to recruit him.

Yuan completed his doctorate in political science in 1972, but stayed on for another two years to finish a post-doctorate thesis. In 1974 he applied for and was offered the post of assistant professor of political science at Berkeley and immediately applied for his Green Card. His application was successful, allowing him to accept the position.

Yuan rented an apartment in Oakland, right across the bay from San Francisco, and close to the university. In 1978 he was promoted to associate professor, and the following year applied for and was granted naturalisation. Then, as an American citizen, he had married another Chinese-American in 1979. But the marriage had lasted less than two years, and was childless. Two years later, in 1983, he had become a full professor, and over the following years had proceeded to slip quietly into early middle-age in the cloistered backwaters of Californian academia.

Then, in 1995, at the age of forty-six, and completely out of the blue, he had applied for a job in the State Department.

Certainly, they would have been pleased to receive him, an ethnic Chinese professor of political science, a naturalised American citizen who spoke fluent Mandarin. And Yuan Tao's life had taken a totally different turn.

He had moved to Washington in the following year. But the papers provided by the Americans gave no clue as to what work he had been involved in there. Then in 1999, he had astonished his employers by applying for a posting to the US Embassy in Beijing when a lowly vacancy had arisen on the visa line. Several internal memos expressed consternation, and a letter had been sent to him suggesting that his abilities would be better employed elsewhere. There was no record of his response, and his application had duly been granted, with reluctance.

Yuan Tao had finally arrived back in China six months ago to take up his job in the visa department at the Bruce Compound at the top of Silk Street.

Li lit a cigarette and watched the blue smoke curl lazily through the light of his desk lamp. A series of facts. A chronology. None of which told him the first thing about the man. Who was he really? What were his hopes and fears? Who did he love, who did he hate, and who hated him? Why had he never returned to his homeland in the early years after the Cultural Revolution when it would have been safe for him to do so? And then why, after thirty-four years, had he suddenly decided to come back after all?

Li's thoughts turned to the apartment at No. 7 Tuan Jie Hu Dongli. Why had Yuan wanted to rent when the embassy provided accommodation? And what had he hidden under the floorboards there that only his killer could have taken? The answers, Li was sure, would not be found in his file.

He wondered how Yuan had felt, returning to the country of his birth thirty-four years after he left it. What incredible changes there had been in that time. China must have been unrecognisable to him, a foreign country. Had he sought to make any contact with relatives? For surely there would be some, somewhere. Li flipped through the pages, coming to the only reference he could find to Yuan's parents. His father had been a teacher, and died, apparently, in 1967. His mother had worked with pre-school children in kindergarten, but there was no record of what had become of her. And then there must have been old school friends. In six months he must have made contact with someone.

It was in Yuan's own résumé that Li finally found what he was looking for. A list of his academic qualifications. He ran his finger down a reverse chronology, stopping finally at the second-last entry, and all the hairs stood up on the back of his neck. Yuan Tao had graduated from the No. 29 Middle School in Qianmen in May of 1966.

Li sat staring blankly at the sheets in front of him for several minutes. The murder victims had *all* attended the same school.

The revelation cast for the first time, in his mind, a shadow of doubt over Margaret's conclusions at the autopsy. For it inextricably linked all four. They had all been doped with the same drug, all had their hands tied behind their backs with the same silk cord. They had all had placards placed around their necks, their nicknames written upside down and crossed through. The placards had been numbered in sequential descending order from six. They had all been beheaded – the first three with a bronze sword – and Li had no doubt that forensic results would confirm this to be the case with the fourth.

And yet ... the nagging doubts still would not go away. Small doubts they might be, but Li could not shake them off. Why would Yuan drink the blue vodka? Why did his killer stand on his right to deliver the fatal blow, when he had stood on the left of at least two of the others? Why had he tied his wrists with a knot which was exactly the reverse of the knots he had used to tie the other three?

There were other questions, too. Why had victim number three been moved from the scene of his execution? It must have been terribly risky, not to mention messy. And why, given the amount of blood that would have been shed, had they been unable to find the place where he had been murdered?

It was, he thought, like one of Mei Yuan's riddles. He wished the solution could be just as simple. It made him think again of the riddle she had set him that morning, about the thirty-yuan hotel room. But he could not get his mind even to begin addressing the problem of the missing yuan. He had a bigger riddle of his own to solve first. And if he immersed himself in it deeply enough perhaps he might finally be able to put Margaret out of his mind.

He leaned back and blew a jet of smoke at the ceiling as the door opened and Chen came in. He was silhouetted against the lights of the detectives' room, and his face was above the ring of light shed by Li's desk lamp, so that Li could not immediately see his expression. Chen closed the door and Li saw that he was wearing a suit. And a tie. It was unheard of for Chen. He was renowned as a casual, even sloppy dresser who would usually shuffle to and from work in baggy pants, an open-necked shirt and an old zip-front jacket. He stepped towards the desk and Li caught sight of the grim set of his mouth.

'You missed the briefing,' Li said.

'I was at the Ministry.' Which explained the suit. Chen pulled up a chair and sat down. 'Got a cigarette?'

Li tossed him one and Chen lit it, inhaling deeply, and then exhaling slowly, allowing his eyes to close. He loosened his tie at the neck. 'I feel so damned uncomfortable in this stuff. How are you supposed to do your job properly if you're not comfortable?' Li knew he wasn't expected to respond. He waited apprehensively for Chen to continue. But Chen was in no hurry. He took several further pulls at his cigarette before turning to meet Li's eye.

'We've been asked to keep the Americans fully apprised of any developments in this case. Access to everything.' He paused, then, 'They have requested and it has been agreed – above my head I might say – that our point of contact with them be Dr Campbell.'

Li was stunned, as if he had just had his face slapped for a second time. 'I thought she was going back to the States?' His voice seemed small and very distant.

'Apparently they have prevailed upon her to stay.' He hesitated. 'I know this is tough for you, Li—'

'Tough?' Li was scathing. 'In one ear the Commissioner tells me to steer clear of her. In the other you're telling me I've got to co-operate with her.'

Chen was annoyed by his tone. He leaned forward and snapped, 'Then you're just going to have to learn how to separate your personal from your professional life.' He stopped and peered strangely at Li. 'What's that on your face?'

Li said, 'The slap you've just delivered.'

Li weaved his way through the night traffic in a daze. His uncle's bicycle, like every other on the streets, had no lights and no reflectors. He relied on motorists seeing him. But right now he didn't care much. If it had been painful seeing Margaret today, how much more so it would be tomorrow, and the day after, and the day after that. He felt as if he had been cast into limbo in which there could be only pain, and the knowledge that there was no foreseeable end to it. How could she have agreed to do it? Wouldn't it be just as painful for her? Or maybe she saw it as some way of gaining revenge, turning the knife in his own, self-inflicted, wound.

At the Chaoyangmen Bridge he turned west, passing a Kentucky Fried Chicken joint on his left before turning south again. He parked up at the corner of Dong'anmen Street and joined the crowds of people thronging the night market. Food stalls stretched off as far as the eye could see. For a handful of yuan, you could eat almost anything deep fried on a stick.

There were grubs the size of human thumbs, whole scorpions, tiny birds complete with heads, all stuck on skewers and ready to be plunged into great woks of boiling oil. But Li was not much interested in the exotic. He bought shredded potato deep-fried in egg and wrapped in brown paper. He ate one and bought another, and washed it down with a can of Coke and wandered through the animated groups of family and friends crushing the length of the street like animals at a feeding frenzy.

He had tried not to think about her, but even here she came back to haunt him. He had brought her here the night she told him about her husband and how he died. Everywhere in Beijing that they had been she lingered, wraithlike, in his memory.

Li finished his Coke and became aware of a small, raggedy man of indeterminate years following him, to his left and slightly behind. His eyes were firmly fixed on Li's empty can. Li turned, and was about to hand it to him when an old woman with tightly bound white hair and a single stump of a tooth grabbed it and made off. The raggedy man howled with dismay and chased after her, hurling imprecations at her back. So many cans returned for recycling earned so many fen. The street scavengers were fighting over them now.

Li retrieved his uncle's bicycle and headed south again. There was beer in the refrigerator back at the apartment, and all he wanted to do now was get drunk. His wheels slithered and slid where reconstruction and rain had turned Wangfujing Street into a quagmire. Mud spattered over his trousers and shoes.

From East Chang'an Avenue he could see the floodlights of Tiananmen Square, where workers had already begun preparing the massive floral displays for National Day in just twelve days' time. But all he wanted to do was escape from lights and people. The dark of Zhengyi Road came as a relief. The first leaves, he noticed, had started to drop from the trees. But autumn had not yet properly begun. These were just harbingers of its inevitable arrival.

The security guard nodded as he entered the gates of the compound, and parked and locked Old Yifu's bicycle. His legs felt leaden as he dragged himself up the two flights of stairs. And then, as he slipped the key in the lock, he froze, and suddenly all tiredness and self-pity were banished. All his senses were on full alert. The door to the apartment was not locked. He always locked it. He hesitated for several seconds before slowly pushing it open. There was a shrill call, and the sound of footsteps, and a small girl appeared in the hallway, black hair tied back in bunches. She stopped dead when she saw Li. And then a pretty young woman in her late twenties appeared and the child immediately clung to her leg, burying her face to hide it from Li.

Li was stunned. 'What are you doing here?' he asked.

'That's a fine welcome after three years,' the young woman said. 'Didn't you get my letter?'

Li hadn't checked his mail in days. He looked at the pile of it on the table, and saw the envelope with the Sichuan postmark. He looked back at the young woman and the child.

'I'm sorry,' he said. 'Life hasn't been that organised.' He

hesitated only for a moment before stepping towards her and taking her in his arms, almost completely enveloping her slight form. She clung tightly to him, and the child tightened her grip on her leg. 'Why have you come?' Li asked.

'We need to talk,' she said.

IV

It was dark outside, and Margaret was making progress on her second vodka tonic in the bar of the Ritan Hotel when Michael appeared. She had almost forgotten about him, so focused was she on the spectre of Li, and the prospect of his returning to haunt her on a daily basis until this crime was solved. Of course, she realised, he would probably feel that he was the one being haunted. She had contemplated refusal to co-operate with the embassy. She could have insisted that she wanted nothing further to do with the investigation and got the next plane back to the States, as originally planned. They had no means of forcing her to stay on. But she hadn't. And she wondered whether it was simply that she was more afraid of what the future held for her back home, than of the barren status quo here in China. It was easier to do nothing and drift with the tide, than to fight against it. Better the devil you knew.

'I'll have what the lady's having.' Michael's voice startled her out of her reverie. The barman moved away to prepare another vodka, and Michael perched on a bar stool beside her. 'Can I get you another?'

'You've heard then?'

'Heard what?'

'Three vodkas and I'm anybody's.'

'And one more for the lady,' he called after the barman.

She smiled. 'Of course, it's not true.'

'Oh.' He feigned disappointment.

'It takes at least four.' She looked at her watch. 'You're early.'

'I never keep a lady waiting,' he said.

'Never?'

He shrugged. 'Well, of course, that all depends on the circumstances. There are certain things you wouldn't want to rush.'

'I agree.' She drained her glass. Then, 'It's a long time since anyone gave me flowers.'

'Did you like them?'

'They were beautiful. I'm just not sure what they signified. Men always have such ulterior motives.'

'And, of course, women never do.'

'Of course they do. But women are more subtle. Flowers are a bit . . . how can I put it? . . . in your face.'

He thought for a moment. 'Let's just say they were an expression of my pleasure at hearing you were staying on – at least for another couple of days. I was just getting to know you the other night when you did your disappearing act. Like Cinderella.'

'And you wondered if I'd turned into a pumpkin?'

He laughed. 'That was her carriage, wasn't it?'

'Oh, I don't know. I'm not very up on my fairy tales.' Their drinks arrived and they raised and touched glasses. 'Cheers,' she said. Then, 'Oh, I know, she shed a glass slipper on the way out. That was it, wasn't it? Then he went round trying it on all the women.' She pulled a face. 'I reckon he was a foot fetishist. I mean, how come he didn't recognise her face?' She took another gulp of vodka. 'It's like Lois Lane and Superman. He puts on a suit and a pair of glasses and she doesn't know who he is. I mean, it's ridiculous.' She caught his expression and stopped, and laughed. 'I'm sorry, it's just so refreshing to be able to sit here and talk absolute crap. And be understood, and not have to worry about giving offence, or losing face, or breaching protocol . . . I've had nearly three months of it. You have no idea.'

He smiled. 'Oh, I think I do,' he said. 'I love China and the Chinese dearly. But after six months here I just can't wait to get home, see a movie, have a hot dog, take in a baseball game. And, yeah, talk crap and have people know what I'm talking about.'

'Oh, my Ga-ad,' a voice drawled excitedly. Michael and Margaret turned to find Dot McKinlay and a group of her Travelling Grannies arriving at the bar. Her face was flushed with excitement. She put her hand on Michael's arm, almost unable to speak. 'Do y'awl know who you are?'

Michael smiled. 'Well, I did the last time I looked.'

Dot turned to Margaret. 'It's Michael Zimmerman. He's on TV.'

'Actually, he's not,' Margaret said, and Dot's face fell. Michael looked puzzled.

'What d'yawl mean?' Dot said.

Margaret shook her head seriously. 'Michael Zimmerman's his twin brother. Well, actually, sister. But that was before she had her sex change. Or should I say "he"? Anyway Daniel and Michela – that's what she called herself before she became Michael – they don't get along. And Daniel doesn't really like being mistaken for her – him.' She finished her drink and took Michael's arm. 'Anyway, we were just going.'

Michael let himself be led away from the bar. He smiled and nodded at Dot's Travelling Grannies, who looked at him as if he had two heads. They were almost at the door before Dot recovered herself and called after Margaret, 'I thought y'awl were leaving today, Miss.' There was the hint of accusation in this.

'Had to stay on unexpectedly,' Margaret called back. 'To meet a man who'd lost his head.'

They made it through the front door and down the steps before their pent-up laughter exploded into the floodlit forecourt.

'Jesus,' Michael said. 'So now I'm a sex-change twin!'

'It's OK,' Margaret said, wiping tears from the corners of her eyes. 'It doesn't show.' Which sent them into a fresh fit of giggles. With the vodka, and the endorphins, Margaret hadn't felt this good in a long time.

'Do y'awl know who you are?' Michael mimicked.

'Oh, my God,' said Margaret. 'We're being watched.'

And Michael turned to see Dot McKinlay's Travelling Grannies glaring at them from the window of the bar. He took Margaret's arm and hurried her out of the gate, past the brown-uniformed guards who were watching them sus-piciously. A taxi driver looked hopefully in their direction, and on a wave from Michael jumped in and started up his car.

'Have you eaten?' Michael asked.

'Sure,' she said. 'In return for my doing an autopsy for them, the embassy treated me to a slap-up meal. In the canteen. Which I had to pay for myself.'

'Wow. These guys really know how to show a girl a good time.'

'Don't they just.'

He paused for a moment. 'So how long *are* you staying on?'

She shrugged. 'I don't know. Could be a day, could be a week, could be a month.' And she saw that this pleased him. 'So where are you taking me?'

He opened the door of the taxi. 'Somewhere a little special,' he said, and he slid into the back seat beside her, then leaned forward to speak to the driver in what sounded to Margaret like fluent Chinese.

As he sat back she looked at him with admiration. 'Your Chinese is fantastic,' she said.

'Not really.' He shook his head solemnly. 'Actually the driver speaks English. I briefed him before I came in to look like he knew what I was talking about.'

She was taken aback. 'You're kidding!'

He turned to her, straight-faced. 'Yeah, I'm kidding.' And then he grinned. 'When I decided to specialise in the archaeo-logical history of China at Washington University in St Louis, I figured I should really learn the language, too. There were more than twenty-five students when I started the class. At the end of the first year there were seven left – and I was the only non-ethnic Chinese among them.'

'Everyone says it's an incredibly hard language,' she said.

He shrugged. 'On paper it's quite easy. The grammar couldn't be simpler. Basically it's all present tense. I go there today, I go there yesterday, I go there tomorrow. The problem begins when you start trying to speak it.'

'It's all in the tones.'

'Yeah. You can apply four different tones to the same word and it'll mean four different things. I used to practise a lot with this girl whose spoken Chinese wasn't really very good. But she was a real doll, so I figured it was worth the sacrifice. Anyway, one day she says to me, "Do you want to have sex?" And I can't believe my good luck. But there's something about the way she says it that doesn't quite convince me that's what she means. That and the fact that she's peeling an orange at the time.' Margaret laughed. 'So I ask her to repeat what she'd said. And she says it again. "Do you want to have sex?" To be honest, all I really wanted to say was "yes". But I asked her to write it down instead. Sadly, there's no ambiguity in written Chinese.' He smiled to himself.

'Well?' Margaret asked impatiently. 'What did she write?'

Michael shook his head ruefully. 'Turned out she was asking me if I was religious. It was a big disappointment.'

'So you never did have sex with her?'

He cocked an eyebrow at her. 'Now that would be telling, wouldn't it? And I never betray a girl's confidence.'

'I'm glad to hear it.'

Their taxi cruised west past the Gate of Heavenly Peace. The portrait of Mao Zedong gazed down on Tiananmen Square where once hundreds of thousands of Red Guards had hailed him as the red, red sun in their hearts. Now the square was filled with tourists, and men working under floodlights to erect massive floral sculptures and a giant mirror ball in time for National Day.

As Michael stared out at the square, Margaret sneaked a look at him. He was dressed casually, in jeans, tan leather boots, and a black open waistcoat over a white shirt that he hadn't tucked in. He was lightly tanned, with a fine clear skin. He had big, strong hands, pale skin beneath immaculate fingernails, and a strong, well-defined jawline. Their car was not big, and his thigh was pressed against hers. She could feel the warmth of his leg, and the firmness of the muscle. He gave off a very distinctive scent that she could not quite place. It had a bitter-sweet, slightly musky, high-pitched note.

'What's your aftershave?' she asked.

He dragged himself back from some distant thought and frowned. 'I don't use aftershave.' Then he realised. 'Oh, you mean the patchouli?' He grinned. 'I hate the smell of after-shave. It's kind of overpowering first thing in the morning. I just smear the tiniest amount of patchouli oil on to my neck, below the Adam's apple. I think there's something fresh about it. He paused. 'Don't you like it?'

'No, I do,' she said. 'It's unusual, that's all.'

'I hope you like jazz,' he said suddenly.

'Jazz?'

'That's where we're going. To hear the best jazz band this side of the Great Wall.'

And she felt a tiny stab of disappointment.

Their taxi dropped them in the forecourt of the *Minzu Fandian* on Fuxingmennei Avenue. But this was not their destination, and they left the lights of the hotel behind them and went down through the underpass. At the other side of the avenue, steps led them up into the deep shadow of trees separating the bike lane from the sidewalk. Margaret began to feel uneasy. Old men sat about on walls playing chess while women stood gossiping in groups, their children laughing and shouting, kicking a ball up and down the grass. The narrowest of *hutongs* led off into a maze of walled courtyards. She had been here before, she realised.

The Sanwei bookstore stood on the corner, its lights spilling out into the dark of the street. They could hear the sound of jazz music drifting lightly on the warm evening air. As they stepped inside, a young girl came forward to sell them entrance tickets for thirty yuan each. Down a couple of steps, staff milled around narrow aisles between shelves of books and magazines. 'Don't be fooled by the bookshop,' Michael said. 'There's the most wonderful tearoom upstairs.'

'I know,' she said, and he stopped on the bottom step, taken aback.

'You've been here before?'

She nodded. 'But not on a jazz night.' And she remembered the stillness of the tearoom: lacquered tables and chairs grouped silently on a tiled floor; vases and sculptures displayed on shelves and cabinets; traditional and modern scrolls hanging on the walls; screens along the window wall dividing it into discreet individual areas, in one of which she had sat with Li on a night when the place was otherwise deserted, on a night when she had opened her heart to him for the very first time.

'Are you OK?' Michael was concerned.

She almost told him she didn't want to go up, but in the end didn't have the heart. 'I'm fine,' she said. He lingered a moment, still concerned, then took her hand and led her up the stairs.

The band was taking a break as Michael and Margaret got to the top of the steps, and the audience in the packed tearoom was still applauding their last number. A bespectacled young man sitting at a table, took their tickets.

'Hello, Mr Zimmerman,' he said in a slow, concentrated English. 'How are you tonight?'

'I'm good, Swanney. How are things at work?'

'We are ve-ery busy just now, Mr Zimmerman.'

Michael introduced Swanney to Margaret, who shook his hand. 'Swanney is a doctor at the infectious diseases hospital,' Michael said, and Margaret had the immediate urge to go and wash the hand he had shaken. 'He works here on jazz nights, partly because he likes jazz, but mostly because it gives him the chance to practise his English.'

'Pleased to meet you,' Margaret said. She looked around. The tearoom was crowded, a mix of Chinese and European faces. It was mostly a young crowd, with the exception of a single elderly man wearing jeans, a tee shirt and baseball cap. He was working hard at charming his way into the pants of a Chinese girl who was young enough to be his granddaughter. She looked exceedingly bored. It was a very different atmosphere from the still and solitary one Margaret had experienced here with Li on an emotionally charged night. Raised voices and laughter, people gathered round tables in animated groups, drinking tea and beer.

And yet there was something odd, something missing. And then she knew what it was. She said to Michael, 'No one's smoking.'

He grinned. 'I know. A jazz club without cigarette smoke. Doesn't seem right, does it? The lady who owns the place is a bit eccentric.' He nodded down a colonnaded corridor to a door at the end. 'She practically lives in there. Hardly ever shows her face. Hates smoking, so she made jazz nights a smoke-free zone.' He steered her towards what appeared to be the only free table in the place. 'Reserved,' he said. 'Wanted to be sure we'd get a seat.'

A girl of about twenty, wearing a white apron, and a big smile on an open, pretty face, materialised out of the crowd. 'Hello again, Mr Zimmerman,' she said, gazing at him with unabashed adoration.

'Hi, Plum,' he said, returning her smile. 'Plum, this is Margaret. She's a doctor.'

Plum turned to Margaret, her smile just as wide and disarming. 'Hello, Miss Margaret,' she said, extending her hand.

'I'm ve-ery pleased to meet you. I am study English at Beijing University. What would you like to drink?'

They ordered beer, and Margaret looked around the young, animated faces and froze, suddenly, as she turned and met the eye of a tall Chinese man pushing past their table. It was Li. She felt the blood colour her cheeks as he stopped, unable to avoid the fact that they had seen each other. And then her eyes flickered past him to an attractive young Chinese woman at his side, and she immediately felt sick. It was as if he had returned her slap ten times over. So this was why they had no future, she thought bitterly. There was already someone else. She wanted to stand up and hit him again. Only harder this time, with a clenched fist, so that it would really hurt. But she remained frozen in her chair. 'Well,' she said, barely able to control her voice. 'This is a surprise.'

Initially it was his embarrassment that left Li at a loss for words, and then his eyes flickered towards Michael, and it was anger that flushed his cheeks. He looked back at Margaret. So this was why she had decided to stay on. It hadn't taken her long to get over her heartbreak.

'Isn't it?' is all he could bring himself to say.

Michael jumped immediately to his feet and extended a hand. 'Hi. I'm Michael Zimmerman.'

Politeness forced Li to take his hand. 'Li Yan,' he said curtly.

Margaret stood up slowly and turned her gaze on the woman with Li. 'And this is?' she asked pointedly. She wasn't going to let him away without having to make an introduction.

Li looked at Margaret steadily for a moment, and the

directness of his gaze disconcerted her. 'This is Xiao Ling,' he said. 'My sister.'

Another slap in the face, this time one of rebuke. Margaret didn't know which was the dominant emotion, embarrassment or relief. But whatever else, she felt very foolish. She tried a smile and shook Xiao Ling's hand. 'I'm pleased to meet you,' she said.

Xiao Ling nodded politely, her eyes meeting Margaret's for only a moment before flickering downward.

'Hi,' Michael said, shaking her hand also. 'Won't you join us?'

Margaret threw him a horrified glance. But Li coldly dismissed the invitation. 'We were just leaving,' he said. 'We made a mistake. This is not usually a jazz night.'

'No,' Michael said. 'It's a one-off tonight. A special event.'

Li nodded, and ushered Xiao Ling past him. 'Enjoy it,' he said, and they left.

Margaret and Michael sat down. 'Wow!' Michael said. 'I feel like I just spent the last few minutes in the freezer.' He examined his fingers. 'I'm not sure I didn't get frostbitten.'

Margaret smiled reluctantly. 'I'm sorry, Michael.'

'Who was that guy? Or shouldn't I ask?'

'No, you can ask,' Margaret said. 'He's just about the most stubborn, difficult and downright discourteous man I think I've ever met.'

'Right.' Michael nodded sagely. 'So you and he were an item.'

She flicked him a quick look. 'That obvious, was it?'

He smiled. 'It was the stamp on your foreheads that said "ex-lovers" that really gave you away.' She grinned ruefully. 'Who is he?' he asked.

'Li Yan is Deputy Section Chief of Section One of the Criminal Investigation Department of the Beijing Municipal Police.'

'A cop?' Michael was clearly astonished.

'Unfortunately, in my line of work, it's very difficult to avoid them.'

He shook his head in amazement. 'What's Section One?'

'Oh, it's kind of like a serious crime squad. They handle all the big robberies and murders.'

Then the penny dropped for Michael. 'So he was the one you were working with during that rice thing?' She nodded. 'And now? This autopsy you did for the embassy? He involved in that, too?'

'Unfortunately,' Margaret said. And she added, with feeling, 'It's just a pity he wasn't the one on the table.'

'Ouch,' Michael said. 'Wouldn't like to get on the wrong side of *your* scalpel.'

She smiled. 'Some people have accused me of having a sharper tongue.'

'Wouldn't like to get on the wrong side of that either.'

She gave him a sheepish grin.

Plum arrived with their beers. Michael took a long pull at his and eyed Margaret thoughtfully. 'So what is it you're working on, a murder? Or is that a state secret?'

'Oh, I don't think so,' Margaret said. She took a swallow of beer. 'Just a guy at the embassy, a Chinese-American, got his head lopped off by some serial killer. Or, at least, that's what the Chinese think.'

Michael made a face. 'Decapitated? That sounds pretty unpleasant. An ancient Chinese form of execution.'

She looked at him, interested. 'Is it?'

'For thousands of years,' said Michael. 'Until quite recently, in fact. And, you know, when they buried their emperors in these huge underground tombs, it was quite common for dozens of the imperial concubines and members of the entourage to be entombed with them. Some of them were buried alive. The lucky ones were executed first. There are plenty of examples of headless skeletons found in tombs that have been excavated.'

Margaret shuddered. 'Wouldn't make working for the emperor the most attractive career.'

Michael shrugged and said, 'It was the price they paid for incredible privilege while he was alive.' He took another draught of his beer. 'So,' he said, 'you don't think the Chinese-American guy *was* killed by this serial killer?'

She shrugged vaguely, her mind still very much on Li. 'Not really. Too many inconsistencies.'

'So who *do* you think did it?'

'Haven't a clue. And neither do the Chinese. And by the time they find out, if they ever do, I'll probably be drawing my pension.' She looked up from her beer and smiled, shaking her head. 'But it's pretty boring stuff, really. Not nearly as interesting as it sounds.' She sipped her beer. 'So how was your day, darling?' She made a determined effort to tear her thoughts away from Li.

'Pretty dull, really,' he said.

'I thought you started filming today.'

'We did. But it wasn't anything very exciting. We're still setting things up. But the sun came out, so we did some aerial shots from a helicopter of the tomb at Ding Ling.'

She burst out laughing. 'Ding-a-ling?' she asked incredulously.

'No.' He smiled at her silliness. '*Ding Ling*. It's the site of the tomb of Zhu Yijun, thirteenth emperor of the Ming Dynasty, Emperor Wanli. It is built into Dayu Hill in the cradle of the Heavenly Longevity Hills, just an hour out of the city. And it looked fabulous today. The first sunshine in ages. We couldn't believe it. So we got the chopper up there fast, and came in very low over the mountains, so that as we traversed the final peak, the tomb opened out below us in all its glory. With the autumn colours, and the light, we got some great pics.'

Margaret said, 'I don't mean to be a killjoy, but pretty pictures aren't going to sustain a whole series, surely? And, well, to be honest I can't say I'd be riveted by the prospect of looking at a lot of tombs.'

Michael smiled indulgently at her ignorance. 'That's not what the series is about,' he said. 'History is about people, Margaret. And this series is about an amazing person called Hu Bo.' He stopped himself. 'But you don't really want to know about this.'

She laughed. 'No, I'm sorry. I do. Honestly. Go on.'

He shrugged, a little embarrassed. 'Hu was a pioneer of archaeology in twentieth-century China.'

'On second thoughts . . .'

Michael grinned. 'OK, I know. That might not sound very interesting in itself. But when you look at his life and what he achieved – in the face of incredible odds, against a backdrop of war and revolution, and political madness – it's an incredible story. A story that started when he was just ten years old, and his father sold him to an entourage of foreign explorers. A story that ended with a final act of will – the publication of the true story of the excavation at Ding Ling, which he and a handful of colleagues had kept safe from the destructive forces of the Cultural Revolution at considerable cost to themselves.'

Margaret said, 'Sounds to me like the voice-over for the start of a TV series about a Chinese archaeologist.'

He chuckled. 'Not far off it. I haven't actually written it yet. It'll be better when I do.' His eyes smiled and twinkled at her. 'Would it make you watch?'

She sucked in a breath through her teeth. 'Well . . . I'm hard to please, Michael. It might make me give it a minute or two.'

He leaned forward. His enthusiasm was infectious. 'If you give me a minute, I'll give you an hour. And if you give me an hour, you'll watch the whole series. I promise you.'

In spite of an in-built resistance to the idea that anything about archaeology or archaeologists might be of the slightest interest to her, Margaret was intrigued. Although she wasn't sure whether it was the story, or the storyteller, that aroused her interest.

He took her hand in his, quite unselfconsciously. 'Come out to location tomorrow. Please. We're staging a recreation of the moment when Hu Bo and his ragtag team of archaeologists and amateur enthusiasts open the emperor's tomb, almost exactly four hundred years after it was first sealed. They don't know what to expect. There are stories of poisonous gases, of mechanical crossbows primed to release poison-tipped arrows if the gates of the underground chamber are opened. As they pull away the first few bricks they are literally terrified . . .' He paused and waited.

'So what happened?' she asked impatiently.

He grinned and sat back. 'You see. Got you already.' She laughed. 'If you want to know, come out tomorrow. I'll have a production car pick you up.'

'Well . . .' she said, almost coyly. 'I'll think about it.'

The jazz band began assembling again at the far end of the tearoom, to Margaret's disappointment. Once the music began, conversation would become impossible, and she had been enjoying the conversation. She liked Michael. He was easy company, and he was entertaining. Then she clouded as thoughts of Li again forced their way into her consciousness. And she wondered if she would ever get over him.

Michael turned his chair towards the band and said to Margaret, 'These guys are a bit special. They're only in town for a couple of nights, that's why they're on tonight instead of the weekend. The sax player is up there with the best anywhere in the world.'

Margaret cast her eyes over the band. The keyboard player

was an American – he was speaking Chinese but she could still hear the American accent. The drummer, sax player and double-bassist, were Chinese. The keyboard player reintroduced the band in Chinese and English, and then counted them into a medium-paced piece, dominated by an endlessly repeating cycle on the keyboard, with diversions and interjections by the sax. They were undoubtedly good, but Margaret's emotions were not really engaged. She saw that Michael was listening intently. Clearly this was an area where their interests diverged.

She let her attention wander around the rest of the tea-room. The old guy with the baseball cap still wasn't getting past first base with the young Chinese girl. Near the front an intense-looking young man sat with eyes fixed on the band, his head moving rhythmically up and down in time with the music. He was transfixed. His pretty girlfriend, ignored by her lover, was keeping herself awake by idly creating the most wonderful origami creatures from a single square of hand-kerchief. Margaret watched, intrigued, as the girl conjured up a peacock with fan tail and cocked head, an intricate and elaborate arrangement of folds in the handkerchief. When she had finished she nudged her boyfriend in search of his approval. He glanced briefly at her creation, nodded and half-smiled, then refocused his attention on the music. The girl shrugged and with a single flick undid all her work and started again on something else.

The band finished their number to enthusiastic applause. The keyboard player spoke for a moment or two in Chinese, and Margaret became aware of heads starting to turn in their direction. Michael was blushing. Then the keyboard player switched to English. 'And for those of you who don't speak Chinese,' he said, 'we have with us tonight a certain Mr Michael Zimmerman.' He waved a hand in Michael's direction and more heads turned and there was a scattering of applause. 'Now, if you know him at all, most of you have probably seen him on TV fronting those popular historical documentaries. But not many of you will know that Michael's real talent is the alto sax.'

Michael half-turned towards her. 'This is embarrassing.'

'I didn't know you played,' Margaret said, suddenly intrigued by this new and unexpected dimension. And then she realised that, in truth, she didn't know anything about him at all.

'So, Michael, how about you come up and play a number with us? Big hand for Michael Zimmerman, everyone.'

The eyes of the entire tearoom were on their table. 'Jesus,' Michael whispered under his breath, but made no move to get up.

'Go on,' Margaret said, nudging him. And she stood up and started clapping. 'I want to hear you play.'

He was trapped. He shook his head, got up reluctantly and made his way forward to join the band. Margaret watched, glowing with a strange and unaccountable pride. She was with him, and she was aware of people looking at her and wondering who she was. Michael fixed his own mouthpiece to an alto sax that the Chinese sax player took out of a case on the floor behind them.

They had a brief discussion, then the drummer counted

them into a slow, dreamy piece, just made for a treacly sax solo. The electric piano reverberated around a simple circular melody, the bass player slipping fingers up and down his fretless board, bending and pulling the strings through the cycle. Michael stood with eyes closed, swaying slightly, letting the music wash over him, before lifting the sax to his mouth and breathing velvet and silk into a creamy solo that swooped and fell and growled around the room.

Margaret felt the hairs stand up on the back of her neck, and across her scalp, and goosebumps raised themselves on her thighs. She had never had much time for music, but occasionally something would move her. And she was moved now. There was a deep, penetrating sexuality in this music, in part spawned by the fact that this was the man she was with, but also because this was talent, raw and real and just a touch away. She watched his intensity, fingers sliding over the keys of his sax in a blur, as his solo soared towards it climax, like a woman towards orgasm. And as he finished, and stepped back, sweat running in rivulets down his face, everyone in the room burst into spontaneous applause. Even the origami girl had abandoned her handkerchief and was clapping her hands with unanticipated enthusiasm.

Margaret's hands were stinging as Michael made his way back to their table to join her. He sat down, mopping the perspiration from his face with the handkerchief the origami girl had offered him on the way past. To the intense annoyance of her boyfriend she was still watching him, a sexual, predatory look in her eyes. Margaret was aware of it, too.

'Sorry about that,' Michael said, and he seemed genuinely embarrassed.

'And I suppose you always carry your mouthpiece with you,' she said. 'Just in case.'

He grinned. 'Always.'

And Margaret decided there and then that she would, after all, take up his offer to go out on location tomorrow.

V

Mei Yuan was sitting on the settee, her arm around Xinxin, a big picture book open in front of them. Xinxin was so engrossed she could hardly tear her eyes away to glance at her mother and uncle coming in.

Mei Yuan did not possess a telephone, but during her illness Li had got to know a neighbour who was willing to pass on phone messages. And so Mei Yuan had come straight away when he called, arriving by bicycle twenty-five breathless minutes later, her face glowing. She had brought a large bundle of colourful picture books for young children, prompting Li to wonder where on earth she had managed to find them. But he did not ask. She was delighted to babysit. She loved children, she said. Her only remaining close family were a cousin and her husband, and their 'baby' was nearly thirty. So it was very rare for her to have the opportunity to be with young children.

Xinxin was still uncertain of her big, strange uncle. She eyed him cautiously with dark, wary eyes. She had not seen him since she was two years old and had no recollection of him at all. But she had taken a shine to Mei Yuan immediately. Li and Xiao Ling had been shooed out the door and told not to worry. Xinxin was in good hands, and they were not to feel they had to hurry back. Mei Yuan understood their need to talk, and if they were late back, then she would just sleep over on the settee. So she was surprised when they returned so early, gone little more than an hour, and sensed a chill in the air they brought in with them.

Xinxin was unhappy about her leaving so soon, and was close to tears before Mei Yuan assured her she would come to see her again, and that in the meantime she would leave the books for Xinxin to look at.

As she left she said quietly to Li, 'Anytime you need me.' He squeezed her hand and nodded his silent gratitude. And when she was gone he sat gloomily in the sitting room listening to Xiao Ling in Yifu's old room trying to persuade Xinxin that it was time for her to go to sleep. At first he heard Xinxin complain that she wasn't sleepy, and then Xiao Ling talked for a long time in low, hypnotic tones, and then there was silence. But it was, perhaps, another ten minutes before Xiao Ling came through. She had removed her cardigan, and he noticed for the first time how much the swelling in her womb was already showing. She looked tired and strained, and Li saw that his little sister was beginning to age.

She was no longer the fresh-faced young girl he remembered from trips home to Sichuan when he was still at university. It brought back a recollection of the time he had returned to discover that she was engaged to a young man he had not even met, a young man who, he was dismayed to discover, he could not bring himself to like. Xiao Xu owned a small farm near the town of Zigong in Sichuan Province, where he and Xiao Ling and Xinxin lived with his parents. In the new China, his privately owned farm had flourished and he was, comparatively speaking, well off. They had just built themselves a new house. Li had never been there. He had never been asked. But neither had he any inclination to go. As far as he was concerned, Xiao Xu was a brutish peasant and not good enough for his sister. Not that he had ever treated her badly – Li would have beaten him to a pulp if he had – but Li had never sensed in him any real affection or respect for his sister. She had been a pretty girl, and come with a respectable dowry, but Li believed that Xiao Xu had simply been in the market for a wife to bear his child, and that his sister had been in the wrong place at the right time. She had deserved so much better. And now this.

'Do you want tea?' she asked. And he nodded. He would have preferred beer, but needed to keep his head clear. She went into the kitchen to boil some water. All that she had told him was that she had not yet decided if she was going to have the baby or not. She was only sixteen weeks pregnant and could still decide up to twenty-eight weeks if she wanted an abortion. Under China's One-Child Policy, the penalties, both psychological and financial, of going ahead with the birth when she already had a perfectly healthy little girl, could be severe. Loss of free education for Xinxin and her unborn brother or sister, loss of free medical care for the whole family, loss of housing benefit and other tax breaks, even a hefty fine.

The psychological pressures that could be brought to bear by the village committee and Party cadres had, in some cases, driven mothers to take their own lives. But at the same time Li abhorred the idea of abortion, of taking the life of her unborn child. It was a dreadful dichotomy, a dark place into which it would have been better she had never ventured.

It was almost the first question he had asked her. 'Why?' And she had been dismissive. It had happened, she said, and that was that. But he knew she had wanted this baby. He knew that she had been dissatisfied with her little girl. She wanted a boy, like every other mother in China.

His decision to take her to the Sanwei tearoom, somewhere quiet where they could talk uninterrupted, had been a disaster. Jazz nights were normally a weekend phenomenon. He thought of Margaret, and his surprise at meeting her there, of his anger and jealousy at finding her in the company of a good-looking American. He had no right, he knew, to be jealous, but he touched his cheek where it tingled still from her slap, and he wondered if her righteous indignation of that afternoon had owed more to guilt than to anger.

Xiao Ling brought the tea through on a tray, and laid out teapot and cups on the coffee table in front of the settee. She poured hot water on to the green leaves in the cups and put their lids on to let the leaves rehydrate and infuse the water with their leafy bitter flavour. Then she perched on the edge of the settee next to Li and waited in tense silence.

'So what did Uncle Yifu say to you?' Li asked, finally, and she immediately tensed further.

Yifu, at the request of their father, had travelled to Zigong by train to talk to Xiao Ling about her pregnancy and had been killed on the night of his return to Beijing.

She clasped her hands together, wringing her fingers as she spoke. 'After all the pressure everyone had been putting me under,' she said, 'old Yifu sat me down and took my hand and told me my destiny was my own to decide.' Her eyes filled with tears. 'He made no judgements or accusations. He took me through all the options and all the consequences. He asked me to tell him why I wanted a boy. He made no comment upon my reply, but he made me think about it and give expression to my feelings. Nobody else cared what I thought, not Xiao Xu, not his parents nor our father, nor anyone. They just wanted me to do what I was told. Uncle Yifu wanted me to do what I thought was right.' She turned to Li as the tears spilled over and ran down her cheeks. 'He was such a lovely old man, Li Yan. Such a good man. We talked for hours and I wanted him to stay for a few days. But he said he had to go.' She bit her lip. 'If only I'd insisted, if I'd *made* him stay, he'd still be alive today.' And the guilt that she had been holding in for who knew how long, rose in great sobs that tore at her chest, and she wept unreservedly. 'I feel so responsible.'

Li put an arm around her and pulled her to him. She felt so small and fragile, he was afraid to squeeze her too hard in case she broke. 'You share no blame for his death,' he almost whispered. His voice was hoarse with emotion. 'If there is someone to blame then it is me. He would not have been killed if it were not for me.'

But this seemed only to distress Xiao Ling even further. 'I don't know why you ever wanted to be a policeman anyway,' she sobbed, and he felt her accusation in it.

'Because I wanted to be like him,' he said, desperate for her understanding. 'Because I believed in the same things he did – in fairness and justice, and the right of people to live in security without fear for their lives or possessions.'

And she turned her tear-stained face to his. 'I'm sorry,' she said. 'I know you loved him, too.'

They sat for a long time then, just holding each other, until their tears had all been spilled. Finally Xiao Ling wiped her face dry with a handkerchief and sat forward to sip her tea. It was only lukewarm by now. Li no longer felt like drinking his, and he went to the refrigerator and opened a bottle of beer. He stood in the doorway watching her, then took a long pull from the neck of his bottle. The ice-cold beer took the heat out of the burning in his throat. Then he asked the question he had been putting off all night. 'Why are you here, Xiao Ling?'

She avoided his eye. 'There is a clinic in Beijing where I can go to have what they call an ultra-sound scan.' Her voice was husky.

He frowned. 'What's that?' Such things were beyond his experience, and he was apprehensive.

'It's where they can get a picture on a television screen of your baby in the womb. They do it with sound, somehow . . . high frequency sound waves. I've been reading up about it.'

'What is the point of that?'

She hesitated. 'Sometimes they can tell the sex of the baby.'

And he knew immediately what was in her head, and he felt sick to his stomach. 'And if they can't,' she said, 'then they can take fluid from the womb and know for sure.'

He stood, motionless, looking at her for a long time. He felt a vein pulsing in his temple. 'And if it's another girl?' He waited for her reply, but she said nothing, and steadfastly refused to meet his eye. So he said it for her. 'You're going to have her aborted, aren't you?' Somehow it seemed even worse when the 'it' had become 'her'.

Xiao Ling seemed to be examining her fingernails with great interest. 'If they have to do the fluid test it'll take about four weeks for the results. I would still only be twenty weeks gone.'

He took a long draught from his bottle and controlled the urge to shout at her. In any case, what gave him the right to judge her? He wondered what Yifu would have said or done, then realised he had no idea. And it came home to him just how different he was in so many ways from the uncle whose standards he had been trying to live up to all these years. Perhaps they were always going to be too high for him. Always just out of reach.

'This clinic,' he said at length. 'It is private?' She nodded. 'Expensive?' She nodded again. 'How can you afford it?'

'Xiao Xu has been doing well these last few years. I have saved some money.'

'And Xiao Xu approves of this?'

There was a long silence before finally she said, 'Xiao Xu doesn't know. He thinks only that we have come to visit you.'

Li was shocked. 'But it's his child, too. Doesn't he have a right to a say in what happens to it?'

Xiao Ling met his eyes for the first time and he saw, to his dismay, something like hate in hers. 'He wants me to get rid of it whether it's a girl *or* a boy.' There was venom in her voice. 'They got to him. I don't know what they said, I don't know what they threatened to do, but suddenly he didn't want it any more. It was *my* fault, *my* problem, and as far as he was concerned it was up to me to get rid of it.'

Suddenly he understood the crushing loneliness she must feel. The whole world against her. Urging a single course of action. And she, driven by some instinct, or by the dreadful weight of five thousand years of tradition, just wanted a baby boy. A desire that, had she lived in almost any other place on earth, would have been the simplest desire in the world to fulfil.

'If this ... scan ... tells you the sex of your baby ...' His mouth was dry, and the question would barely form in it. 'What will you do if it is a boy?'

This time she returned his gaze, steady and sure. 'If it's a boy I will have it, and give Xinxin up for adoption.'

CHAPTER FOUR

I

A large kitchen knife came down twice in quick succession, and the heads of the fowl dropped from the rung of the ladder and into the ditch. For a few manic moments, the two headless chickens ran blindly around, blood spurting from their necks. The peasant who had delivered the fatal strokes stood watching breathlessly as the life ebbed from the creatures and they toppled over and lay still in the bloodied earth. A hand clamped itself on his shoulder and spun him round. He found himself staring into the perplexed face of Hu Bo.

'What the hell do you think you're doing, Wang Qifa?' Hu demanded.

Wang Qifa held himself erect and said, boldly, '*Mr Hu, you were the one who warned us about the dangers of the hidden weapons. The old men in the village told me that chicken blood would protect me from harm. "As long as two chickens are killed, all hidden weapons are powerless," they said.*'

'OK, cut and check.' The man beside Margaret spoke into a walkie-talkie, and Margaret saw the image on the screen spool rapidly back to the moment before the knife fell. The exchange between Hu Bo and the peasant had already been shot three times – a master shot and two close-ups. The chickens had only been added when they were happy with everything else. They would only have one shot at them. The sight of their headless frenzy was sickening in itself, but there was additional resonance in it for Margaret.

'Won't the animal rights people be after your blood for this?' she asked.

The man beside her grinned. 'The chickens belong to a couple in the village. They were always destined for the dinner table. All we did was pay them a lot of money to let us kill them on camera. Now they'll be guests of honour at a banquet tonight, the main item on the menu.' He turned to watch the playback.

Margaret had liked him immediately. In spite of the enormous pressure he was under to meet schedules and deadlines, he seemed relaxed and easy-going, even when everyone else on set appeared tense. Michael had introduced them when the production car he had sent for her arrived at Ding Ling.

'Charles has directed all my series to date,' Michael had said.

Charles had shaken her hand. 'Pleased to meet you, Margaret. But call me Chuck. Mike's the only person I know who calls me Charles.'

'Maybe,' Michael had said, grinning wickedly, 'that's because you're the only person I know who calls me Mike.'

Chuck had shrugged hopelessly at Margaret. 'What can you do? The man's impossible to work with.'

The shot had finished replaying on the monitor and a voice on one of the walkie-talkies said, 'Clear.'

'OK,' Chuck said. 'Set up the next shot, Dave. Quickly please. These people are waiting for their chickens.' He turned to Margaret. 'Anyway, I'm shooting the blood and guts in such a way we can cut around it if the network thinks it'll put an early evening audience off its pizza and French fries. But, you know, this is how it happened. We're just trying to show it like it was.'

They were in a truck that had been kitted out as a video control centre and lowered by helicopter on to a wall thirty feet above the set. Cables spewed out a rear hatch like the entrails of a dead animal, and hung down into the long stone corridor that led to the entrance of the underground palace of the tomb of Emperor Wanli.

'I still can't believe they let you shoot this in the actual tomb,' Margaret said.

'Hey,' said Chuck. 'It took Mike six months to talk them into it. That and a very large cheque. The Chinese are big capitalists at heart. They'll have worked out exactly how much additional tourist revenue this series is gonna generate. And they must have figured it's worth it, 'cos they're having to close it to the public for six weeks – so we can set it up, shoot it, then clean it up. And from our point of view, this is the centrepiece of the series, so if we're gonna spend the money somewhere, this is where it's gonna go.'

On the monitor, Margaret saw that the camera had been moved into a low position with the dead chickens in centre frame. She watched as twice, the shot panned up, and then the camera rose more than ten feet as it moved back, so that the whole of the paved passageway leading back between high walls towards the steps of the stele pavilion came into shot. It was one smooth, flowing movement.

'That looks good, Jackie,' Chuck said into his walkie-talkie. 'Dave, is Mike ready yet? Does he want to do a walk-through?'

Dave's soft Irish voice crackled back across the airwaves. 'Michael's ready, Chuck. He says he's happy to rehearse on tape. It's a long speech.'

Chuck grinned. 'OK, if everyone else is ready, let's try one.' He said to Margaret, 'We'll probably only use Mike in vision at the beginning of this, and at the end. In between we'll lay over various pictures we haven't shot yet. We'll probably re-record the whole speech back in sound dubbing, but it's nice to get location sound. It's more authentic.' And into the walkie-talkie, 'Jackie, remember once you've got Mike waist-high and centre frame, keep him there as the dolly moves back, and only when you bring the camera back down again do I want to see him walk into close-up. When you're ready, Dave . . .'

Margaret heard the first assistant director's voice over the foldback warning everyone to be quiet. Then, 'Roll VT,' a pause and, 'Action!'

The camera was close on the dead chickens. Then it started to drift back and lift. Chuck whispered into his walkie, 'Cue Mike.'

Then she heard Michael's voice. '*Whatever superstitions there may have been about the kinds of defences the Emperor had built into his tomb, the fears of the archaeologists and their peasant labourers were based on historical record and the fatal experiences of grave robbers through the centuries. The Indiana Jones world of concealed traps and hidden weapons was not so fantastical.'*

As he walked into shot he waved his arm upwards towards a high brick wall sealing the entrance to the tomb. Clearly visible was an inverted 'V' shape in the brick.

'When, on May 19th, 1957, after a year of digging, the archaeologists discovered the "diamond wall" that sealed the gate to the tomb, the rumours that grew about what might lie behind it fed very real fears. Science and superstition, culture and ignorance coexisted in the minds of the team members as well as the peasant diggers. People spoke of crossbows operated by a hidden mechanism that would send poison arrows to pierce the flesh of anyone who tried to open the gate. They indulged in talk of toxic gases that would be released to strike down the tomb's invaders, sabres that would fall from the vaulted ceiling of the interior. No one could survive.

'Then, ten days after the discovery of the "diamond wall", their fears were further fed by the sudden appearance of a mysterious old man . . .'

Chuck said to Margaret, 'We'll see the old guy at this point, talking to the peasants.'

'He was dressed in ragged clothes and a straw hat, and had a long white, wispy beard. He told the peasant diggers that he possessed an ancient genealogy passed on to him by his ancestors. This document, he said, told of a stream running through the underground palace of the tomb. To reach the coffin they would have to cross the stream, at the other side of which they would find a chasm one hundred thousand

feet deep. At the bottom of the chasm were barbed wires bridged by a stepping board. Only those born on a certain auspicious day could cross it. All others would lose their lives.

'Such was the effect of his story, that the old man made a tidy sum from the peasants who were falling over themselves to have him tell their fortune. But the next day, when the archaeologists heard of it and went in search of this person who was spreading panic among their workers, the "immortal" was nowhere to be found.'

Michael smiled at the camera, reflecting his audience's scepticism about the old man. *'Ridiculous? You and I might think so. But Hu Bo and the other archaeologists on the team, educated men all, were not prepared to dismiss anything. For they were studying an ancient account of the construction of the tomb of the first emperor of China, Emperor Qin Shihaung, more than two thousand years ago. Qin not only unified China and built the Great Wall, he constructed a vast army of life-sized terracotta soldiers to guard his mausoleum.'*

'Shots of the Terracotta Warriors here,' Chuck said. 'We've got loads of stock.'

'The account of the construction of his tomb told of pearls, jade and all kinds of treasures. Candles made of dugong grease were lit and kept burning. Hidden crossbows and arrows were installed inside with an automatic propulsion system to prevent robbery. The coffin was surrounded by a river of mercury, kept flowing mechanically. Above was a celestial body with the sun, the moon and the stars, and below was a landscape with rivers and mountains . . .'

Michael walked into close-up and looked very earnestly at the camera. He was incredibly photogenic, Margaret thought. He looked good in the flesh, but the camera made him beautiful. The camera loved him. A tiny, involuntary, frisson made her shiver.

He said, '*Rivers of mercury? If they existed, they would certainly be rivers of death for anyone trying to enter Qin's tomb. So has anyone tried? Well, actually, no. They have dug up the Terracotta Army, ranged in battalions around the tomb. But to this day, no one has had the courage to attempt to enter the tomb itself. Why? Because soil tests show a dangerously high level of mercury. So was it any wonder that Hu Bo and the others, under the direction of the venerated Xia Nai, approached the opening of the Emperor Wanli's mausoleum with fear in their hearts?*'

He turned away from the camera. 'Shit! I missed out the bit about the stones painted with cinnabar.'

Chuck leaned forward. 'That's OK, Mike, we're off you at that point. We can pick it up in dubbing. But, really, I don't think we miss it.'

Michael turned back to camera. 'We miss it,' he said firmly. 'I want to do it again.'

'Goddamn perfectionist,' Chuck muttered. Then, 'OK, cut it and set it up from the top.' He turned to Margaret. 'What did you think?'

'Sounded good to me.'

'Me, too.' He sighed. 'We could be some time at this.'

She stood up. 'I think I'll take a wander. Catch up with you later, if that's OK?'

'Sure,' Chuck said. 'Mind if I join you?' He grinned. 'If only.'

Outside, the hot September sun beat down, throwing the mountains that rose out of the north-west into sharp relief. The sweet smell of pine rose from the spruce trees all around. Margaret walked away from the activity surrounding the technical wagons, through the shade of the trees, to the outer crenellated wall that encircled the tomb. A bleak and barren landscape, bleached white by the sun, surrounded this walled oasis. The foothills of the mountains were dotted with the tombs of Wanli's ancestors, symbolising the desperate attempts of history's rich and powerful men to maintain their status over the rest of us, even in death. Futile attempts at immortality. And now, centuries later, they served only to provide entertainment for the MTV generation. If only those rich and powerful men had known.

Margaret pushed her hands deep into the pockets of her trousers and scuffed her way idly along the paved top of the outer wall, pushing a pine cone in front of her as she went. It was all interesting enough, and Michael was charming and attractive, but she was still emotionally raw. She would almost certainly recoil from the merest hint of romantic interest. She still ached when she thought of Li.

As she approached the stele pavilion, the third assistant director, a young Chinese girl, put a hand up to stop her, and placed a finger to her lips warning her to be silent. To her right, in the deep slash that cut through the hill to the stone façade of the tomb's entrance, she saw Michael in the glare of lights mounted all around him doing his piece to camera again. The camera dolly tracked back from him as he approached the design team's re-creation of the diamond wall. She could hear his voice echoing back from the walls that leaned over him. *'If they existed, they would certainly be rivers of death for anyone trying to enter Qin's tomb . . .'*

Ahead, up a flight of broad steps, the stele pavilion towered over everything, one roof atop another, curling eaves supported on ancient wooden beams. The stele itself, a standing stone tablet inscribed with ancient script, stood more than twenty feet high, framed by open arches in each of the four sides of the red-painted pavilion.

Thirty feet below it, in a tree-shaded square, extras in period costume sat round stone tables on seats carved in the shape of elephants. A long paved walkway led off, across three marble terraces, to the distant gates, and the parking lot beyond where production vehicles – make-up, wardrobe, a catering wagon, Michael's Winnebago – clustered in the shade of the trees around its fringes.

She heard someone shout, 'Cut!', and then the third assistant listened intently to a garble of instructions coming over the walkie, before relaying them in Chinese to a cluster of production runners in the square below, who began rounding up the extras. She waved Margaret on, and Margaret walked up the steps to the stele pavilion. From here she could watch the activities in the square below as well as the crew resetting at the diamond wall. Months of preparation, she reflected, dozens of people, hours of filming, all to put a few minutes on screen. She was not sure she would have the patience to survive in a business like this.

When Margaret got back to the control truck Chuck was more animated than she had seen him all morning. A tall, lanky man, with a shock of prematurely grey hair, he seemed to have folded himself over the control console and was talking rapidly into his walkie-talkie. 'We get one shot at the master, guys,' he was saying. 'We get it right, or we spend the rest of the day setting it up again.' He had lit a cigarette, the first she had seen him smoking. He waved it at her apologetically when he saw her. 'Sorry about this,' he said. 'I only smoke when extremely stressed. So if you ever see me with a cigarette in my hand you know I'm about to implode. Design have been setting this up for days. It's cost an arm and a leg, and I don't want to have to reshoot.'

'What's the scene?' Margaret asked.

'It's the moment when they remove the first bricks from the diamond wall and open the tomb. Special effects are great.' He paused. 'I hope.' Then he grinned and puffed some more at his cigarette. 'I've got three cameras on it, so it had better be good.'

Margaret saw that two other monitors, which had previously been black, now showed the pictures being fed from the other two cameras. The master shot was set wide and showed the ladder leading up to the top of the inverted V. Dozens of extras dressed as peasants in blue cotton Mao suits were gathered around the foot of it. The actor playing Hu Bo stood at the top of it, a trowel-like implement in his hand, ready to start digging out the bricks.

Another camera had been set somewhere higher up the wall, giving a view from above Hu Bo, down to the upturned peasant faces. The third camera was set low, among the legs of the gathering at the foot of the ladder. In the background

Margaret could see camera and crew. She said to Chuck, 'Are we meant to see them?'

Chuck laughed. 'They're supposed to be the film crew that shot the real opening of the tomb. That's how we know exactly what it was like. We're going to intercut our stuff with some of the original footage.'

It was another forty-five minutes before they were ready to go for a take. Hu Bo and the peasant Wang Qifa had run through their lines several times, going through the actions of removing the first brick without actually doing so. Sound recordist, camera operators, lighting director, all seemed happy to go for it.

'OK, Dave,' Chuck said. 'When you're ready . . .'

Dave, a burly young man with long red hair beneath his baseball cap, gave a thumbs-up to camera and ducked out of shot. Then Margaret heard him on foldback. 'OK everyone, quiet please. Roll VT. Very still. And . . . action!'

Wang Qifa, clutching a trowel, climbed the ladder to join Hu Bo. '*What are you doing?*' Hu Bo asked.

'*I thought we might remove the first bricks together,*' Wang Qifa replied.

'*Ah, but there might be hidden weapons,*' Hu Bo replied. '*And chickens' blood is not always foolproof. You'd better wait at the foot of the ladder and I'll hand down the bricks. That way only one of us will get killed.*'

That was enough to send Wang Qifa back down the ladder. It was deathly silent as Hu began scraping with his trowel to remove the first brick. The overhead camera caught, in close up, the concentration on his upturned face. The brick slowly came loose and, using both hands, he pushed and pulled it from side to side until finally it came free of the wall. There was a loud pop and a sucking sound like the rushing of air. A voice shouted, '*Poisonous gas!*' And almost immediately a thick black mist came belching out of the opening, accompanied by a noise like the growling of an animal.

Hu put his hand to his mouth, dropping the brick, and slid down the ladder, choking and coughing. The peasants had all thrown themselves to the ground as the mist descended and engulfed them. The air was filled with the sound of choking.

Then Margaret saw, on the third monitor, a figure emerging from the mist, incongruous in white shirt and jeans. On some signal she couldn't see, the coughing stopped and the set became quiet. Michael addressed himself to the camera in an eerie silence while still walking towards it, the black mist billowing around his legs. '*But it wasn't poison gas. It was simply an accumulation of rotten organic materials released by the inrush of air after nearly three hundred and forty years of decay. Vile and unpleasant, but not toxic. And if there were hidden weapons within, they were still to be encountered.*'

'Cut!' Chuck shouted. 'Brilliant! Check it. Sound, do you need a wild track?'

A voice came back from somewhere. 'Yeah. Lots more coughing and choking.'

'OK, we'll do it after we've checked tape. Dave, kisses all round. Tell Design I owe them a very large drink.'

*

It was cold in the Underground Palace, and damp, and Margaret shivered. Michael put his jacket over her shoulders, covering her thin cotton blouse. And she wasn't sure whether it was the cold or his touch that raised goosebumps on her forearms. She shrugged the thought aside and looked around the vast chambers with their arched roofs and shook her head in amazement. 'I had no idea this would be so big.'

'Built from giant stone blocks, each one hand-cut and polished,' Michael said. 'The cost of building the tomb nearly bankrupted the country.'

'And there were no hidden weapons after all?' Margaret was disappointed.

'I'm afraid not.'

'Well, isn't that a bit of a cheat? Building your audience up to think there were?'

'No,' Michael said earnestly. 'I want the audience to experience the same sense of the unknown, of hidden dangers, as Hu Bo and the others. So the tomb wasn't booby-trapped, but they weren't to know that. And then once they were inside they had other problems. They couldn't open the huge marble doors to any of these chambers, including the door to the central vault.'

Margaret looked at the doors. They were massive studded affairs that must each have weighed several tons.

'They were locked, apparently from the inside,' Michael said.

'You mean people locked them and then stayed in here to die?' Margaret was shocked.

Michael smiled. 'For a while they thought that might be the case. Then Hu discovered the secret of a hook-shaped key that could be slipped between the doors to move a stone buttress on the other side, and one by one they managed to open all the doors. To find the chambers empty.'

'Empty?' Margaret was surprised. 'So the emperor wasn't buried here after all?'

'For a time they thought perhaps the tomb had already been robbed. They found three white marble thrones, one for the emperor and one for each of his empresses. There were various sacrificial objects, but no coffins. Until,' he said, 'they opened the very last chamber at the far end.' And he led her past the marble thrones to the end chamber. 'And there, on a raised dais, each on its own golden well, sat the coffins of the emperor and his two empresses, surrounded by twenty-six red lacquered wooden chests.'

Three huge red lacquered boxes sat on the dais before them, surrounded by the twenty-six chests.

'And that's them?' Margaret asked.

Michael shook his head. 'Reproductions.' He sighed. 'You must remember when it was that these tombs were being opened up. The late fifties in China was a time of political purges and great social upheaval. The director put in charge here was a political appointee. He knew nothing about the history of the place, and couldn't care less about the contents of the tomb. The original coffins had deteriorated with age, and reproductions were made to go on public show. So the director ordered the originals to be thrown away.'

'You're kidding!' Margaret was appalled. 'They didn't, did they?'

'When the archaeologists objected, the director ordered some soldiers to throw them over the outer wall where they were smashed on the rocks below.'

In spite of herself, and to her great surprise, Margaret found herself full of furious indignation. 'But these things were hundreds of years old, priceless historical relics.'

Michael looked sombre. 'Unfortunately, much worse was to happen to the contents of the coffins. Wonderful, irreplaceable artefacts.' He put his arm around her shoulder, and she felt his warmth, even through his jacket and her blouse. 'But you're cold down here. And the rest of the story can wait. I think we should go and get some lunch.'

It required the fifteen minutes it took them to walk the full length of the paved walkway, down to the parking lot, for the warmth of the sun finally to reach and banish the chill that seemed to have set in Margaret's bones.

On the walk she asked him, 'Why are you so fascinated by this Hu Bo?'

He smiled, a little sadly. 'Because all his life he was a victim. Of circumstance, and of history. And every time fate knocked him down he got up and hit right back.' His hand clamped itself around her upper arm. 'Think about it, Margaret. At the age of ten he was *sold* by his father. Sold to work in the camp of a Swedish explorer, Sven Hedin, who was just setting off on an exploration of the remote western regions of China. A disaster for a young boy, forced to become what was little more than a slave. He suffered great hardship, trekking across the western deserts, crossing uncharted mountain ranges. He lost three fingers to frostbite. But he also learned tailoring, and cooking, and barbering, how to bake bread, how to ride and shoot, how to collect samples of ancient relics in the field. He became familiar with the methods of survey, and the essential principles of excavation. He developed the skills needed to restore and preserve disinterred relics.' Michael's eyes were shining with wonder and admiration. 'He took a disastrous sequence of events, and turned them to his advantage. By the age of twenty, a peasant boy from nowhere, he was studying archaeology at the university in Beijing.'

He became aware that he was gripping her arm and let go immediately. 'I'm sorry.' He smiled. 'I get carried away sometimes.'

Margaret looked at the light in his eyes. His enthusiasm was boyish, verging on the immature. But it was also infectious, and quite compelling. She rubbed her arm, smiling ruefully. 'I'll be all bruised tonight.'

'I'm sorry,' he said again, suddenly self-conscious.

They walked in silence for a few moments. Behind them, the mountains shimmered in a blue haze, and the double roof of the stele pavilion rose above the blue-green needles of the spruce trees. Ahead of them the parking lot was crowded, and crew and cast and extras clustered around the catering wagon. Out of the blue he said, 'Have you been to Xi'an to see the Terracotta Warriors?'

She laughed. 'I've hardly been out of Beijing.'

He said, 'But you must see them. You can't come to China and not see the Eighth Wonder of the World.'

'A bunch of ceramic figures?'

He gasped in frustration. 'Margaret, they are awe-inspiring! Thousands of ancient warriors, my height and bigger. Each one individually cast and hand finished. Every face unique. Made by craftsmen two thousand, two hundred years ago. Just to stand among them, to feel their presence, to touch them, is to be touched by history in a way I can't even begin to describe.'

That infectious enthusiasm again. She smiled and shook her head. 'Michael, you're wasting your time with me. I'm a cultural cretin.'

'Listen,' he said. 'I have to be in Xi'an tomorrow. We're arranging for the shipment of more than five dozen warriors to the United States as part of an exhibition I've organised to coincide with the broadcast of my latest documentary series. It's called *The Art of War*, and it's going to be the biggest exhibition of Terracotta Warriors ever seen outside of China.' He paused. 'Come with me.'

'What?' She was completely taken aback.

But there was no restraining his alacrity. 'I'm travelling down on the sleeper tonight. I'm there all day tomorrow and tomorrow night, then fly back first thing the next morning. I can't afford to be away from the production for any longer.'

'I couldn't possibly,' Margaret laughed. 'I'm involved in a murder investigation here.'

'One day, that's all you'd be away.' He stopped and took

both her hands in his. 'My production office will book your travel and accommodation. And I can get you right down there among the warriors, touching them, brushing away the earth of two thousand years. Something only a handful of people will ever experience.' He stopped for breath. 'Say yes. Don't even think about it. Life's too short for that. Just say yes.'

For a moment she looked into his eyes, felt his hands, big and strong, enveloping hers, and was aware of something both painful and pleasurable stirring deep inside her.

II

Blood, and headless bodies, and disembodied heads, and hands tied with silk cord, swam in front of his eyes. Photographs were spread across his desk like the pieces of a jigsaw that were all the same size and gave no clue as to where or how to begin piecing them together. Li had spent the morning sifting through reports and pictures, interviews and statements, all the while distracted by unrelated thoughts that crowded his mind and blurred his focus. *You're just going to have to learn how to separate your personal from your professional life*, Chen had told him last night. But Li was finding it impossible.

During his early morning *jian bing* stop at the Dongzhimennei corner, he had told Mei Yuan about his sister and her intentions. Mei Yuan had listened with grave intensity, making no comment, offering no advice. She understood that all he needed to do was talk. She expressed her sympathy for his troubles with no more than a slight squeeze of his arm.

Somehow, even that had been reassuring, and he had remembered her words of the previous evening. *Anytime you need me.* It was not until he had reached his office that he realised she had forgotten to ask him about the thirty yuan riddle. It was just as well, for he had given it little thought and had no answer.

He had left Xiao Ling, first thing, preparing for her appointment later that morning at the clinic where they would perform the ultra-sound scan. Xinxin, still sleepy and puffy-eyed as she woke from her slumbers, had forgotten that she was being strange with her uncle, and had given Li a hug and a kiss before he left. His sister, huffy and alienated by his disapproval, had not. Neither of them had slept as Xinxin had. And now Li found himself almost afraid to return home tonight, for whatever the result of the scan, his sister's response to it would be unthinkable.

He screwed up his eyes to try to banish the thought from his mind, and found a picture of Margaret there, staring at him with that knowing, challenging look of hers. How was he going to be able to deal with her in a professional capacity without being affected by his personal feelings? *You're just going to have to learn how to separate your personal from your professional life.* How? How is it done? he wanted to ask Chen. And who, he wanted to ask Margaret, was the man she'd been with at the Sanwei the night before?

He opened his eyes and found four victims staring up at him from his desk, almost accusingly. Why had he not found their killer?

A secretary from downstairs knocked on his door and came

in with a large brown envelope. 'That's the translations of the autopsy reports you requested,' she said. 'And copy prints of the crime scene pics.' She set it down on his desk.

'Don't put it there,' he barked uncharacteristically, and she jumped. 'They're for Dr Margaret Campbell at the American Embassy. Get them sent over straight away by dispatch rider.'

'Yes,' she said timidly, her face flushing. And she backed out as Zhao came in.

'What is it, Zhao?' Li was terse and impatient.

Zhao said, 'I've only been able to track down one teacher who was at No. 29 Middle School back in the early sixties, boss. He's nearly eighty.'

'What about the others?'

Zhao shrugged. 'I don't know. Some of them are probably dead by now. A lot of the school records were destroyed during the Cultural Revolution, so getting information of any kind hasn't been easy. It's the same thing trying to get anything on Yuan's family.'

'What about Qian? Is he making any progress?'

Zhao said, 'He's having the same problem, boss. We're having to go by word of mouth. But he's got the names of some of the victims' classmates, so it should only be a matter of time before we manage to track down the rest.'

'Time,' Li said, 'is something we don't necessarily have a lot of, Zhao. The timescale between each of these killings is anywhere between three and fifteen days. And if there are another two victims out there, then we want to find them before the killer does.'

'You want me to set up interviews?'

Li thought for a moment. 'Yes,' he said. 'But let's do them at the school. Tomorrow morning. Ask the headmaster to give us a couple of rooms. I'd like to get a feel for the place.'

Wu's voice called from the detectives' office. 'Boss? You got a moment?'

Zhao stepped aside as Li went to the door. 'What is it, Wu?'

Wu was at his desk, holding his hand over the telephone receiver. 'That's the forensics boys out at Yuan Tao's embassy apartment. There's some stuff they think you should have a look at.' He raised his eyebrows. 'You want to go?'

Li nodded. 'You'd better sign out a car.'

Wu said into the telephone, 'We'll be right there.'

Li went back to his desk. At least *something* was moving.

Qian came in, almost at his back. He had a sheet of paper in his hand, and his eyes were alive with anticipation. 'Just in, boss. Fax from the Evidence Determination Centre. The result of those tests that Dr Campbell suggested we do on the signature of the murder weapon . . .'

Li snatched the sheet and ran his eyes over the tightly printed characters of the report. He felt the skin tighten across his scalp.

The diplomatic compound where Yuan Tao had been allocated an apartment was set just behind the Friendship Store on Jianguomenwei Avenue. Wu parked their dark blue Beijing Jeep in the cycle lane at the front, and he and Li got out on to the sidewalk and looked up at the relatively new apartments.

A long-haired beggar with no legs sat on the pavement, leaning against the wall of the compound. A straggling beard grew on his dark, gaunt face and he looked up at them appealingly and rattled a tin cup he held in his hand. Beside him, his tricycle had been fitted with an elaborate mechanism that allowed him to drive the wheels by hand-turning a crank handle. His skin was streaked and dirty, his clothes and hair matted. His face was a mask of disappointment when he saw that they, too, were Chinese.

A few yards further along, propped against a tree, a blind woman with a withered hand called out to them for money. There were others spread out along the length of the sidewalk. Li felt sick to see poor souls like this on the streets.

Wu looked at them with undisguised disgust. 'What are they doing here?' he asked, looking along the sidewalk. 'There must be half a dozen of them.'

Li took out a ten-yuan note and stuffed it in the cup of the beggar with no legs. 'Foreigners,' he said, nodding towards the diplomatic compound. 'Embassy staff and tourists. The guilt of the "haves" when faced with the "have-nots". It's fertile ground.'

Wu looked in horror at the note Li had given the beggar. 'In the name of the sky, boss, what did you do that for?'

'Because life has no guarantees, Wu,' he said. 'One day that could be me. Or you. And that's not guilt. Just fear.' He headed off towards the entrance to the compound.

At the gate a po-faced guard of the armed police stood sentinel. 'Who are you looking for?' he asked unceremoniously.

'CID. Section One,' Wu said, and pushed his ID in the guard's face.

'You know this guy?' Li showed him the picture of Yuan Tao that had come with his file.

'Sure,' the guard said, and he pulled a gob of phlegm into his mouth and spat it out. 'Yuan Tao. Second floor. He's the guy that got himself murdered.' He jerked his head towards the building. 'Some of your people are in there just now.' A grey forensics van was parked in the forecourt.

'How well did you know him?' Wu asked.

'As well as I know any of them,' the guard said. 'Which is not at all. They don't like us very much.'

'Why's that?' Li asked.

'They think we're spying on them.'

'And are you?'

The guard flicked a look at Li to see if he was joking and decided he wasn't. 'We're told to keep an eye on who goes in and out. If they get Chinese visitors they got to come down and pick them up here at the gate. And they got to see them out again when they leave.'

'And they don't like that?' Wu said.

'No, they do not.'

'But you knew Yuan Tao by sight?' Li asked.

'Sure. He was unusual. He was Chinese.'

'And was there anything else you thought was unusual about him? Anything that made him stand out from the others?'

The guard shook his head slowly. 'Nope. Can't say there

was.' He hesitated. 'If anything, I'd say I saw him less than the rest. Don't remember him ever having any visitors.'

'Ever?' Wu was astonished.

'Not that I can remember. Course, you'd have to ask the guys on the other shifts.'

'Would you know,' Li asked 'if he didn't stay in his apartment for a night, or even two?'

'Not necessarily. He might already be in when you came on shift. And he might not.'

'You don't keep records?'

'Nope.'

Li produced photographs of the other victims. 'Ever seen any of these guys?'

The guard took a long look, then shook his head. 'Nope.'

They climbed the stairs to the apartment on the second floor and found the door lying open. The place was tiny: one central room for living, eating and cooking, a stove and a sink set on a worktop over cheap units against the far wall. Through a half-glazed door was a tiny toilet with a shower that drained into an outlet set into the concrete floor. The bedroom was just large enough for a bed, a bedside cabinet and a single, mirrored wardrobe. Apart from the fact that it was smaller, the contrast with the apartment Yuan Tao had rented in Tuan Jie Hu Dongli was stark. Books were stuffed into sagging bookshelves, and piled up on the linoleum beneath the window. Piles of Chinese newspapers were stacked under a gateleg table folded against one wall. There was food decaying on dirty plates on the table, and dirty dishes were soaking in the sink.

There was a smell of body odour and cooking and old clothes, a faint, distant hint of some exotic scent that seemed vaguely familiar. The kitchen cupboards were groaning with tinned and packet food. Dirty washing was spilling out of a laundry basket in the bedroom, washing hanging up to dry on a line in the toilet. Unlike the apartment at Tuan Jie Hu Dongli, Yuan Tao had lived here. He had left his smell, his personality and all his traces in this place, and perhaps, too, a clue as to why someone should want to kill him.

There were two officers there from the forensics department at Pao Jü Hutong. They were dusting for prints. The senior officer, a small, wizened man called Fu Qiwei, said, 'Be with you in two minutes, Deputy Section Chief.'

Li ran his eye along the shelves of books. They were mostly academic volumes, some fiction, almost all of them in English, well-thumbed pages and broken spines.

'He must have had them shipped over,' Wu said. And Li wondered, not for the first time, why a professor of political science at a prestigious American university would give up his career to work on the visa line at the US Embassy in Beijing. Was there more to all this than met the eye? More to it than he was being told? Had Yuan Tao been a spy for the Americans, or even the Chinese? But he quickly dismissed the thought. If there were the slightest suspicion of that, he thought, the investigation would have been taken very quickly out of his hands.

All along the tops of the bookcases was an accumulated clutter of miscellaneous personal items and dust: a paperweight, pens and pencils, a dried-up eraser, a couple of unused notebooks, an antique dominoes set picked up at a market somewhere, a chipped and cracked but otherwise clean ashtray filled with fen coins on top of what appeared to be a picture frame lying face down. Li took out a handkerchief and shifted the ashtray so that he could turn over the frame. It contained a haphazard montage of old black-and-white family snaps – a couple in their early thirties with a young boy standing awkwardly between them grinning shyly at the camera; a passport-sized photograph of a teenage boy; a portrait picture of each of the adults, a little older, wearing Mao caps and staring earnestly out from the mists of history.

Wu peered over Li's shoulder. 'His family?'

'Looks like it.' Li always found pictures like these depressing. He had ones just like them. His sister, his mother and father, himself as a young boy, family groups with aunts and uncles and cousins, reminders of a time when he was still a part of a family, happy and whole, before history had torn them apart. 'We'll want these for the file,' he said, and carefully he opened up the back of the picture frame and tipped the faded and dog-eared photographs out on to the table. On the backs of them someone had written dates and places – Ping Zhen, Ye and Tao, Tiananmen, 1952; Tao, aged seventeen; Ping Zhen, Qianmen, 1964 . . . Li turned over the family group taken in Tiananmen Square in 1952. In the background, he saw, *hutongs* and *siheyuan* where now the Great Hall of the People stood. People were flying kites back then, just as they did today. For a moment or two he scrutinised the faces of Yuan's parents, Ping Zhen and Ye, as if there might be some answer in their dull, staring eyes. They did not look like happy people in their button-up tunics and Mao caps. They did not look like the same carefree couple who had posed, smiling unselfconsciously with their son in Tiananmen Square twelve years earlier. In just twelve short years life had etched its unhappiness indelibly on their faces. And no doubt, Li thought, the worst had still to come.

He left Wu to slip the pictures into a plastic evidence bag, and looked around the room again. There was a single, well-worn armchair, acquired second-hand, no doubt. The cushion and the chair back still bore the imprint of Yuan Tao's body. A few short, black hairs clung to an antimacassar. There was a single dining chair at the gateleg table. *Don't remember him ever having any visitors*, the security guard had said. He had clearly furnished his tiny apartment in the expectation that he would be its sole occupant. He had not anticipated receiving visitors.

They went into the small toilet. There was no curtain, nor any other attempt to cover up the window in the toilet door. Another indication that Yuan Tao had lived here in absolute isolation. He had had no need to protect his privacy. There was more of his hair trapped in the shower drain in the floor. A small cabinet on the wall contained the usual toiletries: shaving foam, a couple of fresh bars of soap, toothpaste, haemorrhoid cream, several packs of Advil – all American branded.

'He bring all this stuff with him, too, do you think?' Wu asked.

'I don't know,' Li said. It was possible now to buy a huge variety of Western consumer goods in ordinary Chinese supermarkets. But these were a little different. '*Unscented*,' he read off the can of shaving foam. And, '*Hypo-allergenic*,' off the soap wrapper.

'What's that?' Wu asked.

Li said, 'Looks like maybe he had an allergic skin reaction to anything highly scented.' He looked again at the contents of the wall cabinet. 'I don't see any aftershave or deodorants either.'

He closed the mirrored door of the cabinet and saw his own face staring back at him, and he was shocked by the dark shadows beneath his eyes and the strain in the lines around them. He looked quickly away, and Wu followed him into the bedroom. The sour smell of body odour and dirty laundry hung in the air. The forensics officers had just finished dusting. 'What did you want to show me?' Li said.

Fu Qiwei beckoned him towards the wardrobe and opened the door. It was jammed with clothes, mostly formal suits and white shirts. Several ties hung from a bar attached to the inside of the door. On a shelf above were a couple of pairs of jeans, some sweatshirts, a pile of tee shirts. The officer crouched down to a row of shoes along the bottom of the wardrobe. Again, the shoes were mostly formal, black or brown leather. There was a single well-worn pair of blue and white trainers. With his gloved hand, the officer carefully lifted one of them and Li saw, in its tread and lying scattered in the bottom of the wardrobe, a small accumulation of dark blue-black dust.

Li whistled softly. 'Is that the same stuff we found on the victim that was moved?'

'The archaeology professor,' Fu Qiwei said, nodding. 'It looks very like it. Same colour and consistency. We'll be able to tell for sure once we get a sample back to the lab.'

Wu crouched down beside Li, peering in at the blue dust, frowning his consternation. 'What does it mean, boss?'

Li shrugged and shook his head, as perplexed as Wu. 'I've no idea.' But they all knew there was significance in it. That Yuan Tao had, somehow, been in the same place, possibly at the same time, as Yue Shi, the professor of archaeology at Beijing University. Here was something else to link them besides the manner of their deaths and the fact that they were former pupils of the same school. A blue-black dust, particles of fired clay – as puzzling and insubstantial as every other piece of evidence they had managed to collect.

'That's not all,' said the forensics officer. He stood up and they followed him through to the living room where he stooped to open the kitchen cabinet below the sink unit. There, amongst a bucket and bottles of cleaning fluid, stood three unopened bottles of Californian red wine.

Li felt the hairs bristling across his scalp. Then wondered why he had reacted in such a way. After all, here was a man who had lived for more than thirty years in the United States. Would it not be the most natural thing in the world for him to keep bottles of wine in his kitchen? To drink a glass or two with a meal was commonplace in the West. He crouched down to look at the labels. They were all the same vintage. A 1995 Mondavi Reserve Cabernet Sauvignon from the Napa Valley. Li knew enough to know that this was no cheap plonk.

He also knew that Yuan Tao could not have purchased them in China and could only have brought a limited amount with him. So why, after six months, did he still have three bottles? And even more curiously, why would he keep his expensive vintage wine with the cleaning fluids beneath the sink?

'Wow!' Wu said. He was chewing furiously on his gum and rolling one of the legs of his sunglasses back and forth between thumb and forefinger. 'Can we tell if that's the same stuff our first three victims had been drinking?'

Fu Qiwei nodded. 'We can compare it to residue found in wineglasses at the first two crime scenes. Give you a result later this afternoon.'

But Li knew that the results would only confirm what his instincts were already telling him. And he felt himself slipping deeper into the mire of confusion in which they were already wallowing.

III

Margaret had thought she would be curious about the place where Yuan Tao had worked. But, in truth, the visa department in the Bruce Compound was just another anonymous legation building. An extension had been built out front to accommodate the queues of applicants, so that they no longer had to clutter up the street, standing in line under the watchful and sometimes intimidating eye of the Chinese armed police guard on the gate. Inside the main building, extensive renovation work had created new, white-walled offices in the US Citizen Services Department where Margaret had been allocated a small room.

Sophie opened the door and waved Margaret through it. 'Your very own office,' she said.

Margaret looked around without enthusiasm. There was a small window high up on the wall that she could not see out of. What little daylight it admitted was supplemented by a naked fluorescent striplight overhead. There was a single desk with a telephone extension, a blotter, a pile of thick brown envelopes and a computer terminal, an uncomfortable-looking office chair, a battleship-grey filing cabinet, a yucca tree in a pot, and a map of China pinned to the freshly painted wall. The place smelled of emulsion paint and new carpet, and the fluorescent light reflecting from the white walls hurt her eyes. She wondered briefly who had been de-camped to make space for her, but knew better than to ask. She was sure she would spot some resentful face glaring at her in the corridor before the day was out.

'You don't look terribly impressed,' Sophie said.

'Should I be?' asked Margaret. The filing cabinet was locked. She tried the desk drawers. They were locked, too. 'I'm obviously not expected to be here very long.'

'As long as the investigation takes.'

'Which is as soon as possible as far as the embassy's concerned.'

'Naturally,' Sophie said. She pointed to the bundle of envelopes on the desk. 'That's all the stuff you asked for from the

Chinese police – copy prints from the crime scenes, translations of the autopsy reports . . .'

'That was quick!' Margaret was astonished. 'They must be as anxious to get rid of me as you are.'

Sophie grinned. 'It *is* quick. Jonathan couldn't believe it. Apparently it would normally take weeks for something like this. Chinese bureaucracy moves at its own, usually very slow, pace.'

'Just shows what they can do when they want,' Margaret said, shuffling through the contents of the envelopes. 'Oh, good,' she said, pulling out a sheaf of reports. 'That's the toxicology results on my autopsy, along with the transliteration of the tape. Means I can get my own autopsy report written up.' She glanced through the toxicology results and nodded. 'Nothing unexpected here.' She looked at her watch. 'Oops, no time to read them just now,' and she stuffed them back in the envelope and starting gathering all the papers and envelopes into a pile that she could carry away.

'Where are you going?' Sophie asked, disconcerted.

'To pack. I've got a train to catch at six fifty.'

Sophie frowned. 'But the Chinese police have set up a briefing meeting for you at Section One.'

Which stopped Margaret in her tracks. 'When?'

'At five.'

'Then it'll have to be a brief briefing.'

She lifted the bundle from the desk and pushed past Sophie and off down the corridor. Sophie chased after her. 'But where are you going?'

'Xi'an.'

'Xi'an?' Sophie was perplexed. 'But . . . what's in Xi'an?'

'The Terracotta Warriors. Didn't you know? Apparently they are the Eighth Wonder of the World and not to be missed.'

'Michael,' Sophie said flatly, as realisation dawned. 'You're going with Michael.'

'He asked,' Margaret said breezily, as she passed the scrutiny of the marine at the front door and was allowed out.

'You lucky bitch!' Sophie grinned. 'He's only after your body, you know.'

'Well, maybe I'm after his, too,' Margaret said with a twinkle. 'Anyway, it's only for a day. We'll be back the day after tomorrow.'

'Well, I hope you don't expect the American government to pay you while you're off gallivanting with Mr Zimmerman.'

'Of course I do,' Margaret said. She crooked her arm around the bundle she was carrying. 'After all, I'll be taking my work with me.'

The tension in the top floor meeting room of the Section One building in Beixinqiao Santiao was almost tangible. Margaret, shown first into the room, had taken Li's customary seat with the window behind her. She knew it was the power seat in the room, and almost certainly the seat that Li would have made his own. Despite anxious glances from the other detectives, however, Li gave no sign of having had his nose put out of joint. He sat directly opposite Margaret and seemed concentrated on sorting out his papers. Also present were

Zhao, Wu, Qian and Sang. To the annoyance of the others, it had transpired that Sang spoke flawless English, and so Li had nominated him official interpreter for the meeting.

'OK,' Li said. 'You have received the prints and copy autopsies we sent you?'

Margaret nodded. 'But, since they have only just come into my possession I have not yet had time to study them.' She paused before delivering the first barb. 'Twenty-four hours does seem a rather excessive amount of time to have to wait.'

Li felt the anger rising in his throat and took a moment or two to control it before speaking. 'But time enough for you to have completed your autopsy report?'

'Without the toxicology results and the transliteration of my tape which, of course, I have been waiting for from your people, that would have been rather difficult.'

Sang struggled to translate this.

Li sat back and exhaled his frustration. 'Then there's not a great deal of point in continuing this meeting,' he said.

'However,' Margaret drew a bundle of stapled sheets from her bag, 'as soon as I received the necessary information this afternoon I booked time in the business centre of my hotel – at my own expense – and produced a preliminary report covering all the essentials.' She pushed the copies across the desk towards him. 'There are no surprises.'

Li pulled the bundle to him, pushed one towards Sang, and flicked through the top copy. Without looking up he said, 'We ran those tests you suggested on the sections of spine, comparing the signature left by the murder weapon on the vertebral bone in each murder.' He paused.

Margaret could not restrain her curiosity. 'And?'

'We matched the first and third murders. Your "sweet spot" theory looked as if it might stand up for a while. But we could not find a match for the other two.' Margaret was about to comment, but he cut her off. 'We did, however, run another test, with the scanning electron microscope. On the bronze residue left by the sword that we collected on the tape lifts. The computer was able to report the relative percentages of the constituent elements. They were exactly the same. Which means that the same weapon was used in all four murders.' He waited long enough to let the frown start to form on her forehead. Then added, 'Which rather gives the lie to your suggestion that Yuan Tao's murder was a copycat killing.'

The other detectives, listening intently to Sang, looked quickly to see Margaret's reaction.

She shrugged. 'Not really,' she said. 'It simply means that the killer had access to the same murder weapon used in the first three murders.' The detectives turned to catch's Li's reaction. But he was impassive. She added, 'Is that all you have to tell me? Is that the sum total of your investigations over twenty-four hours?'

'Of course not.' Li looked more composed than he felt. She had been unfazed by the revelation about the murder weapon, and her calmly suggested explanation was so simple he wondered why he had not thought of it himself. But he knew the answer to that almost immediately. He had found it virtually impossible to believe that Yuan Tao had been murdered by a copycat, and in admitting that to himself now, realised he had been making a basic mistake for which his uncle would have derided him. He had made an assumption, and was trying to make the evidence fit the assumption. *Assume nothing*, his uncle used to tell him. *Let the evidence lead to you the conclusion, do not jump to it yourself.*

Margaret glanced at her watch with ill-concealed irritation. 'Well?' she asked.

And Li told her about the blue-black powder found in Yuan Tao's apartment and the forensic confirmation, received less than an hour ago, that it matched similar coloured powder found on the trousers and in the treads of the shoes worn by Professor Yue. This caught her interest and she leaned forward. 'And this powder is what, exactly?'

He pushed a small sample in a clear plastic evidence bag across the table. 'Particles of fired clay. A kind of ceramic dust. You'll find a more detailed breakdown among the documents we've provided.'

She frowned, examining the dark blue dust in the bag and thinking for a moment. Then, 'What else?' she asked.

Li said, 'We found three bottles of vintage Californian wine in Yuan Tao's apartment. Tests carried out this afternoon show that it is almost certainly the same wine that our first three victims had been drinking. The stuff that their killer spiked with the flunitrazepam.'

Margaret's interest was well and truly ignited now. She forgot about the time. '*Three* bottles?'

Li nodded.

She scratched her chin thoughtfully. 'So . . . one for each of the remaining victims.'

'We already have *four* victims,' Li said. 'And the countdown began at six.'

'Humour me,' Margaret said. 'Assume that Yuan Tao was never on the hit list—'

Li interrupted. 'You still think he was killed by someone else?'

She nodded. 'I'm sure of it. I can't tell you by who, or why, but the evidence seems quite clear to me. And if you rule him out, then there are still three victims out there, not two. And that's why there were three bottles of wine.'

'But why was the wine in Yuan Tao's apartment?' Everyone was startled by Sang's sudden intervention. He seemed taken aback himself, and became immediately self-conscious. The other detectives asked him what he had asked. Still blushing, he told them.

Margaret smiled. 'I have no idea,' she said. 'But that question is still relevant whether or not you believe that he was one of the original intended victims.' She turned back to Li. 'Was there anything else in the apartment?'

He shook his head. 'Nothing relevant. Books, clothes, personal possessions.'

'And this apartment that he rented privately – have you any idea why?'

Again, Li shook his head. 'Detective Qian tracked down the owner. We interviewed him this afternoon. He claimed he had no idea that Yuan worked at the embassy – he was Chinese, had a Beijing accent. The owner says Yuan told him that he was lecturing at the university and only required the apartment for a few months. He was prepared to pay well over the going rate, so the owner didn't ask too many questions.'

'Do you believe him?'

'Yes,' Li nodded. 'He's in breach of several public security regulations, but nothing more than that.'

'Which brings us back to the question of why Yuan Tao felt the need to rent another apartment. Was he keeping a mistress?'

'No.' Li had no doubts. 'There are no female traces in either apartment. But, in any case, Yuan Tao was not the type.' He lit a cigarette, and wondered what it was he had gleaned about this man that made him so sure he had not been having an affair, or entertaining prostitutes. Instinct, he decided. 'If I was to make a guess, I would say he rented the apartment so that he could come and go without being seen or questioned. Or perhaps receive visitors he didn't want the authorities to know about.'

'And he couldn't do that at his embassy accommodation?'

'There is a twenty-four-hour guard on the gate to the compound.'

Margaret nodded thoughtfully. 'So why would he want to come and go without being seen or questioned, or have secret visitors?'

Li blew a jet of smoke at the overhead fan. 'If we knew that, we probably wouldn't be sitting here.'

Margaret suddenly stiffened and checked the time. 'Oh, my God, I'm going to be late!' She stood up quickly and lifted her bag on to the desk. 'Is it possible for you to call me a taxi?'

Li and the other detectives were taken by surprise. They had anticipated that their meeting would go on for some time yet. 'Where are you going?' Li asked.

'Beijing West Railway Station,' she said. 'My train leaves at ten to seven.'

Li looked at his watch. It was a quarter to six. He shook his head. 'You'll never make it. Not at this time of night. The traffic will be at a standstill. It'll take at least an hour and a half.'

'But the station's not that far,' she protested. 'I could walk it in twenty minutes from my hotel. We got the train to Datong from there.'

'No,' Li shook his head. 'That's *Beijing* Railway Station. Beijing *West* Railway Station is way on the other side of town.'

'Shit!' Margaret cursed.

Li stood up and gathered his papers together. The other detectives took their cue from him. 'Where are you going?' he asked, trying to sound as if he was indifferent to the answer.

'Xi'an,' she said. 'To see the Terracotta Warriors.'

Li looked at her in astonishment. 'On your own?'

'No.' She hesitated for just a moment. 'Michael Zimmerman's taking me.'

Li felt the colour rise on his cheeks, and he heard Sang translating for the others. He turned to them. 'That's all,' he said curtly. Disappointed, they lifted their papers, nodded politely to Margaret and went out. Still feigning indifference, he said, 'Michael Zimmerman . . . That's the man you were with at the Sanwei tearoom last night?'

In spite of her anxiety about her train, Margaret had derived some small pleasure from seeing the colour rising on Li's face at the mention of Michael's name. 'That's right,' she said. 'Are you going to call me a taxi or not?'

But he was in no hurry. 'Who is he, exactly?'

'I don't really figure that's any of your business, exactly,' she responded tartly.

He shrugged. 'Well, if I'm going to stick a flashing light on the roof of a police Jeep and get you to the station in time for your train, I think I have the right to expect a civil answer to a civil question.'

She smiled ruefully. He had trapped her. And if she wanted to catch her train . . . 'He's a TV archaeologist,' she said.

'A what?' He had no idea what she meant.

'He makes documentaries for television about archaeology,' she spelled it out for him. 'China is his speciality. He's very popular in the States.'

'And why is he taking you to Xi'an?'

'Now that,' she said, 'is not a civil question. So do I get my ride or not?'

Dusk fell over the city like a grey powder slowly blotting out the light. For a time, as their Jeep careered in and out of cycle lanes, siren wailing, red light flashing, the sun had sent long shadows to meet them and blinded them through the windscreen. Now it was gone, and the red streaks in the sky were fading through blue into black. There were times when Li, squeezing between buses and taxis, had turned the three lanes of the westbound carriageway of the third ring road into four. Margaret watched his concentration as he leaned frequently on the horn to supplement the siren, muttering to himself in between drags on his cigarette, almost as if she wasn't there. He had not spoken to her since they left Section One. And her naked fear had banished all thoughts of conversation as he drove, like a man possessed, through the evening rush hour.

He checked his watch and appeared to relax a little. He glanced across at her for the first time. 'We might just make it,' he said.

'I'm glad,' she said, a hint of acid in her tone. 'I'd hate to think I'd aged ten years in vain.'

'And I would hate to think,' he said, looking straight ahead again, 'that a mere murder investigation would get in the way of your love life.'

'You know what your trouble is?' she said, controlling the urge to tell him exactly where he could go. 'Your grasp of English is far too good. Your uncle taught you well, but he should have told you that sarcasm is the lowest form of wit.'

'Who said I was being witty?'

'Well, certainly not me!' She glared at him, then relaxed. 'Anyway,' she said, 'since you are clearly so anxious to know, the relationship between Michael and me is strictly platonic. You know what platonic is, don't you?'

He nodded. 'It's the word people always use to describe their relationship with someone just before they sleep with them.' But he wasn't smiling. His mouth was set in a grim line as he swung the Jeep off the ring road on to the flyover leading to the Tianningsi Bridge.

Margaret was stung. Not so much by the barb in Li's words, but by the truth of them. And she wondered just why she had agreed to go to Xi'an with Michael, and knew at once that it wasn't to fulfil a life's ambition to see the Terracotta Warriors. She felt a churning in her stomach, and that fear that fluttered so elusively in her breast. What in God's name was she doing? She stole a glance at Li. She had stopped seeing him as Chinese again. Just as Li Yan. And she had seen the warmth and sparkle return to his eyes as they had fenced verbally at Section One, and again in the Jeep. She knew, without daring to let the thought crystallise in her mind, that she still loved him. But what point was there in it? It was as foolish and impossible as a teenager falling for a rock star. Li had made it clear. They had no future.

His focus appeared to be entirely on the traffic as he weaved between vehicles along Lianhuachidong Road. Suddenly he leaned forward and pointed out to their left. 'Beijing West Railway Station,' he said.

Margaret looked out, and in the fading light saw a vast structure rising out of sweeping flyovers to east and west, outlined in neon and dazzling in the glare of coloured arc lights. Huge towers rose in ascending symmetry to a colossal centre-piece of three roofs, one atop the other, curling eaves raised on towering columns. 'Jesus,' she whispered breathlessly. 'It's vast!' It was bigger than most airports she had been in.

'Biggest railway station in the world,' Li said. And he swung off the road on to a ramp that swept them up and round to a multi-lane highway running parallel with a main concourse thick with arriving and departing passengers. He drew the Jeep into the kerb, jumped on to the concourse and lifted Margaret's bag out for her as the siren wound down and tailed off to a throaty splutter.

Margaret grasped her bag and looked up in awe at the station looming over her. 'My God,' she said. 'How will I ever find Michael?'

But to Li's disappointment he saw an anxious-faced Michael pushing through the crowds towards them. 'I think he's found you,' he said.

Michael arrived breathless and flushed and immediately took Margaret's bag. 'Thank Heaven, Margaret. I thought for a while there you weren't going to make it.'

'With my own personal police escort, there was never any danger,' Margaret said, glancing at Li.

Michael looked at him and nodded. He held out his hand. 'We meet again, Mr Li.'

Li was taken aback that Michael remembered his name and wondered if he had been a subject of discussion between Michael and Margaret. 'Mr Zimmerman,' he said politely. Their hands clasped firmly. Perhaps a little too firmly, and the air between them stiffened with an electric tension. And Li became aware, vaguely, almost sub-consciously, of something familiar about this man. He searched his face for some sign, some clue, but the familiarity, strangely, seemed somehow not quite physical.

The moment passed, as quickly as it had come, and they let go each other's hands. Michael checked his watch and said to Margaret, 'We'll have to hurry.' And to Li, 'Thanks for getting her here on time.'

Li resisted a powerful urge to punch him and turned instead to Margaret. 'Enjoy your trip.' His words seemed stiff and formal.

She nodded. 'Thank you,' she said, and then she and Michael were off, hurrying through the crowds towards the main entrance. Li stood for a moment, watching them, and a cloud of depression, as dense as the darkness that had fallen, enveloped him.

The interior concourse of Beijing West Railway Station was daunting, cavernous and crowded with people responding to a bewildering array of electronic information displayed from gantries on all sides. Above the hubbub of thousands of passengers rose the soft voice of a female announcer, hypnotically repeating the arrival and departure times of trains in Chinese and English. A huge, gaping hole fed escalators up and down to lower levels. Along either side, between banks of ticket desks, shops sold everything from pomegranates to pop sox. You could buy what Margaret thought were polystyrene containers of noodles smothered in spicy sauces from an array of fast-food joints. The polystyrene, Michael assured her, was not polystyrene, but compressed straw. Biodegradable. China's contribution to world ecology.

A broad corridor shimmered off into the multicoloured neon distance, feeding left and right into huge waiting rooms for the various platforms. Giant multiscreen television displays were playing environmental awareness ads in between pop videos. Michael took Margaret's hand and led her quickly through the crowds, past the escalators, turning left towards the entrance to the No. 1 Soft Seat Waiting Room.

At the door, a young girl in green uniform and a peaked cap several sizes too large, checked their passports and tickets before granting them access to the rarefied atmosphere and spacious luxury of the soft sleeper waiting room where only the privileged and wealthy were allowed. Comfortable green leather seats were ranged around coffee tables beneath a copper-coloured mural depicting scenes from Chinese history. Margaret caught a whiff of burning incense as they passed the toilets, before being whisked to the far end of the waiting room. There a ticket attendant clipped the tickets that Michael presented, and they were waved through. They ran along a corridor, past hard-class waiting rooms, before turning left down a steep flight of steps leading to platform six.

'Wait!' Margaret said suddenly. 'Your luggage!'

Michael smiled. 'It's already on board.'

As soon as she reached the platform, Margaret recognised the smell of coal smoke funnelling back from the impatiently chuffing steam engine that stood somewhere up ahead in the blackness. Michael hurried her along the platform to coach number seven where they climbed up into a long, narrow corridor. Patterned nets hung on the windows, and blue floral curtains were draped on either side. A red carpet with a gold patterned border led them up to their compartment. It was a far cry, Margaret thought, from her only other experience of travelling by train in China. Then, she had been in hard class, in cold uncomfortable compartments where people spat on the floor and crowded together on butt-numbing hard seats.

'Here we are,' Michael said, and waved her into their compartment. Here there was more netting and blue curtain, lace covers on the four berths, and antimacassars on the seat backs.

'Oh,' Margaret said, surprised. 'We're sharing.'

Michael shrugged apologetically. 'I'm sorry, the production office wasn't able to get you another compartment at this short notice.'

Margaret laughed. 'I don't mean you and I,' she said. 'I mean with someone else.'

Michael looked at the bunks and smiled. 'Well, actually, no,' he said. 'I've bought all four berths, so we've got it to ourselves.'

It was then that she noticed the ice bucket on the table, the gold-wrapped neck of a champagne bottle jutting from it, and a large wicker hamper on the top berth.

Michael slid the door shut. 'It's a fourteen-hour journey,' he said. 'So I thought a little good food, washed down with some fine champagne, might help pass the time.'

IV

By the time Li returned the Jeep to Section One and cycled home on his uncle's old bike, his depression about Margaret had turned to apprehension about having to face his sister. If the scan had been successful, then she would know the sex of her unborn child and her decision would have been made. If the scan had been ambiguous in any way, then they would have had to draw fluid from her womb, and a decision would be delayed for four weeks. It was not in Li's nature to procrastinate, but right now he was praying to his ancestors that the scan had been inconclusive. Much could change in four weeks.

He parked his bicycle in the compound, beneath a corrugated plastic roof, and wearily climbed the two flights to his apartment. He had seen the lights in the windows from the street below, so he knew that Xiao Ling and Xinxin were home. They had probably been back for hours.

Li thought about the sleepy little five-year-old who had kissed him before he left that morning, cuddly, affectionate, pretty – a sweet-tempered little girl, bright and full of life. How could his sister even contemplate having her adopted? She had tried, desperately, to justify it to him. There were thousands of childless Western couples, she said, who were just desperate to adopt little Chinese girls. Xinxin would have a much better life than Xiao Ling could ever give her. Li had shaken his head in despair. He could only assume that Xiao Ling had succumbed to some kind of hormonal insanity that was robbing her of her senses.

He could hear Xinxin crying even before he unlocked the door to the apartment. In the hall, he called out to Xiao Ling, 'Is everything all right?' But she did not reply, and Xinxin's wailing became, if anything, more plaintive. The living room was empty. He hurried down the hall to his uncle's old bedroom and found Xinxin sitting on the bed alone, breaking her heart. Her eyes were swollen and red, and her voice hoarse. The little bib front of her dress was wet from her tears. In consternation, Li called back down the hall, 'Xiao Ling?' But there was no reply. He crouched beside Xinxin and pulled her to him. Her little arms went around his neck and clung on tightly. 'Where's your mummy?' he asked. But the sobs that tugged at her chest made it impossible for her to speak.

Then he saw the envelope on the bedside table, his name written on it in his sister's hand. He freed an arm from Xinxin's grasp and tore it open with trembling fingers. 'Li Yan,' it said. 'Please forgive me. I know you will do what is best for Xinxin. I have gone to the home of a friend in Annhui Province to have my baby boy. No one knows me there, so there will be no trouble. All my love, Xiao Ling.'

CHAPTER FIVE

I

An occasional cluster of distant lights broke the endless stream of darkness outside the window as their train ploughed slowly but surely south towards the heartland of the Middle Kingdom, and its ancient capital of Xi'an. The empty champagne bottle floated on melted ice, its neck gently clunking on the rim of the bucket. A bottle of Bordeaux, a St Emilion, stood breathing on the table beside two crystal goblets. The debris of their starter, small nuggets of foie gras with salad and toast, on china plates, had been cleared away back into the hamper where a selection of exotic cheeses awaited. Michael had disappeared off to the dining car to organise their main course.

Margaret leaned against the window, the glass cool against the champagne-induced flush of her face. Already it seemed like a lifetime since the train had left Beijing. Flashing glimpses of the floodlit station had illuminated the sky between towering new buildings as they rattled west and south through the city across a great confluence of railroad tracks. She knew she was being romanced and was enjoying every minute of it. It was flattering and exciting, and a little frightening. And it was doing her self-esteem a power of good. She had very deliberately pushed all thoughts of Li off to some distant place where he could not haunt or hurt her. She did not deserve to have to feel guilty. She had to get on with her life. And this seemed as good a starting point as any.

The door slid open and Michael came in smiling. 'Success,' he said, and slipped into his seat opposite Margaret. Behind him, a pretty girl in blue uniform with a short-sleeved white blouse and black bow tie carried in a tray with two whole fish on oval plates. The smell of soy, and ginger and onion filled the compartment, rising with the steam from the fish. The girl placed the tray on the table and smiled at Michael. The girls all smiled at Michael, Margaret had noticed. Even the surly attendants who had come to check their tickets and passports. While they had glared at Margaret, their faces had lit up with wide smiles and sparkling eyes when they saw Michael. He had an easy way with women, full of charm and humour. He always made them laugh. When he spoke Chinese to them Margaret had no idea what he said, but they would invariably giggle coyly, responding to the pleasure he so clearly got from flirting with them. She knew that she should feel good about being with someone that other women found so attractive. And she did. But she also knew that it could very quickly become tiresome, breeding insecurity and jealousy.

Michael slipped the girl a few yuan and said something that elicited a giggle before she drifted out into the corridor and slid the door shut behind her. He lifted fish forks and knives out of the hamper and passed a set to Margaret before filling her glass with the pale red St Emilion. 'I guess the purists would say we should be drinking white with fish,' he said. 'But when it comes to Chinese flavours like these, I figure you need something a little more robust to hold its own.' He raised his glass. 'To a successful trip.'

Margaret touched her glass to his. 'You wouldn't be trying to get me drunk, would you?'

He grinned. 'If I had to do that,' he said, 'it would take the fun out of the chase. Try your fish. It's usually excellent.'

She took a forkful of soft white flesh and crispy skin, dipping it in the juices before taking her first, tentative taste. The flavours filled her mouth, rich and spicy and sweet. 'It's wonderful,' she said, and washed it over with a sip of wine. 'So . . . you do this often, do you?'

'I've made the trip a few times,' he said. He paused before adding, 'But this is the first time I've had company.'

'So what's it like?' Margaret asked. 'Xi'an.'

'Ah,' said Michael, his eyes widening. 'Don't get me started on my favourite subject or we'll be here all night.'

'We're here all night anyway,' Margaret said. And, then, with a twinkle, 'Unless you had something else in mind.'

He met her eye very directly, and held her gaze for what seemed like a very long time. The butterflies that had earlier fluttered in her breast were now swarming in her stomach, and she felt the first faint stirrings of desire. 'Xi'an,' he said suddenly. 'Capital of Shaanxi Province. The beginning, and the end, of the Silk Road. Founded before the birth of Christ, and the capital of China for more than eleven hundred years. Once known as Chang'an – the city of everlasting peace – it became the city of western peace, Xi'an, more than six hundred years ago.' And his eyes shone. 'All my life, Margaret, I have wanted to reach out and touch the past, to feel history and run it through my fingers. Like desert sand. In Xi'an I can do all that at a single point in space and time.'

Margaret said, 'Yes, but do they have a McDonald's?' And for a moment she wondered if she had misjudged his sense of humour. Then he burst out laughing.

'You know, for everything I know about Xi'an, that's one thing that's escaped me. They do have a Kentucky Fried Chicken, though, I can tell you that. The Colonel and I go back a long way.'

'I'm glad to hear it.' She stuffed some more fish in her mouth. 'The fish is fantastic, by the way. Don't think I don't appreciate this.' She took another sip of wine. 'What's the Silk Road?'

'It was a trade route,' he said, 'covering thousands of miles across some of the most barren and inhospitable terrain in the world.' He refilled their glasses. 'The peoples of the Middle East and Central Asia sent great caravans of traders to bring back the mysterious silk from China. Only the Chinese knew how to make it. The route was flourishing at a time when the Chinese and Roman empires were in full bloom, each with only the vaguest notion of the other's existence. Before the Silk Road ultimately led to Rome, the Romans thought the

Chinese grew silk on trees. Their name for it was serica, and they called the people who made it the Seres, or Chinese. The silk people.' By now he'd forgotten about his fish. 'The thing about the Silk Road is that it brought all manner of culture and literature and religion to China. Chinese Buddhism took root in Xi'an, carried from India on ancient scriptures. At one time the old city had a population of more than two million, including foreigners from Arabia, Mongolia, India, Malaya. You will see the influence of their facial features tomorrow in the faces of the Terracotta Warriors.'

'Your fish is getting cold,' Margaret said, nodding towards his plate.

'Oh. Yes.' He awoke almost is if from some distant dream, and began attacking his fish again.

'I guess that must be why you're not married,' she said, and he looked at her, frowning his consternation. 'You reserve all your passion for your history and archaeology.'

'Not all of it,' he said, and took another mouthful of fish. 'Anyway, what makes you think I'm not married?'

Her fork paused midway to her mouth, and the piece of fish on it fell back to the plate. She blushed, caught completely unawares. He leaned forward and gently wiped her blouse with his napkin where soy had splashed from her plate. 'That'll stain,' he said.

But Margaret was oblivious. 'You're married?'

'No.' He shook his head. 'Who told you that?'

'You bastard!' She grinned and blushed again, only this time with embarrassment. 'Never?'

'Never. I did live with someone for nearly ten years. She was an actress.'

'Anyone I'd know?'

'I doubt it. She had bit parts in movies and TV shows, but mostly she worked in theatre. She did well for a few years. We hardly saw one another. It was only when she started getting unemployed and we got to spend more time in each other's company that the relationship started falling apart. Turns out we never really knew one another at all. The relationship had been . . . how can I describe it? . . . convenient. But there comes a time when you look for more than that.'

'And are you anywhere near finding it?'

He shrugged. 'Who knows? I'm still looking.'

Their eyes held again for a few moments before hers flickered back down to her plate and she picked the final pieces of fish from the bone.

He said, 'What about you? I see you're wearing a ring.'

Her right hand went instinctively to the band of gold on her wedding finger. She wasn't sure why she still wore it. For protection, perhaps. Men were more guarded in their approach to a woman wearing a wedding ring. 'I was married for seven years,' she said. 'His name was Michael, too.'

'Oh,' he said. And she saw the colour rising on *his* cheeks this time. 'I'm not sure how I'm supposed to feel about that.'

'You're not supposed to feel anything. You're nothing like him.'

'Divorced?'

'Separated,' she said. And then, after a long moment, 'By death.'

He was clearly shocked. 'Oh. I'm so sorry, Margaret. I had no idea.'

'Don't be. I'm not. It's history. And I don't really want to talk about it.'

They concluded their meal in silence then. Somehow a spell had been broken. Margaret declined the cheese, saying she was too full. But they finished the wine, sitting staring out into the darkness, trying to focus beyond their reflections in the glass. Margaret was angry at allowing herself to be ambushed again by the man who had already brought so much pain and misery to her life. She wondered if she would ever be able to excise him finally from her mind, to prevent him from creeping up on her when she least expected it and dumping all his misery on her once more.

The champagne and the wine was having its effect. She felt sleepy and sad, and when Michael slipped across the compartment to sit beside her, she allowed him to pull her gently into his shoulder and close his hand around hers. It was comforting and warm, and she smelled his patchouli, and something in its musky sweetness was distantly arousing. She felt his breath on her forehead and she inclined her head to find his face very close to hers. His eyes, earnest and deep, seemed somehow filled with genuine concern, and she felt safe in his arms, and contented in a way she had not known for a long time. He lowered his head and kissed her. Not a kiss full of passion, but a long, lingering soft kiss full of care and tenderness. She responded, savouring the taste and the smell of him. She ran a hand through his fine, shiny brown hair, and was alarmed suddenly by a sexual awakening that came from somewhere deep inside her. And she remembered Li's firm, hard body pressed into hers in that distant railway carriage.

She pulled away, flushed and a little breathless. 'I'm sorry, Michael. I don't think I'm ready for this.'

He looked at her for a long moment, then smiled and brushed her hair out of her face. 'It's OK, Margaret,' he said. 'If there's one thing you learn as an archaeologist, it's patience. It can be a lifetime, or a millennium, before you finally get what you're looking for.' He paused. 'You tired?' She nodded.

He stood up and arranged her pillows at the window end of her berth, and gently swung her legs up so that she reclined along its length. She felt him removing her shoes, slowly, carefully, his fingers brushing the unstockinged skin of her ankles, the arch of her foot. And she felt a rush of desire. But it was too late now. The moment had passed, and she felt incredibly sleepy and warm as he drew the quilt over her, tucking it in around her neck. Then his lips brushing gently over hers.

She drifted for a time, somewhere between sleep and wakefulness, aware of him clearing away the debris of their dinner before undressing, and then climbing into his berth and turning off the light.

A final thought, as she drifted into darkness, was a tiny stabbing moment of fear that she might start snoring.

*

Sunlight slanted over the peaks of mountains to the east, falling in long yellow slabs through the window of their carriage as Margaret opened sleepy eyes and found Michael sitting opposite, watching her.

'Good morning,' he said. 'We'll be there in under an hour.'

'Oh, my God,' she sat up suddenly, remembering her final thought before drifting off to sleep the night before. 'I wasn't snoring, was I?'

He shook his head and smiled. 'Not too loudly.'

'I wasn't!' she said.

His smile widened. 'That's for me to know. But don't worry. Your secret's safe with me. You know I never betray a girl's confidence. Would you like coffee?'

'Talk about changing the subject!' She grinned sheepishly. 'I thought the Chinese only drank tea.'

'They do. But I always travel equipped for any eventuality.' He took a glass jug and a filter funnel and paper filter from the hamper and set it up on the table. He opened an airtight tin and Margaret immediately smelled fresh ground coffee – an olfactory experience that seemed as far away and long ago as the United States itself. He spooned a generous quantity of it into the filter and reached under the table for a large silver flask. He opened the top and steam exploded out of it. 'It's not exactly boiling,' he said. 'But it'll make a passable cup or two.'

She took her toilet bag and went to the washroom to wash the sleep from her eyes, and to brush her teeth and apply a touch of colour to her lips. She examined her face in the mirror. It was still a little puffy from sleep, and the skin was pale, so that her freckles seemed more prominent than usual. Somewhere behind her eyes were the vague traces of a hangover. She remembered the taste and the touch of Michael from the night before, and a small shiver ran through her. She was embarrassed by her reticence, but grateful that he had not pushed her. And she had a sense now, that this day that lay ahead of her could be a defining one in her life.

When she returned, the smell of fresh coffee filled the compartment. 'That smells wonderful,' she said. And the taste of it and the caffeine hit kick-started her day.

Outside, fields of cropped corn stretched away into the distance, while on the slopes of the hills that rose around them, every contour of the land had been terraced and cultivated, every feature of it man-made, carved from nature by the blood, sweat and tears of men. A blue wisp of smoke rose into the morning sky from a bonfire of dried corn stalks, an ox led by a bare-chested peasant pulled a plough through stony ground. Occasionally they passed clusters of large standing hoops of what looked like pink and white paper flowers. 'What are these?' Margaret asked. 'They look like giant wreaths.'

'That's just what they are,' Michael told her. 'Wreaths on fresh graves, or to mark the anniversary of a death.'

'I thought everyone in China was supposed to be cremated,' Margaret said.

'They're supposed to be. The Chinese government believes burying the dead wastes fertile ground. And they are probably right. But old habits die hard.'

He turned suddenly to business and told her that she

was not to worry about her luggage when they got to Xi'an. His production company had employed a runner to pick up their bags and the hamper, and they would be met outside the station by a car and driver. They would go first to their hotel to check in, and then drive out to the museum of the Terracotta Warriors just beyond the town of Lintong, about an hour from the city. He would have to leave her with the warriors for a time while he went to conclude his business with the director of the museum, but he would see that she was in good hands.

Gradually the fields and the rolling hills gave way to the industrial outskirts of the sprawling conurbation that was Xi'an, and within fifteen minutes their train had pulled into the station.

Jostled and pushed by crowds anxious to be on their way, frowned at by railway staff inspecting their tickets, pursued by touts selling maps and tourist guides, they made their way across a chaotic concourse and out into the brilliant sunshine of the Xi'an morning, where a frenzied throng of passengers and bicycles and vehicles was fighting its way towards the exit. The runner who had retrieved their luggage materialised from nowhere with a trolley. She looked about sixteen, and barely big enough to lift their bags. But she had managed without help.

'Car by gate,' she said. 'You follow me.' And they passed through narrow gates, out into a square filled with buses and flanked on one side by high-rise blocks, and on the other by the ancient crenellated city wall that rose twelve metres into the sky and ran twelve kilometres around the old city centre. A large black limousine stood purring outside the gate.

'Welcome to Xi'an,' Michael said, and Margaret felt a tiny thrill of expectation run through her.

II

Li watched thoughtfully as Xinxin wolfed down the lotus seed buns that he had steamed for her breakfast. She had already, it seemed, developed a taste for tea, and she washed down the sticky sweet buns with large gulps of steaming green tea from a dragon mug. It was a treat, and for the moment she had forgotten that her mother had gone, leaving her in a strange house with this stranger who was her uncle.

Eventually, the night before, after he had calmed her down, she had slept. Xiao Ling had not even made up a story for Xinxin to explain her absence. She had simply told the child to wait in her room for her uncle. He would not be long. Xinxin had been on her own for nearly three hours before Li turned up.

For the second night in succession Li had barely slept, and this morning had had to concoct a story about how Xiao Ling was not well, how she had had to go unexpectedly to a special hospital somewhere far away. And that Xinxin was to stay with her uncle until she returned. This had elicited a fresh burst of tears, and Xinxin had simply wailed that she wanted to go home. And home, Li had decided, was where she had to go. This was a problem for her father, not for him. He would write to him, explaining the circumstances, and tell him to come and fetch his daughter at once. But this would take time. A week, or more. And he was at a loss as to what to do with the child in the meantime. The only solution he had arrived at during long, sleepless hours, was to seek the advice of Mei Yuan. And the only problem with that was that he would have to take Xinxin with him.

But another, greater, problem awaited.

As Li cycled north, Xinxin sat side-saddle on the bag carrier over the rear wheel of his bicycle, gaping in wonder at the people and traffic in this huge and seemingly never-ending city. She watched the children on their way to school with a wide-eyed fascination, the boys who toiled up the *hutongs* with their three-wheeled coal carriers, the unbelievable numbers of people on foot and on bikes and clambering off and on buses. Li felt the unaccustomed burden of responsibility for the child on his bike, and now, as he pulled in beside the *jian bing* stall at the Dongzhimennei corner, his heart sank as the woman at the hotplate turned to greet him, and it was the face of a stranger.

'Where is Mei Yuan?' he asked, perplexed.

The woman said, 'She had to go to the public security bureau to renew her licence. So she asked me to make her *jian bings* this morning.'

'When will she be back?'

'I don't know. In a few hours, perhaps.' The woman paused. 'Who are you?'

'Li Yan,' he said, and her face opened up in a smile.

'Ah, Li Yan. She has told me all about you. I am Jiang Shimei, her cousin.' She held out her hand to shake his. 'You looked after Mei Yuan when she was not well.' She looked at Xinxin. 'Is this your daughter?'

'No.' Li was embarrassed. 'She is my niece.'

'She is very beautiful.' Jiang Shimei stooped to run fingers lightly down Xinxin's cheek. 'What is your name, little one?'

'Xinxin.'

'Xinxin? What a lovely name.'

'Can you put my hair in bunches?' Xinxin asked suddenly, and she dug into the pockets of her little green pinafore to produce two pink elasticated bands with plastic cartoon fox heads. 'My Uncle Yan is hopeless. He says he doesn't know how.'

'Of course,' Jiang Shimei said, and Li shuffled awkwardly while she quickly arranged makeshift bunches high on either side of Xinxin's head. 'There,' she said. 'Just perfect.' And Xinxin's little round face beamed with pleasure. And she did look perfect, Li thought, with the red piping on her white blouse matching the red tights she wore beneath her green pinafore, her red satchel slung over her shoulder, tiny feet secured in open white sandals.

'Tell Mei Yuan,' Li said, 'that I need her advice. I will come back later.' He lifted Xinxin on to the bike behind him.

'Do you not want a *jian bing*?'

'I have no time today.' And he pushed off across the road, weaving through the stream of traffic, whose horns blared angrily. He cycled up the slope, past fruit and vegetable stalls on his left, a barber's shop open for business already, the smell of wet cut hair and scented oil drifting out of the open door. He parked under the trees next to the front entrance of Section One and took Xinxin by the hand, leading her with great apprehension to the side door, and up three flights to the top floor. The pair drew curious glances from secretarial staff and detectives. Apart from nodded acknowledgements, no one made any comment. Li hesitated briefly outside the door to the detectives' room, then summoned all his courage and walked in, little Xinxin trotting wide-eyed at his side, as if it were the most natural thing in the world.

Zhao was just putting down the telephone. He turned and caught sight of Li. 'Boss, I've got a car waiting downstairs to take us to the Middle School . . .' His voice trailed off as he saw Xinxin. Other heads turned. The hubbub of voices died down.

Wu pushed his sunglasses back on his head. 'Um . . . is there something you haven't been telling us, boss?'

Li decided to brazen it out. 'Guys, this is my niece, Xinxin. Her mom's not very well right now, so I told Xinxin that you would keep her amused this morning while I conduct those interviews.'

There was a moment's stunned silence before Qian, whose own little girl was nearly ten, took the initiative. 'Hello, Xinxin,' he said, rounding the desk. 'Those are beautiful bunches you've got. Did your Uncle Yan do them for you?'

Xinxin tutted and raised her eyes to the ceiling as if he was mad. 'Of course not,' she said. 'Uncle Yan's useless.' Which elicited much laughter from around the room. She went on, warming to her reception, 'It was a lady in the street that did it.'

'Yeah,' Wu said, 'we all think Uncle Yan's pretty useless, too, don't we, guys?' There was a general chorus of consent as Li drew Wu a look.

Qian lifted her up to sit on the edge of the desk and looked in her satchel. 'What have you got here?' And he pulled out the books that Mei Yuan had left two nights previously, and a jigsaw puzzle in a cardboard box.

'It's dead easy,' Xinxin said. 'Do you want me to show you how to do it?'

'Sure,' Qian said. The other detectives started gathering around, indulging the age-old adoration that the Chinese have for their children. 'Has Uncle Yan tried it yet?'

Xinxin laughed so infectiously it got all the detectives laughing with her. '*Silly!*' she said. 'How could someone who doesn't know how to do bunches do a jigsaw?' More laughter at Li's expense.

'Li!' The voice was sharp and imperative, and brought the room to silence. Li turned to see Section Chief Chen Anming standing in the doorway. Chen flicked his head towards Li's office. 'A word.' And he went through. Li pulled a face at the other detectives and then followed Chen through.

Chen turned. 'Shut the door,' he said. 'What the hell's going on, Li?'

Li shrugged. 'I've got a problem, Chief.' And he explained how his sister had abandoned Xinxin, literally on his doorstep. It would take a week or more, he explained, to write to her father so that he could come and get her. Meantime he didn't know what else to do.

'Well, you can't turn the detectives' office into a crèche,' Chen said. 'In the name of the sky, Li, we've got a serial killer on the loose!'

Li was at a loss. 'I know,' he said lamely.

Chen glared at him for a moment, then shook his head, giving way at least a little to the sympathy he felt for Li's predicament. 'Where does her father live?'

'Near Zigong, in Sichuan Province.'

'I'll call the police chief there and have him get in touch with your brother-in-law. He could be on a train to Beijing by tonight.'

Li nodded, abashed. 'Thanks, Chief.'

There was a burst of laughter from the office outside, and Li grinned, embarrassed. 'She seems to be a big hit with the guys.' He paused. 'You've got a couple of kids, haven't you, Chief?'

Chen grunted. 'A long time since they were that age. My daughter's in publishing, and my son teaches quantum physics.'

The door to Li's office swung open and Xinxin strutted in holding out one of Mei Yuan's books. 'Will you read this to me, Uncle Yan?'

Li glanced beyond her to the expectant faces of the detectives outside and knew that she'd been put up to it. 'I can't, honey,' he said. 'I have to go and interview some men. I'm late already.'

Xinxin turned to Chen. 'Will you read it to me, Uncle Anming?'

Chen flushed, and narrowed his eyes at the detectives in the next room, realising that he, too, had been set up. He flicked a look at Li who was somehow managing to keep his face straight. 'I'm very busy, little one,' he said.

Xinxin frowned. 'What's that yellow mark on your head?' she asked, gazing up at him, and the sound of stifled laughter drifted through from the next office.

Chen flushed. 'That's from smoking too much,' he said.

'Oh.' Xinxin's face fell and she said, very seriously, 'Smoking's ve-ery bad for you.'

'Yes, I know,' Chen said.

Xinxin giggled. 'Good. So now you stop smoking and read to me, OK?'

She took his hand, quite unselfconsciously, and he blushed to the roots of his hair.

Li said quickly, 'Now you take good care of Uncle Anming while I'm away, Xinxin.' He glanced quickly at Chen, hardly daring to meet his eye. 'Sorry, Chief. Got to dash. Late already.' And he turned and hurried out, before Chen had time to object. Li collected Zhao as he went, grabbing him by the arm and whisking him through the door.

The two of them stifled their laughter all the way down the corridor, before it finally burst forth in the stairwell and resounded around the building.

'Oh, shit, Zhao,' Li said, wiping the tears from the corners of his eyes. 'I'm going to be in big trouble when we get back.'

*

No. 29 Middle School was hidden away behind a plain white-tile entrance at the far corner of a bus park just off Qian Men Xi Da Jie, a spit away from the south-west corner of Tiananmen Square. Above the heavy green metal gates, a photograph mounted on a long board showed the school's original elaborate stone entrance. Zhao parked the Jeep outside, and a janitor hurried out from a brick gatehouse to let them in. As the metal gates swung closed behind them, they entered a strange oasis of calm in the centre of the city. Two-storey, brick-built classroom blocks stretched off to left and right, shaded by neatly cropped trees. Through a tunnel lined with school noticeboards and potted plants with luxuriant leafy fronds, the sun shone directly on to a tree-lined quadrangle with basketball and badminton courts. Classrooms overlooked it from all sides. The sounds of traffic in the street had become a distant rumble.

Li looked around in amazement. 'I had no idea this place was here,' he said.

'It used to be a university,' the janitor said.

Zhao frowned. 'What do you mean?'

'University of China.' The janitor grinned and nodded. Li thought, perhaps he was a little simple. 'Sun Yat-Sen founded the university in 1912. We have an exhibition. Come and see.'

And he ushered them into a classroom that had been converted into an exhibition room. Blue panels mounted all around the walls exhibited photographs of the school's founders and teachers, and other historic memorabilia. The janitor was not simple. It had been founded by the President of the first Chinese Republic, Sun Yat-Sen, and it had indeed been the University of China. Faces from history stared down at them from the walls: the balding Sun Yat-Sen with his neatly clipped silver moustache; the crop-haired Li Da Zhao with his Stalinesque whiskers, a professor of economics there in the twenties who had translated the works of Marx into Chinese for the first time, before being hanged by Chiang Kai-Shek in 1928; the honorary headmaster, General Zhang Xüe Liang, who betrayed Chiang Kai-Shek to the communists in the infamous Xi'an incident of 1936. In a glass case stood the bell that had called the first students to class at the start of the previous century. And it had hung from a tree that today still stood sentinel over the quadrangle outside.

The story of the school's history written on the walls revealed that when the communists came to power in 1949, the University of China had become 'The New Beginning Middle School', then three years later, more prosaically, the No. 29 Middle School.

A young man wearing jeans and a dark zip-neck sweatshirt over a grey tee shirt, hurried into the room, a little short of breath. 'How do you do?' he said, shaking their hands. 'The headmaster asked me to take care of you this morning. I have no classes till the afternoon.'

'You are a teacher?' Li asked, surprised. Teachers had not dressed like that in his day.

'Sure,' said the teacher. 'I am Teacher Huang.'

'There's quite a history to this place,' said Li.

'Sure. We are very proud of our history,' Teacher Huang

said. 'But now we are just a Middle School. We have six hundred students and one hundred and fifty teachers. Follow me. You can have my classroom for the interviews.'

Teacher Huang's classroom had four rows of six desks, with a long blackboard at either end. Tall windows opened out on each side of the room. Li lifted a chair down from a desktop. 'Are there no classes this morning?'

'Sure,' said Teacher Huang. 'There are plenty of classes. You will know when they have a break, because the students will make plenty of noise.' He grinned. Then, 'An old teacher from here, Lao Sun Lian, and some former pupils are waiting in another room. When you want to speak to them let me know.'

'Send in Teacher Sun,' Li said. And then as Teacher Huang went to the door, asked, 'By the way, what happened to the original school gate?'

'It was destroyed by Red Guards during the Cultural Revolution,' Teacher Huang said.

'The same ones who destroyed the school records?'

Teacher Huang shrugged. 'I don't know. Possibly. But I am only twenty-eight. I don't remember.' And he went out.

Li and Zhao arranged three desks with two chairs for themselves on one side, and a single chair on the other. The smell of the classroom, of stale food and chalk dust, reminded Li of his own schooldays. It had the same pale green and cream walls, the same sense of something institutionalised, uniform and dull. Nothing, it seemed, had changed much over the years.

It was hot in here. Li wandered to the nearest window and opened it as wide as it would go. He looked out on the

THE FOURTH SACRIFICE | 218

quadrangle. They had all played here, all four victims. They had shared the same experiences, suffered the same doubts and ignominies, the same hopes and aspirations. Something in this place, in its classrooms, or its quadrangle, something that had happened here more than thirty years before, had sown the seeds of destruction that someone with a bronze sword had harvested all these years later. Somewhere, here, in this cradle of modern Chinese academic history, lay a motive for murder. Li was sure of it.

Teacher Sun was seventy-nine years old, with thin, iron-grey hair scraped back across a scalp spattered brown with age spots. He wore an old blue cotton Mao suit. Not because it signified anything political, he told them, but because he had got used to wearing them, and they were cool and comfortable. It did not look as if there was much flesh on the bones beneath the baggy blue cotton. He walked with a stick and was dragging on the stump of a hand-rolled cigarette. He sat down on the other side of the desks and looked at them reflectively, a light shining still in his dark old eyes.

'This makes me think,' he said, 'of the bad old days.' And he stamped his cigarette end on the floor.

'What days were those?' Li asked.

'When they brought me into classrooms like this and sat me down and talked rubbish at me for hours. And then wanted me to talk rubbish back.'

'During the Cultural Revolution?' Li said. The old man nodded. 'You had a bad time?'

He nodded again. 'Not as bad as some. But bad enough.

Struggle Sessions, they called them.' He chuckled. 'They would struggle to make me confess and I would struggle not to.'

'What did you have to confess to?' asked Zhao.

'Whatever it was they decided to accuse me of. If I didn't confess I was accused of being arrogant and an active counter-revolutionary. If I did confess I was pilloried and abused. It was like those women accused of being witches in medieval Europe. They threw them into the river, if they survived they were witches, if they drowned they were innocent. There was no way you could win.'

'But why would they want to accuse their teachers?' Zhao was curious. Li glanced at him, surprised, then realised that the Cultural Revolution would have been over by the time Zhao started school, and it had been a long time after that before people spoke about what had happened. And now there was a whole generation profoundly ignorant about the events of those twelve tragic years.

But the old man just smiled sadly at Zhao's ignorance. 'Had you been here, you could have read why,' he said. 'The Red Guards came and pasted *da-zi-bao* posters all over the walls out there in the square, great handwritten propaganda posters denouncing us all as revisionists.' He chuckled and shook his head. 'Of course, usually it was the stupid ones who led all the attacks, and they just copied their slogans from the newspapers. Apparently, although we did not hold bombs or knives, we teachers were still dangerous enemies. We filled our students with revisionist ideas. We taught them that scholars were superior to workers, and promoted personal ambition by encouraging competition for the highest grades. It seems the authorities believed that in trying to raise the standards and expectations of our students we were changing good young socialists into corrupt revisionists. In truth, it was simply that an ignorant peasant was less of a threat than an intelligent thinker. So the leaders believed that the invisible knives wielded by the teachers were much more dangerous than any real knives or guns.'

Li sat back and lit a cigarette. He said, 'You know why we are here, Teacher Sun?'

Teacher Sun shrugged. 'I hear rumours.'

'Four of your former pupils,' Li said, 'have been murdered.' Teacher Sun nodded. 'I want to know if you remember them.' And Li rattled off their names.

As he did so, the old man raised an eyebrow, then shook his head. 'Very sad,' he said. 'I remember Yuan Tao well. He was a brilliant student. By far and away the best in his year. A likeable boy, shy and unassuming.' His eyes flickered and focused somewhere in the middle distance as he remembered Yuan with clear affection. And then a cloud descended on him, and all the light went out of his black eyes. 'The others . . .' he said, 'I only remember for one reason. Dull students, except for Yue Shi. He went on to become a professor of archaeology, I believe. Brighter than the others, but an unpleasant boy, easily led.' He shuddered at some disagreeable memory. Then he looked very directly at Li. 'They were all members of a group of Red Guards who called themselves the Revolt-to-the-End Brigade. Part of the

Red-Red-Red Faction. Stupid, brutish boys, manipulated by much cleverer people much higher up.'

Li felt his pulse quicken. It was the connection they had been looking for. Red Guards! They had all been Red Guards! He leaned forward. 'Were they the ones who smashed down the school gate and destroyed the school records?'

Teacher Sun nodded. 'They had already left the school. Most of them were unemployed and simply used the Cultural Revolution as an excuse not to work. They came back to take revenge on their teachers. They went through the school records, destroying any evidence of their poor exam results. And school reports we had written criticising lack of effort, or lack of discipline, were then used against us. In their eyes we were responsible for all their failures, not them. If they were lazy, or stupid, or incompetent, or badly behaved, it couldn't be blamed on them. It was our fault.

'They made us wear dunce hats and parade around in the square out there with signs around our necks. *Reactionary Monster Sun Lian*, they scrawled on mine. They made us beat gongs and shout, "I am a reactionary teacher. I am a reactionary monster." And they would kick us and whip us with their belts. They tore my classroom to pieces looking for black material.'

'Black material?' Zhao asked, puzzled. 'What's that?' Li glanced at him and saw that he had gone very pale, shocked by what he was hearing.

Teacher Sun said, 'The Communist Party was symbolised by the colour red. Black, being the opposite of red, was used to represent anything or anyone opposed to it. Chairman Mao declared that the Five Black Categories were the worst enemies of the people – landlords, rich peasants, counter-revolutionaries, criminals and rightists.

'Anything foreign was black. I was a teacher of history, and so of course I had many foreign books and magazines, and many more books on world history. The Revolt-to-the-End Brigade declared all that material *black*, and I was made to drag it out into the square, all my books and papers, and make a big bonfire of them all.'

Li glanced out of the window and saw that a couple of students were playing badminton. He tried to picture what it must have been like out there. Red-faced adolescents screaming at their teachers, abusing and beating them; teachers with tall, pointed dunce hats banging gongs and denouncing themselves; the smoke from burning books drifting across the court where two students now whipped a shuttlecock back and forth. And he remembered how his own primary school teacher had been beaten to death in the lunch hall. To his surprise he realised that Teacher Sun was chuckling now.

'It started to rain,' he said. 'Quite heavily. And it was putting out the bonfire of my books. The Revolt-to-the-End Brigade were getting agitated, and one of them told another to go and get my umbrella from the classroom. *Yang-san* he called it. And one of the others accused him of spreading the *four olds*. The boy didn't understand why. And the other, I think he was their leader – a big, coarse boy that they all called Birdie – he said that *yang* meant foreign, and so *yang-san* meant foreign umbrella. He claimed they were called that because before the Liberation umbrellas were imported from abroad. He said that now they were made in China they should no longer be called *yang-san* and anyone who did was a xenophile.' The old man shook his head. 'No doubt he learned the word from the newspapers. Anyway, I burst out laughing and told him he was just an ignorant boy who had not worked hard enough at school. His face went purple with anger and embarrassment. In the first place, I told him, *yang* meant sun, not foreign. A *yang-san* was a sun umbrella, or parasol.'

The smile faded from Teacher Sun's face. 'The rest of them went very quiet, everyone wondering what he would do. For a moment, I don't think he knew himself, then suddenly he flew into a terrible rage and grabbed me by the neck and dragged me back into my classroom. The others followed, and he ordered them to smash all the windows in, and then spread the broken glass across the floor. I was the xenophile, he screamed, and I had to be taught a lesson. And he pushed me down to my knees and forced me to cross the classroom on them, from one side to the other. The broken glass splintered beneath the weight of me, cutting through my trousers and into my flesh.' He leaned over and pulled up his right trouser leg above the knee, and Li and Zhao saw the intricate lace-pattern of tiny scars where the glass had cut into him all those years ago. 'There are still some splinters of the stuff in there yet,' he said. 'Sometimes they work their way out and I start bleeding again.'

He rolled down his trouser leg and looked at the two

detectives. 'So, yes,' he said, 'I remember these boys. I am not likely to forget.'

'They were all in this Revolt-to-the-End Brigade?' Li asked. And he went through the names again – Tian Jingfu, Bai Qiyu, Yue Shi, Yuan Tao.

Teacher Sun nodded. 'All except for Yuan Tao, of course. I heard that he got out and went to some university in America just before the Cultural Revolution began. He was one of the lucky ones. One of the very few, very lucky ones.'

III

The air was thick with huge pennants fluttering in the smoke of battle as armoured soldiers rushed forward, swords raised, the thunder of horses hoofs filling the air behind them. Margaret flinched involuntarily as the soldiers surrounded her, rushing past, the sound of bronze blade on bronze blade ringing out above the bloodcurdling cries of anguish. She felt the warmth of Michael's body pressed against her as she clutched the rail. A soaring orchestral score, like something from a Hollywood musical, reached fever pitch as the battle neared its climax. And then the pennants flew in her face, one by one, as the flags of the conquered states were laid out before the all-powerful first emperor of China, Qin Shi Huang.

'Impressive, isn't it?' Michael whispered.

Margaret nodded. It was the first time she had experienced surround cinema. Screens entirely circled the auditorium, the action moving freely from one to the other and continuing on behind. The sense of being in the middle of it all was extraordinary, standing clasping metal rails and listening to a surround soundtrack that completed the illusion. 'This must have cost a fortune to make,' she said. 'There's an incredible number of extras.'

Michael smiled. 'If there's one thing the Chinese have in plentiful supply, it's people.' Thousands of coolies carrying baskets of earth on bamboo poles, moved all around them. 'That's them starting work on Qin's tomb,' Michael said. 'One hundred and twenty thousand craftsmen, labourers and prisoners. It took them forty years. In those days people believed that when you died your soul lived on underground. That's why Qin built his Terracotta Army and buried them in three different pits, or chambers, around his mausoleum – to guard his underground empire.'

On the screen, semi-naked labourers tramped clay underfoot before pounding it with great clubs and setting it in moulds to make the warriors and horses. The body parts were then assembled, and overlaid with hand-carved armour and delicately shaped faces – each one different, unique. Hair was sculpted in pleats or piled high, fine detail worked even into the treads of their boots. Warriors were divided into generals and officers, foot soldiers and kneeling archers, charioteers, and then fired in huge kilns. All around her Margaret saw Terracotta Warriors standing in rows as artists painted them in vivid primary colours.

'Are these real?' she whispered.

Michael laughed. 'No. They are exact reproductions,

handcrafted from the same clay as the originals, and fired at the same temperature. You can buy them, full-sized, have them shipped to America for a couple of thousand dollars to stand in your garden. Most people wouldn't be able to tell the difference between the reproduction and the real thing. They did paint the originals, though. Just like that,' he said, nodding towards the screen.

Margaret said, 'In all the photographs I've seen, they just look sort of clay-coloured.'

Michael said, 'The warriors were buried for more than two thousand years. The paint simply didn't survive. The clay colour is just a coating of dry, dusty earth. Underneath they are a sort of bluish black, as they were when they came out of the kilns.'

Labourers, their bodies glistening with sweat, dug the pits to house the warriors. Great beams were raised to support the roofs. Then the warriors were put in place, arrayed in battle formation, between high walls of rammed earth. Real weapons were placed in their hands – swords, bows, spears – and then logs laid overhead to form the roof which was covered with straw matting and then buried under tons of earth. The shadowy figures of the warriors were swallowed into blackness.

And then suddenly the screen was afire with battle again. The voice of the commentator relating the story rose above orchestral crescendos.

'What's happening now?' Margaret asked.

'A peasant uprising, a year after Qin died. They sacked his

palace and broke into the three chambers containing the warriors and stole their weapons to use against the real army of Qin's successor.'

The blackness burst violently to life as the peasants smashed their way into the warriors' chambers, carrying flaming torches that cast long shadows among their terracotta counterparts. As they took the swords and spears from an opposing army fired in clay, they began smashing the serried rows of warriors. The distinctive sound of breaking pottery was sickening. All that work and artistry. All the years it had taken to achieve. Smashed in a few moments of mindless vandalism. Margaret watched, wide-eyed, as the peasants set fire to the pits, roof timbers blazing and then caving in on the army below.

From its pitch of excitement, the orchestra swooped to a meandering, tranquil melody of violins to match the sudden pictures of peaceful, open countryside that now surrounded them in the shadow of a hill that rose to a central peak.

'That's the tumulus of Qin's mausoleum,' Michael said. 'The one they are afraid to open because of the rivers of mercury. The year is 1974. China is still in the throes of the Cultural Revolution.' A group of peasants in Mao suits was digging in an open field. 'These guys were digging a well, when suddenly they started unearthing terracotta heads and hands. The first fragments of a great army that had remained buried for more than two millennia.'

Margaret said, 'You know, you should think about doing this sort of thing for a living. You might be quite good at it.'

He laughed and took her arm. 'Come on,' he said.

'But it's not finished yet.'

'Doesn't matter. Let's go see the real thing.'

Outside the auditorium, they blinked in the bright sunlight. The huge concourse was crowded with tourists come to see the Eighth Wonder of the World: busloads of Western tour groups, parties of Chinese schoolchildren, families from all over the Middle Kingdom, from every walk of life; all drawn by the extraordinary phenomenon of the Terracotta Warriors, housed in three huge halls constructed over the pits where they had been found.

As they crossed the concourse Michael said, 'What happened after they discovered the warriors was a comedy of errors. The officials and cadres at the local cultural centre didn't seem to think the find was worth telling anyone about. They dragged some bits and pieces off to the centre and started reassembling three of the figures, patching them together and then putting them on display. It was only when a visiting journalist wrote an article about it, months later, that the authorities found out. They immediately put the whole site under state protection, and in 1976 built the first of the exhibition halls over the biggest of the pits – Pit No. 1.' He inclined his head towards the huge domed construction that loomed over them, and took Margaret's arm, led her up steps and through the pillared entrance.

He spoke to an attendant, who hurried off, and they took a seat in the entrance hall, beneath big squares of yellow light that fell through the glass roof and dazzled on the marble floor. 'Someone will come and get you in a minute,' he said. 'Then I'm going to have to go off to my meeting.'

Margaret flipped through the pages of a book she had bought on the way into the auditorium. It was filled with photographs of the three pits, and an account of the excavations by the lead archaeologist, Yuan Zhongyi. She said. 'I thought there were only three chambers.'

'There are,' Michael said.

'That's not what it says in here.' She read from Yuan Zhongyi's account: *'Our drilling also revealed a fourth pit at about 20 metres north of the middle part of Vault 1.'*

'Sure,' Michael said. 'But the pit was empty, filled with sand and silt. They figured that the fourth chamber was never finished because the workers all got sent off to fight against the peasant uprising.'

She read on, *'As no clay figures have been found in this pit, it is not counted in the vaults of the terracotta army. Generally we speak only of the other three.'* She cocked an eyebrow at Michael. 'Bet that pissed them off. All that digging and the damn thing turns out to be empty.'

'That's archaeology,' Michael said. 'You can spend years on something and get nowhere. Then start again a couple of metres to one side or the other and discover a whole civilisation.'

A small man with a shock of spiky black hair laced with streaks of steel-grey, came smiling through the squares of sunlight, his hand outstretched. He shook Michael's hand warmly and they exchanged greetings in Chinese. He was a man perhaps in his middle fifties, with square tortoiseshell glasses on a smooth, unlined face. He wore an open-necked white shirt loose over dark slacks, and blue-cloth rubber-soled shoes.

'Margaret,' Michael said, turning to her, 'this is Mr Lao Chuanfang. He is one of the most experienced archaeologists working on the excavation.'

His handshake was dry and firm, and his eyes sparkled. 'How d'you do, Miss Margaret,' he said, bowing his head slightly.

'It's very good of you to look after me like this,' Margaret said, embarrassed. 'But it's really not necessary. I could just as easily wait here for Michael.'

'No, no,' said Mr Lao. 'It my pleasure. Mr Michael is ve-ery good friend of Chinese people.'

'Well, one or two of them, anyway,' Michael said, grinning. He checked his watch. 'Look, I've got to go, Margaret. I'll come and get you when I've finished my business. Take good care of her, Mr Lao.' He winked at her and hurried off.

Mr Lao led Margaret into the main hall. 'I didn't realise excavations were still going on,' she said. 'I thought it was all finished.'

Mr Lao laughed. 'It ma-any years before we finish, Miss Margaret. There are maybe six thousand warrior and horse in here. We uncover, maybe, one third.' And they stepped out on to a gantry that ran all the way around the pit.

Margaret was not certain what she had been expecting, but it had been nothing on this scale. An intricate network of scaffolding supported a roof that arched over an excavation site that shimmered off into a hazy blue distance. Immediately below them, between high walls of rammed earth that stretched away both left and right, stood the warriors. Some two thousand of them, in battle formation. In gaps between the ranks, horses stood patiently, harnessed to wooden chariots that had long since decayed and disappeared. Sunlight fell in angled slabs through occasional windows in the roof, and lay across the silent soldiers, casting shadows across ancient faces.

The hair rose up on Margaret's neck and arms, and she felt tears prick her eyes. She blinked, surprised at her reaction. She had not anticipated anything like this. But there was something startling in the sight of these life-sized figures, something extraordinary in their silent dignity, in their patient vigil. They stood, still guarding their emperor's tomb, with a mute determination. All around, the voices of chattering tourists filled the hall, and Margaret was consumed by an almost irresistible desire to shout at them. To tell them to shut up. There was something here that deserved the dignity of silence, the awe and respect of all who cast eyes on it. This was a privilege, a rare glimpse of a priceless heritage, an insight into the minds of men, their fears and beliefs, their endless futile attempts to transcend death. And in a way, the men who had created these figures had achieved a kind of immortality. For here their warriors still stood, a testament to their makers' existence, silent witnesses to a dawn that predated Christ.

She turned to find Mr Lao smiling at her. 'You are impressed,' he said.

'I don't know what I am,' Margaret said. 'Speechless, really. They are . . .' she searched for the right word, 'fabulous,' she finished lamely, unable to find an adjective that could adequately describe her feelings.

'You come,' he said. 'I show you more than tourist see.' And she followed him around the gantry, gazing down on the figures below as they went.

There was a sudden clamour of raised voices, and she turned to see a green-uniformed police officer snatching a camera from a struggling Chinese tourist. The man and his wife screamed at the officer, waving their arms belligerently, as he opened up their camera and ripped out the film, exposing its entire length to the light.

'It forbidden to take photograph here,' Mr Lao said. He shrugged philosophically. 'It happen all the time.'

At the far end of the site, raised on an area that had not yet been excavated, Margaret could see now that there were hundreds of pottery figures crowding together, archaeologists moving amongst them, piecing together the broken bits and pieces that would make them whole again. A large motorised conveyer belt was removing great piles of excavated earth out through a large rear hatch. But this was an area not open to the public. And below them now, crouched in the dust, white-shirted archaeologists of all ages worked among dozens more figures, still immersed in earth, and emerging centimetre by centimetre from their ancient graves as brushes and knives scooped and swept away the layers of time that had buried them.

Mr Lao opened a gate and Margaret followed him into an area off limits to tourists, down stippled metal steps to where a small group of archaeologists was at work: two men, and a young woman perhaps a little younger than Margaret. Mr Lao made introductions in Chinese, and they all shook her hand and bowed their heads and smiled. Mr Lao handed her a short, round-bladed knife with a curved handle that fitted the back of the hand behind the thumb and forefinger. 'Now you be archaeologist, too,' he smiled. 'Miss Zhang show you how.'

Miss Zhang smiled and handed her a black-bristled brush and led her among a cluster of pottery bodies emerging at strange angles from the soil. Some of them were cracked and broken at the shoulder. Others had heads lying crookedly to one side or another. Some had no heads at all – a strangely evocative image, bringing back to Margaret a sudden recollection of why she was still here in China.

These were armoured warriors, elaborately carved squares of studded armour draped across their chests, hair piled high in knots on their heads, silk scarves around their necks. Miss Zhang squatted down beside two figures still waist-deep in the earth. One lay at a crazy angle, his head resting on the shoulder of his companion, as if he had wearied of his two-thousand-year existence. Their features were still partially obscured by caked mud.

Miss Zhang worked carefully with her knife to scrape the earth away to reveal the clean line of the jaw, then brushed away the dust with her brush. She indicated, with a smile and a nod, that Margaret should do the same. Margaret crouched beside her and nervously, very tentatively, scraped away the earth gradually to reveal the good strong features of the warrior: fine, full lips, a moustache that curved up to his cheekbones, almond eyes beneath strong brows. She brushed away the debris and looked at him. He was beautiful. She touched his cool, smooth pottery features and felt a sensation like electricity run through her fingertips. She was touching more than two thousand years of history. A man had carved these features at a time when the Romans had ruled Europe, nearly seventeen centuries before her own country had even been discovered. And for the first time she really understood Michael's passion. There was more life in this pottery creation of fired clay than in any of the bodies that had passed through her autopsy room; cold, dead, decaying flesh that would simply have vaporised in the kind of temperatures that had brought these ancient warriors to life and preserved them across the millennia.

There were still occasional traces of the original paintwork, and Margaret saw now that beneath the orange-coloured earth, the figures were a deep blue-black, the dark blue dust shed by their broken bodies gathered around them like the dust of time.

IV

Chang Yichun might have been a child of the Communist Liberation, but he was a highly successful capitalist of the post-Mao era, as he took great delight in telling Li and Zhao. The bell had rung some time ago, and through the open windows came the sounds of children playing out in the quadrangle.

Chang was a short man, but powerfully built, with close-cropped hair and big, callused hands. He considered himself better than all his more academically minded classmates of the sixties. He had done all right here at the No. 29 Middle School, he admitted grudgingly, but what good were qualifications when you just got sent to labour in the countryside? Such had been his fate in the Cultural Revolution.

He drew on an expensive Western cigarette. 'Irony was, it turned out to be the making of me,' he said. 'Learned my trade as a carpenter, and when I came back to the city in '72 I got a job on the maintenance and building team of the Xichang Street Committee.' He scratched his head and then brushed the dandruff off the lapel of his designer suit. 'There were twenty others, unemployed like me, and six women. We mended central heating systems, built chimneys, did odd jobs around all the houses. It was a farce. Totally unprofessional. It was the social monkeys – you know, the ones who hung around the streets all day – that got us the jobs. They fixed the worksheets, took extra wages, and then kept everything that was left after paying the wages. In seven years we ran up debts of nearly ninety thousand yuan.'

He cleared his throat and spat unselfconsciously on the floor of the classroom. 'But I could get us jobs, too,' he said. 'And in '79 they put me in charge. The difference was, I wanted to run it as an enterprise, with control over finance and personnel. Proper contracts, proper structure of management and pay. Made seventy-six thousand yuan in the first year. Within four years we were a properly registered construction company with a workforce of more than two thousand, fixed assets of three million, and liquid assets of more than seven.' He sat back grinning, pleased with his own success, proud to brag of it and bask in the sunshine of their admiration. 'I count my cash in dollars now. Deng Xiaoping said, "To be rich is glorious." Welcome to fucking Gloryville, PRC.'

He snorted noisily and spat on the floor again. He leaned forward and jabbed a finger at Li. 'So where are they now, these fucking Red Guards? Well, let me tell you. Nowhere. Bunch of no-use dead-heads!'

'Do you know how many were in the Revolt-to-the-End Brigade?' Li asked.

'Sure,' said Chang. 'The leader lived in my street. An ugly big bastard called Ge Yan. He was a moron. Thick as pig shit. Always at the bottom of the class, always getting disciplined by the teachers. But as soon as their backs were turned, he was beating shit out the other kids. He might have been the school bully, but he never laid a finger on me. I'd have cracked his fucking skull if he had. And he knew it.' He paused. 'What was it you asked? Oh, yeah, how many? There were six of them.' He stroked his chin trying to remember. 'There was Birdie . . .'

'Birdie?' Li asked.

'Yeah, that's what they called Ge Yan.' He scratched his head again, frowning, as if trying to sort out some conflict in his memory. 'Funny thing. A big, hard bastard like him. He loved his birds. He had dozens of them, all sorts of colours. He hung them in cages in his yard. I was in there once, saw him with them. You never saw hands that could punch your lights out handle anything so gently as he handled those birds. Like they were the most delicate things in the world. Breathe on them and you'd break them. Only he loved them. Spent all his spare time in his yard or down the bird market.'

'Do you remember who else?'

'Yeah, sure.' Chang lit another cigarette. 'There was Monkey, and Zero, and Pauper . . . She was the only girl among them. But you wouldn't have known it to look at her. Ugly bitch. Then there was Tortoise, and . . . oh, yeah, Pigsy. How could I forget big fat Pigsy?'

'And Yuan Tao?'

Chang looked at Li and Zhao as if they were mad. 'Yuan Tao? You're kidding. He was a nice guy, bit bookish, you know? Bit of a swot. He'd never have been involved with those guys. They were creeps and wasters. The ones with the chips on their shoulders were the worst. Took all their inadequacies out on anyone smarter. Like it was your fault they were born stupid.'

'Yue Shi wasn't stupid,' Zhao said.

'No, but he was sleekit, you know? A creep. One thing to your face, another behind your back.'

'How did Yuan Tao get the nickname Digger?' Li asked.

Again, Chang cast him a withering look. 'Where do you guys get your info? Yuan was never called Digger. His nickname was Cat. You know, short for Scaredy Cat.'

Li frowned. 'You're sure about that?'

'Sure I'm sure.'

'Why'd they call him Scaredy Cat?' Zhao asked.

'Because the other kids were always picking on him, you know? Making a fool of him, kicking the shit out of him behind the bike sheds. And he never fought back, never once. I felt sorry for him, but if he wasn't going to be big enough to stand up for himself I wasn't going to do it for him.'

'So how come everyone picked on him?' Li wanted to know. 'Just because he was clever?'

'Naw,' Chang said. 'There were other clever kids no one never went near. But when your old man's a teacher at the school . . .' Chang shrugged. 'What can I tell you?'

Li sat for a moment in stunned silence. 'His father was a teacher here?'

'Sure,' Chang said. 'Old man Yuan. He was our English teacher.'

The detectives' office was busy when Li and Zhao got back, a cocktail of voices and telephones and shuffling paperwork. In spite of all the windows lying open, the air was thick with cigarette smoke.

'Qian,' Li shouted as he went straight through to his office.

Qian appeared at his door. 'Yes, boss?'

'Imperative you track down as many of the classmates as you can. Turns out our first three victims were members of a Red Guard faction called the Revolt-to-the-End Brigade. There's another three. Concentrate on them.' He consulted his notes. 'A guy called Ge Yan, nicknamed Birdie. A bird fancier. Apparently he was always hanging around a local bird market when he was a kid. A girl they called Pauper, but nobody seems to be able to remember her real name. And another guy named . . .' He searched through his notebook. 'Gau Huan. They called him Tortoise, apparently because he was so slow.' He tapped his head. 'Up here. Suspicion he might have been retarded in some way.'

Almost without pausing for breath he called, 'Wu!' And Wu appeared beside Qian. Li didn't even look up. 'Yuan Tao's father taught English at the No. 29 Middle School. According to our information he died in '67. But we still don't know what happened to his mother. I think it's pretty damned important that we find her. And any other relatives still living. That gets priority, OK?'

'Right, boss.'

Li looked up and Wu and Qian still lingered hesitantly in the doorway. 'Well?'

They exchanged glances, and Qian said, 'The Chief wants to see you, boss. The minute you came in, he said.'

And his tone brought memories of Xinxin flooding back. 'Oh, shit,' Li said. 'I'd forgotten about that.'

Chen's office was a shambles. His blotter and all his paper-work had been removed from the desk and piled along the windowsill. Xinxin's jigsaw puzzle, half-finished, was spread across the desktop. Her books lay opened on the floor, and all the chairs had been drawn together in the middle of the room, and an array of soft toys – a panda, a rabbit, a tiger, a lion – arranged side by side.

As Li entered, Xinxin was sitting on Chen's knee, and he was reading to her from a big picture book. He looked up and glared at Li over Xinxin's head. He closed the book, handing it to Xinxin, and lifting her down on to the floor. 'I need to talk to your Uncle Yan now, little one,' he said.

Xinxin pulled a face and she, in turn, glared at Li. 'He's *always* spoiling things,' she said.

'You go next door and ask Uncle Qian to finish the story for you,' Chen persisted gently.

Xinxin's face lit up. 'Oh, yeah. Uncle Qian. He's brilliant.' And she headed off down the corridor clutching her book, without so much as a second glance at Li.

'I've often heard people speak of the Little Emperor syndrome,' Chen said. 'All these only children spoiled by over-doting parents. And here I am participating in it. Shut the door.'

Li closed the door behind him and moved the lion to get a seat. 'Where did all this stuff come from?' he asked.

'Uncle Qian,' Chen said with a tone, 'took her down to the market stalls on Ritan Lu, where they sell all those soft toys. The guys had a whip round, and that's the result.' He nodded towards the collection of furry animals. 'You were a hell of a long time, Li.'

Li nodded. 'But I think we made a breakthrough, chief.' And he told him about the Revolt-to-the-End Brigade and Yuan's father, and the fact that whoever had killed Yuan Tao had got the nickname wrong.

'But Yuan Tao wasn't a Red Guard. Couldn't have been. He wasn't even in the country,' Chen said.

'No,' Li agreed. 'But they were all classmates, and they were all taught by his father, and maybe something else, Chief. Something we're not seeing yet. But we're looking in the right place now, and if we look hard enough, and keep on looking, we will. I'm sure of it.'

'And I'm sure,' Chen said glumly, 'that the situation with your niece cannot continue like this.' He waved a hand around his office. 'Look at this place!'

Li stifled a smile. 'I thought it looked like you and Xinxin were getting on like a house on fire, chief.'

'That's got nothing to do with anything,' Chen snapped. He paused and took a breath, then, 'I phoned the police chief at Zigong and he spoke to Xinxin's father.' He paused again.

'And?' asked Li.

Chen said grimly, 'He says that as far as he's concerned his wife has left him and taken the little girl with her. He doesn't want anything to do with either of them.'

Li wheeled his bike through the afternoon heat, dodging the traffic on Dongzhimennei Street. Xinxin sat in a huff on the rack over the rear wheel, clutching her satchel and panda to her as if she expected someone to try and tear them away. She was distinctly displeased with Li for removing her from all the attention she was getting at Section One, and she was becoming increasingly aware now of how much she was missing her mom. Her lower lip was petted, and tears were welling in her eyes.

Li felt sick. How could Xinxin's father expect him to look

after her? Li was single, working long hours for a very modest salary. He would have to employ someone full time to look after the child until he could straighten things out with the man. And God knew where her mother was! It was so unfair. There was too much in his head to deal with, without having to cope with this.

Mei Yuan spotted him crossing the street, and her face lit up when she saw Xinxin on the back of the bike. Xinxin was just as delighted to see Mei Yuan, and she jumped down and ran into the open arms of the street vendor, and burst into tears.

'Uncle Yan won't let me play,' she sobbed. 'And my mommy's not well, and I want to go home.'

Mei Yuan squatted down and held the child tightly to her, looking up over her shoulder to see Li's helpless expression. He shrugged and shook his head. 'You know what?' Mei Yuan said suddenly, holding Xinxin at arm's length and brushing the tears from her face. 'I bet you could go a *jian bing* right now.'

Xinxin frowned. 'What's that?'

'It's a big pancake.' She looked at Li. 'Without the chilli?'

Li smiled. 'She comes from Sichuan, remember.'

'Of course.' Mei Yuan grinned and stood up, taking Xinxin's hand. 'Here,' she said, 'you watch me make it.' And Xinxin, for the moment, forgot her tears as she watched Mei Yuan spread the liquid mix over her hotplate and then break an egg on to it and smear it over the bubbling pancake as it formed. 'My cousin said you came earlier,' Mei Yuan said to Li. 'I'm sorry I was not here.'

'I have a problem, Mei Yuan. But it is not easy for me to tell you right now.'

She nodded. 'How is your Cantonese?'

'Rusty,' he said. Six months in Hong Kong had provided him with the basics, but he had not used it in a long time.

'Mine, too,' she said, in Cantonese. 'So where is her mother?'

'Pregnant,' Li said. 'She had a ... I don't know the word for it in Cantonese.' He thought hard for another way to say it. 'They made a picture of the baby with sound. She knows it's a boy. She's gone to stay with some friend somewhere in the south to have it. I don't know where. And Xinxin's father doesn't want to know.'

Mei Yuan finished the *jian bing* and wrapped it carefully to give to Xinxin. 'There we are, little one. Careful. It's hot.'

Xinxin bit into it. 'Hmm,' she said, her face brightening up immediately. 'It's good.' And she took another big mouthful. 'How come I don't know what you're saying?' She gazed up at Mei Yuan, a perplexed look in her eyes.

Mei Yuan smiled. 'Oh,' she said, 'we were just practising another kind of Chinese. I'll teach you some of the words tonight if you like.'

'Tonight?' Xinxin's face lit up. 'Are you coming to Uncle Yan's house again?'

'No,' said Mei Yuan. 'You're coming to stay with me for a day or two. Would you like that?'

'Oh, yeah,' Xinxin said, all the sparkle back in her eyes now. 'That would be brilliant.'

Mei Yuan looked at Li. 'My cousin will look after the *jian bing* for a while.' She paused. 'Until things get sorted out.'

Li found his eyes filling with tears, and he had to blink them back hard. He reached out and squeezed Mei Yuan's hand.

'So, have you worked out my riddle yet?' she asked.

He shook his head. 'I still haven't had a chance to think it through.'

'OK, but you only get one more day,' she chided him. She paused to think, then added, 'But the answer is staring you in the face, if only you will stop believing what I tell you.'

CHAPTER SIX

A warm breeze drifted across the green water of the Nine Dragons Pond, rippling its surface. Beyond it, high above the Sunset Glow Pavilion, ski lifts carried tourists to the summit of a tree-clad mountain.

'The water remains a constant forty-three degrees centigrade all year round,' Michael told Margaret. They were walking slowly along the water's edge towards a white marble statue of a semi-naked woman at the centre of a fountain. On their left a huge green-roofed pavilion rose up on rust-red pillars. 'In the depths of winter, when the wind blows across the water from the south, it gathers heat and lifts the frost from the roof of the pavilion. And if the sun is shining the air above the roof sparkles and dances with tiny particles of coruscating light. They call it the Frost Flying Pavilion.'

They had arrived here at the hot springs after a short drive along a highway punctuated by peasants selling pomegranates from big bamboo baskets. Margaret had spent more than an hour with the archaeologists excavating warriors, before Michael had returned and taken her on a tour of the other two pits. She had been flushed from the power of her experience of excavation, and her enthusiasm had amused him.

'What was it you said the other night?' he had reminded her. '*Can't say I'd be riveted by the prospect of looking at a lot of tombs*? Something like that?'

She punched his arm playfully. 'Are you trying to make a fool of me?'

He grinned. 'Do I have to try?'

'OK,' she said. 'So I was wrong.' She shook her head ruefully. 'I guess I just spend too much time with the dead. I had no idea that archaeology could be such a . . . such a living thing.' She looked at him very directly. 'I envy you, you know.'

'Why?' he laughed.

'Because you can do that. You can bring things to life. Reanimate history. I can't do that for the people who end up on my table. All I can do is cut them up and say how they died. Not very constructive.'

He had suggested that on their way back to town they stop off at the Huaqing Hot Springs, the winter playground of the emperors who had made their capital at Xi'an. It would be quiet there, he had said, after the crowds in the exhibition halls of the Terracotta Warriors, and the feeding frenzy of touts and tourists surrounding the market stalls outside.

And it was. In the weeks before the national holiday to celebrate the anniversary of the Liberation, tourism dipped to its lowest point of the season. Only a few souls wandered among the paths and terraces of these centuries-old gardens that climbed into the foothills of Li mountain.

'Who's the bimbo?' Margaret asked, nodding towards the scantily clad statue.

Michael smiled. 'Yang Guifei,' he said. 'One of the Four Beauties of Chinese history. She was one of three thousand, six hundred concubines of the Tang emperor Gao Zong. He fell in love with her. Passionately. Blindly. They spent all their winter months here, warming their love in the hot springs. He became obsessive, began ignoring the affairs of state. All he wanted to do was spend every waking and every sleeping hour with the woman he loved. Then when her adopted son led an uprising against him, his ministers told him that his army would not fight unless she were put to death.'

Margaret said, 'He didn't, did he?' Michael shook his head and she grinned. 'You had me worried there for a minute.'

'She saved him from having to do it by taking her own life,' he said.

She gasped in frustration. 'Do you have to spoil every story?'

He laughed. 'I don't make them up. It must be the way I tell them.'

She wondered if it was a true story and decided it probably was, although romanticised by time, and by storytellers like Michael. All the same, it cast a slight cloud of sadness over the place. Even the privileged lives of emperors could be touched by tragedy. They were, after all, only human.

'But there's another story associated with this place,' he said, 'that is not quite so tragic. Although I'm sure Chiang Kai-Shek probably wouldn't agree.' He took her hand, without any apparent self-consciousness, and led her away from the lake over a hump-backed bridge, through scholar trees and up steps to a paved terrace. His hand felt warm and strong, and Margaret found herself responding to his touch. 'You do know who Chiang Kai-Shek is?'

She shook her head apologetically, and she felt the overwhelming scale of her ignorance. It made her feel small, and insignificant. 'Any relation to Barry?' she asked.

He drew her a look. 'When the Qing Dynasty was finally overthrown in 1911,' he said, 'the first Republic of China was born. But its founder, Dr Sun Yat-Sen, did not live long, and the country was torn apart by factional warlords. His successor was Chiang Kai-Shek, a brilliant and ruthless leader who crushed the warlords in 1928, and then spent the next two decades engaged in a civil war with the Communists.' They stopped and leaned on a stone balustrade, looking down on the jumble of stairways and terraces below, and watched the first amber leaves of fall float down on to the water. 'Am I boring you?' he asked.

'Don't worry. I'll let you know.'

'Good.' He turned her round, taking her hand again, and led her across the terrace to a shady villa on the far side. 'Because in December of 1936 Chiang Kai-Shek lived here, in this house. The Japanese had invaded and were occupying large tracts of the country. But some of Chiang Kai-Shek's generals thought he was spending too much time fighting the Communists when the real enemy was the invading foreign devils. They wanted him to join forces with the Communists to fight off the Japs. So, with a small band of soldiers, they came here to kidnap him. There was an exchange of fire.' They were now on the covered terrace that ran the length of the villa. 'See,' he said. 'They have covered the windows here with plastic to protect the bullet holes in the glass.'

Margaret peered beyond the perspex and saw the round bullet holes in the fractured windows. 'Yeah,' she said sceptically. 'Like these are the original bullet holes.'

Michael said, 'You're such a cynic, Margaret.' She grinned and he smiled and shook his head. 'Anyway, they didn't get him without a chase. He had been in his bed when they attacked, and when they finally caught up with him in a tiny pavilion up on the hillside there, he was still in his pyjamas, wearing one shoe, and without his false teeth.'

Margaret laughed. 'So much for his dignity. And did he join forces with the Communists?'

'Reluctantly, yes. Then after the Japs were finally defeated in '46, the two sides went at it again until the Communists won in '49, and Chiang Kai-Shek fled to Taiwan where he set up the Republic of China.'

'As opposed to the *People's* Republic of China.'

'Exactly.'

'There,' she said. 'I'm learning something. Three months in this goddamn country and I'm finally learning something about it.' She smiled up at Michael and found a curious intensity in his eyes and immediately felt a churning sensation in her stomach. He cupped her face in his hands and tilted it towards his. For a moment he hesitated, almost as if giving her the chance to draw back before he either made a fool of himself, or committed them both to a course of action that would take them deep into unknown territory. But she did not draw back, and he kissed her. A long, tender, lingering kiss, and she felt her body drawing into his, felt its hardness and its warmth against her.

They broke apart and for a moment she closed her eyes, breathing hard, feeling his breath on her face. When she opened them again, she found him looking at her very intently. Then she grinned, and then laughed.

'What's so funny?' he said, almost a sense of hurt in his bewilderment.

'Oh, I don't know,' she said. 'Some girls get romanced under starlit skies and told how beautiful they look. Me? I get seduced with tales of Chiang Kai-Shek and his missing dentures.'

He laughed, too, then, and as gradually his smiled faded he said, 'OK, so tonight we'll find a starlit sky somewhere, and I'll tell you just how beautiful you are, and just how much I want to make love to you.'

She was a little shocked, a little pleased, a little scared. 'Better be careful,' she said. 'I might just take you up on it.'

The faces of dead men looked up at her from the bed. Four men who had all been separated from their heads by a single sword. They had all been sedated with the same drug, but only three of them had swallowed it with red wine. The same three had been executed by a swordsman standing on their left, and had their hands bound by a length of silk secured with a conventional reef knot. The fourth had been killed by an assassin standing on his right, and tied with a reverse reef knot. He had drunk vodka turned blue by a drug he could not have failed to notice. In every other detail the killings were identical.

Margaret shook her head. Her initial conclusion, she remained certain, was correct. Yuan Tao had been murdered by someone who had attempted to make it look as if he had been a victim of the same person who had killed the other three. And yet, they had all attended the same school, so there was clearly a link. So what was she missing? What were they all missing?

She ran the other evidence through her mind. The three bottles of wine found in Yuan Tao's apartment. *Three* bottles, three more victims. But what were they doing in his apartment? The dark blue dust there too, that matched the substance found on the shoes and trousers of one of the other victims. Another link. But what was the connection? And what had been hidden beneath the floorboards in the illegally rented rooms? She looked again at the photograph of Yuan Tao's body, the blood draining into the hole in the floor where the linoleum had been ripped back and the floorboards removed. Li had said the linoleum was torn. That suggested a search. Someone looking for something.

Margaret had spent an hour or more reading the autopsy reports, looking at the photographs. She had felt a sense of guilt when she and Michael arrived back at their hotel in the late afternoon. Four men had been murdered, the fate of perhaps another three depending on their killer being found quickly. And here she was in Xi'an, hundreds of miles away, flirting with a man who found her attractive and wasn't afraid to say so, but who had nothing whatsoever to do with the investigation. She had told herself that this was not her investigation. She had been drawn into the whole thing quite against her will. But still she felt guilty.

She wondered what fresh developments there had been today, and toyed briefly with the idea of trying to phone Li to find out. But she quickly dismissed the thought. She knew that Li would probably be difficult with her, and that she would probably be awkward with him. Which, in turn, made her wonder if her feelings of guilt were not so much about the investigation as about Li and her relationship with Michael. But, damnit, why should *she* feel guilty? Li was the one who had turned his back on her. An anger flared briefly in her breast, and then subsided, leaving her feeling empty and sad. And she knew that whatever she felt for Michael she was still in love with Li.

She dropped the autopsy report she had been holding on to the bed, and one of the photographs flipped over. She turned it the right way up and looked at it for a moment. It showed the blood-stained placard that had been hung around the neck of the second victim. She looked at the strange and impenetrable Chinese characters, which meant nothing to her, and was struck by a sudden revelation. Handwriting! Surely the Chinese would have experts in calligraphy able to tell if the characters on the cards had been drawn by the same hand. It had not occurred to her before, she realised, because normal practice would be to compare a written specimen with the handwriting of a suspect, not to compare specimens from different crime scenes. She quickly laid out the photographs of the four placards. But even as she did, her excitement gave way to disappointment. There were only two characters on each one – a nickname and a number. And each was different. The sample was not big enough to make any definitive comparison.

What about the ink? It might be possible to establish that the same ink had been used in each case. But what conclusion could they draw from that? Only, she supposed, that the killer had access to the same ink, in the way that he had access to the same murder weapon. Which simply raised more questions than it answered.

But what if – her mind kept returning to the Chinese characters – what if a calligrapher *had* been able to establish that they had all been written by the same hand? What would that have meant? There was something in the thought that was only just eluding her.

She tutted with frustration and got up off the bed, catching sight of herself for a moment in the bedroom mirror. With a shock she realised she was still naked. She had not dressed after her shower. And something in her nakedness brought images of Michael into her mind, and she felt the stirrings of sexual desire deep inside. And immediately the guilt returned and she moved quickly away from the mirror to slip into her panties, and the jeans and white blouse she had laid out on the chair. She forced her mind back to blood and headless bodies. She had, she knew, been close to something, something that would make sense both of the things that were different and of the things that were the same.

She had almost given up, and had started clearing away the autopsy and forensics reports when suddenly she realised what it was. It seemed, somehow, so obvious that she wondered why she had not thought of it before. Quickly she searched her purse for her address book, and found the telephone number for Section One that she had previously tried in vain. She hesitated for a long moment, her heart pounding somewhere up in her throat, almost choking her it seemed. Then she sat on the bed, lifted the telephone and called the Beijing number.

There were three long, single rings before a telephonist answered in Chinese. Margaret said, very slowly and carefully, '*Qing. Li Yan.*' A gabble of Chinese came back at her. She tried again. '*Qing. Li Yan.*' She heard an impatient intake of breath, another burst of Chinese, and then the line was put on hold. After what seemed like a very long time, she heard a man's voice.

'*Wei?*' he said.

'Li Yan?'

There was a pause. 'Margaret?' Something in the way he said her name brought goosebumps up on her arms.

'Li Yan, I've thought of something,' she said. 'To do with Yuan Tao's killer . . .' She waited for a response.

'Well?' he said eventually, and there was a tone in his voice that this time raised hackles rather than goosebumps, and she remembered just what a frustrating man he could be. She drew a deep breath.

'You know how you said no one outside of the investigating team and the murderer could possibly know all the details of the killings?' She didn't wait for his answer. 'Well, suppose Yuan Tao's killer was an accomplice, or at the very least a witness, to the other murders. That would explain how he knew what the *modus operandi* was. And if he was simply left-handed instead of right-handed, that would explain why that was the only difference in Yuan Tao's case.'

Another long silence, then Li said, 'Well, thank you for the thought. I'll make a note of it in the file.'

She felt her anger rising. 'And that's all you've got to say?'

'How is Xi'an?' he asked, and when she didn't, couldn't, respond, added, 'You and Mr Zimmerman still just good friends?'

'None of your fucking business!' she said, and slammed down the phone. And in a single, furious movement, she swept all the photographs and reports off the bed and on to the floor. Why had she even bothered? He didn't care about her. He didn't want her sticking her nose into his investigation. He was just a typical chauvinistic, xenophobic Chinese male! She felt tears springing to her eyes, and turned her fury on herself. *Why* was she upset? *Why* was she feeling guilty? *Why* was she wasting her time on this man?

There was a knock at the door, and she jumped up quickly, brushing the tears from her eyes. 'Yes?'

'It's me. Michael.'

She took a deep breath, blinked furiously and checked her hair in the mirror before going to open the door. His smile of greeting was warm and open and friendly, and after her brief exchange with Li she just wanted him to take her in his arms and hold her there. But 'Hi' was all she said. 'Come on in. I'm nearly ready. Just got to put on a little make-up.' He came into the room and she saw, with embarrassment, his eyes drawn to the pictures and papers strewn over the floor. 'A bit of an accident,' she said. 'I'll just pick these up.'

'Here, I'll help you.' Michael crouched to gather up the scattered files.

'No, it's OK,' Margaret said quickly. But it was too late. He was already looking at a photograph of one of the headless bodies.

'Oh, my God!' He turned away from it, his face screwed up in disgust.

She snatched it from him. 'Big mistake,' she said, 'letting you see stuff like that. Men usually find what I do for a living a big turn-off.'

He stood up, his face pale and shocked. 'I'll try not to think about it,' he said. 'It's just a bit of a jolt seeing someone you know with their head cut off.'

'Someone you know?' Margaret frowned and then looked at the photograph she had taken from him. It was Yue Shi. 'Of course,' she realised. She had not made the connection before. 'He was a professor of *archaeology* at Beijing University.'

'It was a terrible shock when I heard about what happened

to him,' Michael said. 'I never expected to actually *see* what happened to him.'

Margaret was concerned. 'I'm so sorry, Michael. Did you know him well?'

He shrugged. 'He wasn't a close friend, but we had a lot of contact while I was researching the documentary series on Hu Bo. He was Hu's protégé. Studied under him at the university and assisted in several major excavations. He knew the old man as well as anyone. He was invaluable in giving me a picture of Hu Bo the man, rather than just Hu Bo the archaeologist.'

Margaret threw her files on the bed. 'I'm sorry,' she said, and she put her arms around his waist and stretched up on tiptoe to kiss him lightly on the lips. 'I didn't want anything to spoil tonight for us.'

He smiled wanly. 'It won't, he said. And he bent to return her kiss, and slip his arms around her. 'I think I could probably do with a drink first. Then I'll show you Xi'an. And then we'll eat.'

'And then . . . ?'

He shrugged. 'I don't know, Margaret. Let's just wait and see.'

And she felt a huge surge of disappointment, and she cursed Li and his investigation. Whatever she did, whichever way she turned, somehow he always seemed to be there spoiling things for her. And now he had driven a wedge between her and Michael, brought home to him the reality of her job, confronted him with the death of a friend. As if, somehow, Li had planned it all, to ensure that her relationship with Michael stayed, as she had described it to him, platonic.

When they stepped out of the Japanese-owned Ana Chengbao Hotel it was dark, and Margaret looked in astonishment at the transformation of this dusty and undistinguished daytime city into a night-time place of light and life. The towering south gate, immediately facing them, and the crenellated city wall that ran off to east and west, were outlined in yellow neon, for all the world as if someone had taken a luminous yellow marker pen and drawn them against the night sky. Multicoloured lights illuminated the elegantly curled roofs of the ancient gate and the watchtowers that shimmered in the distant darkness.

Michael grinned. 'A bit Disneyesque,' he said. 'Come on.' And he took her by the hand and flagged down a taxi.

Their car followed the route of the great moat, which was separated from the wall by a park full of quiet walkways and peaceful pavilions completely encircling the city. Above it, for mile after mile, the crenellations of the wall were drawn yellow on black. The sidewalks of the streets outside, empty during daylight, had turned into endless open-air eateries. Row upon row of tables was laid out under the trees, lit by low-hanging red lamps strung from loops of electric cable. Braziers and barbecues burned and smoked in the dark, while people congregated in their thousands, families, friends, eating together beneath fleshy green leaves in the balmy autumn evening.

'They are night people, the inhabitants of Xi'an,' Michael said. 'When the sun goes down this is an exciting city.'

'Where are we going?' Margaret asked.

'To the Muslim Quarter.' He smiled. 'An experience not to be missed. I know a little place where we can get authentic Muslim cuisine.'

Margaret raised her eyebrows in surprise. 'Muslims? In China? I thought religion was banned here?'

'Ah,' said Michael sagely. 'You've been listening to the anti-Chinese propagandists back home. The God botherers. The truth is, in the last twenty years people have been free to worship whatever god they want. But, then, after the appalling religious persecution of the Cultural Revolution, it's not really surprising that it's taken a little longer for people to become open about it again.'

'But is religion not a threat to the Communists?' Margaret asked. 'I mean, communism's an atheist philosophy, isn't it?'

'The thing is, Margaret,' Michael said, 'Communism's kind of like the state religion here. It has about fifty million members – the numbers go up and down when the corrupt ones get weeded out and shot, and the next batch of young urban technocrats sign up. But, you know, The Word according to Mao, or even Deng Xiaoping, is not what it used to be. Nowadays the Party's more like a big club. People don't join it because they've seen The Light. They join for the same reasons a businessman in Chicago signs up for the Rotary. To make contacts and connections. To get on in life.'

Margaret watched him talk, eyes twinkling, his voice

animated by enthusiasm. He took pleasure in what he knew, in passing it on to others. She saw exactly why he was such a success on television, regardless of his subject.

A couple of whiskies had relaxed him after the shock of seeing the photographs on her bedroom floor. He had been genuinely shaken by the sight of things that Margaret viewed as routine. It made her wonder again if there was something wrong with her, if she had been desensitised by her job, made indifferent by years of exposure to the horrors of death in all its guises. But whatever effect her work might have had on her, she knew that she was not impervious to the emotional slaps in the face that life seemed constantly to deliver: a husband who had betrayed her and died bequeathing her all his guilt; a lover from an alien culture who would neither accept her fully into his life, nor make the transition to be accepted into hers.

She wondered if Michael would be any different. If she succumbed to those desires that pulled and taunted her, would she just end up being hurt again? And yet she felt so comfortable with him. Safe. There was something wonderfully reassuring in his hand holding hers in the back of the taxi. Here was someone taking care of her, guiding her gently through a strange and fascinating world. A world from whose dangers, she felt certain, she would be protected in his company. And after so many years of being the independent, hard-assed career woman, there was something deliciously appealing in the idea of simply delivering herself into his care.

They turned east now, through the west gate along Xi Dajie,

and Margaret watched a whole family on a motorbike overtake them. A small boy nestled between the father and the front handlebars. A slightly bigger girl was sandwiched between the father and the mother who was riding pillion. Four of them on the one bike. Margaret was so taken aback by the sight, that it was several moments before she realised how rare it was to see a family of four in a country whose social structure had been so dislocated by the One-Child Policy.

Ahead of them, a huge floodlit building rose up into the night sky.

'The Bell Tower,' Michael said. He spoke to the driver and they pulled in at the edge of a large square, neatly manicured lawns crisscrossed by paths and walkways, a broad flight of steps leading down to the bright lights of an underground shopping centre. They got out and Michael paid the driver. Margaret looked around. At the far side, a great long restaurant built in traditional Chinese style, was traced against the sky in neon. The square itself was crowded, families out for an evening stroll, children playing on mini-dodgems on a concrete apron, people sitting on a wall by a pond reading newspapers and books by the light of an illuminated fountain. A woman tried to sell them a giant paper caterpillar that rippled across the concrete with unnerving realism at the tug of a length of string. But Michael just smiled and shook his head.

As he led Margaret across the square people openly gawped and called, 'Hello,' or, 'So pleased to see you,' in strange English intonations. They passed beneath the shadow of what Michael told her was the drum tower, and turned into a narrow covered alleyway lined on both sides by hawkers' stalls filled with tourist junk and religious trinkets.

On the other side of the wall, to their left, Michael said, was the Great Mosque. Religion and commerce, it seemed, went hand in hand. They ran the gauntlet of traders trying to sell them everything from teapots to ornamental swords. Occasionally Michael would stop and speak to one of them. You could see the astonishment on their faces as he spoke in fluent Chinese, and whatever he said would invariably make them laugh.

The alleyway was crowded with shoppers and kids on bicycles, the occasional motorbike inching its way past, and soon they turned left, past the entrance to the mosque itself, and into the comparative quiet of a crumbling, dusty *hutong*.

'It must be wonderful to speak Chinese as well as you do,' Margaret said. 'It must open up the whole culture of the place to you in a way that most people could never hope to experience.'

Michael inclined his head doubtfully. 'It can be a double-edged sword,' he said. 'China was once described to me as being like an onion. It is made up of layer upon layer upon layer, with only subtle differences between each one. Most people usually only get two or three layers deep. People and places, a little history, a little culture, become familiar to them. But the heart of the onion, the very core of China itself, is still many more layers away. Out of reach, almost untouchable.'

He thought for a moment. 'When I first started learning the language people were great. The Chinese love it if you can pay them a compliment, or give instructions to a taxi driver, or order up a meal in Mandarin. But when you've been here a while, and your grasp of the language gets good enough so you can start talking politics and philosophy, suddenly they get cautious. The encouragement stops. You're getting too close to something the Chinese don't really want foreign devils like you and me getting too close to. The heart of China, the core of Chineseness.'

'Wow!' Margaret was taken aback. 'I always thought the Chinese were very welcoming.'

'They are,' Michael said. 'I love them. They are warm and friendly and wonderfully loyal.' He paused. 'Just don't get too close, that's all. Because you're not one of them.'

And Margaret wondered if that's why her relationship with Li was doomed to failure. Because she was not Chinese, because she could never hope to understand him the way another Chinese could.

A couple of chickens, startled by their approach, skittered away up an alley. A Chinese labourer humping coal into a *siheyuan* shouted, '*Ni hau*,' and then laughed raucously as if he had said something funny. They passed a tiny girl displaying remarkable skill in keeping a weighted pink ribbon in the air by kicking it up repeatedly with the instep of her foot. A group of her friends watched patiently waiting for her to make a mistake so that they could take their turn. At the far end of the *hutong* they turned into the outer edges of the Muslim Quarter, passing beneath a large character banner that straddled the street. Up ahead, shop fronts and food stalls blazed light into the road. Tables, with the now familiar red shades hanging over them, were set out down the middle of the street as far as you could see, lost in a blur of lights and people.

As they approached the frenzy of eating and cooking, they passed a wagon piled high with ox livers crawling with flies. A little further on another wagon groaned with great heaps of stinking intestine. Other smells rose to greet them on the warm night air. The ripe stench of an open sewer, the stink of dead animals as they walked past lines of pelts hung between trees. Then, as they left the gloom on the outer fringes of the Quarter, and wandered deep into the very heart of it, the olfactory sensations became a little more pleasant. Indian spices. Cumin, coriander, garam masala. The smells of cooking. Spiced lamb and roast chicken. Braziers were pumped up to extremes of heat and light by electronic blowers placed directly beneath them. Long troughs of charcoal glowed and smoked and filled the air with the mouthwatering smells of barbecued meat. Savoury chestnuts and black beans were being roasted together in huge woks, great vats of brown sesame sludge brought to high temperatures on fiercely burning fires to separate the oil from the tahini. There were barber shops, seed stores, sweet sellers, hardware stands. A boy was rolling out noodles on a sidewalk cooking table while a woman behind him washed dishes in a big stone sink. Through a doorway, Margaret saw a man stretched out on a barber's chair, sleeping under green covers as he waited for the barber to finish reading his paper and give him a shave.

In a butcher's shop, men in white coats hacked at carcasses

with great cleavers, and a boy threw joints of meat through the open doors of a van backed up to the shop. They passed racks of barbecued chicken legs, and tables laid out with tray upon tray of candied fruits and baskets of nuts.

Old men in round white hats sat eating at tables and watched with a dull-eyed curiosity as Michael and Margaret strolled by, hand in hand. This circuit was not on the tourist itinerary, and white faces were almost unheard of here. But all the young children, clinging to mothers' hands, were desperate to try out the English they were being taught in school. 'Hello,' one of them said. And then, bizarrely, 'So happy you could come.'

Banners and flags fluttered in profusion overhead in the evening breeze. And above them, the leaves of overhanging trees whispered into the night sky.

'Told you it was an experience,' Michael said.

Margaret was wide-eyed and held his hand tightly. 'That's the thing about you, Michael,' she said. 'You never take me anywhere interesting.'

'Come on,' he said suddenly, and drew her off the street, past a young man tending a brazier, and into a tall, narrow room that opened directly on to the street. Hanging fluorescent strips reflected light harshly off cracked white tiles lining the walls and floor. There were several round fold-up tables with melamine tops and low wooden stools. An open concrete staircase led off, it seemed, to nowhere.

'What are we coming in here for?' Margaret asked, alarmed.

Michael grinned. 'To eat,' he said.

'You're kidding!' Margaret was shocked. She had recurring visions of flies crawling over piles of ox liver and intestine.

'It's OK,' Michael said. 'Muslims are very particular about preparing and cooking their meat.'

'Yeah, I'd noticed,' Margaret said. She remembered the boy throwing joints of meat into the back of his van. 'Like the health inspector would be redundant here.'

Michael was amused by her fastidiousness. 'It's perfectly safe,' he said. 'Honestly. I've eaten here many times and lived to tell the tale.' He sat down on a low stool, and reluctantly she followed suit. A gaggle of graceless young girls in pink and white immediately flounced around their table, bringing dishes of plain soy and chilli soy for dipping. They couldn't take their eyes off Margaret. One of them spoke quickly to Michael and he grinned. He said to Margaret, 'They want to know if they can touch your hair.'

'Sure. I suppose,' Margaret said apprehensively, and they all tentatively touched her soft, blonde curls, withdrawing their hands quickly as if it might burn them. They giggled and gabbled excitedly. Another one spoke to Michael and drew a laugh from him. He shook his head and spoke quickly, making them laugh in return. 'What was that about?' Margaret asked, a little put out by her sense of exclusion.

'They wanted to know if I was a film star,' Michael grinned.

Margaret snapped her fingers. 'I knew I'd seen you some-where before. *The Creature from the Black Lagoon*, wasn't it? Must be sickening being so good-looking, huh?'

He smiled. 'And they want to know if you want chicken feet.'

Margaret pulled a face. 'No thank you. I'm quite happy with the ones I've got.'

He sighed patiently. 'To eat.'

She pulled another face. 'Why would I want to eat chicken feet?'

'The Chinese believe they are good for your skin. Make you look younger.'

'Oh, yeah? Ask them how old they think I am?'

He asked them and they looked at her and had an animated discussion. Then, 'Twenty-two,' Michael said.

Margaret laughed. 'Yeah, well, I'm thirty-one.' She stuck a finger in her face. 'And if they want to know how I keep this looking so young, you can tell them it's McDonald's. Quarter-pounders with ketchup and French fries.'

First they brought steaming bowls of soup filled with noodles and pieces of chicken and mushroom. It was scalding hot and full of flavour. And then came a plate piled with fried dumplings filled with pork and spring onion and beansprouts and coriander. Margaret struggled to handle them with her chopsticks. But they were worth the effort, spicy and delicious dipped in chilli soy.

'What do you want to drink?' Michael asked.

She said, 'Something cold and plenty of it to cool down my mouth. Beer would be good.'

'Sorry,' Michael said. 'No can do. Muslims don't drink. No alcohol in the Muslim Quarter.'

'Of course,' Margaret said. 'Coke, then.'

Michael spoke to one of the girls who ran across the street to an old woman selling soft drinks off the back of her bike and returned with two plastic bottles.

'Love the glasses,' Margaret said, and she took a long pull from the neck of the bottle. But, then, she thought, it was probably more hygienic this way.

The lamb arrived. Great bunches of metal skewers laden with tiny pieces of barbecued lamb, half of them marinaded in a chilli sauce. They were tender and sweet and full of flavour. Margaret watched Michael as he stripped the meat from a skewer and into a dish of soy with his chopsticks, and then delicately picked out the pieces to eat one by one. This *was* an experience, she thought. Extraordinary, exciting, unlike anything she could have imagined. And yet Michael seemed completely at home, confident and relaxed. She watched how dexterous he was with his chopsticks, and felt the butterflies starting up again in her stomach. She had been attracted to him from the first moment they had met, but now she found herself being drawn inexorably towards him, like a moth to the light.

He caught her eye and smiled. 'Enjoying it?'

She nodded. She wanted to get closer to him, draw him in, drink from the vast pool of his knowledge, find out everything there was to know about him, his life, his dreams.

'You were going to tell me about the stuff they found in the coffins at the Ding Ling tomb,' she said.

He waved a hand dismissively. 'You don't want to hear about that.'

'I do. You said much worse was to happen than the smashing of the coffins.'

Lights shone in Michael's eyes as he leaned towards her and took her hand. 'They found the most wonderful things in the coffins, Margaret. Beautiful Ming vases, Buddhist scriptures, dozens of pieces of jade, which the ancient Chinese believed would stop the bodies from decaying. But most extraordinary of all was an array of stunning hand-embroidered quilts and brocades. In the coffin of one of the empresses they found an exquisite jacket embroidered with one hundred boys at play. In the other, they found the body of the empress dressed in a jacket and skirt embroidered with dragons and bats and swastikas. All in perfect condition.'

'Swastikas?' Margaret was taken aback. 'Ancient oriental Nazis?'

Michael smiled. 'No. Hitler only borrowed it from the Chinese. It was the ancient Chinese character for long life. The cretin even managed to get it the wrong way round.' He paused, and she saw that intensity in his eyes again. 'The thing is, all these wonderful embroideries, quilts and jackets and skirts, gold brocades – they had been in there for hundreds of years at a constant temperature, never exposed to the air. No one knew what the effect of oxygen and different humidity levels would be. Hu Bo and the others were still pioneers. They had no idea how to preserve materials like this.'

'Oh, God,' Margaret groaned. 'What happened?'

'Politics happened,' Michael said grimly. 'The great Anti-Rightist Movement of 1958. The leadership ordered work on the tomb to stop. And it ground to a halt for six whole months. The brocades, which the team had tried to preserve by sticking down to plexiglass, hardened and turned brittle. Their colours faded. The wonderful embroideries developed large black spots and began to rot.

'Hu Bo and his mentor, Xia Nai, had been summoned to Beijing to take part in the political movement. But when they heard what was happening, they hurried back to the tomb. There they found the warehouse, where they had stored the treasures, filled with the smell of mildew. The brilliant colours of the brocades and embroideries had turned into dark clouds. The materials had puckered and shrunk, and when Hu reached out to touch them, they disintegrated in his fingers. Lost for ever. All that remains now are a few sketches made and photographs taken when the coffins were first opened.'

Margaret let out a tiny gasp. 'It's unimaginable.' She shook her head. 'It must have broken their hearts.'

'It did,' Michael said. 'But there was worse to come.'

'Jesus,' Margaret breathed her exasperation. 'Don't any of your stories have happy endings?'

Michael shook his head. 'Not really. After all, are there any really happy endings in life? There may be heart-warming tales en route, but the journey always ends in death, doesn't it? No one should know that better than you.'

Margaret thought of her poor dead husband, of the murder victims whose photographs she held in her hotel room, of the conveyer belt of corpses that had passed through her autopsy suite. He was right. She herself, Michael, Li, all of them would end up on a cold slab somewhere, sometime. It was a depressing thought. 'Sure,' she said. 'But none of us would ever embark on the journey if we thought too much about where it was going to end.'

Michael smiled. 'Which is why people invented gods. To give meaning to their lives, and the hope that death was not the end.'

'So you're an atheist?'

'No.' He shook his head.

'You believe in God, then?'

'I don't know what I believe in. The indomitable spirit of man, perhaps. Of his will to survive, his ability to create, of his propensity to destroy. I believe in history, and that in history we all live on in some small way.' He chuckled. 'Anyway, this is all getting a bit serious.'

'So what was the worse still to come,' she asked, 'for poor old Hu Bo?'

Michael smiled and shook his head sadly. 'Poor old Hu Bo,' he said. 'When they were finally allowed to restart work on the tomb, a very important member of the government, and his wife and son, came to visit. It just happened that while they were there, Hu and some others were spraying the place with a mixture of formalin and alcohol to prevent further mildew. The man's wife started choking and crying, and the boy complained that Hu had tried to poison him.

'Within a week, Hu was accused of releasing toxic gases, of being the recipient of undeserved privileges. They had also discovered that as a boy he had been in the Youth League of the Kuomintang, Chiang Kai-Shek's party. Poor old Hu was sent to the countryside for re-education.'

'Didn't have much luck, did he?' Margaret said. 'And what happened to the tomb?'

'It was turned into the museum that you see today. Except that what you see today is minus what was destroyed during the Cultural Revolution.'

'For heaven's sake, Michael, what next?' Margaret was incredulous.

'The museum was stormed by Red Guards,' Michael said. 'They dragged the remains of the emperor and his empresses out into the square in front of the stele pavilion and smashed them to pieces, then made a huge pile of everything they could get their hands on and set it on fire. The contents of the tomb represented the Four Olds, you see – everything that the regime was trying to wipe out. We're filming a re-creation of that scene tomorrow. You should come out and see it.'

'I'd love to,' Margaret said, and she realised he was still holding her hand.

'Everything would have been destroyed,' Michael said, 'if it hadn't been for the courage of the museum's caretaker. Li Yajuan was just a housewife. She had four children at home. But she defied the Red Guards and refused to give up any of the other relics. They beat her and kicked her until she bled, and finally she locked herself away in the warehouse with the relics, day and night for nearly three years.' Margaret was shocked to see his eyes filling up. 'She was a real heroine, Margaret. She had extraordinary courage.' He paused. 'It's people like her that I believe in. That's the spirit that I was talking about. Just an ordinary housewife. But her life had meaning, and she has her place in history. She died in 1985, anonymous and unsung. She should have been declared a Hero of the People.'

Margaret was uncertain whether it was the story he had told, or the effect it had had on him, but she too found herself deeply moved. She squeezed his hand. He blinked back his tears and smiled, embarrassed. 'Stupid!' he said. 'I'm sorry.' He took a gulp of Coke. 'Let's get out of here.'

They left the Muslim Quarter through an elaborate gate over the entrance to the main *hutong*, and turned east to the bell tower, and then south down Nan Dajie to where a Kentucky Fried Chicken joint had insinuated itself between a supermarket and a department store. Michael put a strong arm round Margaret's shoulders and drew her close to him. But they walked in silence. All the shops were still open, and the streets were full of families and young lovers, and teenagers of both sexes on the prowl for partners. The Colonel smiled past them as they entered the fried chicken shop, and Michael bought them a couple of ice creams to cool their still burning mouths. They sat at a table by the window. On the other side of it life streamed past in a never-ending blur.

'How the hell did you ever get into all this?' Margaret asked. 'I mean, television.'

He shrugged. 'Pure accident. It's certainly not what I set out to do in life.' He toyed with his plastic spoon, pushing the tasteless pink ice cream around in its carton. 'I did a video project at university. A friend showed it to someone on a small cable network which had a few bucks to make a documentary on a local archaeological landmark. They asked me to do it.' He shook his head. 'Don't ask me why, but it got really good figures, and the cable company sold it on all over the States. They got more money, we made a couple more shows, then I got asked to do a series for the Discovery Channel. That was it. Someone did a piece on me in *Cosmopolitan*, a picture spread. Suddenly archaeology was sexy. Ratings went through the roof and I got offered a deal by NBC. The rest is history.' He examined her face for a moment or two. 'Now you know nearly everything about me, and I know virtually nothing about you.'

She smiled. 'I wouldn't want to disillusion you.'

'You mean you don't want to tell me.'

She cocked her head. 'It amounts to the same thing.'

'That's not fair, Margaret.'

'Maybe not. But that's how it is.'

He pursed his lips. 'Sometimes animals curl up to protect themselves when they've been hurt. Is that what you're doing?'

'What if I am?' she said defiantly. 'I'm not like you, Michael. You're open and honest and . . . I don't know, just you. Like you've never been hurt. Like you've no reason not to trust people. Me? Every time I open up someone puts the knife in. And turns it. You're like the big friendly dog that comes running up to a stranger looking to get its ears tickled. I'm the dog that cowers in the corner if someone looks at it the wrong way.'

'Or growls if anyone gets too close.'

She smiled reluctantly. 'You got it.'

'So if I get any closer, do you think the dog'll bite?'

She met his gaze. 'I'm not sure if the dog knows that yet, Michael.'

'So . . . approach with caution.'

She nodded. 'That would be the sensible course.'

He scratched his chin thoughtfully. 'You know, usually I'm pretty good with dogs. Never been bitten yet.'

She grinned. 'There's always a first time.'

A profusion of white and pastel green and pink flags hung down from the atrium-style glass roof seven floors above the sprawling marble foyer of the Ana Chengbao Hotel. A scattering of guests looked down from the Wisteria bar on the second floor, their desultory conversation a distant whisper. Margaret glanced at the full-size bronze reproductions of two Terracotta Warriors just inside the sliding doors, and remembered the sense of wonder she had experienced in the burial chambers earlier that day as she had slowly brushed away the dust of history to reveal the features of an ancient general. Had it really only been that morning? Already it seemed like a faraway, magical memory.

Michael steered her past the lifelike statues of a Silk Road trader and his Bactrian camel to the elevator, and they rode up to the top floor. From the open corridor, they could see down through the flags to the white marble below, the bronze warriors reduced to tiny, insignificant figures. At the far end they reached her room first and stopped at the door. They had said virtually nothing on the long walk down Nan Dajie, under the south gate and out to the vast circle that led them round to the hotel. Now the easy conversation of earlier seemed to have dried up. This was good night, awkward and stilted, nothing resolved. *Let's just wait and see*, he had said earlier, still affected by the photograph of his friend's headless body.

'Well,' Margaret said. 'I guess it's an early start tomorrow.'

He nodded. 'Got to be at the airport for seven.'

'I hope I don't sleep in.' But she thought it was highly unlikely that she would sleep at all.

'Better set your alarm.'

She shook her head. 'I'm hopeless with these things. They never go off at the right time.'

'I'd better do it for you, then,' he said. And he stood expectantly, and she realised he was waiting for her to open her door.

Her mouth was dry as they walked into her hotel room. The curtains were still open on French windows leading to the balcony. Below, they could see the yellow tracery of the city wall and the floodlit south gate, the reflected lights of Xi'an casting a soft glow around the room. Margaret went to switch on the light, but Michael put a hand out to stop her, and his hand held hers. 'I want you, Margaret.' His voice was little more than a hoarse whisper.

The wave of desire that washed over her almost made her buckle at the knees. 'Aren't you afraid I'll bite?' she said.

He smiled. 'I don't care,' he said. 'I figure your bark's much worse.' And he kissed her. Slowly at first, gently. Then, as she responded, their passion and hunger took control, and their mouths and bodies pressed hard together. To her sudden surprise she found her feet swept away from under her, and he had her in his arms, carrying her across the room to the bed as if she were no more than a rag doll. No man had ever carried her like that before, and she felt as if all control had been taken from her. But, still, she felt completely safe.

He laid her on the bed and kissed her again and stripped off his shirt. She saw light reflecting on the curve of his pectoral muscles, the concave arch of his belly as he slipped out of his trousers. Then she felt his breath on her face, his hands on her breasts, and she fought to rid herself of her blouse and her jeans in her haste to feel his flesh on hers, warm and firm and smooth. And finally they were naked and he was poised over her, his face looking down into hers, a light in his eyes. She reached up and grabbed his buttocks and pulled him towards her. His mouth fell on hers again and then she felt his lips warm and wet on her neck, on her breast, sucking, biting, teasing the nipple. And the breath escaped from her in a long sigh as she felt him slip inside her and all memories and thoughts of Li were finally banished.

CHAPTER SEVEN

I

Li took a bottle of beer from the refrigerator and wandered through a cloud of depression, bare-footed, to dropped himself into an armchair in the living room. His shirt was unbuttoned and hanging loose over his jeans. He swung one leg up over the arm of the chair and took a slug at the bottle. It tasted cold and sharp. A drip of condensation fell from the bottle and landed on the flat, hard muscle of his bare stomach, making him wince. The light from the streetlamp outside cast the long shadow of the window frame across the room. He had no desire to turn on the light, to see Xinxin's little jacket hanging on the chair opposite, to be reminded that Mei Yuan's generosity could only be a temporary solution.

He lit a cigarette, letting his head fall back, and blew smoke at the ceiling. *None of your fucking business*, Margaret had told him. And she was right. It wasn't. He had no right to be jealous, no right to be hurt, no right to hurt her. So why had he treated her that way on the phone? She had clearly been thinking about the investigation, about the myriad conflicting evidence, and had called him, excited by a fresh thought. A valid thought. If Yuan Tao's murderer was indeed a copycat, it was entirely possible that he had been there at the previous three murders, and therefore knew exactly how to make the fourth one look the same. It was an intriguing thought but, if anything, muddied the waters even further. Who was the other murderer? There was no clear motive in any of it. The first three victims had been members of the same Red Guard faction, but Yuan had not even been in the country then, nor for thirty years afterwards.

Li was still not convinced that Yuan's was a copycat murder. One of his team – it was Sang, he recalled – had suggested that the murderer had deliberately adopted a left-handed stance and tied the knot differently in order to confuse the investigation. It was entirely feasible, even if Margaret thought it unlikely.

His mind drifted back to Margaret. He drained his bottle and went to fetch another. Why had he been so short with her when he had wanted so much to say, *Margaret, I was wrong, forgive me, we can still find a way*? Why, instead, had he deliberately taunted her, provoking her angry response? *None of your fucking business!* And the sound of the phone slamming in his ear. He slumped again in the chair and lit another cigarette. Was this his destiny? To be alone and in the dark, smoking and drinking and regretting the might-have-beens? He saw his life stretching ahead of him, an endless repetitive cycle of working days and lonely nights. He thought of his uncle and how he had used his work to fill the void left by the death of his wife.

But for Li there had never been anything but work. There had been no one in his life who'd left a void to fill. Until now.

He shook his head and sat up. This was ridiculous! Morbid and self-pitying. He tried to clear his thoughts, and Mei Yuan's riddle found its way into them. What was it again? Three men had paid thirty yuan for the room. But it only cost twenty-five, and when the bell-boy went to return the five they had overpaid, he pocketed two and only gave them back one each. So effectively they had paid nine yuan each, which was twenty-seven, and the bell-boy had pocketed two. Which was twenty-nine. So where had the other one gone?

Li frowned and scratched his head, then tipped it back to drain his bottle. What was it Mei Yuan had said to him that afternoon? *The answer is staring you in the face, if only you will stop believing what I tell you.* What had she told him? That they had given ten each and each got one back, which meant they had paid nine each. Which was twenty-seven. Li turned it around for a moment and then suddenly he saw it. Of course! How stupid of him! They didn't get one back each from thirty, they got one back each from twenty-eight because the bell-boy had taken two. So among them they had paid twenty-five, plus the three yuan that had been returned to them. Which was twenty-eight. Plus the two the bell-boy had pocketed. Which was thirty. Mei Yuan was right. He had made the mistake of taking her suggested calculation at face value. And, of course, it was nonsense. So nothing else made sense.

The thought stopped him in his tracks. He sat frozen for several moments. Wasn't that exactly what was happening with the Yuan Tao murders? All the evidence was suggesting things to them that didn't add up. They were making assumptions that they couldn't reconcile. Perhaps the assumptions were wrong. Any of them, all of them. Li cursed himself. He had even recalled to himself the previous day his uncle's own philosophy. *Assume nothing. Let the evidence lead you to the conclusion, do not jump to it yourself.* And yet he had continued, for another day, to do exactly that.

He stood up, agitated now, and lit another cigarette and moved out into the glassed-in balcony. Outside the occasional yellowing leaf drifted to the sidewalk below. Stupid! His head had been so full of Margaret and Xiao Ling and Xinxin, he had not concentrated his mind properly at all. What other evidence was there? What had they been overlooking in their attempt to make the big evidence fit the picture they had formed for themselves? Something small, something insignificant. What?

He searched his mind, gathering together all the details, big and small, sifting them, rearranging them. The placards, the nicknames, the numbers, the bronze weapon, the silk cord. What else? Yuan Tao's illegally rented apartment. What was it for? He walked himself through the apartment again in his mind, as he had done physically the night they found Yuan Tao. He saw the head and the body, the pool of blood draining into the hole in the floor. He paused. The hole in the floor. Boards that had been lifted. A secret cache. Hiding what? Then suddenly he remembered Margaret's question at the autopsy. *Had the linoleum been lifted, or was it torn?* It appeared to have been torn, he had told her. Why had she asked? He thought about it. If you had hidden something under the floorboards, you would be very careful with the linoleum that covered them. A tear would draw attention. So it wasn't Yuan Tao that had opened up his hiding place. It was someone else. Someone who had searched his apartment and didn't care if they tore the linoleum. Someone who knew he *had* an apartment.

What had they been looking for? And had they found it there, under the floorboards?

Li paused to think again, rewinding his thoughts. If his murderer knew he had an illegally rented apartment, then he would also know that he had an embassy apartment. Had that been searched, too? Li drew on his cigarette and thought back to the embassy apartment in the diplomatic compound behind the Friendship Store. He and Wu had covered it pretty thoroughly. Forensics had been over it from top to bottom. There were no obvious signs of a search. Li tried to picture the floor, pull it back from somewhere in his memory. He saw a standard, grey linoleum floor covering. He was pretty certain that's what it had been. And he would have noticed if it had been torn. But there was something else in his memory. Something vague and elusive, just beyond his reach. Something about the apartment.

In his mind's eye he retraced the steps Wu and he had made through it. The living room with all its personal bric-a-brac, the photographs of Yuan's parents, the books . . . The toilet, the shelf above the washbasin crammed with toothpaste, shaving foam, a couple of bars of soap . . . And suddenly Li knew what it was. The shaving foam and soap had been hypo-allergenic. Unscented. There had been no aftershave or deodorant. And yet, Li recalled, there had been a faint, distant smell of some exotic scent, like an aftershave, lingering on the air. It had only registered at all because it was unfamiliar to him. So the scent could not have been Wu's or belonged to Forensics. Or to Yuan Tao.

Of course, he realised, it might have been someone from the embassy. Their security officer, perhaps. Americans were fond of their aftershave. But it left Li feeling uneasy. If someone *had* searched the apartment in the diplomatic compound, had they found what they were looking for? He quickly gulped down the last of his beer and went in search of his shoes, buttoning his shirt and tucking it into his jeans as he went. He was damned if he was going to sit here feeling sorry for himself. If Yuan Tao had hidden something in the apartment he was renting illegally, he might also have hidden something in his embassy apartment. Something that may, or may not, still be there. But it was worth a look.

Li glanced at the time. It was a quarter to midnight. But it didn't matter. There would be a guard on the gate of the compound all night.

II

Li wheeled his uncle's bike through the gates of the diplomatic compound, and looked up at the windows. There were lights still on in quite a few of them – embassy staff and their families watching television or working late.

'Where the hell do you think you're going?' The guard hurried out from behind the hut where he had been having a cigarette. He stamped it out under foot as he approached Li. It was not the same guard who had been on duty during his last visit.

Li played dumb. 'What d'you mean?'

'I mean, what makes you think you've got the fucking right to just waltz in there?' The guard swaggered up to him. He was young and cocky, and a sneer curled his lip.

'I'm going to visit a friend.'

'No you're not.' The guard pushed his face close to Li's. 'Not unless I say you can.'

Li ignored the guard's aggression and asked innocently, 'Why not?'

The guard looked at him as if he had two heads. 'Because this is a diplomatic compound, dickhead. And Chinese like you don't get in unless I say so.'

Li drew out his Public Security ID wallet and thrust it in the guard's face. 'I don't know if they taught you to read where you come from – *dickhead*.' The guard's startled face recoiled, almost as if from an electric shock. 'But in case they didn't, you're talking to a senior ranking CID officer of the Beijing Municipal Police. And if I ever catch you talking to another Chinese like that again I'll see to it that you spend the rest of your career on border patrol in Inner Mongolia.' The guard blinked and gulped. His face had gone pasty pale.

'Understand?' The boy nodded. 'Good,' Li said. 'And is that how you speak to foreigners?'

'No, boss.' The guard shook his head vigorously, completing his transformation from snarling hound to grovelling mongrel.

'So if I was a *yangguizi* and I told you I was visiting a friend, what would you say?'

'I'd check who it was you were going to see and then let you in.'

'Wouldn't they have to come down and get me?'

'Only if you were a Chinese.' He looked at the ground and wouldn't meet Li's eye. So it would be difficult, Li thought, for anyone who did not live in the apartment building to gain access to it, unless he was a foreigner.

'Look at me, son,' Li said, and the boy reluctantly raised his eyes. 'That uniform doesn't make you any better than anyone else. Treat people the way you would have them treat you.' He tucked his ID into his back pocket and wheeled his bike on into the compound.

There was tape stuck across the door – black on yellow: 'CRIME SCENE, DO NOT ENTER'. Li opened the door and ducked under the tape. He was struck immediately by the familiar smells of stale cooking and body odour. But there was no hint of the scent he had detected on his first visit. So it had been fresh. One of the Americans probably. The light in the entrance hall did not work, and he fumbled in the dark into the tiny living room and felt for the light switch. A fluorescent strip hanging from the ceiling flickered into life and washed the room in its cold, harsh light. It seemed very sad and empty. A lonely place where a single man spent long hours with only his books for company. What on earth had drawn him back to China? From a job of position and prestige at a top American university, to a lowly visa clerk in Beijing. What kind of life had he lived, processing paperwork at the Bruce Compound during the day, cooped up here alone at night with his books? And yet there had been another life. A secret life. Why had he needed another apartment? According to his neighbours he spent hardly any time there. It was not a meeting place. If he had received visitors his neighbours in the apartment building would have known. But *someone* had visited. Someone had entered late at night, unobserved. Someone had torn up the linoleum and found something hidden beneath the floorboards. Someone had murdered Yuan Tao there and left unseen.

Li examined the linoleum in the living room. Bookcases stood along one edge of it, piles of books and magazines along the other. One could not have lifted it without moving almost everything in the room. There were no creases or tears obvious to the naked eye. He felt a tiny stab of disappointment.

He turned his attentions then to the bedroom, stripping the bed and checking the mattress and the base. There was nothing. He moved the wardrobe and tapped it front and back for hidden panels. But it was a utilitarian piece of furniture. What you saw was what you got. The linoleum in here had been tacked to the floor.

He went through to the toilet. But it was too small to hide anything. Plaster walls, concrete floor, one tiny cabinet on the wall. Li unscrewed the top of the cistern and looked inside. A cheap plastic mechanism winked up at him from the clear cold water that filled it. He stooped to remove the hair that had gathered in the drainer in the floor beneath the shower head and tried to prise it loose. But it was stuck fast. He washed his hands and went back through to the living room. He checked the armchair, pulling all its cushions away, then tipping it on to its side and tearing the hessian base to reveal the springs within its frame. Nothing.

He looked around, disappointed. Frustrated. All that remained were the books. He squatted down and began lifting them out in batches of six or eight, piling them on the floor at his feet. There were dozens of political volumes. Books on the history and development of the Communist Party in China, a Chinese translation of the works of Karl Marx, a series on the development of democracy in Taiwan, a fat volume on political changes in Hong Kong since the handover. There was a history of the Kuomintang and the legacy of Chiang Kai-Shek, another on the Chinese Secret Service written by two French journalists. Almost an entire shelf was devoted to the bloody events that had occurred in Tiananmen Square in '89: *The Long March to the Fourth of June*; *Cries for Democracy*; *Voices from Tiananmen Square*; *Death in Beijing*. Yet another shelf seemed devoted to books on the Cultural Revolution. Li picked one out. Like most of the others it was in English. *A Memoir of the Chinese Cultural Revolution*. He opened it and saw that it had been first published in China in the late 1980s by the Workers' Publishing House, before an American company had published this translation in the mid-nineties. There was a bookmark near the back of the book, and Li wondered if Yuan had been reading it in the days before he died. He flicked through to the marked page and the bookmark fell to the floor. He scanned the pages, but there was nothing of significance in them, and he lifted the bookmark to put it back and realised that it was in fact a sheet of paper twice folded. He put the book down and unfolded it. It had yellowed slightly and was a little brittle. There were handwritten Chinese characters scrawled across it, and Li realised that it was a letter. It was addressed to Yuan Tao c/o the University of California, Berkeley. The sender lived at an address at Guang'anmen in south-west Beijing. Li glanced to the foot of the page and saw that it was signed by Yuan's cousin, Yang Shouqian.

His mouth was dry as he righted the armchair and sat on the edge of it to read the letter. It was dated May 15th, 1995.

My Dear Cousin Tao,
I wrote to cousin Liu in San Francisco in search of your address, but since the death of his father he was no longer sure where you were living. He was, however, almost certain that you were still teaching at the University of Berkeley, and as I was able to confirm this on the Internet I am writing to you now.

You are probably not aware that my mother died about six weeks ago. She was nearly ninety. She had had a good life, and the end was peaceful. It was only when I was going through her things last week that I came across the enclosed diary. There was a letter with it, from your mother, dated 1970, which I have kept. In it she asked her sister to see that you got her diary. It covers the years after you went to America.

At first I did not understand why my mother had not done as her sister requested. That is, until I started to read the diary. I am sorry that I did so. I did not mean to invade your privacy. As you will see, it is written as a personal account to you. I did not read it all. In truth, I think I would have found it difficult to do so.

I suppose my mother was trying to protect you, but I think she should have sent it, none the less. Although it might be she was afraid that it would not have reached you at that time. And perhaps with the passage of time she thought it better to leave well alone.

However, it all now seems like such a very long time ago, and I think you have the right to know what happened. So here is the diary.

Please write to me to let me know how you are. Did you ever marry? Do you have children? I have a daughter who is at university now. If you should ever return to Beijing, I would very much like to see you again after all these years. I remember you only as a teenager, when I was not much older myself.

With all my very best wishes.

Your faithful cousin,

Yang Shouqian

Li was aware of the letter trembling slightly in his hand. Somewhere, just ahead, there was a door that he felt certain must open on to enlightenment. And in his hand he held, if not the key, then the intimation of its existence. He had the letter, but where was the diary? He had no idea what it looked like, whether it was large or small, black, red, blue . . . He laid the letter carefully on the table and cleared the bookshelves, checking each and every book, stripping the covers off hardbacks in case they concealed the diary underneath. Nothing.

He turned then to the piles of books and magazines under the window. Again he found nothing that remotely resembled a diary. He stood in the centre of the room and looked hopelessly around the disarray. He could not think where else it might be concealed. He crossed to pick up the letter again and felt the faintest of creaks beneath his foot. And paused. He stepped back and then rocked forward again. But this time there was nothing. Had he imagined it? And, anyway, what if he hadn't? Floors creaked. Li followed again the line of the linoleum around the edges of the room with his eyes. If Yuan Tao had hidden anything under it, he had not envisaged requiring quick or easy access. But still, Li figured, if he had hidden something under the floor in the other apartment, might he not have done the same here? His earlier stab of disappointment became a spur of hope and anticipation.

It took him nearly twenty minutes to clear all the furniture and books to one end of the room so that he could pull back the linoleum. It had stuck a little to the floorboards around the edges, then as he rolled it back, he saw that there was a layer of old newspapers underneath it. He checked the dates and saw that they were all about six months old – just around the time Yuan Tao would have taken possession of the apartment. He rolled the linoleum right up to the furniture, then swept the newspapers aside, clearing a space in the middle of the floor where he had felt the boards creak underfoot. Immediately he saw where a single board had been lifted at a join, cut about twelve inches from it, and then nailed down again. Li had no idea whether Yuan had cut it, or whether it had been done long before by some tradesman accessing cables or pipes. He had no idea, either, how he was going to lift it again.

He searched the apartment for something with which he could prise up the floorboard, eventually finding a small box of tools in the cupboard under the sink. Taking a stout screwdriver, he drove it between the boards and forced them apart, levering the cut board upwards. The wood splintered, and the nails groaned as they were forced free of the joist. Eventually the twelve-inch length of board sprang free and clattered away across the floor. Li found himself looking into a space made dark by his own shadow. He moved so that he was not in his own light and saw, among the deadening rubble, the gleam of something plastic and shiny. He took a handkerchief from his pocket and reached in to lift out a small red book wrapped in clear plastic. For a long time he kneeled there, staring at it, hearing the sound of his own breath rasping in the silence of the apartment. A tiny rivulet of sweat ran down his forehead and dripped from his brow on to the bare floorboards.

The duty officer at Section One was astonished to see Li coming down the corridor on the top floor. He checked his watch. It was after 2 a.m. He had just been to refill his flask with hot water and was on his way to make a mug of green tea. He hurried into the detectives' office after Li. A couple of detectives looked up in surprise. 'Either you're very early boss, or you're very late,' the duty officer said.

But all Li said was, 'I don't want to be disturbed. For *any* reason.' And he slammed the door of his office shut behind him.

III

July 17th, 1966
A boy whom I recognised as one of your old schoolfriends came to our house this morning. His name is Tian Jingfu, a pudgy boy whom I seem to remember you called Pigsy. Your father remembered him, too, as a former pupil. Not a very bright one, he said. Anyway, now he wears a red arm band. He is one of the *hung wei ping*, the Red Guard activists who are spreading the word of Chairman Mao. He told us that all teachers were to report back to the No. 29 Middle School. Your father has not been there since classes were suspended in June. I do not know why Tian Jingfu was sent. He is no longer at the school.

When your father returned, he told me that *da-zi-bao* posters had been pasted up on all the walls by the pupils, who are being encouraged to criticise their teachers.

When he and the other teachers got there the children were all painting slogans. They stopped what they were doing and watched their teachers with great caution, as if they were afraid that they might be punished. But your father said that when they realised the teachers no longer had power, they started to taunt them, calling them 'rightists' and 'counter-revolutionaries'. There were several posters that mentioned your father by name.

You probably do not recall that your father was denounced as a 'rightist' in 1958 and sent to work in the countryside for six months. We thought that was all behind us – until today.

A meeting was held in the square and a cadre from the party addressed the whole school and told them it was now the duty of every student and every teacher to take part in the 'Anti-Four Olds' campaign. The 'Four Olds', he said, were old ideas, old superstitions, old customs, old bourgeois life-styles. The worst exponents of the Four Olds, he said, were persons in authority taking the capitalist road. Then everyone was told to go home.

Your father believes he will be all right because he has already been punished as a 'rightist' and can claim that he has been reformed through labour. But he is always the optimist. I am not so sure. I am just happy that you will not be a part of this. And although you are far away, at least I feel I can talk to you by keeping this record of what is happening. I will try to keep it up to date so that like a photo album you will have a record

of your family. But I am scared, Tao. Not so much for me
as for your father.

Li rubbed his eyes with gloved hands. The concentrated light
of his desk lamp on the white pages of the diary were making
them water. He sat back and lit a cigarette, blowing smoke into
the darkness that lay beyond the ring of light. Then he leaned
forward again, and with his white gloves he turned each page
with great care in order not to disturb whatever forensic evidence the diary might yield. Reading it was depressing, like
a journey back through time to a distant memory of his own
childhood and an experience shared with millions of people
all over China. July 1966. It was only just beginning.

He did not read it all, flicking carefully forward through the
pages, August, September, stopping here and there to read the
increasingly harrowing account, as the fate that befell Yuan
Tao's parents unfolded.

September 15th, 1966
Your father and I watched from our window today as Mr
Cai from across the landing was attacked in the street
by Red Guards. They took his shoes and made him squat
on a stool in full view of the street and shaved his head.
I do not know why. It seems more and more that they
can do what they like to you on whatever pretext they
dream up.

Your father has not been at the school for nearly two
weeks. His angina attacks are less frequent now, and he

has learned to sit quietly and wait with great patience for the pain to pass. It is an awful thing for me to think, but I am glad of his heart condition. It keeps him away from the school. I fear for his life every time he goes there.

October 21st, 1966

They came to the house today. Six of them. All former pupils of your father. To look for 'black' materials, they said. This is anything that they believe is opposed to the Communist Party. The leader is a boy who lives in our street, Ge Yan. I think you know him. He is the boy who keeps birds in his yard. It is strange to think of someone who can love such delicate creatures being so violent and filled with hate. He screamed and shouted at me when I refused to let him see your father. He was very red in the face, with veins bulging at his temples. I was very frightened. But your father had not been well earlier, and he was in his bed.

Finally, when he heard all the shouting, he came out in his dressing gown and asked them what they wanted. He was quite angry with them for shouting at me, and they seemed quite taken aback. I don't think they knew how to deal with him. They still remembered him as their teacher and I think were still a little afraid of him.

The girl that the others called Pauper was the boldest. She told your father that as a teacher of English, he was a lover of things foreign, and all foreigners were opposed to the Great Proletarian Cultural Revolution. His interests, therefore, were 'black', she said, and he must give up all his 'black' materials. I do not think they knew what these materials were, but your father was clever. He said that of course he would give them anything they considered 'black', as he wanted to do everything he could to help the revolution. He went into our front room and took all his old magazines from England and America that he has been collecting for years and told them to take them away. They were undoubtedly 'black', he said, because they were all in English.

The one they called Zero, whose name your father says is Bai Qiyu, took your bicycle. He said that you had betrayed the revolution by going to study abroad, and that your bicycle must be confiscated. I did try to stop him, but there was nothing I could do. Your father said to let them go.

When they were gone, I asked him if it did not break his heart to lose his prized collection of magazines. But he said they were just paper and ink, and that flesh and blood were more important.

I am so sorry about your bicycle.

February 2nd, 1967
Tao, do you remember Mrs Gu, my friend Gu Yi from the kindergarten? She is dead. When she finished mourning the death of her husband she tried to find herself another man, because she still had two children, and her job at the kindergarten did not pay much. She wore pretty

clothes and make-up to make herself attractive. But all she did was attract the fury of the *hung wei ping*.

Last week they came to her door in a procession, banging drums and gongs and carrying scarlet banners. They made her paste a *da-zi-bao* on her door, denouncing herself as a capitalist whore. They dragged her into the street and forced her to 'confess' and promise to remould herself conscientiously. They hung two torn shoes around her neck, which is a sign of immorality, and made her wash her face publicly, and tore off her 'black' bourgeois dress.

Last night she hanged herself.

April 15th, 1967
Your father's condition continues to deteriorate. He has been in his bed for several days. Still, I am glad he is safe here at home instead of at the school. We hear terrible stories. Your old headmaster and some of the senior teachers have been made to do manual labour. They are supervised by the Red Guards of the Revolt-to-the-End Brigade, who are all former pupils at the school. I think they were all in your year.

We hear that Headmaster Jiang and the others were forced to demolish the school's lovely old stone gateway with sledgehammers provided by a group of construction workers. And then they had to parade around the square wearing pointed paper dunce hats, just like the landlords during the Land Reform Campaign in 1951. They were made to wear signs around their necks branding them 'cow-headed ghosts' and 'snake spirits'. The schoolchildren, apparently, took delight in calling them 'monsters'.

I was surprised that Headmaster Jiang was treated in this way, because he is a member of the Communist Party. But your father says many of the people targeted are Party members. They are seen as the persons in authority who have taken the capitalist road. He says he is glad now that he never joined the Party.

April 29th, 1967
They came again today. Oh, Tao. I am so afraid. They have found out that I attended the American university in Beijing before the Liberation, and that my father owned a little land in the north.

They are horrible, these children. Their faces are twisted by anger and hatred. They screamed and shouted at me in our own house. They made Gau Huan, the slow-witted boy they call Tortoise, tear up our family photo album. I don't think he really knew what he was doing, but he is like a hungry devil who feeds on destruction. I pleaded with them not to do it, and when I tried to stop Gau Huan, the girl, Pauper, struck me with her hand across my face. She hit me so hard I saw stars and black spots in front of my eyes. One of the others, a clever boy called Yue Shi, shouted in my face that I did not have a good class status. I was the daughter of a landlord. I could not choose my class status, but I could choose my future. I was to denounce my family and destroy their 'black' history.

They asked about you, Tao. They wanted to know when the 'black whelp' was coming home. I screamed at them. I told them you would not be back because you were smarter than they were. I told them they were stupid, and all they could do was destroy things. The girl, Pauper, hit me again.

Hearing the raised voices and my sobbing, your father came out from the bedroom. His face was grey. He had your grandfather's big, stout walking stick in his hand and he bellowed at the little bastards and told them if they raised a hand to me again he'd beat them to within an inch of their lives.

I think they were startled by his appearance and his anger and the threat of violence. They left, then, but said they would be back. I cried for nearly an hour after they had gone, and your father just sat in the chair by the window and gazed out in silence. I could not get him to speak for the rest of the day.

Oh, Tao, much as I would love to see you again, whatever you do, never come back here.

May 1st, 1967
I went to the square today to see Chairman Mao. There were hundreds of thousands of students there, most of them Red Guards. I have never seen so many people in Tiananmen before. On the *guan bo* public address

system, they were playing 'The Helmsman' and 'The Eight Disciplines', then 'The East is Red' just before the great man appeared on the rostrum in front of the Forbidden City. Then everyone was chanting 'Long live Chairman Mao'. The atmosphere was extraordinary, like some fanatical religious gathering. I did not know what to feel. It is hard not to be swept up in the emotion of it all. But all I really wanted to do was weep. I do not think anyone noticed my tears.

June 5th, 1967
This was what I had been dreading. Yue Shi came to the house this morning and sneered as he told us your father must attend the school today. I told him he was not well enough. But the boy just said that if your father did not turn up, others would be sent to fetch him. He would be forced to go on his knees, if necessary.

Oh, Tao, I am so glad you are not here to see this. But I miss you so much. You are so clever, I am sure you would have known what to do. I wish I could just talk to you and hold your hand for comfort.

Li paused. There were three small round blisters on the paper, yellow and raised, and a fourth that had blurred the ink on the character of Tao's name. Tears, Li realised, spilled more than thirty years ago. A simple statement of the hopelessness felt by Yuan Tao's mother as she wept for the son that she knew she would never see again. More eloquent than any words she could have written. And then, with a slight shock, Li realised that they might not be her tears after all. And he thought of Yuan Tao reading his mother's words all those years later. Of the pain and the guilt that he must have felt. It was more than possible that they were the tears of a son spilled for his parents. He read on.

Although it was hot, your father was shivering, and I dressed him warmly for the walk to the school. He had your grandfather's stick in his right hand, and I held his left arm, but he could hardly walk, and we had to stop every ten metres for him to catch his breath. It is a terrible thing to see the strong, young man you married reduced to this.

When we got there, there was a big crowd in the square, gathered around a small wooden stage they had built alongside the basketball net. The geography teacher, Teacher Gu, was standing on the stage, bent over with his hands on his knees and his head down. There was a sign hanging around his neck with his name painted on it upside down in red and scored through.

The students and the Red Guards were roaring, 'Down with Teacher Gu.' Every time he tried to lift his head one of the Red Guards would push it back down. They kept screaming questions at him but wouldn't let him answer. And then they screamed at him again for refusing to speak.

When they saw us arrive, some of the Red Guards

– Pauper and Yue Shi and Pigsy and Tortoise – came and grabbed your father from me. They hung a sign around his neck like Teacher Gu's and pushed him through the jeering crowds to the stage. I tried to go after him, but children swarmed all around me like bees, calling me a 'landlord's daughter' and the 'mother of a black whelp'. I saw your father trying to get on the stage, and when he couldn't, the big boy, Ge Yan, hit him on the back of the neck with a long cane and he dropped to his knees.

Eventually they lifted him on to the stage and Teacher Gu was pushed aside. Your father became the centre of attention. I could see the tears in his sad, dark eyes, but there was nothing he or I could do about it. One of the girls who used to come to our house for extra tuition took my arm and led me away to a classroom. She wore a red arm band, but I think she was only pretending to be one of them. She got me some water and told me I should not look. But I could not leave my husband to face this alone.

When I went to the door of the classroom, I could see him on his knees on the stage, his head bowed, the sign swinging from his neck. They were shouting, 'Down with Teacher Yuan.' They demanded to know why he had neglected his students, why he refused to work. Did he think he was too good to serve the people? What could he say? Even if he were capable of answering, how could he answer such questions? He was ill, so very, very ill.

But each time he failed to answer, they would take it

in turns to hit him across the back of his neck with the cane. I could hear the sound of it. I could feel his pain with every stroke. Then Ge Yan pulled his head back by the hair, and the one called Zero forced him to drink a pot of ink. He gagged and was sick, but still they forced it down his throat.

I screamed at them to stop, but no one could hear me over the noise, and the girl who had taken me to the classroom stopped me from trying to reach him. I have the bruises of her fingers on my arms as I write.

It was just their revenge. Because he had shouted at them and threatened them with his father's stick if they hit me again. I feel so guilty, Tao. It is my fault they did this to him. If I had not tried to stop them tearing up our family photographs, if I had just accepted there was nothing I could do, perhaps they would have let him be.

When he fell over, at first they tried to get him back to his knees, but he was quite unconscious and I think they thought then that he was dead.

It was strange, because suddenly the whole square went quiet, as if somehow the game had all gone terribly wrong. Just children. They had no idea what they were doing.

I ran to the stage, and they all moved aside to let me past. No one stopped me as I got up and removed the sign from around your father's neck. His mouth and face were black from the ink, and there was vomit all down his tunic. But I could hear him breathing. Short, shallow breaths.

I kneeled down and drew him up into my arms, but he was too heavy for me to lift on my own. I called out, 'Will anybody help me?' But no one moved. And then Ge Yan, the bird boy, ordered some of the children to give me a hand to take away this 'black revisionist'.

When, eventually, I got him home and into bed, I went to get the doctor. But when I told him what had happened he did not want to come, and so I have sat here alone with your father for hours now, keeping him cool with cold compresses, tipping his head forward to make him take some water.

It is dark. I don't know what time it is. Sometime after two. Outside it is very quiet, and the house is very still. And yet I can barely hear your father breathing. I don't know what he has done to deserve this. You know what a kind and gentle man he is. Oh, Tao, I am so, so weary.

June 6th, 1967
Tao, your father is dead. Sometime after four this morning, I fell asleep in the chair by the bed, and when I awoke he was quite cold. He died alone, while I slept. I don't know if I can ever forgive myself. I am so sorry, my son. Please know that I love you. I hope you will make a better life for yourself than this.

It was the last entry, although there were many blank pages after.

Li sat with tears filling his eyes, and saw that the first grey light of dawn had appeared in the sky. As a young boy he had been devastated by his mother's death in prison, shocked and distressed to see his father reduced to the palest shadow of his former self. But he could not imagine how Yuan Tao must have felt, nearly thirty years on, reading his mother's harrowing account of his father's death. Of the sickening humiliation and brutality meted out by barbarous, ignorant youths whom his own father had taught. He could picture tears, and anger, and knew that in reading those lines the seeds of revenge had been sewn deep in Yuan Tao's heart.

And he also knew now who had killed Zero and Monkey and Pigsy. And why.

He swivelled his chair and sat for a long time staring out of the window at a grey sky shot with streaks of pink. Li felt inestimably sad. How empty Yuan Tao's life must have been for it to have been consumed so quickly by hate and revenge. A failed marriage. No children. An undistinguished academic career that was going nowhere. How often, Li wondered, had he regretted leaving his home country, destined always to be a stranger in a strange land? What guilt must he have felt, on reading his mother's diary, to realise that what he had escaped had cost his father's life? That while he was safe on the far-off campus of an American university, his father had been persecuted and hounded to his death by Yuan's own classmates. And so hate had filled his emotional void. And revenge had given his life a purpose.

And for five years he had planned his revenge. Engineered his return to Beijing, and methodically set about the execution of his father's tormentors, in a ritual that closely replicated the manner of his father's final humiliation.

Although the diary in no way provided conclusive evidence, it made perfect sense. Li had no doubts. But it still left one deeply puzzling question unanswered. Who killed Yuan? And why?

There was a knock at the door and Qian poked his head in. He seemed surprised to see Li. 'Someone said you were in.' This, as if he hadn't believed it. 'You're early today, boss.' And then he noticed the fog of cigarette smoke that filled the room, and the deep lines etched under Li's eyes. He frowned. 'Have you been here all night?'

Li nodded and slipped the diary into its plastic bag and held it out to Qian. 'Get this checked for fingerprints, Qian. Then get copies made for everyone on the team.'

Qian took it and looked at it with curiosity. 'What is it, boss?'

'A motive for murder.'

IV

Yang Shouqian lived in a crumbling apartment block just south of Guang'anmen Railway Station. He was, Li reckoned, somewhere in his middle fifties, with thinning hair and a long, lugubrious face. His wife was a short, round-faced woman with a pleasant smile who invited Li into their kitchen. They were just having breakfast, she said, before Yang went to work at the nearby Ministry of Hydroelectricity. She was steaming some lotus paste and red bean buns. Would Li like some? Li accepted the offer and sat with them at their table, trains rattling past every few minutes on the southbound line, which they overlooked from the rear of the apartment. He was grateful for the hot green tea and the sweet buns, and felt the fatigue of a night without sleep sweep over him. The burden of his news weighed heavily.

Yang looked at him curiously. 'My wife says you have word of my Cousin Tao.'

Li nodded. 'Have you seen him in the last few months?'

Yang was astonished. 'Seen him? You mean he is in Beijing?'

'For about six months.'

Yang's initial delight turned quickly to confusion, and then to hurt. 'No,' he said. 'I have not seen him. He has not been in touch.' His wife put a concerned hand over his.

She looked at Li, sensing immediately that something was wrong. Why else would he be here? 'What has happened?' she asked.

'I'm afraid he has been murdered,' Li said.

Yang went quite pale, and his wife squeezed his hand. 'I don't understand,' Yang said. 'Murdered? Here in Beijing?' It seemed extraordinary to him that such a thing was possible. 'Who by?'

'We do not know,' Li said. 'Was he in touch with you at all? At any time over the last few years?'

Yang shook his head. 'Never. I have never heard from him in all this time. He was a spotty teenager when I last saw him, shortly before he left for America.'

'But *you* wrote to *him*?'

Yang looked up quickly, surprised. 'How do you know that?'

'Because I have the letter you sent him in 1995.'

'I didn't know you'd written to Cousin Tao, Shouqian,' his wife said.

He nodded. 'You remember, when I sent him the diary?'

'Oh, yes.' She looked at Li and shook her head sadly. 'Such a tragedy.'

'You read it?' Li asked.

'Not all of it. Shouqian showed me it before he sent it.'

Li said, 'You told him that you were keeping the letter Tao's mother had written to your mother.' He paused. 'Why?'

'Because, as you say, it was written to *my* mother,' Yang said. 'It belonged to her, and therefore to me, not Cousin Tao.' He examined his nails for a moment in studied silence. 'Besides,' he said eventually, 'it was probably better that he never saw it.'

'Why?'

'On top of the diary . . .' He shrugged. 'It would have been too much.'

Li said, 'May I see it?'

Yang darted him a quick look, and Li saw something that was almost like shame in his eyes. He nodded and got up and crossed to a dresser against the far wall. He opened a drawer and began searching through a bundle of papers.

'Did you know any of the Red Guards who hounded Tao's father?' Li asked.

Yang shook his head. 'No. They were all younger than me, and we went to different schools.'

Li said, 'In the last month three of them have been murdered.'

Yang's wife gasped. Yang turned to look at Li, and the shame Li had seen in his eyes had turned to something else that he could not quite identify. 'Dear God,' Yang said. 'Tao killed them, didn't he?' And Li knew that it was fear in his eyes.

'I think it is very possible,' Li said.

Yang's wife was quickly on her feet, and she held his arm as he staggered momentarily before steadying himself. He moved back to the table, clutching an old yellowed envelope in his hand and sat down heavily. 'Because I sent him the diary,' he said, his fear realised and turning quickly to guilt. 'I might as well have killed them myself.' And he was struck by an even more horrifying thought and looked up at Li. 'Is that why Cousin Tao was murdered?'

Li shrugged hopelessly. 'I don't know.'

Yang's head dropped. 'I should never have sent it to him. But after all these years I thought he had a right to know. I never for a moment thought ...' He broke off, his voice choked with emotion.

His wife hugged him and said, 'How could you possibly have known, Shouqian?'

'Is that the letter?' Li asked and held out his hand.

Yang nodded and handed it to him. The envelope was unstamped. There was no address, just the name of Yang's mother in clear, bold characters. Li slipped the letter out from inside. The paper was thin and close to tearing at the fold. Li opened it carefully. It was dated July 1970.

My dearest sister, Xi-wen,

I have received word today that my son, Tao, has graduated in the subject of political science at the University of Berkeley in California and is to stay on for another two years to complete his doctorate. I am so pleased for him. His success is assured and he will have no need ever to return here. In a sense it is all I have lived for since the death of my beloved husband. But it is still hard to think of him living somewhere on the other side of the world, watching the same sun rise and set, the same moon as I see on a clear night in Beijing, and not be able to speak or touch. I still remember the feel of him curled up inside me. But he is as removed from me now as my husband.

The Great Proletarian Cultural Revolution seems to be entering a new phase of madness, with faction fighting faction. I am still disgraced because of our father's history and my education and I have not been allowed to work at the kindergarten for nearly two years now. I am so weary of it all and wonder where it will end.

I have spent long hours going through the scraps of our lives before it all began. There is not much of it that has survived. A few photographs, some treasured letters that my husband and I exchanged in the months before we were married, a letter from Tao that, miraculously, reached us not long after he arrived in the United States. And this. It is the diary I kept for Tao after he left. It was meant to be a record for him of the things he missed and could catch up on when he returned.

I could not bring myself to continue with it after his father died. But I would like him to have it. He should know what happened to his family. I entrust it to you, because I know that you will keep it safe and see that Tao gets it when future circumstances allow.

Please tell him I love him. I am sorry for the trouble.

Your loving sister,

Ping Zhen.

Li looked up and found Yang watching him, that sense of shame returned to his eyes. 'It was a crime back then,' Yang said. 'Chairman Mao described it as "alienating oneself from the people".' A tiny explosion of air escaped from his pursed lips. 'Quite a euphemism. In reality what it meant was that we were not allowed a private room at the crematorium, we could not wear mourning armbands, or play funeral music. The whole family was made to feel the shame.' And Li saw that he still felt it, even after all these years.

'What happened?' Li asked.

Yang shook his head. He could barely bring himself to recall the horror of it. 'She threw herself out of the window and was impaled on the railings below. No one would go near her. Apparently she took hours to die.' He met Li's eye. 'Tao never knew.'

CHAPTER EIGHT

I

Margaret's ambivalence was more emotional than consciously thought out. And it wasn't so much ambivalence as a sense of pleasure edged with guilt. But it was a serrated edge that made its presence felt disproportionate to its size. The net effect had been to cloud her pleasures of the night before with embarrassment the morning after.

She was annoyed, because she still felt warm and satisfied by a sexual encounter that had been all she could have hoped for. Michael had been a caring and sensitive lover, and she had surrendered herself completely to his ministrations. They had lain for a long time afterwards in each other's arms and talked. About themselves, about their lives, although Margaret had still avoided the subject of the other Michael in her past. But he had not pressed her, and she had felt comfortable and relaxed with him, until she drifted off to sleep, aware as she did so of the myriad tiny kisses with which he was peppering her face and neck and breasts.

The difference a few short hours can make. Awakened from

a deep sleep by their early alarm, she had been awkward and embarrassed with him. It was extraordinary how the day could cast such a different light upon events. Michael, on the other hand, had been attentive and affectionate, and if he was aware of her awkwardness, gave no sign of it.

Now, as their plane circled to land at Beijing Capital Airport after the seventy-minute flight, the embarrassment was passing, and in its place Margaret felt a growing apprehension. For thirty-six hours she had escaped from her life, had been able to pretend she was another person in another place. Now reality was racing up to meet her at several hundred miles an hour. She heard the squeal of tyres and the heavy jolt and swing of their China Northern aircraft as it touched down clumsily on the tarmac. Thoughts of Li, of the four murders and the continuing investigation, flooded back, and she wondered if she could achieve a less bumpy landing in life.

All hopes of a smooth transition, however, were quickly swept away as Margaret and Michael passed into the arrivals hall and saw Sophie's anxious face scanning the crowds. Instinctively, Margaret withdrew her hand from Michael's, like a schoolgirl caught in an indiscretion. Michael smiled. 'Ashamed to be seen with me?'

Margaret was annoyed with herself. 'Of course,' she said. 'What self-respecting girl wouldn't be?'

Sophie caught sight of them and pushed her way through the crowds. Her face was flushed. 'I've got a car waiting for you,' she said to Margaret. She flicked a look at Michael. 'There have been developments.' And she steered Margaret a discreet distance away and lowered her voice. 'Your friend Deputy Section Chief Li now seems to think that Yuan Tao committed the first three murders.'

'What?' Margaret was caught completely off balance. And as she recovered a little, she said, 'I suppose they think he cut his own head off.'

'I doubt it very much,' Sophie said with a tone. 'The point is, an American citizen now stands accused of the murder of three Chinese nationals.'

'He must be shaking in his grave,' Margaret said. 'What do you want *me* to do about it?'

'The Chinese police have set up a briefing meeting at Municipal Headquarters in . . .' she checked her watch, 'forty-five minutes. We can't afford to hang around.'

'You can give me one minute,' Margaret said, and she headed back towards Michael.

He was engaged in conversation on his mobile phone and looking at his watch. 'Yeah, OK, Charles, I should be on location by ten thirty at the latest . . .' He saw Margaret approaching. 'Hang on,' he said and put his hand over the receiver.

'Michael, I'm sorry, I've got to go straight to a police briefing. I won't be able to make it out to location after all.'

He shrugged and smiled ruefully. 'Can't be helped, I suppose.' He paused. 'What's happened?'

Margaret gasped her frustration. 'Apparently they seem to think that victim number four killed the other three.' He frowned. She laughed. 'Don't even think about it. Will you give me a call?'

'Tonight,' he said, and to her surprise he lowered his head and gave her a long, soft kiss. 'We must do that again sometime,' he said ambiguously.

She nodded, aware of Sophie's eyes watching them from somewhere behind her. 'Soon.'

In the car, Margaret found Sophie looking at her curiously. She turned to meet her gaze.

Sophie said, 'So you slept with him.' It was a statement, not a question.

'None of your business,' Margaret said.

Sophie shook her head ruefully. 'You lucky bitch. You know you'll be the envy of half the women in America? And to think I introduced you.'

'Well, you were right about one thing,' Margaret said.

'What's that?'

She grinned. 'He has got a great ass.'

II

Commissioner Hu Yisheng rose to shake Margaret's hand across his desk. The divisional head of CID was dressed formally in a dark green jacket with two gold stripes on the sleeves above gold cuff buttons, and a pale green shirt with dark blue tie. The Ministry of Public Security police badge at the top of his left sleeve seemed disproportionately large, as did his head on a small body. But he was a handsome man for his age, she thought, with his dark-streaked grey hair swept back from a smooth, unlined forehead. His smile, however, was strained as he waved Margaret to a chair.

'I would like to offer, Dr Campbell, my sincere thanks for your most excellent work on behalf of the Chinese people,' he said stiffly.

Margaret was about to tell him the only reason she was here was because of her loyalty to the American people. But Sophie, sensing an imminent breach of etiquette, said quickly, 'Dr Campbell is more than happy to help, Commissioner.' Margaret could almost see the Commissioner wondering why she had not been able to say so for herself.

Jonathan Dakers was already there, as was Section Chief Chen Anming. There was a distinct chill in the air as he and Margaret were reacquainted. It was Chen, she recalled, who had first involved her in a Chinese police investigation back in June. He had asked her to perform an autopsy. A perfect example of the Chinese phenomenon of *guanxi* in action. He had presented her with a lavish gift while a pupil on a course in criminal investigation in Chicago, where she had been lecturing the previous year. A favour was owed, and he had called it in. But as that investigation had escalated beyond anything either of them could have imagined, she knew he had begun to regret involving her. Now it was clear from his manner that he did not want her anywhere near this new investigation. But the decision had not been his to make. She wondered if it was Chen who had ordered Li to stay away from her.

Sophie sat between Margaret and Chen, as if aware of the tension between them, and chatted animatedly to the

Section Chief while Dakers made desultory conversation with Commissioner Hu. Margaret sat like a lemon, wondering what she was doing here and how long she was going to give it before making an exit. But she was spared from having to take that decision by the arrival of Li.

He knocked and entered, a little flustered she thought. He was in uniform, as she had seen him the very first time they met. Pale green short-sleeved shirt over dark green trousers. His epaulettes bore the three gold stripes and three stars of a Class Three Senior Supervisor. His gold-braided cap sat square on his head, its peak casting his eyes in deep shadow. Seeing him like that made something in her stomach flip over, and her guilt returned to haunt her. He saluted the Commissioner, apologised for being late, removed his hat and drew in a chair. He opened the briefcase he had been carrying and took out some papers.

'Well,' Hu said, 'now that we are all here, why don't you brief us, Deputy Section Chief?'

Li cleared his throat awkwardly and glanced at Margaret. There was something utterly sad and disconcerting in his eyes. She wondered if she was imagining it, but she also felt she saw betrayal there. As if he knew that only a few hours ago she had been lying in another man's arms, sexually sated, all memories of Li wiped from her mind. And suddenly she felt utterly exposed, as if she was sitting there naked, on view to everyone in the room. She felt herself blush.

Li said, 'Following up on our investigations, I last night discovered a diary hidden under the floor of Yuan Tao's embassy apartment. The diary was that of Yuan's mother, and covered the period from May of 1966, when he left for the United States, until the death of his father in June of 1967.' He broke off to hand around several photocopied sheets. 'These are photocopies of the relevant passages from it. They detail the harassment of Yuan's parents by a group of his former classmates who comprised the six Red Guard members of the so-called Revolt-to-the-End Brigade. They were part of the then Red-Red-Red Faction which existed during the Cultural Revolution.' He paused and looked around. 'I should make it clear now that the first three victims were all members of the Revolt-to-the-End Brigade.'

This was news to Margaret, Sophie and Dakers, and the significance of it was not lost on them. 'We are having a translation made of the diary in its entirety,' Li said. And Margaret listened in fascinated and horrified silence as he then outlined the nature of the harassment as described in it, culminating in the final humiliation of Yuan's father in front of a jeering crowd at the No. 29 Middle School, and his death just a few hours later.

Li concluded, 'The sign hung around his father's neck, his name written upside down in red and scored through; the kneeling position and the blows to the back of his neck inflicted with a cane; even the enforced drinking of the ink – all of these can be seen as a template for the *modus operandi* used in the killings. For ink, read red wine. The administering of the drug flunitrazepam, through the medium of the wine, made it easy to place the victim in a kneeling position. The blow to the back of the neck, only this time with a sword, brought death through decapitation. All three victims had their names written upside down in red ink on white card hung around their necks.

'Remember, also, that decapitation was an ancient form of capital punishment in China. The killer almost certainly saw himself as an executioner, performing just retribution for crimes committed.'

Margaret said, 'But if you're right, then this wasn't justice. It was revenge.'

Li inclined his head slightly, indicating agreement. 'True,' he said. 'But what is capital punishment but society's collective revenge on those who commit crimes against it? And history is littered with individuals who have taken matters into their own hands when they feel that society has let them down.'

Margaret wondered if these were the thoughts of Uncle Yifu, carefully collected, and polished and preserved by his nephew to be trotted out on appropriate occasions. She said, 'It's an interesting theory, Deputy Section Chief. But aren't you rather flying in the face of conventional methods of Chinese police investigation?' She felt ice forming in sheets around her. 'I understood that only after the painstaking collection of evidence would you even start to form a picture of the crime and who had committed it. I mean, what evidence do you have that puts Yuan Tao at any of the other crime scenes?'

Li was unfazed. 'The particles of dark blue dust found in Yuan's apartment are an exact match for the particles found on the body of Yue Shi.'

'Are you suggesting Yue Shi was murdered in Yuan's apartment?'

'No.'

'Then there is no direct connection.'

'The wine, then,' Li said evenly. He was determined not to be rattled by her. 'The red wine found in Yuan's apartment was the same as the wine the other three had been drinking before being murdered.'

'But that still doesn't place Yuan at any of the other crime scenes, does it?'

'No,' Li conceded.

'And we know that Yuan was killed with the same weapon.'

'Are you suggesting,' asked Li with the hint of a sneer in his voice, 'that Yuan cut his own head off?'

Margaret laughed. 'Actually, I thought maybe that's what you were suggesting. Although I think he might have had trouble disposing of the murder weapon afterwards, don't you?' But her amusement was not shared by anyone else in the room.

Li said, 'You suggested yourself that he might have been murdered by someone who was a witness to the other killings.'

Margaret shook her head. 'That was before we had a motive. A witness would have had to be an accomplice. If, as you suggest, Yuan had gone on a spree of revenge killings, an accomplice would have had to share his sense of revenge. What other motive could he have had? And, then, what would have been his motive for murdering Yuan?'

'This is all very interesting, Margaret,' Dakers broke in.

'But we're not here to start picking over the evidence. This is a briefing meeting.'

'What?' Margaret almost snapped at him. 'So we're supposed to just sit here and accept what we're told without question?'

'Of course not,' Dakers said smoothly. 'We very much want to participate in the scrutiny of the evidence. Which is why we have asked our friends in the Ministry of Public Security if they would allow you the privilege of participating full time in the investigation – at least until Yuan Tao's involvement in it has been cleared up to everyone's satisfaction.' He had stopped addressing himself to Margaret and had turned towards Commissioner Hu. 'I know that the American ambassador has already broached this subject at a higher level.'

The colour rose slightly on the Commissioner's cheeks as he interlaced his hands on the desk in front of him. Margaret noticed that his knuckles were white. He did not like anyone going over his head. 'I understand this to be so,' he said. 'I spoke to the Minister myself less than thirty minutes ago. Your ambassador has already been informed of his decision to grant your request.'

For once, Margaret was speechless. She glanced at Li and saw that he was staring, stony-faced at the floor.

A burned-out sun in a pale sky reflected white off the dusty compound outside the redbrick building that housed CID headquarters. Margaret struggled to keep up with Li as he strode across the compound to where he had parked his Jeep in the shade of a line of trees.

'You knew about this, didn't you?' she said.

'Would it matter if I did?' he said without turning. 'The decision was not mine to take. And if it had, you know what it would have been.' He opened the driver's door and threw his briefcase inside.

'Well, of course,' she said. 'God forbid that you should need help. Or even ask for it if you did.'

Li turned on her, his face pale with anger. His eyes were shaded by the peak of his cap and she could not see them. 'I do not,' he said, 'appreciate having my inquiry called into question in front of my section chief and the divisional head of CID.'

'Ah!' Margaret threw her hands in the air. 'Of course. *Mianzi*. That's what all this is about, isn't't? Face. Or rather your loss of it in front of your boss. To hell with the evidence, let's not lose face! That it? How very Chinese of you.'

His fury was palpable, but he controlled his voice, albeit with difficulty. 'This *is* about the evidence,' he said. 'The most important piece of evidence we've come up with, and you just ... dismiss it.' He waved his hand dismissively towards the trees.

'I didn't dismiss anything.'

'Well, you made it perfectly clear that you don't believe Yuan Tao was responsible for the other murders.'

'Of course he is,' Margaret said. 'The diary provides us with the perfect motive. It's obvious he did it.' Li was stunned to silence. And she was on a roll. 'He had both motive and oppor-tunity. And the wine and the blue dust provide us with good circumstantial evidence. But the point I was making is that we don't have a single scrap of evidence actually tying him to any one of the crime scenes. And we need that.'

'We?' he asked.

'Well, whether we like it or not, it looks like you're stuck with me and I'm stuck with you until we put this one to bed.' She stumbled momentarily over her unfortunate choice of metaphor, then added quickly, 'So the sooner we find out whodunnit, the sooner we'll be out of each other's hair.'

'And the sooner you can get back to your archaeologist.' It was out before he could stop himself. He could have bitten his tongue off.

'Oh,' she said, 'so that's what all the hostility's about. My relationship with Michael.'

He became immediately defensive. 'Why should I care about your relationship with "Michael"? After all, it's strictly platonic. That's what you said, isn't it?'

Margaret struck back. 'And what was it *you* said? Platonic is how you describe your relationship with someone just before you sleep with them?'

He flinched, as he had done when she slapped him in the face after the autopsy. But this was no slap in the face. It was a knife in the heart, and she immediately regretted it. But there was nothing she could say now that would undo the damage. They stood glaring at each other in a tense silence until she could no longer bear to meet his eye and looked away towards the towering municipal police headquarters at the far side of the compound.

'It's a pity the AFIS didn't come up with a match for the fingerprint found at number two,' she said for something to say.

Li forced his mind back through the red mist of pain that filled it and tried to focus on what she had just said. 'What?'

'Your Automated Fingerprint Identification System. If it had matched that bloody fingerprint to Yuan, it would have placed him at one of the crime scenes.'

The red mist cleared as Li remembered the bloody fingerprint found on the edge of the desk in Bai Qiyu's office. He had forgotten all about it. Margaret clearly had not. But he did not understand her question. 'Why would the AFIS come up with a match for Yuan Tao when his fingerprints haven't been entered into it?'

'What?' Margaret was shocked. 'You mean you don't enter the prints of victims as well as criminals? That's standard practice in the States.'

In other circumstances Li might have been defensive. But his mind was racing. He said, 'The system's new. It's not fully operational yet.'

'So no one's crosschecked to see if there's a match?' He shook his head. She said, 'Well, don't you think someone should?'

'Hey, good to see you guys are getting right into it.' They turned to find Dakers and Sophie approaching across the compound. Beyond them, Li saw Chen getting into an unmarked Section One saloon car.

Dakers was all smiles and bonhomie. He addressed himself to Li. 'Just been going over the ground rules in there. I think we're gonna get along just fine. Anything you need, anything we can help you with, you just ask.' Li nodded curtly. Dakers touched Margaret's arm. 'Talk later,' he told her.

He and Sophie were about to turn away when Li said, 'Were any of your people in Yuan's embassy apartment before our forensics people got access?'

Dakers turned back. 'Sure,' he said. 'I checked it out myself.' He grinned. 'Just in case there was another body in there we didn't know about.' None of the others smiled.

'Nobody else?' Li asked.

Dakers shook his head, a little puzzled now. 'Nope. Just me.' He paused. 'Am I missing something here?'

'No,' Li said. And then, unexpectedly, 'Have you always had a beard?'

Dakers' hand went instinctively to his fine-cropped whiskers and he ran it through the bristles, surprised by the question. 'Sure have,' he said. 'Always had a heavy growth. Had to start shaving when I was fifteen. Brought me up in a nasty rash. So I couldn't wait to grow a beard. Soon as I finished school.' He paused again. 'Sure I'm not missing something?'

Li managed a smile of what he hoped was reassurance. 'Just curious.' But he was thinking that men who don't shave don't use aftershave. So it wasn't Dakers who had left his scent in Yuan's apartment.

Dakers gave him an odd look. 'OK,' he said. 'See ya.' And he and Sophie went off towards the embassy limo, parked in the shade with its large red *shi* character prominent on the registration plate.

'What was all that about?' Margaret asked. She watched carefully for his response. Li never asked questions for no reason. But he just shrugged. 'Nothing.' He reached into the Jeep for the police radio. 'I'd better get Yuan's prints entered into the AFIS.'

She watched him as he spoke rapidly in Chinese into the radio handset and a strange metallic voice crackled back at him. She wanted to touch him and tell him she was sorry. Not that she had slept with Michael, but that she had told him – or as good as told him. It was cruel and unfair, and the colour that had risen high on his cheekbones was still there. But she knew it was not something she could discuss with him. To admit his hurt would be to lose face. And that was something he would never do. He finished his call and turned to her. 'It seems Detective Wu was one step ahead of us. He's already asked for the prints to be crosschecked.'

'Well, at least one of your team's on the ball,' Margaret said.

He ignored her barb. 'But the result may be superfluous,' he said. 'It looks like we might have found the dealer who sold him the sword.'

III

Li's Jeep nosed its way along the narrow *hutong* of Xidamochang Jie running east off Qianmen. It was crowded along its length by pedestrians and cyclists, traders with barrows, lorries, boys delivering coal briquettes. Small restaurants spilled tables and chairs out into the street where men sat barbecuing meat and chicken over hot coals, the smell of it hanging in smoke that obscured the narrow strip of blue sky overhead. Women sat in groups on tiny stools, preparing dumplings or just chatting. Through an open doorway, Margaret saw a man stretched out on a plastic-covered divan, hands tucked behind his head, fast asleep. In another, a woman stood chopping vegetables on a wooden board with a huge cleaver. 'Where on earth are we going?' she asked Li.

'The Underground City.'

She frowned. 'What's that?'

'In the sixties,' he said, 'when Mao fell out with Stalin, he thought the Russians were going to drop atomic bombs on Beijing. So he encouraged the population to dig tunnels and shelters under the city. Over ten years, working in their spare time, and with whatever tools they had, the people dug hundreds of kilometres of tunnels and dozens of shelters. Below us right here, there are about thirty-two kilometres of tunnels running in all directions.' He snorted. 'But it's just as well the Russians didn't bomb us. The tunnels aren't nearly deep enough. They would have been worse than useless.'

'So why's it called the Underground City?'

'Because the Chinese people are very practical.' Li swerved to avoid a boy on a bicycle who careered out of a side street without looking. He blasted his horn. 'Since they had dug out all that space down there, they thought they might as well make use of it. So now there are shops and warehouses, even a one-hundred-bed hotel. The views are not very good, but it is cheap, and at least you get away from the traffic.' He blasted his horn again, this time at a delivery truck blocking the way. As he edged past it he said, 'The dealer in reproduction arte-facts that we want to speak to has a shop down there.'

A column of primary school children wearing royal-blue trousers and tunics with white shirts and red scarfs marched in ragged single file towards them. They shouted and waved, smiling at Margaret when they saw her in the Jeep. 'Hello,' they shouted. 'Pleased to see you.'

She waved back. 'An incredible number of these kids speak English,' she said. 'It was the same in Xi'an.' She had men-tioned Xi'an without thinking and wished immediately that she hadn't.

But Li appeared unconcerned. 'Children are being taught to speak English in all the schools,' he said. 'All over China. Soon they will speak three languages. The local dialect, which is the one they grow up with, then Mandarin, then English.'

They pulled up outside a white-tile building with a pas-sageway leading through to a school yard from which children were wandering in and out. At the west side of the building, adjoining an old single-storey block, stood a dusty doorway built in the traditional style, with pillars and crossbeams sup-porting a sloping green tiled roof. An ornately painted fascia was almost obscured by grime. Dozens of bicycles were parked against the wall on either side of it.

'This is it?' Margaret said as they climbed out of the Jeep. 'The entrance to the Underground City?'

Li shrugged. 'One of them. My uncle once told me there are about ninety entrances to this particular complex, some of them in shops, others in people's homes. They say there are many tunnels and entrances the authorities do not even know about.'

As they approached the entrance, Detective Sang stepped out to meet them. He rattled off something quickly in Chinese to Li, and then turned politely to Margaret. 'This way, please. You follow me.'

In a plain room with scarred, green-painted walls, a young man looked up briefly from his paper as Li, Sang and Margaret passed through from the street. There was nothing unusual about the sight of foreigners here. Up to five hundred of them a day paid to see the Underground City. A staircase with red handrails and paint peeling from the walls led down into the tunnel complex below. The smell of damp, fetid air rose to greet them, and Margaret felt the cold, clammy touch of it on her skin and in her clothes. The tunnels were arched and stippled with white plaster stained by dirt and damp. Fluorescent tubes hung at intervals from a single electric cable running the length of the ceiling. On a concrete ledge, the tools and paraphernalia of the workers who had dug the tunnels were laid out like exhibits in a museum: a broken-handled pickaxe, a knife with a wooden handle, a shovel, three tin mugs, a lunch box. They took a right turn, and in the distance, through several arched supports, they saw an illuminated red map of the tunnel complex beneath a green sign that read 'beijing air raidshel ter'. An incongruous group of Scandinavian tourists sat on hard seats listening to a lecture on the history of the complex given by a bored-looking Chinese guide.

Sang led them through the group and they turned left along a stretch of tunnel where the supports had been painted a fresh, bright red, and the walls were covered with hand-painted murals. Inset, below two spotlights, was a white bust of Mao Zedong set against a red background. Almost within touching distance, ironically, stood a Buddhist shrine. Marble statues of women riding lions lined the final stretch of tunnel leading to a huge, brightly lit emporium of tourist junk: everything from jade Buddhas and silk dressing gowns to scroll paintings and imitation Ming vases. Attendants raised hopeful eyes as they entered, and then lost interest immediately they saw Li's uniform. Red lanterns hung from a high arched roof above fluorescently lit glass display cabinets and rack upon rack of silkware.

The visitors passed a tunnel that led off into a dark, misty gloom, and Margaret shivered as she felt the cold breath of it billowing into the comparative warmth of the shop. She saw a sign with an arrow. In both Chinese and English it said, *To the Station.* But she had no desire to venture into the dark abandoned network of tunnels that ran on deep into the icy bowels of the city, and was relieved when Sang led them through a doorway into a long, narrow shop displaying all manner of reproduction artefacts in tiered glass cabinets. This was, she thought, an extraordinary place. Unless you had prior knowledge, you would have no inkling of its existence from the streets above.

A small, shiny, round-faced man with his hair scraped across his bald head from a parting above his ear, came forward to meet them. There was an exchange of Chinese, then Li turned to Margaret. 'Mr Ling tells us he speaks English.'

'Just little, just little,' Mr Ling said, beaming at Margaret. 'No get much practice.' He shrugged his shoulders in theatrical apology.

Li said, 'You told Detective Sang that you sold a bronze reproduction sword about three months ago to a man asking for a very specific kind of weapon.'

'Sure,' said Mr Ling. 'Usually we sell sword for ceremonial purpose, or maybe for *wu shu*. But this man, he want real bronze sword, like real artefact. Of course, I have no sword like this. But I tell him I can arrange have one made for him. Only, it ve-ery expensive, and it take time.'

'Did you ask him what he wanted the sword for?' Margaret asked.

'Sure, I ask,' said Mr Ling. 'He say sword for exhibition.'

'And he gave you exact measurements?' Li said.

'Sure. I don't remember exactly now, but Mistah Mao in Xi'an, he will still have mould.'

'Mr Mao?' Li asked.

'Mistah Mao Ming Fu of the Xi'an Craft Artistic Products Factory. He ve-ery clever man. He restore bronze chariot found with Terracotta Warrior.'

Li turned to Margaret and with a slight tone said, 'Of course, you will have seen the bronze chariots at Xi'an.'

'Of course,' Margaret said. She addressed herself to Mr Ling. 'What kind of measurements did he ask for?'

'Oh, you know. Length. I think one metre maybe for sword. Maybe little less. And he want handle some certain length. And wood. He want wood handle. And he want the weight just so.' He moved his hands up and down as if weighing an invisible sword. 'And, you know, this sword he want in style of Warring States period. Mistah Mao make ve-ery good job. He charge only one thousand yuan. Ve-ery good price.' He grinned. 'So I make a little on top.'

Li took a photograph of Yuan out of his breast pocket. 'Is this him?'

Mr Ling put on a pair of spectacles and peered at it. 'Sure, that him.' He nodded thoughtfully. 'You know, not every day someone order sword like that. But I also remember this man for two other reason.'

'Oh?' Li tucked the photograph back in his pocket. 'What were they?'

Mr Ling said, 'He Chinese man. OK. He have Beijing accent. OK. But he don't act like Chinese man. I don't know how describe. But he just not like Chinese man.'

'And the other reason?' Margaret asked.

Mr Ling's face lit up. 'Oh yeah. He recommend to me by my good friend. Ve-ery famous American archaeologist. Mistah Zimmerman.'

Sang stood at a discreet distance pretending not to listen, but heads in the street were turning, and a group of small children stood by the entrance to the schoolyard staring with gaping mouths as the *yangguizi* shouted at the policeman.

'It's just ridiculous.' Margaret's voice rose to a shrill pitch. 'How can you possibly figure Michael has *anything* to do with this?'

'Who said I did?' Li's calm was all the more infuriating. He walked off towards the Jeep, and Margaret followed like a dog snapping at his heels.

'Why else would you want to question him?'

'To eliminate him from our inquiry, of course.' He reached the driver's door and turned back. 'I mean, you must admit,' he said, 'it's a very strange coincidence that he just happened to know the victim. And not only did he know him, but he recommended a place where he could buy a sword, which in all probability will turn out to be the murder weapon.'

'It might be a coincidence,' Margaret came back at him. 'But there's nothing strange about it. Yuan worked at the embassy. Michael spent a lot of time there in the last six months. It's a small community. I mean, there's nothing more sinister about that than Michael knowing the professor of archaeology at Beijing University.'

Li frowned at her. 'Yue Shi? Zimmerman knew Professor Yue?'

Margaret could have kicked herself. All she had succeeded in doing was giving him more ammunition. 'Well, of course,' she said defensively. 'He's an archaeologist. China's his speciality. Yue Shi was a protégé of the archaeologist Hu Bo – the guy Michael's making his documentary about. I happen to know that he was deeply shocked by the professor's murder. It's not every day someone you know gets their head cut off.'

Li lit a cigarette as Margaret took a breather. He stared hard at the ground for a moment, gnawing reflectively on the inside of his cheek. Then he looked at her very directly. 'How come Zimmerman knew how Professor Yue was murdered?'

Margaret frowned. 'What do you mean?'

'I mean, how did he know the professor had been decapitated? Stuff like that doesn't make it into the papers here. Very few people know the details of how any of these people were murdered.'

Margaret raised her hands to the heavens in frustration. 'How the hell do I know? He knows lots of people at the university.' She stopped, steadied herself, took a deep breath. 'You're enjoying this, aren't you?' He cocked an eyebrow at her. 'And don't pretend you don't know what I'm talking about. You're jealous and angry and hurt, and here's a heaven-sent opportunity to get right back at me.'

Li took a long pull at his cigarette, his face impassive. 'I don't know what you think I have to be jealous of,' he said evenly. 'But even if I did, I'm smart enough not to let my personal feelings cloud my professional judgement.' He paused for effect. 'Unlike someone else I could mention.' She glared at him, seething inside, but knew that his position was unassailable. He pushed home his advantage. 'So why don't we just go and ask Mr Zimmerman all those questions that neither of us has the answers to?'

IV

A large brush in a clenched fist daubed red paint over the two characters representing Ding Ling, and as the camera pulled back, a young peasant appeared on the screen, clutching his pot of paint and scrambling down the ladders that leaned up against the huge stele. Chuck ruffled his white hair excitedly, never taking his eyes off the monitor. 'Of course, we covered the stone in clear plastic,' he said, as if anyone might believe the vandalism was real.

Margaret looked out from the open door of the truck and saw, at the far side of the stele pavilion, the camera and camera operator on a cherry picker at the end of a huge crane. The crane swung back from the pavilion and started slowly delivering the camera towards the ground. She glanced back at the screen and saw the shot pan away from the pavilion to the steps leading down to the square. Michael was already descending the stairway. He looked straight into the lens as it moved down with him.

'Already they had smashed the stone bridge leading to the square. Then they vandalised the proud stone tablet that had stood sentinel over the imperial burial chambers for centuries. And as the peasants gathered in the square were whipped up to a frenzy by the Red Guards, they were about to deliver the most devastating blow of all. An act that would haunt the young Red Guard leader for the rest of her life, as night after night the Emperor and his Empresses returned in her dreams to try to kill her with a sword.'

The camera stopped moving, and Michael walked out of shot.

'Cut,' Chuck shouted into his walkie-talkie. 'Brilliant!' He turned to Li and Margaret. 'When we pick up the reverse of that we'll be following him down into the square. Of course, by then, there'll be about fifteen hundred extras there baying for blood.'

'What happened?' Li asked. 'I mean, in reality.'

'Didn't they teach you in school?' Margaret said. 'Surprise, surprise. I don't suppose the Cultural Revolution was on the curriculum.'

Li said, 'When I was as school, the Cultural Revolution *was* the curriculum.'

There was a moment of stand-off between them, and Chuck leaped in quickly. 'They smashed up the skeletons of the Emperor and the two Empresses,' he said and nervously lit a cigarette.

'Then they made a big bonfire,' said Margaret, never taking her eyes off Li, 'of all the royal remains.'

Chuck said, 'Then it started to rain and everything got washed away in the mud. Lost for ever.' He sighed. 'We're going to have to simulate that rain later today. Not the best of weather for it.' He nodded towards the door and the palest of clear blue skies outside. The mountains beyond shimmered in the heat.

'You seem to know a lot about it,' Li said to Margaret. 'And I *know* the Cultural Revolution wasn't on the curriculum at your school.'

'Michael told me,' she said. 'He knows more about it than most Chinese.'

Li bristled.

Chuck was uneasy with the tension between the visitors to his control truck. 'Listen, you guys,' he said. 'You want to talk to Mike, I can give you about twenty minutes while we're setting up the next shot.'

To Li's annoyance, Michael stooped to give Margaret a quick kiss before reaching out his arm to shake Li's hand. Li felt his face colour. Margaret, too, was embarrassed by this show of affection in front of Li. Only Michael seemed oblivious. And, again, as he had been at Beijing West Railway Station, Li was aware of something curiously familiar about Michael, something he couldn't quite identify.

'Hey, guys,' Michael said. 'Great you could make it. I didn't think you were going to manage out, Margaret.' He seemed genuinely pleased to see them.

'No, neither did I,' she said self-consciously.

Michael caught her look and paused. 'Something wrong?' He glanced from one to the other.

'Why don't we take a walk,' Li said, and the three of them headed away around the curve of the wall in the dappled shade of the spruce trees that climbed all around them. The sound of crew shouting to each other as they set up the next shot, and ADs marshalling the hundreds of extras waiting patiently in the square below, faded into the distance. Instead, the sound of birdsong and small creatures scuttling through the undergrowth came into earshot, and beyond there was a strange silence hanging in the haze that shimmered across the valley in the lee of Dayu Hill.

'What's this all about?' Michael asked Margaret.

She raised her hands in her own defence. 'I'm sorry, Michael,' she said. 'This is not my idea.'

Li flicked her a look of annoyance. Then he turned to Michael. 'We understand that you were acquainted with a Mr Yuan Tao who worked in the visa department of the United States Embassy, as well as a Professor Yue Shi of the archaeology department at Beijing University.'

Margaret saw the skin darken behind the tan on Michael's face, and then felt the full force of hurt and accusation in his eyes as he looked at her, like a dog whose trusted master has just kicked it. He turned back to Li. 'That's correct,' he said. 'In fact I knew Professor Yue quite well. Though Mr Yuan barely at all.'

Li said, 'Well enough to advise him on where to purchase a reproduction sword.'

'Only because he asked. Which is the one time I ever had any contact with him. Someone at the embassy recommended me to him. So he sought me out, and I pointed him in the direction of a dealer in the Underground City. But that was months ago. I haven't even seen him since.'

'So you have no idea if he was successful in finding the sword he was looking for?'

Michael shook his head. 'No.'

'But you are aware that his is one of the murders we are investigating?'

He sighed. 'Yes, I am.'

'How do you know?'

This time Michael looked at Margaret again. 'Sophie told me,' he said.

'And Sophie is . . . ?' Li asked.

Margaret said, 'Sophie Daum. She's the assistant RSO at the embassy. You met her this morning.'

'Oh. Yes,' Li said.

The walkie-talkie on Michael's belt crackled. A voice said, 'Michael, are you there?'

Michael raised it to his face. 'Yeah, Dave.'

'That's your make-up call.'

'OK. Be there in a minute.' He clipped it back on his belt. 'Is there anything else?'

'Yes,' Li said. But he took his time in asking. 'Are you aware how Professor Yue was murdered?'

'Yes,' Michael said. His expression now was resentful, and he was volunteering no more than he was asked.

Li remained impassive. 'Well, would you like to tell me?'

'He was decapitated.'

'How do you know this?'

'Jesus,' Michael said, his exasperation finally getting the better of him. 'Everyone in the department knew what had happened to him. Apparently the place was crawling with cops for days. It was common knowledge.' He paused and looked at Margaret. 'Besides, I saw the photographs.'

Li was startled. 'What photographs?' And Margaret blushed to the roots of her hair.

'The photographs that Margaret took to Xi'an with her.'

Li turned an icy stare on Margaret, and clenched his jaw.

She couldn't meet his eye. He said to Michael, 'Can you tell me where you were and what you were doing the night Yuan Tao was murdered?'

'Oh, for God's sake, Li—' Margaret wheeled on him, patience at breaking point.

But Michael interrupted, 'Why don't you ask Margaret?' he said.

Margaret was momentarily perplexed, and then with a huge sense of relief, realisation dawned. 'The pre-production party at the ambassador's residence,' she said.

'As I recall you left about ten,' Michael said. 'The party went on until about eleven thirty, and then a bunch of us went on to the Mexican Wave bar in Dongdaqiao Lu. It must have been about two when we left.' He turned his focus briefly on Li. 'Frankly, I resent these questions, Detective.' Then he turned back to Margaret. 'And I'm disappointed that you should even think that I could have any connection with this.'

'I don't,' Margaret said flatly. She turned to Li. 'I think we should go.'

Michael's walkie-talkie crackled again. 'Michael?' The voice was insistent.

'On my way,' he said, and with a curt nod he headed back along the top of the wall.

Li and Margaret stood for a long time saying nothing, before finally Margaret turned away to lean on the crenellation and stare out bleakly over the sun-scorched valley.

'You let him see confidential photographic evidence?' Li's

voice was very level, but there was no mistaking the anger in it.

She closed her eyes and gritted her teeth. She was in the wrong and knew it. 'I didn't mean to.'

'Oh, I see,' Li said. 'You just happened to show him the photographs by accident?'

'Actually, yes.' She spun to face him. 'I'd been going through all the evidence in my hotel room. The stuff was spread all over the bed. You might remember, I phoned you. You more or less told me to fuck off.' Li did remember. He had spent several hours regretting it afterwards. She said. 'Michael came to fetch me. We were going to dinner. I'd dropped some stuff on the floor and he helped me pick it up. That's when he saw the photograph. And he was pretty shaken up by it.'

'Not enough to spoil your night out, though.'

It took a great effort of will to stop herself from slapping him again. 'You bastard,' she said. 'All that stuff about not letting personal matters cloud professional judgement? Crap. You kicked me off like an old goddamn shoe. OK, I've had to accept that. But you can't stand to see me with anyone else, can you?' She glared at him. 'Well, congratulations. You've probably just ruined my relationship with Michael. And for what? To confirm what we both always knew. That he has absolutely no involvement in this whatsoever.' And she turned on her heel and marched angrily away.

He stood for a moment, reeling from the force of her tirade. Of course, he knew she was right. Zimmerman's connection to the killings was tenuous at best. And Li wondered exactly why he had wanted to come out here and press those questions about Yuan and Professor Yue. Was he really letting jealousy cloud his judgement?

Margaret was halfway across the square, pushing her way through the mass of extras, before he caught up with her. He fell into step beside her, and they crossed the little stone bridge that the Red Guards had smashed thirty-four years earlier.

'So what now?' he said.

It was a long time before she responded. Finally she said, 'I think it's probably about time we talked to those people with a motive for wanting to kill Yuan Tao.'

'And who would that be?'

She stopped, and he was a couple of paces past her before he realised it, and could turn back. 'Who do you think?' she asked contemptuously.

She clearly was not going to share her thoughts with him, and he realised that he had not given it any serious consideration. The discovery of the diary, tracing the vendor of the weapon, the connection with Zimmerman, had all distracted him from focusing on the question that the diary itself had thrown into sharp focus by revealing Yuan as the killer of the other three. Who had a motive for killing Yuan? And even as the thought formed, the answer seemed obvious. 'The remaining members of the Revolt-to-the-End Brigade.'

'Congratulations,' said Margaret. 'You have just won a sunshine holiday for two in Florida.' And she marched off down the paved and cobbled walkway.

Li hurried after her. 'But how would they have known about the other three being murdered?'

Margaret breathed her exasperation. 'Oh, for heaven's sake, don't give me that stuff about murders not appearing in the papers. You and I both know just how efficient the Chinese grapevine is. There's no way those three didn't know about their old Red Guard pals getting whacked. And it wouldn't take too much intelligence to work out who was next.'

V

Margaret sat staring at the computer screen, aware of the eyes that flickered in her direction in constant curiosity. Most of the girls in the computer room had probably never seen a *yangguizi* this close up before. And here was a particularly good example of the species. Fair, curling hair, startling blue eyes, pale freckled skin. There was a strange hush in the room, broken only by the soft chatter of keyboards and the occasional giggle.

Li was upstairs somewhere taking a meeting of his detectives. Full co-operation, it seemed, stopped short of admitting her to the holy sanctum of the inner circle. But since virtually none of the detectives spoke any English, Margaret was not inclined to push the point. She had asked instead for the use of a computer with access to the Internet.

Li's attitude towards her since their return from Ding Ling had been cool and formal. But there had been the faintest tinge of a smile in his expression when he took her to the computer room and asked one of the girls to vacate a computer for her use. It had not taken her long to find out why. Every pull-down menu was in Chinese, an incomprehensible collection of character pictograms that left her struggling to find her way about a computer screen that was otherwise very familiar. Finally she had found the Internet Explorer icon, clicked on it with her mouse, and found herself dumped on to the home page of an equally impenetrable Chinese server. She clicked on the Stop symbol to prevent the computer downloading more Chinese, and typed in *www.altavista.com*, and was quickly transported to the comfortingly familiar territory of the main page of the Alta Vista search engine. She typed in *tameshi giri*. Less than half a minute later, the search for references on the Internet to Tameshi Giri threw up more than twenty thousand Web pages, links to the first ten of which came up on the screen.

She shook her head. It would take her hours to sift through. She thought for a moment, and then clicked in the *New Search* box and typed in *Yuan Tao*. Her request was fired off across the ether, through a mind-boggling inter-connection of telephone lines and computers around the world, returning a few seconds later with a response. To her astonishment and dismay there were links to nearly one hundred and sixty thousand Web pages. She scanned the first ten which came up on the screen. The *yuan* and *tao* all seemed to be reversed. There was a link to a place called Tao Yuan in Taiwan, another to a Web page at an American university, several more to pages on an ancient Chinese poet called Tao Yuan-ming. But, then, at the head of the list, the best and only exact match for her query: *Yuan Tao*. It was a link through to a news-sheet on Japanese martial sword arts.

'Yes!' she said out loud, as her mood swung immediately from despair to elation. And she was aware of half a dozen heads turning towards her. She smiled, embarrassed, around the quizzical and astonished faces, then turned her concentration quickly back to the screen. She clicked on the link, and her computer whirred and chattered as it downloaded the contents of the *North California Review of Japanese Sword Arts*. Somewhere in here was a reference to Yuan Tao. She scrolled down the pages, through adverts for genuine Japanese cutting swords, an account of a Tameshi Giri competition in Kyoto, Japan, during Shogatsu in 1997, the list of winners at the 34th Annual Vancouver Kendo Taikai . . . Margaret stopped scrolling and backed up. There it was. *Yuan Tao*. Joint second place in the category Forty-one Years and Over. At the foot of the list were brief biographies of the winners.

Yuan Tao, according to his notes, had joined a San Francisco-based Kendo club affiliated to the Pacific North West Kendo Federation in 1995, later switching membership to a club in Washington DC. He had taken part in several competitions, achieving extraordinary results in a very short period. One judge at a competition had described him as 'the most focused competitor I have seen in a very long time'.

Margaret sat back and wondered what Yuan had been focused on. Had it been his role as executioner of the Red Guards who had driven his father to a premature death?

And what images had he held in his mind as he practised his Tameshi Giri on those rolled up bundles of straw? She shook her head in wonder at the extraordinary lengths he had gone to in order to exact revenge for his father's murder – for that's clearly how he saw it. He had planned it coldly, meticulously, practising the means of execution until he had achieved a high degree of expertise, changing the course of his life, following a new career plan that would bring him back, in anonymity, to the Old Country and his old home town. Revenge, she had always heard it said, was a dish best served cold. Yuan Tao had placed his carefully in the freezer and brought it halfway around the world to dish it out with chilling effect.

But that revenge had been cut suddenly, and unexpectedly, short. Someone had done to Yuan as he had been intent on doing to others. Someone who knew in exact detail how Yuan had dispatched his first three victims. Could it really have been one of the remaining three Red Guards? Certainly, they would have had the motive. But how could any of them possibly have known the details of Yuan's *modus operandi* well enough to have replicated the murders so precisely? She had glibly thrown at Li the idea of Yuan being murdered by one of his intended victims, but wondered now just how well it would stand up to detailed scrutiny.

'Are you finished?' Li's voice startled her out of her reverie.

She turned to find him standing in the doorway. 'Just a moment,' she said, and she selected Print, and crossed the room to the printer as it spewed out two copies of the half-dozen pages of the *North California Review of Japanese Sword Arts*.

Li appeared beside her. 'What's this?'

'Report on a sword arts competition in Vancouver two years ago. Yuan Tao came second in his category. Apparently he took up the practice of the Japanese sword art of Kendo shortly after he got his mother's diary in 1995. Seems he was pretty good at it by the time he got here.' She handed the copies to Li. 'Not much doubt now about Yuan being our man.'

'None,' Li said. 'That bloody fingerprint in Bai Qiyu's office? It was Yuan's.'

Margaret clicked her tongue. 'That's it, then. We've got motive, opportunity, a whole bunch of circumstantial evidence – the blue dust, the wine, the sword expertise – and now evidence that puts him at one of the crime scenes. Enough to get a conviction in any court.'

'Except that someone beat us to it and took the law into their own hands. Here,' he handed her a loose and weighty folder and turned towards the door.

She headed after him, struggling not to spill its paper content all over the floor. 'What's this?'

He strode off down the corridor. 'All the latest updates for your records,' he called over his shoulder. 'Transcripts of all the interviews we conducted with teachers and former pupils of Yuan's old school, a translation of the diary, profiles on the remaining Red Guards . . .'

'Could you not just have had these sent over to the embassy?'

Li turned at the top of the stairs and there was something in his smugness that infuriated her. 'I wanted to deliver them personally into your hands, so no one can ever accuse me of failing to keep you fully informed.' He started off down the stairs.

'Where are you going?' A bunch of papers slipped from the folder and fluttered down the steps in his wake. But he didn't turn.

'We.' His voice reverberated around the stairwell.

'We what?' she gasped in frustration as she tried to retrieve the dropped sheets.

'Where are *we* going.' His voice rose up to her as he started on the next flight down.

She picked up the last of the papers and ran after him. 'OK, where are *we* going?' She caught up with him at the foot of the stairs, the file clutched to her bosom, arms wrapped around it. She was breathing hard.

He stopped and tucked a copy of the computer print-out into the top of the folder. 'To see Pauper,' he said.

'Who's Pauper?'

But he seemed lost in thought for a moment before tentatively meeting her eye. 'You might as well know, I did a check on Michael Zimmerman's whereabouts during the first three murders.'

'Jesus Christ!' Margaret exploded.

Li said, 'Chinese police work requires meticulous attention to detail, Dr Campbell.' He paused, but before she could tell him what she thought of his Chinese police work, he added, 'You'll be pleased to know he wasn't even in the country when the first two murders took place.'

And he went out into the glare of afternoon sunshine. She

caught up with him again at the Jeep. The few moments it took allowed her temper to cool just a little, enough at least for good sense to prevail. There was no point in pursuing it. It was over. 'So, who's Pauper?' she asked again.

'One of the Red Guards.' He opened the driver's door and got in behind the wheel, then watched as she struggled to keep her folder intact and open the passenger door at the same time.

'Don't help or anything,' she said as she finally slipped into the passenger seat and unloaded the files on to the floor behind her. 'So you think this Pauper person's a potential suspect?'

He shook his head. 'Not a chance.'

'Why not?'

'She's blind.'

CHAPTER NINE

I

Pauper's *hutong* meandered through a quiet maze of traditional *siheyuan* courtyard homes in a leafy area north of Behai Park. Li parked at the end of the lane, and they walked along the narrow alleyway between high crumbling brick walls, past a trishaw with a single bed strapped to the back of it. Stout wooden gates, left and right, opened on to secluded courtyards where as many as four families shared living space on each side of the square. Through the dark openings, Margaret could see bicycles and pot plants, brushes and buckets, and all manner of the accumulated junk of *siheyuan* life.

Ahead of them, a large crowd of tourists wearing silly baseball hats was gathered around a Chinese tour guide with a red flag and a battery-operated megaphone at his mouth. In a strange metallic monotone, the guide was pointing out the features associated with the *siheyuan*. 'This *traditional* black tile roof,' he said, then repeated for emphasis, '*traditional* black tile roof. In ancient times, black tiles for *ordinary* people, for *ordinary* people.' And using his rolled up flag on a stick as a pointer, he jabbed at a square brown box mounted on the wall at the top right of the doorway. A thick black cable fed in and out of it. 'Another traditional feature of *siheyuan*,' he said. 'Traditional feature of *siheyuan*. This box for cable TV.' And he giggled at his joke. 'For cable TV. We have fifteen channel of cable TV going into traditional *siheyuan*.'

Li and Margaret drew a few curious glances from bored-looking tourists as they passed the group and Margaret heard a middle-aged American lady whisper to her companion, 'Why does he have to repeat everything? I just don't know why he has to repeat everything.'

After another twenty yards, beyond a small shop window displaying cigarettes and soft drinks, they turned into an open doorway, stepping over a wooden barrier and then down steps into Pauper's courtyard. Round coal briquettes were stacked three deep and two metres high against one wall. An old broken chair lay at an odd angle on the stairs. Bicycles rested one against the other. Potted plants bloomed on every available space. Two canaries sang in a bamboo cage hung from a shady tree that seemed to grow out of a crack in the slabs. The atmosphere was curiously still and restful. The city seemed to have melted away into some unpleasant dream somewhere just beyond reach. Margaret saw inquisitive faces peering out of windows and doors at the far side of the courtyard. Li saw them, too. 'I'm looking for Blind Pauper,' he called. A woman pointed at a door to their left. It was lying open. Li turned to Margaret. 'This way.'

They passed another door to a tiny cluttered kitchen with

a two-ring gas stove and a charred extractor. A microwave sat incongruously on a melamine cabinet opposite an old white porcelain tub and an electric water heater.

Li paused at the door to the apartment and was about to knock when a woman's voice called, 'Who's looking for Blind Pauper?'

'Police,' Li said, and Margaret followed him in.

Pauper was sitting knitting on a two-seater settee opposite a television set mounted on a white-painted wall unit. There was a small table with an ashtray on it, a bookcase, an electric fan. Through a glass-panelled door they could see into her tiny bedroom, bare and cell-like with a single bed. Everything was neatly arranged, fastidiously clean. There were, Margaret noticed, no pictures on the walls.

'Who's the woman?' Pauper said. She was a shrunken old lady with silver hair tied back in a bun. She wore a traditional blue Mao suit and small black slippers on her tiny feet. Margaret would have taken her for seventy, before realising with a shock that she must be the same age as the others. Only fifty-one. Her round, black-lensed spectacles gave her a faintly sinister air.

'How do you know there's a woman with me?' Li asked.

'I can smell her.' Pauper's lips curled in an expression of distaste. 'Wearing some cheap Western perfume.'

'She's an American.'

'Ah! *Yangguizi!*' Pauper spat out the word like a gob of phlegm.

'I take it you don't speak English,' Li said.

'Why should you think that?' Pauper said in perfect English, startling Margaret with the sudden change of language, and the vitriol in her tone. 'You think I am stupid because I come from a poor family and didn't do well at school?'

'No,' Li said evenly. 'But I know that not many schools taught English in the sixties.'

'I learned English to read braille. There is not enough of it in Chinese to feed a mind without eyes.' She paused. 'You have come about the murders?'

'Yes,' Li said. He slipped a book out of the bookcase and started leafing through it, running his fingers over the raised patterns of dots that could be 'read' like words. 'What do you know about them?'

'Please do not touch my books.' she said. 'They are very precious to me.' Li was startled, and peered at her closely, as if believing for a moment that she could actually see. 'I can hear you,' she said as if she could read what was in his mind. 'You may be a policeman, but it doesn't give you the right to touch my stuff. Who is the American?'

'I'm a pathologist,' Margaret said. 'I am helping with the investigation.'

'Since when did the Chinese need help from the Americans?' Pauper's disgust was patent.

'We don't need their help,' Li said. 'But one of the victims was an American.'

Pauper frowned. 'An American?' She was clearly caught off balance. 'I only know about Monkey and Zero and Pigsy. What American?'

'A Chinese-American,' Li said. 'He was born here. You went to school with him. His name was Yuan Tao.'

What little colour there was drained from Pauper's face. 'In the name of the sky,' she said. 'Cat!' And there was a sudden dawning in her expression. She put a hand to her mouth. '*He* killed them. We knew it was someone out to get us. One by one. But Cat,' she said again in wonder. 'I never would have thought him capable of it.'

'Who's we?' Li asked her.

'Birdie and me. The only ones left.'

'What about Tortoise? We haven't been able to track him down.'

'You'd have to go to hell to find him,' she said. 'He's been dead more than ten years now. A stupid boy. He was simple, you know. He went down to Tiananmen Square the first night of the trouble, to see what it was all about, and got himself squashed by a tank.' She was struck by another thought. 'But, then, who killed Cat?'

'We thought you might be able to tell us.'

'Me?' Pauper laughed a humourless laugh, and then she pursed her lips and her eyes wrinkled shrewdly. 'You think it was one of us.' And she laughed again. 'Maybe you think I killed him.'

'What about Birdie?'

'Birdie?' she chortled, and chuckled to herself, unable to contain her mirth. 'Birdie? Are you serious? Have you spoken to him?'

'Not yet.'

'Birdie couldn't kill anyone. He's a pathetic, harmless old man.'

'I thought he was the leader of the Revolt-to-the-End Brigade,' Li said. 'The one who led the attack on the teachers, the one who ordered the school gate destroyed.'

'That was a long time ago,' Pauper said. 'More than thirty years. He was brave and strong and I thought the world of him then. But when the Red-Red-Red Faction split, they turned on him. You've heard the old saying that the wheel of fate turns every sixty years. Well, it turned on poor old Birdie. They beat him and kept him in a room for nearly two years, making him write self-criticisms and dragging him out for struggle sessions. They killed all his birds and finally sent him to Inner Mongolia to labour, building frontier defences. I met him again a few years later, and he was a changed man.' She laughed, but it was a sour laugh, filled with bitterness. 'Of course, I was a changed woman by then, too. I had lost my eyes.'

'How did that happen?' Margaret asked.

Pauper swivelled her head in Margaret's direction and sniffed as if making some olfactory assessment. 'They thought I was stupid at school,' she said eventually. 'Because I could not see right. I kept telling them I had headaches, but they thought I was just malingering. I told them I had a black cloud in my eyes, that I could not see the blackboard any more.' She shook her head. 'It was another two years before my father took me to the hospital. But not before I had collapsed. They said I had a tumour in my right eye and that it was malignant and they would have to take the eye away.' The sour laugh again, lips stretched over yellow teeth. 'They believed me then.' She snapped her mouth shut and Margaret saw her lower lip tremble. 'All I could think was how ugly I would look without an eye. But they said they could give me a glass one and no one would know the difference.'

'Were you still in the Revolt-to-the-End Brigade then?' Li asked.

'No. Birdie had been arrested and we had broken up and gone our separate ways.'

'So what happened to your other eye?' Margaret was curious.

Pauper turned a sneer on her. 'You're a doctor, can't you guess?'

'Not my speciality,' Margaret said.

'Hah,' Pauper said. 'Doctors! What do they know?' Her tiny hands clutched her knitting tightly. 'After about six months the headaches came back. At first I thought it was the glass eye, because it was not so bad when I took it out. But it kept getting worse and the doctors said I had a tumour in the other eye. It would have to go, too, they said. But my father wouldn't let them. I wasn't even twenty years old, he said. What had I seen? Of life, of my country.' Again, her lower lip trembled, and Margaret believed if she had had eyes, tears would have spilled from them.

'My father was a packer in a factory,' Pauper said. 'My mother was dead. We were very poor. But he borrowed money from the other workers. Six hundred yuan. It was a lot of cash in those days. He told the doctors they could have my other eye in two months. But first I was going to see my country.

We took the train and went to Xi'an and Chongqing, and then down the Yangtse to Nanjing and Shanghai. And then he took me to his home town of Qingdao, where I had been born. He took me to the top of a hill above the town so that I could look down on it and see the sun rise in the east across the Yellow Sea. But the sea wasn't yellow. It was red. The colour of blood, and Chongqing looked like it was on fire. I'll never forget it. I can still see it now, in my mind's eye. I can never see it again any other way.'

She took a moment or two to steady her breathing, and Margaret saw her grip on her knitting relax just a little. 'By the time we were on the train home, everything was milky and blurred, like a mist had come down. And then they took my other eye, and I had to learn to "see" in other ways. With my ears and my nose and my fingers. Sometimes I think I can see things better without my eyes.' She waved a hand towards the other side of the room. 'That is why I have a television. I see with my ears, and make pictures in my head. I can tell from a voice the expression on a face. I don't need my eyes any more.'

They sat in silence for what seemed like a very long time. Then Li said, 'How did you get your nickname?'

'Pauper?' The bitterness was back in her laugh again. 'How do you think? My father could barely afford to clothe me. My mother was dead and he was no good at patching things, so all my clothes were worn and torn and badly patched. Other kids were poor, too. But they didn't look it. They called me Pauper to make fun of me, and it stuck. All my life. Only, now, I'm Blind Pauper. Poor *and* blind.'

Li scratched his chin thoughtfully. 'Have you ever heard the nickname, Digger?'

She frowned. 'Digger? No, I have never heard that name. Who is Digger?'

'We thought it might have been Yuan Tao.'

'Cat? No. He has always been Cat. Scaredy Cat.' Her lip curled into its habitual sneer. 'I am glad someone killed him. What right did he have to a better life than us? What right did he have to revenge?'

They heard a familiar metallic voice buzzing through a megaphone. 'This traditional *siheyuan* courtyard. *Siheyuan* courtyard. In ancient time only *one* family live here. Only *one* family. Now there are *four* family. *Four* family.'

Pauper put her knitting aside and got stiffly to her feet. 'How else does a blind person make a living these days?' she said. 'They bring tourists to my house to see the curiosity, how an old blind Chinese lady lives. They pay me more money than my father earned in his factory. And at least I am spared from having to look at them.'

Li and Margaret moved to the door. Li said, 'Do you see Birdie often?'

'I have not seen Birdie since they took my eyes,' Pauper said. 'But he comes to visit me often and his birds sing to me, and chatter and make a wonderful noise.'

'And he knew about Monkey and Zero and Pigsy as well?'

'Of course. We spoke several times about which of us would be next.'

The megaphone arrived at the door. 'Only *six* people at a

time, please. *Six* at a time. This is traditional *siheyuan* home. *Ve-ery* small inside. *Ve-ery* small.' He glared at Li and Margaret.

Li said to Pauper, 'We have an address for Birdie in Dengshikou Street. Does he still live there?'

She nodded. 'But you won't find him there now. He has a stall at the Guanyuan bird market. That is where his life is. Where it has always been. With his birds.'

As Li and Margaret pushed out, the tour group was pushing in, chattering excitedly at the prurient prospect of invading an old lady's privacy.

II

Li manoeuvred his Jeep slowly west through the traffic. Beneath the sprinkling of shade cast by the trees, bicycles weaved precariously in and out of narrow lanes, overtaking tricycle carts, avoiding buses and taxis. The sidewalks were alive with activity in this busy shopping quarter, stalls piled high with fruit and vegetables and great baskets of chestnuts outside shops whose windows were crammed with computers and hi-fis and DVD players. In the hazy distance, they could see the flyover at the junction with the second ring road. Horns peeped and blasted, not so much in anger as frustration. Li leaned on his wheel, his mouth set in a grim line. Soon, he thought, Beijing would slip into permanent gridlock and bicycles would become fashionable again, not just as the fastest, but as the only way of getting around.

'Do you want to tell me about the nickname?' Margaret's

voice broke into his thoughts, and he immediately detected the hint of accusation in it.

'You'll read all about it in the statements we took at the school,' he said. And, in a voice laden with meaning, added, 'When you were in Xi'an.'

He heard her sigh, but kept his eyes on the traffic ahead. 'I'll probably get around to reading them sometime,' she said in that acid tone that was so familiar to him. 'Maybe next year, or the year after. But right now it might save time if you just told me.'

He shrugged. 'Like Pauper said, Yuan's nickname was Cat, not Digger.'

'And anyone who knew him at school would know that?'

He nodded. 'Which kind of punches a hole in your theory about his killer being one of the remaining Red Guards.' He turned to look at her, but she was frowning into the middle distance, lost in thought.

'It's looking less and less likely anyway,' she said. 'One of them's dead, the other's blind. That just leaves Birdie. And he would know Yuan's nickname. Unless . . .'

'What?'

'Unless he deliberately used another name to confuse the police.'

'I don't think so,' Li said.

'Why not?'

'You would have to be pretty smart to think of something like that. From all accounts Birdie would have trouble getting his IQ up to room temperature.'

'So why are we going to see him?' But before he could respond, she answered for herself. 'No, don't tell me, I know. "Because Chinese police work requires meticulous attention to detail."' She sighed again and looked at the traffic ahead of them. It was at a standstill. 'Chinese police work also requires great patience,' she said. 'Since it takes so goddamn long just to get from A to B.'

But Li's patience had already run out. He opened the window and slapped a flashing red light on the roof, flicked on his siren and squeezed across the line of on-coming traffic into a narrow lane. He pulled the Jeep in beside a railing and jumped out. 'Come on,' he said. 'We'll walk the rest. It's not far.'

A hundred yards down, the lane was crowded with people buying tropical fish from roadside vendors. Jars of exotic marine life were piled on stalls and carts, plastic trays filled with terrapins and tortoises laid out along the sidewalk. An old lady was selling goldfish in water-filled plastic bags hung from the handlebars of her bicycle. They passed a long, corrugated shed stacked from floor to ceiling with tanks full of brilliantly coloured fish fighting for space in green, bubbling water. Margaret had never seen so many fish. There was an ocean's worth. Whole shops were devoted to selling accessories – tanks, stands, lighting, feed. The shed and stalls and shops were jammed with customers. *Feng shui* was back in fashion. Fish were in. Business was good.

They turned west, leaving the fish market behind, past demolition work behind high hordings, then south again at

Chegongzhuang Subway Station. On South Xizhimen Street, on the sidewalk beyond the tree-lined cycle lane, they saw the first clutches of old men gathered around their birdcages. Bicycles parked by the hundred lined the sidewalk on either side of the entrance to the market. Men with birds of prey tethered to the handlebars of their bicycles showed off new, brilliantly coloured purchases in bamboo cages. Budgerigars, canaries, hawks, parakeets. The collective sound of ten thousand birds drowned out even the roar of traffic on the second ring road.

Li and Margaret turned under a red banner into a covered courtyard stacked high with thousands of cages filled with the most extraordinary dazzle of coloured birds. Yellow, green, vermilion, black with yellow flashes. Old men and young boys bargained noisily with loquacious venders selling everything from kittens and hamsters to grasshoppers caged in tiny bamboo mesh balls. A bald man in a blue shirt and grey waistcoat stood behind a counter laden with a hundred different tobaccos, fine-rolled, rough shredded, black, yellow, green. Great bundles of whole dried leaf hung from the wall behind him between racks of rough carved wooden pipes with curling stems. Margaret was wide-eyed. As with so many things in China, she had never seen anything like it before.

Li stopped at an antiques stall sandwiched between rows of hanging cages and had to raise his voice almost to a shout to ask an old woman where they could find Birdie. She pointed towards a stall at the bottom of the row but said, 'You won't find him there now. Only in the mornings. At this time of day he'll be in Purple Bamboo Park.'

It took them another half-hour to get to Purple Bamboo Park through late afternoon traffic that was gathering itself for the rush hour frenzy. Margaret recognised the entrance to the park, with its tiers of curling bamboo roofs, topiary elephants and incongruous European mannequins standing amidst a profusion of flowers. She had passed it daily, on the cycle from the Friendship Hotel to the People's University of Public Security when she first arrived in Beijing.

At the gate Li spoke to the ticket collector who knew Birdie well. He came every day, she said. Bicycles were not normally allowed in the park, but his tricycle was a carrier for the birdcages that he piled upon it, one tied to the other, or hung from the handlebars. The birds were his constant and only companions, so they let him in with his tricycle, and he wheeled it to a cool bamboo pavilion east of the lake where he practised *wu shu*.

Li and Margaret walked in silence through the gloomy green shade of the early evening, through thick groves of the purple bamboo that gave the park its name. Beyond the weeping willows at the far side of the lake the sky glowed pink as the day slipped slowly towards night. They turned off the main thoroughfare and followed a narrow path that curved up under leaning pine trees to an open pavilion overlooking a brackish brown pond. A dozen cages filled with chattering, singing birds, hung from a bamboo roof supported on stout, lacquered posts. Beneath it, a man in black pyjamas and canvas slippers brought his silver sword arcing through the gloom to pierce and slash the thick, warm evening air in the ancient Chinese sword art of *wu shu*. He was tall and gaunt, with thin wisps of fine dark hair, and a straggling beard that clung precariously to his sunken cheeks and swept to a point at the end of his chin.

Li and Margaret stopped for a moment, as yet unseen by the man in the pavilion, and watched as he took his sword through all its motions with a bold confidence that belied his appearance. Margaret flicked a glance at Li. Here was an echo of his Uncle Yifu, who had been practising sword strokes in Jade Lake Park when Li had first taken her to meet him. Li's face, however, gave nothing away.

The birds had betrayed their presence to their master, chatter increasing at the approach of strangers, and the swordsman stopped in mid-stroke and glanced towards them. He seemed alarmed, and Margaret saw fear in his black eyes. And although he relaxed a little as they approached the pavilion and he saw Li's uniform, gone was all the poise and confidence he had shown in his handling of the ornamental sword.

Li held up his Public Security ID. 'Police,' he said. 'You speak English?' Birdie shook his head. 'You know why we're here?' Birdie shook his head again. Li took the sword from him and examined it. It was a cheap, lightweight effort that concertinaed for ease of carrying. 'You seem pretty good with this thing. You get a lot of practice?'

Birdie nodded. 'Every day,' he said. 'It helps me relax.'

'Just for the record, do you want to tell me your full name?'

'Ge Yan,' Birdie said. 'But no one calls me that.'

'What do you know about what happened to Monkey and Zero and Pigsy?'

The colour drained from Birdie's face and he sat down on the narrow bench that ran between the lacquered posts.

'I don't suppose he speaks English?' Margaret interrupted impatiently.

Li flicked her a look. 'I'm afraid not.' And with a tone, 'What a pity you don't speak Chinese.'

She deserved that, she realised, and backed off to the edge of the pavilion to watch from a distance. Birdie cast a nervous eye in her direction.

'Never mind her,' Li said. 'Answer the question.'

Birdie's eyes darted back towards Li. 'They were murdered,' he said, almost in a whisper, as if afraid to say it out loud.

'Do you know who by?'

He shook his head. 'But we are next.'

'Who are next?'

'Me and Pauper.'

'How do you know that?'

'Pauper said that someone is trying to kill us all. All of us who were in the Revolt-to-the-End Brigade.'

'And why would someone want to do that?'

'I don't know.'

Li paused to think for a moment. He was still holding Birdie's sword. He retracted the blade and threw it to him.

'Here.' Birdie caught it adeptly with his left hand. Li glanced at Margaret. She had not missed the significance. 'Left-handed,' Li said.

Birdie shrugged. 'So what?'

'No reason.' Li lit a cigarette and watched the blue smoke curl slowly up in the still evening air. The light was beginning to fade.

'What has he told you?' Margaret asked.

'The same as Pauper. He knew about the murders and figured they were next.'

'Does he know about Yuan Tao?'

'I haven't asked him yet.'

Birdie seemed alarmed by this exchange in English. 'What are you saying?' he asked nervously.

'We were talking about an old schoolfriend of yours. Yuan Tao.'

Birdie's eyes opened wide. 'Cat?'

'We found him dead in an apartment on the east side of the city. Murdered just like the others.'

For a moment Birdie just stared at him, and then unexpectedly his eyes filled and big teardrops spilled from them and rolled down his cheeks. Li was stunned by his reaction. Margaret moved towards them. 'What did you say to him?'

'I just told him about Yuan.'

Birdie put a hand to his mouth to try to stifle his sobs. He drew in a breath in a series of small gasps and then issued a deep, animal moan, and the tears streamed down his face to gather among the whiskers of his beard. He looked up at Li with pain and hopelessness in his eyes. 'I am sorry,' he said. 'I am so sorry.'

Li stood stock still. 'Did you kill him, Birdie?'

Birdie shook his head, and when he found the breath to speak again, said, 'No. I did not kill him. But we took his life away all those years ago. Back in the Cultural Revolution.' A string of sobs pummelled his chest. 'When we killed his father. In the school yard, with his mother watching.' His eyes appealed pathetically for an understanding he knew would not come, his upturned face glistening with tears. 'We did not mean to. We were just children.' He broke down again, and held his face in his hands, weeping like the child he had once been. Li and Margaret waited in silence for his sobs to subside. There was something faintly shocking in watching a grown man cry so freely.

Finally, he regained some measure of control. 'I have spent my life regretting the things we did then,' he said. 'China had gone mad, and we were carried along by the insanity. And now China has healed itself, but you cannot bring back the lives that were taken, or take away the pain from the wounds that will not heal.' He wiped the tears from his face with the palms of his hands. 'It has left me with a nervous condition now. I cannot work, except with my birds.' He gazed up at his beloved birds singing in their cages. 'They have no past, no future. They know nothing of my guilt. They make no judgements. I am free only with them. I have been free only ever with them.' And after a moment, 'Poor Cat,' he said.

'Cats and birds don't really mix, do they?' Li said, unmoved by Birdie's display of remorse. His reading of the diary was still too vivid in his memory.

Birdie looked at him, confused. 'What do you mean?'

'It was Cat who murdered the others. Revenge for the killing of his father. You and Pauper were almost certainly next on his list.'

'You *still* think I killed him?' Birdie looked at him in disbelief.

'Kill or be killed.'

Birdie shook his head. 'I didn't even know it was him. And even if I had, how could I have taken his life again?' He ran his hands through his thinning hair in abject despair. 'I only wish I had come higher on his list. At least, then, I would not have had to live with the guilt any more.'

'Where were you on Monday night?' Li asked.

Birdie looked at him, and there was a mix of panic and fear in his eyes. 'I don't know,' he said. 'Monday? At home maybe.'

'And you live on your own?'

'Yes.'

'So there wouldn't be anyone to back that up?'

Birdie was becoming increasingly agitated. 'No. Yes. The girl in the lift. She must have seen me coming in.'

'At what time would that be?'

'I don't know . . . Perhaps about seven.'

'And when does the lift girl finish for the night.'

'Ten usually.'

'So, if you'd gone out after ten no one would know.'

'I didn't go out after ten!' Birdie's protestation was shrill and fearful.

'What's happening?' Margaret asked.

'He doesn't have an alibi for Monday night,' Li said.

'Wait a minute!' Birdie's eyes had suddenly lit up. 'Monday night. Monday night,' he said excitedly, and a residue of sobs momentarily robbed him of his ability to speak. 'Monday night I was playing checkers on the wall down at Xidan with my friend Moon. Usually we play Tuesday, but he had something else on and we played Monday instead. We sat and talked and smoked till maybe about twelve, when we finished playing. And then I went to his place for a beer before I came home.'

'And he'll confirm that if we ask him?' Li felt unaccountably disappointed. However pathetic Birdie might have become, it did not alter the dreadful things he had done, and Li had found himself *wanting* it to be Birdie who had taken the life of his old classmate.

Birdie said. 'Old Moon, he'll remember for sure.' And then his excitement subsided, and he stared dejectedly again at the cobbled floor of the pavilion. 'Poor Cat,' he said.

III

It was dark as they drove east on West Chang'an Avenue. Up ahead the lights erected in Tiananmen Square for National Day reflected hazy colour in the misty night air. A long line of red taillights snaked off into the distance. Li and Margaret had not spoken much since they left the park. He had asked her where she wanted to go, and she had said back to her hotel. And then they'd lapsed into silence.

Suddenly she said, 'So what do you suppose it was that Yuan Tao had hidden under the floorboards in that apartment?'

He glanced at her, surprised that her mind was still turning around the investigation. 'The sword, I guess,' he said. 'It is not the sort of thing he would have wanted to carry in and out of the foreign residents' compound.'

Margaret fell again into silence. In spite of her question, she was rapidly losing interest in the investigation. As they passed Tiananmen Square her thoughts turned to Michael. She wanted to find him and tell him she was sorry. To try to make him believe that it had not been her idea to question him over his knowledge of the murder victims, or his whereabouts on the night of Yuan's death. She tried to analyse the feelings that had swept over her in the moments after they discovered that Michael had recommended Yuan Tao to the dealer at the Underground City. Shock. And, momentarily, fear. Why had she been afraid? Surely she could not, in her wildest dreams, have imagined that Michael was in any way involved in these murders? And yet that is what Li had thought – or wanted to think. Or wanted *her* to think. He had leaped so eagerly on her revelation that Michael had known Professor Yue. She knew it was only his jealousy, but still she had felt relief when Michael had reminded her that the night of Yuan's murder was the night she had met him at the ambassador's residence. It was impossible for him to have been involved.

She remembered the hurt in his eyes when he realised why Li and Margaret had driven out to the Ming Tombs that morning, and she felt sick. A traitor.

Li sneaked a look at Margaret. But she seemed preoccupied. A long way away. And he was overcome by a sudden depression. He had loved her so much, it had been painful to be with her. And then it had been painful to be without her. And now he was condemned to some state of limbo where he could neither possess her nor escape her. It was as if, somehow, she had died but her body kept coming back to haunt him. And this spectre that was his constant companion, cast a deep shadow over his memories of how good they had once been together, how sweet it had once felt.

His thoughts were interrupted by his call sign on the police radio. He unhooked the receiver and responded. A radio operator's voice from Section One crackled across the airwaves, and Margaret heard Li's voice flare briefly in annoyance, and then subside to a reluctant acceptance of the response that followed. He rehooked the receiver and drove on in silence. But she could see the tension in his grip on the steering wheel.

'Bad news?' she asked at length.

He glanced at her and hesitated for a long moment before deciding that it didn't really matter whether he told her or not. 'You met my sister the other night,' he said. 'At the Sanwei tearoom.' She nodded. 'You remember I told you before that she was pregnant?' She nodded again, and he told her how Xiao Ling had abandoned Xinxin at his apartment and gone south to have the baby at the home of a friend, and how Xinxin's father didn't want to know about any of it.

'Jesus!' Margaret said. 'How on earth are you coping?'

He looked grim. 'I'm not.' He sighed. 'You remember Mei Yuan? The *jian bing* seller?'

'Of course.'

'She was going to keep Xinxin for a few days until I got something else arranged. She phoned the office this afternoon to say that her cousin's husband has had to go into hospital for an operation.'

Margaret shook her head, perplexed. 'What's that got to do with anything?'

'Her cousin was looking after the *jian bing* while Mei Yuan looked after Xinxin. But with the cousin's husband in hospital she can't do the *jian bing* because she has to take him his meals.'

Margaret was astonished. 'Doesn't the hospital feed its patients?'

'In China,' Li said, 'many people prefer family meals to hospital food. So tomorrow Mei Yuan will have to take over the *jian bing* again from her cousin because she cannot afford to lose the income. Which means she cannot look after Xinxin. When I have dropped you at the hotel I will have to go and pick her up and take her back to the apartment.'

The huge, red neon CITIC sign rose out of the mist ahead of them above the lights of the teatime traffic. 'I'd like to meet her,' Margaret said, taking both Li and herself by surprise. She had no idea why, but just the thought of Li's niece, and that he was responsible for her, made him somehow more human again, more vulnerable, more like the man she had known. It was meeting his uncle that day in Jade Lake Park that had first changed her view of him, from a surly, xenophobic Chinese policeman, to a man who blushed easily, who got embarrassed and was sensitive to the feelings of others.

He looked at her and frowned. 'Why?'

She just shrugged.

Without another word, Li did a U-turn at the next junction and headed east again, and then north towards the northern lakes and Mei Yuan's *hutong*.

Yingdingqiao, or Silver Ingot Bridge, was a tiny hump-backed marble bridge, spanning the narrow waterway linking Houhai Lake in the north and Qianhai Lake in the south. It was an ancient commercial crossroads in the comparative backwaters of Beijing's Northern Lakes district. The lights of a mini-market in an elegant five-sided traditional building blazed out across the water. In brick hovels with tin roofs, old women clattered woks over fiery stoves, sending steam and smoke and wonderful cooking smells issuing into the night air. Li nosed the Jeep carefully over the bridge. Further along the lake to their right, a children's playground stood silent and deserted in the darkness. And as they turned south along the southern shore of Qianhai Lake, they saw the dazzling spectacle of the 140-year-old Kaorouji restaurant that had been the favourite eating place of Manchu princes in the nineteenth century, serving up roast mutton hotpot and other Muslim delicacies. Its lights twinkled and danced on the other side of the water behind the swaying fronds of weeping willows.

Mei Yuan's *siheyuan* was unusually fronted by a small

strip of garden with cut grass, shrubs and trees behind a low fence. She and Xinxin were sitting at a table making dumplings when Li and Margaret came in. She was delighted to see Margaret, and hugged her like a mother might hug a daughter she has not seen in months. It was a very un-Chinese show of affection. She beamed and told them both to sit, and apologised profusely to Li for the inconvenience. Her cousin's husband would only be in hospital for a couple of days, and she could take Xinxin again the day after tomorrow anyway, since it was Sunday and she always took Sundays off. She stopped to draw breath, and they all noticed Xinxin sitting in wide-eyed amazement, her jaw slack, mouth open, as she gazed in wonder at Margaret. This was possibly the first non-Chinese person she had ever seen, or certainly the first she had seen in the flesh.

'Xinxin, this is Margaret,' Li told her. 'She is an American.' He was not sure if she would even know what an American was. Zigong, in Sichuan Province, where she had grown up, was deep in the heart of rural China. Not many, if any, foreigners would ever have ventured there. And Li had no idea how well acquainted, if at all, she was with Western television programmes. If she had heard Li, she gave no sign of it, but kept staring at Margaret as if unable to believe her eyes.

'Hello, Xinxin,' Margaret said. And she held out her hand. 'I am very pleased to meet you.'

If it was possible, Xinxin's eyes widened further, and she recoiled from Margaret's outstretched hand and looked at Li with something like fear in her eyes. 'I don't know what she is saying,' she said. 'Is it a different kind of Chinese, like you and Mei Yuan speak sometimes?'

'No, Xinxin,' Mei Yuan said. 'It is another language. She has different words to describe the things you and I have the same words for. Sometimes Chinese people learn their words, too. And sometimes they learn ours.'

Li thought how good Mei Yuan was with the child.

'What's an American?' Xinxin asked.

'The name of your country is China,' Mei Yuan explained. 'So you are called Chinese. An American is someone who comes from the country of America.'

Margaret smiled apprehensively, feeling shut out of the conversation. 'What's going on?' she said.

Li said, 'Xinxin's getting a lesson in geography and linguistics.'

'Can I touch her hair?' Xinxin asked.

Li looked at Margaret. 'She wants to touch your hair.'

'Sure.' Margaret remembered with a jolt that it had been in the Muslim quarter in Xi'an with Michael that she had been asked the same thing by the waitresses.

Xinxin tentatively reached out to run her fingers through the silky gold of Margaret's curls. Her face broke into a wide, and completely disarming smile. 'It's so soft,' she said. 'Is it real?'

'Of course it's real,' Li said.

'Can . . . what did you say her name was?'

'Margaret.'

'Can Mar-ga-ret help us make dumplings?'

Li looked doubtful. 'We can't really stay long, Xinxin. We have to get you home to bed.'

'Oh, please ...' She widened her eyes to try to look her most appealing.

Li said to Margaret. 'She wants you to help make dumplings.'

Margaret smiled, delighted. 'I'd like that.'

For twenty minutes or more they sat drinking green tea and rolling round thin pancakes from pieces of dough cut off a roll. Xinxin showed Margaret how to spoon a little of the dumpling mixture into the centre of the pancake, fold it over and then crimp it around the edges, so that it looked a little like a seashell. The secret of the perfect dumpling was to finish it off by squeezing the mixture into the very centre by applying pressure with both thumbs and forefingers. The first few times Margaret made a mess of it, and the mixture came squirting out over the table, to Xinxin's endless mirth and delight. Her giggling was infectious, and finally Li and Mei Yuan and Margaret were all reduced to helpless laughter, too.

Oblivious to the fact that Margaret could not understand a word, Xinxin chided her for getting it wrong and explained how it should be done, demonstrating as she went and producing perfect dumplings every time. Eventually, Margaret, too, was producing dumplings that were passable, if not perfect.

Xinxin nodded her satisfaction and began counting the dumplings they had made, making Margaret count with her. Mei Yuan helped with the numbers, and Margaret very quickly discovered that you only had to learn to count to ten to make almost any number. Ten-five was fifteen, five-ten was fifty. Fifty-nine was five-ten-nine. They had made ninety-five dumplings, so she never got to learn what a hundred was.

'You will stay and have dumplings before you go,' Mei Yuan said. 'They will cook in ten minutes.'

But Li became suddenly self-conscious. 'Another time, Mei Yuan,' he said. 'I must get Xinxin home. And I don't want to keep Margaret back any longer.'

Xinxin said, 'Is Mar-ga-ret coming, too?'

'I'm afraid not, little one,' Li said. 'We have to drop her off at her hotel.'

A black cloud cast a shadow over Xinxin's face and her mouth turned down in a sulky temper. 'Won't go without Mar-ga-ret,' she said.

Li sighed.

'What's wrong?' Margaret asked.

'The Little Emperor syndrome,' Li said. 'She won't go unless you come with us.'

Margaret shrugged. 'OK. I'll go back with you.' For a moment their eyes met and she felt strangely uncomfortable, and flushed with embarrassment. To his annoyance Li blushed too, and he turned to find Mei Yuan watching them appraisingly.

Xinxin's good humour returned immediately she learned the good news. Mei Yuan gathered her things together and put them in a bag along with the books she had brought the other night. 'A book is like a garden carried in the pocket,' Xinxin told Li.

Li frowned his surprise and looked at Mei Yuan who smiled. 'I've been teaching her old Chinese proverbs,' she said. 'You'll probably hear a few more of them.'

'That reminds me,' Li said. 'I have the solution to your riddle.'

Mei Yuan smiled and raised an eyebrow. 'You do?'

'You deliberately misled me,' Li said. 'You planted a whole set of figures in my head that did not make sense. You had me wasting my time trying to make them work.'

'What was the riddle?' Margaret asked.

Mei Yuan told her. 'That's easy,' said Margaret. 'Your arithmetic doesn't add up.'

'I just told you that,' Li protested.

But Margaret gave them the solution anyway. Starting with the twenty-five and adding the three and the two to make thirty. Mei Yuan clapped her hands in delight. She said, 'I give you a stone, you give me back jade.'

'What about me?' Li said. 'I got the answer, too.'

'But you took so long,' Mei Yuan said, 'the stone I gave you turned to stone.'

Margaret laughed. 'OK,' she said. 'Here's one for both of you.' She thought for a moment. 'It is National Day in Beijing. The middle of the day. Everyone is out in the streets. Li Yan walks from Xidamochang Street to Beijing Railway Station, and yet not a soul sees him. How is this possible?'

Both Li and Mei Yuan were silent for a moment as they considered the puzzle. Mei Yuan shook her head. 'This I will need to think about.' She opened the door and ruffled Xinxin's head, turning to Li. 'You have a very clever lady, Li Yan. Take care not to let her go.'

And they both blushed fiercely.

Xinxin's face was relaxed and beautiful in the repose of sleep. Margaret sat on the edge of the bed and brushed a few stray strands of hair from her cheek and gazed down on her innocence. Xinxin had 'read' to her from her picture book when they got back to the apartment. And although she could not really read, she had been read the story so often by Mei Yuan in the last couple of days that she knew it off by heart. She still did not fully grasp that Margaret could not understand what she said, and gabbled to her constantly, tutting with irritation whenever Margaret responded in English. 'You must teach her to speak Chinese,' she had said to Li in annoyance.

Now, as she lay sleeping, Margaret's heart went out to her. Abandoned by her mother, rejected by her father, landed on an uncle who had not the first idea of how to look after her. And she felt for Li, too. It was an awesome responsibility, the life of another person. Particularly one so young and utterly dependent. And it was not a responsibility for which he had asked. Somewhere, Margaret became aware, deep inside of her there was a latent desire to share in that responsibility. Something hormonal, she supposed. That chemical spark that fired a woman's desire to have children. She was thirty-one years old, and she had never once felt the desire to have children. Until now. Absurdly. Inappropriately. Impossibly. And yet, as she gazed on the sleeping child, some primeval instinct was conjuring a longing to hold her to her breast, to protect her from all the dreadful slings and arrows that life would throw at her.

Suddenly aware that a constriction in her throat was causing her to breathe erratically, she looked up to find Li standing watching her from the doorway. Her face coloured in embarrassment, as if she believed he could somehow read her thoughts. She looked away, and saw the photographs of Old Yifu on the wall, and unaccountably felt tears filling her eyes. She blinked them quickly away, looking down at the bed to hide them from Li. She picked up Xinxin's picture book and stood up, pretending to scrutinise the pages. Her eyes fell on the vertical columns of large Chinese characters that ran up the right margin of each page, and clutching at something to say to hide her emotion she said, 'Do you really read from right to left?'

Li took the book from her and closed it gently. 'Only when the characters are on the vertical. When they are horizontal we read left to right.' He seemed very close now. She could hear his breathing, and the familiar smell of him made her heart beat a little faster. He said, 'They say that Chinese children learn to read up and down because they are very obedient and always obey their parents.' He made an up and down nodding motion with his head. 'But Western children are very disobedient and never do what they are told. That is why they read from left to right.' And he moved his head from side to side as if shaking it.

She smiled. 'When you say "they" say, I take it you mean the Chinese.'

'Of course.' He dropped the book on the bed and she felt an arm slip around her waist. He lowered his head to kiss her, and she tipped her face towards him in an instinctive response. It was only the shock of his lips on hers that suddenly made her pull away.

'No!' she said, and then suddenly remembered Xinxin and lowered her voice to a whisper. 'No, Li.' They stood staring at each other for a moment. Then she said, 'I'd better go. I'll get a taxi in the street.' And she hurried past him, stopping in the living room to pick up her folders, before running out and down the stairs. He heard the door slam behind her, and felt the tears run warm on his cheeks.

IV

Margaret struggled out of her taxi, laden with the files that Li had dumped on her. She fumbled to pay the driver, then hurried into the Ritan Hotel, past the deserted lobby shop with its display of overpriced trinkets, and turned right towards the elevators.

In the short taxi ride from Li's apartment to her hotel, her distress had turned to anger. How dare Li play with her emotions like that? How could she ever hope to accept his rejection if he could not accept it himself, if he became jealous of any relationship she had with another man, if he was going to succumb to his own weakness every time they were together? And she was just as angry with herself for almost having given way to desires she had been trying to sublimate. Desires she had been *forced* to sublimate. What had seemed clear and easy and right with Michael just twenty-four hours before was suddenly thrown into confusion again. She needed time to think.

'Margaret.' She turned at the sound of Michael's voice just as the elevator doors slid open.

'Michael. What are you doing here?'

'Waiting for you.' He approached across the vast expanse of marble looking at his watch and smiling ruefully. 'For the last two hours. You people work long days.' His face clouded. 'I wanted to talk to you, Margaret. About this morning.'

'I wanted to talk to you, too, Michael.' Margaret sighed. 'I can't apologise enough. It was just Li Yan being jealous. Trying to get back at me through you.' The elevator doors slid shut again.

Michael frowned. 'I thought you and he were history.'

'So did I.'

He shuffled awkwardly. 'Look, Margaret. The thing is, if it gets around that I'm some kind of suspect in a murder investigation, it could completely ruin my connections here in China.'

Margaret couldn't stop herself laughing. 'Oh, Michael,' she said. 'You're not a suspect. Li was just playing silly games with the most tenuous of links. There's no question of anyone thinking you had anything to do with this. You were with me the evening Yuan was killed, you weren't even in the country when another two of the murders took place.' She paused, gasping her frustration. 'What can I say? Forget it. It's not even an issue.'

He seemed to relax a little then, and smiled. 'Have you eaten?' She shook her head. He said, 'Good, 'cos I booked us a table at a little place I know.' He checked his watch again. 'They should still be serving. Just.'

She glanced down at herself. 'Michael, I'll have to change first. Fifteen minutes. That's all. I promise.'

He grinned. 'OK. Starting from . . .' he raised his wrist and began pushing buttons on his watch, 'now.' He started the stopwatch function. She pressed the call button for the elevator.

He held open her hotel room door as she staggered in and dropped her files on the bed, papers spilling out across the bedspread and dropping on the floor. He stooped to start picking them up. 'Just leave that stuff,' she said. 'I'll get it later.' She grabbed some fresh underwear from a drawer, and took a pair of jeans and a lemon tee shirt from hangers in the wardrobe. 'A quick shower,' she said. 'I promise I won't be long.'

He grinned and tapped his watch. 'Still counting.'

She hurried into the bathroom and quickly stripped off and started the shower running. She caught a glimpse of herself naked in the mirror and remembered being with Michael the night before, his hands gentle on her breasts and buttocks, the great sense of his contained strength and control as he slipped inside her. The steam from the shower misted her reflection and she turned to step into the stream of deliciously hot water.

'So if I'm no longer the prime suspect, who is?' she heard Michael call through from the bedroom.

'It's a long story,' she called back.

'Better make it quick, then. You've only got another ten minutes.'

She laughed and started lathering herself with a big soft sponge drizzled with shower gel. 'Yuan's father was killed back in the sixties by a group of six Red Guards during the Cultural Revolution.' She spluttered briefly as she pushed her head back under the shower and let the water run down her face. 'Yuan was at university in America and didn't know about it till he got his mother's diary thirty years later. Seems he came back to take his revenge.'

Michael said something but she couldn't hear him.

'What was that?'

He raised his voice. 'So who killed Yuan?'

'The best bet is some guy they call Birdie. Works at the bird market.'

'Why would *he* want to kill Yuan?'

'Because Birdie's the last surviving member of the group of Red Guards that killed Yuan's father. He was sure to have been on Yuan's hit list.' She rinsed the shampoo out of her hair. 'Mind you, he might be the best bet, but he's a pretty poor one. The guy's a misfit. Lives on his own with a bunch of birds. Suffers from nerves and can't do proper work . . . and a whole bunch of other reasons I wouldn't even bore you with.'

She turned off the shower and stepped out of the bath reaching, eyes closed, for the bath towel on the rail. She felt a hand touching her and screamed with fright, opening her eyes with a shock. Michael stood grinning in the steam-filled room, holding out the bath towel. 'Jesus, Michael!' she said. 'You gave me a fright.' She snatched the towel and wrapped it around herself.

He cocked an eyebrow and said, 'That's not what you said last night.' And he slipped his arms around her waist and drew her towards him.

'You'll get all wet,' she protested.

'Tough.' And he leaned in to her and dropped his head to kiss the softness of her neck. She felt a wave of pleasure and desire weaken her knees, and smelled the heady scent of his patchouli lacing the perfume of her bath gel. She took his face in both her hands, feeling the scratch of his whiskers, and raised it to meet hers. They kissed. A long, passionate kiss, and she felt his erection press against her belly. And suddenly she thought of Li, stooping as he bent to kiss her. The touch of his lips. Her sudden fear, and flight from the apartment. She broke away from Michael, breathing hard, and her smile was a little strained. 'Better hurry if I'm going to beat that clock,' she said.

The Ya Mei Wei restaurant was tucked away down the unpromising Dong Wang *hutong* off Kuan Street, opposite the AVICS space technology building. As Margaret stepped from the taxi she had to dodge a phalanx of cyclists without lights, jostling for space in the strip of road left to them by manic night drivers freed from the constraints of daytime and rush-hour traffic. With bicycle bells still ringing in her ears she made it to the sidewalk and peered down the dark, misty *hutong*. 'We're eating down there?' she asked. And when Michael just nodded, she said, 'This isn't another place like the one you took me to in Xi'an?'

'No,' he said confidently. 'It's nothing like that.'

Fifty yards down, crumbling brick walls rising above them on either side, two forlorn red lanterns hung outside a maroon-painted wooden doorway that was firmly shut. Michael rapped on the door.

'This is it?' Margaret said.

Michael smiled. 'You should never judge a book by its cover.'

A handsome woman of about forty, wearing a pink silk suit, opened the door. Her face lit up in a smile when she saw Michael and she stretched out her hand to shake his. 'Mr Zimmerman,' she said. 'I am so pleased to see you again.' She glanced at her watch. 'You are a little late.'

Michael raised his hands in abject apology. 'I am so sorry, Zhao Yi. Are we *too* late?'

'Of course not,' Zhao Yi said, her smile broadening. 'Never too late for good friend.'

Michael made the introductions and Zhao Yi ushered them inside. The contrast with the *hutong* outside could not have been more startling. This was another world. The centrepiece was a reproduction of a traditional Beijing-style courtyard with sloping green tile roofs and a tiny bridge over a small stream.

Along one side, doors led off to a huge dining lounge. Along the other, more doors led off a narrow corridor to private rooms behind screen windows. Zhao Yi led them across the courtyard and into their own private room where a table was set for two, candles burning, soft classical Chinese music playing from discreetly hidden speakers. It seemed they had the whole restaurant to themselves. It was nearly ten o'clock, long past Beijing evening meal time.

Immediately several girls in matching silk buzzed around them like bees, bringing hot and cold starter dishes to the centre of the table. 'Just help yourself,' Michael said. 'As little or as much as you want. They're only appetisers.' He nodded towards the stainless-steel pots that stood beside each place on circular racks above big purple candles. 'Have you had Mongolian hotpot before?' She shook her head. 'It's a real treat here.' He said to Zhao Yi, 'We'll have a bottle of that Rioja you have. The '93.'

She nodded and melted away, leaving Michael and Margaret to pick at the selection of starters: spicy lamb, roasted peanuts in chilli, fish in sweet and sour sauce. The wine came and Michael raised his glass to touch Margaret's. The light from the candles flickered and refracted red in the wine, and danced in Michael's eyes. 'To us,' he said.

'To us.' And Margaret found that irritating sense of guilt returning. She took a big swallow of wine and determined not to let Li ruin her evening in the way he had spoiled her day.

Michael said, 'There's one thing puzzling me.' He paused. 'No, two actually.' He thought for a moment. 'This Birdie character ... If there were six Red Guards, and only three murders, how is he the last surviving member?'

Margaret laughed. 'That's your training, isn't it? You don't miss thing. Every tiny detail's important.'

'I told you. Archaeology is just like police work. A slow, painstaking process of digging into the past, uncovering and recreating an event, or a place.'

'You should have been a Chinese policeman. They like their detail, too.' She took a sip of her wine. 'I was just talking short-hand, Michael. He's not the last surviving member. There's another one. A woman, but she's blind. The third one was killed at Tiananmen Square.' She took some more fish. 'This stuff's fantastic.' She washed it down with more wine and said, 'So what was the other thing?'

Michael put both elbows on the table and leaned towards her, maintaining a very steady eye contact. 'If it's over between you and Detective Li, why is he jealous of me?'

Margaret wished with all her heart that Michael had not raised the spectre of Li again. It was hard enough for her to keep him from her thoughts without Michael constantly reminding her. She sighed. Honesty was the best policy. 'The reason we broke up was because his bosses told him our relationship was ...' she searched for the right words, 'inappropriate for a high-ranking Chinese police officer.'

'You or his career, in other words.' She nodded. 'And he chose his career.'

Margaret felt a stab of annoyance. 'It's not that simple, Michael.'

He held up his hands. 'I'm sorry. Things never are.'

'I guess,' said Margaret, 'he's just finding it very hard to live with his decision.'

'And what about you?'

'It was hard, I'll admit. It wasn't what I wanted. But it's history now. I'm only looking forward.'

He smiled at her fondly and reached out to squeeze her hand. 'I'm glad,' he said.

The girls came then and lit the paraffin candles, and filled the pots above them with boiling spicy stock that bubbled and steamed at the table. Plates of raw meat – marinated lamb, wafer-thin sliced pork, strips of beef, marinated prawns still in their shells – were placed before them along with plates piled high with crispy lettuce. They cooked everything themselves, a piece at a time, in the boiling stock, and then dipped it in hot soy dips before letting the flavours explode in their mouths.

'This is *wonderful*,' Margaret said. 'I've never tasted meat or prawns so tender.' And she copied Michael, cooking the lettuce in the stock as well. It cleansed the palate between meat or fish.

They finished the wine and Michael ordered another bottle. Margaret felt warm, and sensuous and sated, and Michael was making her laugh a lot with a story about a misunderstanding of French-farce proportions during a dig in Egypt. Then, after a while, she realised she had got a little drunk, and that Michael had stopped talking and was leaning his chin on his hands and gazing at her across the table.

'I know it's too soon to tell you I love you,' he said suddenly. 'But I don't care.'

And just as suddenly, Margaret felt very sober and her heart was pounding. 'What?'

He produced a small red jewellery box from his pocket and opened it to reveal a rose-gold ring set with a diamond solitaire. 'If someone had asked me a week ago I'd have told them I never expected to marry. But I hadn't met you then.' He paused and she saw that his eyes were moist. 'That's why I wanted to know about Detective Li. I'm crazy about you, Margaret. I want you to marry me.'

She sat and looked at him in stunned silence for what seemed like an eternity. Then she laughed in disbelief and shook her head. 'Is that a proposal?'

'It sounded like one to me.'

'Well, then, the answer's no.'

His face coloured. 'Why?'

She laughed again. 'Because I hardly know you, Michael. We only met a few days ago.'

He held her gaze for a long time, then smiled and snapped the box shut. 'How did I know you were going to say that?'

'Because you know it's true.'

'Well, if that's the only problem, it's easily remedied. With a little time and a lot of exposure.' His smile faded and he looked at her very seriously. 'I mean it, Margaret. I've never felt like this about anyone before.' Then he shook his head, laughing at himself. 'And you're making me feel like a clumsy schoolboy getting his first refusal.'

'Oh, Michael.' She reached out to put her hand over his. 'This is all just too soon for me. I need time. To get over Li. To sort out my feelings about you.' She paused. 'Last night was wonderful. But I've got to know there's more to it than that. I threw away seven years of my life married to the wrong man. I don't want to make the same mistake again.'

He nodded. 'I understand. I do. So I'll put the ring on ice, as well as your answer. Because I'm not going to give up on you, Margaret. I'm just not letting you get away that easily. So if you really want to close the door on the past, I'm going to be right there helping you do it.'

CHAPTER TEN

I

He left Xinxin waiting in the Jeep. And then the Chinese security guard in the gatehouse took great delight in exercising his authority over Li by keeping him waiting until Sophie arrived. Officially this was American soil, and Li had no jurisdiction here. It was not often that an ordinary Chinese could thumb his nose at his superiors with impunity.

Sophie shook Li's hand warmly. 'Hi,' she said. 'We met the other day downtown, at CID HQ.'

'Yes, of course,' Li said, and he was aware of her inspecting him with interest. No doubt she knew that he and Margaret had been lovers. Probably the entire embassy knew.

She led him around the side of the Chancery building, and they headed towards the canteen. 'Have you been here long?' he asked.

'Not long. Just about a month.'

'How's your Mandarin?' he asked in Mandarin.

She smiled. 'I'm Vietnamese. But I don't speak that very well either.'

Li looked at her appraisingly. 'How long have you been in America?'

'Born and bred,' she said. 'You don't think I'd make Assistant RSO at a foreign embassy if I wasn't, do you?'

He smiled. 'I guess not.'

Dakers was waiting for them at a table in the canteen. It was crowded with embassy staff tucking into breakfast of waffles and pancakes drowned in syrup and washing it all down with strong black coffee. He stood up and shook Li's hand firmly. 'Mr Li,' he said. 'Good to see you again. Wanna coffee?' Li shook his head. 'Take a seat. What can I do for you?'

Li said carefully, 'I wanted your permission to ask a few of your embassy people about the whereabouts of Michael Zimmerman last Monday night.'

Sophie's face flushed and she said, 'Why do you want to know that?'

Li smiled and waved a hand dismissively. 'Nothing sinister. It's routine stuff. We're just establishing where anyone who knew Yuan Tao was on the night he was murdered.'

'It's hardly routine for a Deputy Section Chief to come calling,' Dakers said shrewdly.

Li grinned. 'I was hardly going to send a junior officer to speak to the Regional Security Officer of the American Embassy.'

Dakers nodded, satisfied. 'Fair enough.' He thought for a moment. 'I guess I have no objection. What about you, Sophie?'

She shrugged. 'None at all. Only you don't need to go any

further than present company. I can tell you exactly where Michael was on Monday night – at least, up until about two.'

'You were at the party, then?' Li asked.

'Sure,' she said. 'It was me that introduced him to Dr Campbell that night.' Li flicked her a look and wondered if she knew what she was saying, if she was deliberately rubbing salt in the wound. If she was, there was nothing in her expression to give her away.

'And after the party . . . ?'

'There were about a dozen of us went on to the Mexican Wave bar.' She turned to Dakers. 'You know the place, Jon . . . where the Hash House Harriers meet up.'

Dakers nodded. 'Sure.'

'And Zimmerman left at two?'

'No, I left at two. I have no idea when he left.'

II

There was a spring in Margaret's step as she strolled past the surly security guards at the gate of the hotel and turned down Ritan Lu past the rows of fur traders. They looked no happier than usual. Business was not any better.

Michael had gone early, before six, to get out to location, and left his smell and his warmth in the bed with her. She had lain for a long time luxuriating in it, wondering what it was she really felt for him. She found him addictive, wanted to be with him all the time. Early signs of the first flush of infatuation. He was attractive, intelligent, a wonderfully sensitive lover. He had talent, as an archaeologist, as a communicator. She remembered the night at the Sanwei tearoom when he had joined the band to play tenor sax. Talent like that was unusual. And sexy. It was only her lingering feelings for Li that still clouded how she felt about Michael. The further removed she became from Li, she was certain, the clearer her feelings for Michael would become. She needed a complete break from him.

The blast of a car horn startled her as she stepped from the sidewalk to cross the street without looking. She turned and saw Li's Jeep pulled up in front of her, Li grinning at her from the driver's seat, Xinxin waving frantically at her from the back. He leaned over and pushed the passenger door open.

She stomped around the bonnet and climbed in with a bad grace. 'What are you trying to do, kill me?'

'Actually,' Li said, 'I was trying to avoid putting a dent in the fender.'

She made a face at him and felt Xinxin tugging at her from behind, repeating the same phrase again and again. She turned and Xinxin planted a big kiss on her lips and then giggled hysterically. Margaret laughed. 'What's she saying?'

'Hello, Auntie Margaret,' Li said with a smirk.

'Oh, my God,' Margaret groaned. 'That makes me sound like someone's ancient maiden aunt.'

'She was very disappointed you weren't still there when she woke up this morning.'

Margaret's smile faded. 'Well, I hope you told her not to expect me to be around for much longer. She's lost too many people already to have her expectations built up about anyone else.' Xinxin bounced around in the back, between the two front seats, waggling her bunches from side to side.

Li pulled out into the traffic again, ignoring a flurry of horns, and said, 'I'm going up to the archaeology department at the university. I thought you might want to come.'

Margaret looked at him suspiciously. 'What are we going there for?'

'I just wanted to ask them about Zimmerman.'

Margaret exploded. 'For Christ's sake, Li Yan, can't you just let it go?' Xinxin was startled by the sudden angry words.

Li said calmly, 'Zimmerman said he heard about what happened to Professor Yue from other people in the faculty. I just want to check on how many people knew what. I already checked his alibi for Monday night. He went on to the Mexican Wave after the ambassador's reception, just like he said.'

'You are such a complete bastard,' she said. 'This is absolutely not fair. Michael has done nothing wrong. Everyone loves him. You talk to anyone who knows him. No one's got a bad word to say about him. They'll all tell you he's really good guy. You can't hound him like this just because you're jealous.'

'I am not jealous,' Li said evenly.

'Like hell!'

'Uncle Li, why is Auntie Mar-ga-ret angry?' Xinxin asked timidly from the back.

'She's not angry with us, darling, it's to do with work,' Li told her.

'What are you saying to her?' Margaret asked suspiciously.

'I'm just telling her not to worry about you shouting at me. And that Americans are always bad-tempered.'

'Jesus!' Margaret hissed.

'The point is,' Li said, 'I'm just tying up loose ends. We follow one line of inquiry until we reach a dead end. Then we move on.' But he was not at all certain that he would be pursuing this particular line of inquiry if it was not for Margaret's relationship with Zimmerman. 'If you don't want to go, that's fine. I'll drop you off at the embassy.'

'Oh, no you won't. I'm going with you, even if it's just to make sure you don't go getting Michael into any more trouble.'

She felt Xinxin tugging at her sleeve. She turned and found herself looking straight into Xinxin's earnest little face as the child spoke directly to her with unusual timidity.

Li said, 'She's asking if you've finished being angry now.'

Margaret pursed her lips in a moment of annoyance, and then found herself forced to smile by the wide-eyed innocent appeal that wrinkled Xinxin's forehead. She sighed. 'Tell her, yes. Tell her that I was never angry with her in the first place. And tell her that the next time her uncle starts letting his personal feelings cloud his personal judgement, I'll slap his goddamn face for him again.'

Li spoke to Xinxin who nodded her head in satisfaction.

'What did you say to her?' Margaret demanded to know. She was frustrated at always being at the mercy of someone else's interpretation.

'That you were very sorry, and wouldn't speak to her Uncle

Yan like that again,' he said. Margaret narrowed her eyes at him and he grinned. 'Only kidding.'

They drove north through Chaoyangmen and Dongcheng District, heading for the third ring road. Li and Margaret sat in silence while Xinxin sang popular kindergarten songs to her panda in the back.

'What did you mean the other night when you talked about "the Little Emperor syndrome"?' Margaret asked suddenly.

Li smiled sadly. 'It is what we call the social consequence of the One-Child Policy.' He thought for a moment. 'Chinese society used to be built around the idea of family and community, the individual putting his responsibility for others first. Now, with most families having only one child, the child is spoiled and pampered and thinks only of itself. They become Little Emperors. The future of China will be in the hands of selfish, self-seeking individuals. Just like in America.'

'Maybe, then, you'll join the rest of us in the twenty-first century,' Margaret said.

'And replace five thousand years of culture and history with the hot dog and the hamburger?'

Margaret was sick of hearing about China's culture and history. Even Michael was full of it. 'Well, maybe it's about time you started looking to the future instead of always living in the past,' she snapped. 'Maybe that's why America ended up the most powerful country in the world. We weren't shackled by five thousand years of tradition. We just looked straight ahead and made it up as we went along.'

'And when you run out of ideas,' Li said, 'you'll have no history to draw on. No lessons you can take from the past.'

Margaret said, 'My old history professor always said the only thing you learn from history is that you never learn from history.'

'But he would be an American.'

Margaret looked at him triumphantly. 'Actually, he was Chinese.'

Li flicked her a look. 'Chinese-*American*. Yes?'

She glared at him. 'You've always got to have the last word, don't you?'

He shrugged. 'I usually do.'

The west gate of Beijing University was a traditional Chinese gate, with sweeping tiled roofs raised on beautifully painted crossbeams and supported on rust-red pillars. Li parked his Jeep in the shade of the trees that lined the street outside, and showed his Public Security pass to the guard on the gate who waved them through, past stone lions that stood sentinel left and right. Little Xinxin trotted at Margaret's side, clutching her hand as if she were in fear of her life. The campus within sat in the cloistered seclusion of landscaped gardens and tranquil lakes behind high grey walls, a million miles, it seemed, from the frantic activity and roar of the city they'd left behind.

Students and lecturers strolled or cycled along leafy paths that meandered through the lush gardens, ancient bridges sweeping over green waterways lined with flowers and dotted with lilies. On rocky outcrops, almost obscured by trees, tiny pavilions provided seats in the shade for undergraduates poring over textbooks or reading newspapers, or just sitting smoking and quietly reflecting on life. University departments were housed in large white pavilions with maroon windows and towering columns below elegantly curling roofs.

Margaret was entranced. 'What a wonderful place to come and study,' she said. 'It's so peaceful. So . . . Chinese.'

'Actually,' Li said, 'it's so . . . American.'

She frowned at him. 'What do you mean?'

'This place used to be the site of the American Methodist Yengching University. Beijing University didn't move here till 1952. All these "wonderful" halls and pavilions were built by the Methodists, designed by an American architect in the Chinese style. In those days, maybe, the Americans still thought there was something they could learn from us.'

The archaeology department stood in a long, two-storey pavilion beyond fresh-cut lawns, lush and verdant from frequent watering. The ground floor had been converted into the Arthur M. Sackler Museum of Art and Archaeology. Administration and lecture rooms were on the floor above. Li took them in through the main door, and they were confronted, across shining marble floors, by two life-sized replicas of Terracotta Warriors standing guard at the far entrance. Margaret was momentarily startled by them, and was transported immediately back to the pit at Xi'an where she had so carefully scraped away the earth to reveal a ceramic face that no one had cast eyes on for more than two thousand years. A bald and wizened caretaker with a speckled face told them they would have to go in by the side entrance and up the stairs to find the head of department.

'Professor Chang's not here right now,' an officious young man in white shirt and dark trousers told them offhandedly in the office. He had a shock of thick hair, dirt under his fingernails, and seemed more interested in the contents of the filing cabinet than in the three visitors.

'Would you like to tell me where he is?' Li asked.

'Not particularly. I'm busy right now.' The young man was clearly irritated by the interruption.

Li produced his Public Security wallet and held it out at arm's length. 'What's your name?'

The young man turned and saw the ID and his face immediately darkened. His frightened rabbit's eyes flickered up to Li. 'I'm sorry, detective, I . . .'

'What's your name?' Li repeated firmly.

'Wang Jiahong.'

'What do you do here?'

'I'm a lab assistant over in the Art building.'

'Do you normally speak to visitors like that?'

'No, detective.'

'I'm glad to hear it. So maybe now you'll tell me where I can find Professor Chang.'

'He's in the conservation lab.'

'Where's that?'

'In the Art building. All the labs are over there.' He tried to make up for his earlier gaffe. 'I'll take you if you like.'

The Art building, opposite the College of Life Sciences, was older and less glamorous, dusty grey brick and ill-painted windows. Dozens of student bicycles stood in the square outside. Inside it was drab and dingy, and Margaret smelled the perfume of stale urine wafting from open toilet doors. A room full of students at the end of the corridor was listening intently to a lady lecturer.

Wang Jiahong opened a nondescript door and led them into the conservation lab and then backed out, leaving them in the company of Professor Chang. It was a big cluttered room with old bookcases and wooden cabinets around the walls, and a huge wooden workbench that stood in the middle of the floor. The table was strewn with bits and pieces of pottery, a vast array of carelessly discarded tools and cleaning materials, and several weapons – two daggers, and a bronze sword held firmly in the jaws of a clamp. The floor was littered with wood shavings and dust and shards of broken pottery. The green-painted walls were scarred and stuck with posters and charts and ancient memos that went back fifty years. Daylight squeezed in through slatted blinds.

Professor Chang was working on the bronze sword, patiently removing layers of verdigris that had accumulated over centuries. He wore a dirty white apron and rubber gloves, and waved his hand vaguely around the room.

'Sorry for the mess,' he said in English when Li had made the introductions. He peered at Margaret over half-moon spectacles. 'We've been restoring the ancient treasures of China in here for decades. I guess it just never seemed all that important to clean up behind us.'

Xinxin went exploring. Li said, 'Do you have many staff in the department?'

'Two hundred students, sixty-seven teachers, twelve professors and nineteen associate professors,' Professor Chang said.

'And how many of them would have known the circumstances of Professor Yue's death?'

The Professor scraped away at the verdigris with a focused concentration. 'Oh, probably all of them,' he said.

From the corner of his eye, Li caught Margaret's head swinging in his direction. He could almost hear her saying, *Satisfied?* He said, 'I understood only a few senior members of the department were privy to those details.'

Chang glanced up at him. 'Well, they were. But you know what people are like. It was a scandal, a gruesome tale. People feed off stuff like that. Archaeologists are no different. It was round the whole department in a matter of hours. Probably the whole of the university.'

Li picked up and examined one of the daggers, still avoiding Margaret's eye. 'Do you know the American archaeologist, Michael Zimmerman?' he asked.

Professor Chang laid down his tools and removed his half-moons. 'What's *he* got to do with this?'

'Nothing,' Li said. 'I just wondered if you knew him.'

'Oh, yes, I know him,' said the professor. He took the dagger from Li and laid it back on the table. 'He came here when he was researching the background for his documentary on Hu Bo. Professor Yue had been a protégé of Hu's. Yue and

Zimmerman became very friendly.' There was something in his tone that gave Li cause for thought.

'You sound as if you don't approve.'

'I don't like Michael Zimmerman,' Professor Chang said bluntly, and Margaret felt the colour rising on her cheeks, stinging as if from a slap.

Li glanced at her. 'Why's that?'

'Because under all that superficial charm, Deputy Section Chief, he's a driven man. I don't know what it is that drives him. Ambition. Greed. But he uses people, manipulates them for his own ends.'

'Is that what he did to Professor Yue?'

'I don't know.' The professor thought about it for a moment. 'But Yue seemed to fall under his spell. They became very close. Too close. I didn't like it. I didn't think it was healthy.'

The sidewalks in Haidian Road were piled high with multi-coloured boxes filled with computers and printers, scanners and modems, monitors and hard drives. Every shop blazed out names like IBM, Microsoft, Apple, Pentium. This was the silicon sales valley of Beijing, awash with computing power: microchips, software, every peripheral imaginable. Unlike the Russian fur trade, business was good. People jammed the stores, and traffic had ground to a halt.

They had left the university in silence and were now grid-locked in the Haidian Road log jam.

Li glanced across at Margaret. The colour was still high on her cheeks and she was sitting staring straight ahead. In the back, Xinxin was mercifully engaged in a complex game of make-believe with her panda.

Finally, Li said, 'I thought no one had a bad word to say about him. They'll all tell you he's a really good guy, you said.'

Margaret's words came back to haunt her. She turned and looked at Li with something close to loathing in her eyes. 'One person's opinion, that's all.' She would never admit to Li how shocked she had been to hear it. Professor Chang had not been describing the Michael she knew. It was as if he had been talking about someone else. But it had hurt.

'Everyone loves him, that's what you said. Talk to anyone who knows him. Well, we did.'

She shook her head. 'You're pathetic, you know that? What did you go to the university for? To find out if people there knew the details of Professor Yue's death. And what did you find out? That they all knew. So, naturally, Michael would have heard, too. But does that satisfy you? Oh, no. Someone doesn't like him. So fucking what? The only thing we've learned here today is that you're a sad, jealous fool.'

Xinxin had abandoned her panda and was staring at Margaret in wide-eyed alarm. 'Fuck,' she said, aping Margaret. 'Fuck, fuck!'

Li glared at Margaret. 'Thank you,' he said. 'You've just taught my niece her first English word.'

The police radio crackled and Li heard his call sign. He unhooked the receiver angrily.

She turned and stared out the window at nothing, biting back the tears. She was determined not to spill them. At least, not in front of Li. It was incomprehensible to her that someone could think so badly of Michael. Was she blind? Were all his other friends and colleagues blind, too? Of course not. It was just the view of one twisted individual, she told herself. Who knew what history there was to it? She heard Li finish his call.

'That was Detective Sang,' he said quietly, and she turned to look at him defiantly. 'Apparently Birdie's alibi doesn't hold up. He wasn't playing checkers at Xidan the night Yuan was killed. We're asking the procurator's office to issue a warrant for his arrest.'

III

Birdie was lost without the creatures which had given him his nickname. He looked naked and vulnerable without his birds around him. It was hard to define, but the man who sat before them was like a human shell, empty and vacant. Almost, Li thought, like a man who had lost his soul. He sat on the edge of his chair, shoulders slumped, hands lying limp together in his lap, staring back at them from behind dark, frightened eyes. His face was streaked by the tears he had spilled when they refused to let him bring his birds. His blue Mao suit was crumpled and dirty, and hung loosely on his gaunt frame. The room was warm and airless, a place devoid of human comfort; naked cream walls scarred and chipped, and scored with the names and thoughts of the thousands of people, both innocent and guilty, who had faced interrogation here during many long hours. Sunlight slanted in through a slit of a window high up on the back wall, slashing the side wall with burned-out yellow. Cigarette smoke, in slowly evolving strands, was suspended in its light. The cassette recorder on the table hummed and whirred in the still of the room. From outside they could hear the distant rumble of traffic from Dongzhimennei Street and, closer, the incongruously innocent sounds of children playing in the *hutong*.

A trickle of sweat ran down Detective Sang's forehead. He leaned forward, strained and intense. He had been very anxious to participate with Li in the interrogation, and Li had allowed him to take the lead while he tried to remain detached and objective. Sang was neither. He was blunt and aggressive, and frustrated by Birdie's apparent confusion over where he had, in fact, been on Monday night. Birdie was certain, he said, that he had been playing checkers with Moon, but if Moon said he wasn't, then he must have been doing something else. He just couldn't think what it was. Usually he spent nights alone at home. Sometimes he would watch television, although he could not remember what programmes he might have watched on Monday night. But usually he went to bed early, when his birds tucked their heads under their wings. He had an early start, he said. He always went to the park before going to the bird market.

'OK,' said Sang eventually. 'So you agree – you don't have an alibi?'

Birdie shook his head despondently. 'But I don't need an alibi. I haven't done anything.'

'Are you saying you didn't know anything about the murders?'

'No. I told you. Me and Pauper talked about them.'

'So you admit you knew that three of the former members of the Revolt-to-the-End Brigade had been murdered?'

'I told you we had heard.'

'And had you heard how they were murdered?'

Birdie winced. 'We heard they were . . . executed.'

'What do you mean by "executed"?'

'That . . .' he shifted uncomfortably, 'that their heads had been cut off.'

'Who told you that?' Li asked.

Birdie shrugged. 'I don't know. People just knew.'

'What people?' Sang pressed him.

'A woman at Zero's factory.'

'That's Bai Qiyu?'

'Yes.'

'What woman?'

'I don't know. I think maybe she was the one who found him. Pauper could tell you. She knew more about it than me. She talks to people, she hears things.'

'So you and Pauper figured that someone was going around killing the members of the Revolt-to-the-End Brigade, and that sooner or later you were going to be next?'

'That's what Pauper thought.'

'Did Pauper always do your thinking for you?' Sang sat back. 'Was it Pauper's idea to kill Yuan Tao before he killed you?'

Birdie was rocking slowly backwards and forwards in his chair. His hands were no longer limp in his lap. They were clasped and wringing one another. 'We didn't kill Cat!' He almost shouted it in tearful defiance. 'We didn't know he was in Beijing. We never even thought of him.'

'There's no point in lying to us, Birdie,' Sang said reasonably. 'We'll find out the truth in the end.' But Birdie just stared back at him. 'How did you find out Cat was back? Did someone see him by chance? Or maybe he contacted you. He must have made arrangements to meet his other victims. Is that what happened? Did he come to the bird market and arrange to meet you somewhere?'

'No!'

'What did he say? That he wanted to talk about what happened back in the sixties? That it was too late now for recriminations, but that he wanted to know why? That he wanted to understand? Is that what he said to the others, do you think? Is that why they agreed to meet him? Because they felt guilty? Even after thirty years?'

'I don't know,' Birdie protested. 'How would I know what he said to them?'

But Sang was on a roll. This was his chance to impress Li, and he was taking it. 'You must have been scared, Birdie. You must have known he was going to kill you, too.'

'No!'

'What did you do? Follow him? That how you found out about the apartment in Tuan Jie Hu Dongli?'

'What apartment?'

'I guess you must have gone there that night and waited for him. How did you know to look under the floorboards?'

But Sang wasn't interested in waiting for Birdie's spluttered protests of ignorance. He pressed on. 'You must have been struck by the irony of it when you found the sword there. The chance to kill him with his own weapon, the same way he killed the others, the same way he intended to kill you.'

'No . . . no . . . !' But Birdie's denials were feeble now, his eyes filling again with tears.

'What else did you find under the floorboards? A killing list, maybe. Silk cord to bind his wrists, the same silk cord he meant to use on you? What did he say when you confronted him? Did he admit it?' Sang leaned forward again, speaking almost softly now. 'Why did you kill him, Birdie? You could just have gone to the police. What happened? Was it anger? Did he spit in your face? Or was it guilt? The only way you could lay the ghost of the past? That dreadful day in the spring of '67, remember it? When you humiliated and beat and hounded Cat's father to his death in the schoolyard in front of everyone, in front of his wife? An old man with a heart condition. You must have felt very proud of yourself.'

Birdie had stopped wringing his hands now. They hung loosely at his sides as he rocked to and fro, and sob after sob ruptured his breathing until Li thought he was going to choke. He stared at his inquisitors unseeingly, and tears ran in rivers of regret down his face.

'Is that why you had to kill Cat, too? Is that why you forced to him to his knees and raised that sword above his head and cut it off with a single stroke?'

Birdie howled like an animal, a deep throaty howl that

rose from his diaphragm and sent a shiver through each of the detectives. 'I didn't mean to,' he shouted. And Li and Sang exchanged glances.

'Didn't mean to what?' Li asked.

'Kill Teacher Yuan.' Birdie clawed at his face with his fingers, trying to wipe away the tears. 'I never meant to do it. Please, please, please, I didn't mean to.'

'It's Cat we're talking about now, Birdie,' Li said softly. He waited for a moment. 'How did you know exactly what it was he had done to the other three?'

But Birdie was shaking his head from side to side, still rocking backwards and forwards. 'I don't know, I don't know,' he kept repeating.

'The placard around his neck. How did you know to do that? The name upside down and scored through.'

Birdie stopped rocking and stared at Li through his tears. 'It's Teacher Yuan you're talking about. That's what we did to him in the Cultural Revolution.' He suddenly banged his fist on the table in frustration. 'How many times do I have to pay for that?' he shouted. 'How many deaths can you die in one lifetime? We were just children. We didn't know what we were doing. Only what Chairman Mao told us. He was the red, red sun in our hearts.'

No, Li thought. He was the blood-red hate in your souls.

They climbed the stairs to the top floor in silence. Sang glanced apprehensively at Li several times. 'You don't look too pleased, boss,' he said. 'For a man who's just cracked a case.'

'We haven't cracked anything,' Li growled. 'Far from it.'

Sang was astonished. 'He as good as admitted it.'

'No he didn't. He was confused. He didn't seem to me able to make a proper distinction between Yuan and his father.'

'But, boss, he had both motive and opportunity. He admitted he knew about the other murders, he doesn't have an alibi – in fact he lied about it.' Sang had to walk quickly to keep up with Li along the top corridor.

Li shook his head. 'The answer's always in the detail, Sang.' His uncle's words fell from his lips as if they were his own. 'And the detail just doesn't add up. Where did Birdie get the flunitrazepam from? How did he know about the placard round the neck, or tying the hands with silk cord?'

Sang shrugged. 'Coercion. He probably forced it out of Yuan. And maybe the flunitrazepam was under the floorboards along with everything else.'

Li stopped suddenly and turned to look at Sang. 'Let me ask you something, detective. Does Birdie look to you like someone who could threaten anyone?' Sang looked uncertain. 'And even if somehow he had managed to force all those details out of Yuan, why did he then write "Digger" on the card instead of "Cat"? How could he get that wrong?'

Sang was at a loss.

Li turned into the detectives' office. Half a dozen detectives were gathered around Margaret and Xinxin, involved in some game with playing cards. They melted away to their desks when Li came in.

'Qian,' Li barked, and Qian jumped.

'Yes, boss.'

'Get a search warrant for Birdie's apartment.'

'Why are we searching his apartment if you don't believe he did it?' Sang asked. He almost tripped on Li's heels as Li stopped and turned on him.

'Police procedure, Sang. I'm assuming you learned *something* at Public Security University. We follow a line of inquiry to its conclusion. I don't expect to find anything incriminating there. I want to eliminate him from our inquiries.'

IV

Five police vehicles brought Li and Margaret, Qian, Wu, Zhao and Sang, along with six uniformed officers to the alleyway leading off Dengshikou Street, where Birdie had his apartment on the ninth floor of a decaying seventies apartment block. This was in the heart of Beijing's shopping district, just off Wangfujing Street, where massive redevelopment was throwing up luxury international hotels and vast shopping plazas. Remnants of the past, however, still survived in little pockets like this.

The lane was dirty and potholed. Women sat behind shabby stalls pedalling lukewarm noodles in a watery sauce. A spotty youth was selling cigarettes and soft drinks from a hole in the wall. The arrival of the police was creating a stir, and a crowd of Chinese, taking a break from the banality of their everyday lives, quickly gathered.

From the lane, the officers entered a courtyard through

a door in an iron gate. Bicycles stood in neat rows under canopies on three sides. Garbage was piled in a heap on steps leading inside where a teenage girl operating the lift viewed the arrival of the police with momentary alarm. She was sitting huddled on a seat, with a pile of cheap romance magazines on her knee, listening to scratchy pop music on a transistor radio. A jar of cold green tea stood on the floor beside her. A fur coat hung on the wall behind her, as if she were anticipating a cold winter. Li and Margaret and two of the detectives, Wu and Qian, squeezed in beside her. The others started up the stairs.

'Do you know Mr Ge?' Li asked the lift girl. She looked puzzled and shook her head. 'He lives on the ninth floor. He keeps birds.'

Her face screwed up in disgust. 'Oh, the bird man,' she said. 'I hate him. He's always bringing his smelly birds in here. It's all right for him. He's used to it, but I can smell them for hours after he's gone.'

'Take us up, please.'

She shrugged and pressed the button for the ninth floor, and the lift jerked and whined and began its slow ascent.

'Do you remember what time he came in on Monday night?' Li asked.

She laughed. 'Are you kidding? Do you know how many people live in this building? Do you think I care when they come and when they go. I don't even look at them.'

'But you'd know the bird man, wouldn't you? You'd smell his birds.'

'He's in and out all the time,' the girl said dismissively. 'And, anyway, I wouldn't know one day from the next. They're all the same to me. You want my job? You can have it.'

'So you wouldn't know if he had any visitors recently?' Li asked hopelessly.

'Gimme a break,' said the girl.

Margaret watched the exchange with an idle curiosity. Beyond her first flush of interest, the lift girl clearly couldn't give a damn and was being less than helpful.

Margaret was not quite sure why she had agreed to come along when Li asked her. After their visit to the university her interest in the investigation was all but dead. She was tired of the emotional roller coaster that sent her hurtling from Li to Michael and back again. It was going nowhere fast. And, if she was honest with herself, she no longer cared who had killed Yuan. What did it matter to her, anyway? Some thirty-year-old vendetta that belonged to another culture in another time. How could she ever hope to understand any of it?

The lift juddered to a standstill on the ninth floor and the door slid open. Li led the way down a corridor with white walls and pale green painted windows that looked down on to the courtyard below. Through a half-glazed door, they turned into a dark hallway, and Margaret saw the number 905 above a door that was shuttered and padlocked. Li stood aside and let Qian unlock it with the keys they had taken from Birdie. After several moments of apparent difficulty, Qian stepped back and shrugged. 'The lock's burst,' he said. 'We didn't need the keys after all.' He pulled back the shutter.

'What do you expect to find here?' Margaret asked.

'Nothing,' Li said, to her surprise.

'If he did it,' she said, 'the chances are there will be some trace evidence here. A speck of blood, a hair. Maybe something more. White card, red ink.'

'*If* he did it.'

'You don't think he did?'

'I am certain he didn't.'

Sang and Zhao and the uniformed officers arrived breathless and perspiring after their nine-flight hike. Li pulled on a pair of white gloves and the others followed suit. 'Bag all the clothes,' Li said, 'clean or dirty. And I want all his shoes. Don't disturb anything unnecessarily, but I want to go through every single little thing in the apartment.' He nodded to Qian who pushed the door open.

They were hit immediately by the smell and the noise. 'In the name of the sky!' Qian took out a handkerchief to cover his nose and went inside, fumbling for a light switch. When he found it, a fluorescent strip hanging from the hall ceiling flickered and hummed and threw a cold light back off walls that had not been painted in twenty years.

'Jesus!' Margaret said.

She looked in amazement at the bamboo cages that hung in profusion from the ceiling. Dozens of them, hooked on to a pulley-type contraption that allowed Birdie to lower and raise them all at the same time. Each of the cages was filled with birds, frantic with the intrusion of light and strangers, squawking and flapping their wings in panic. The noise was deafening. Immediately to the left, a scullery kitchen was caked in grease, old bottles of sticky cooking sauce fighting for space with dirty dishes on the top of an old wooden cabinet. A blackened wok and a couple of filthy pans stood on a two-ring gas stove. Further down the hall, on the left, laundry hung on lines strung across a stinking toilet. Dirty linen lay all over the floor. A fridge-freezer and a top-loading washing machine made it difficult to squeeze past to the far end of the passage where Wu pushed open the bedroom door. More cages hung from the ceiling and stood on every available space: a desk, a wardrobe, a dresser. The din was unnerving. Margaret almost gagged from the stench. It was practically impossible to believe that someone actually lived here.

On their right, a door led into a tiny living room. More cages, more birds. Some of them in here were flying free, and the detectives ducked as frantic wings beat the air about their heads. There was bird shit all over the floor. Through a screen door, the air of a glassed balcony was almost black with flying birds. Birdie had rigged up old branches, and bits and pieces of furniture to try to recreate some kind of natural habitat in there.

'My God!' Margaret shouted above the noise. 'This is unnatural! The man must be insane.'

Li nodded grimly. Somewhere, somehow, Birdie had lost his grip on reality, his ability to relate to the world, to people. His love of birds had become an obsession, a substitute for life. What was it about these creatures that so fascinated him? Was it the illusion of freedom created by their ability to fly?

And yet, what freedom was there for a bird in a cage? Perhaps in robbing them of their freedom, he took some for himself. Freedom from the past. Freedom from guilt. Freedom from reality.

Officers began piling clothing and footwear in large plastic bags, checking through drawers and cupboards, peeling back brittle grey lino to check the floorboards below.

'I'm going out to the landing,' Margaret said, and with her hand over her nose she pushed her way back up the hall towards the door. As she reached it she heard a shout of excitement, and several officers hurried into the bedroom. Curiosity got the better of her, and she made her way back down the hall. Li pushed past the uniforms, and she saw Detective Wu standing holding a bronze sword in his gloved hands, like a trophy.

'It was hidden in the bottom of the wardrobe, boss,' he told Li. Margaret pressed into the room and looked at it. It was about a metre long, with a glazed wooden handle inlaid with mother of pearl. There were no obvious traces of blood. It was clean and sharp.

Sang looked triumphantly at Li. 'That looks like a pretty impressive detail to me, boss.' And Li thought he detected just a hint of smugness in his tone.

It was very bright in here, fluorescent light reflecting off white tiles. On the walk down a long, cool corridor, they could see through windows into labs on either side. They looked, Margaret thought, much like forensic science labs anywhere, the trophies of difficult or gruesome court cases lining the walls. On the back wall of the electron microscope lab there were photo-enlargements of a monstrous hairy-looking insect. Another showed the tip of a screwdriver next to a close-up of the wound it had caused. Through another window, they saw pasted to the wall a series of white linen sheets, about a foot square, each with a small bullet hole surrounded by rims of black soot. In another room, a table was laden with the hardware of death – handguns, rifles, shotguns, each labelled with an evidence tag. In yet another, the paraphernalia of illicit drug use; small metal spoons, bent and blackened; syringes; bottles of pills.

Like many forensic lab technicians, Mr Qi took positive pleasure in the macabre. He was a small man with thinning hair and a cheery face. His white lab coat was several sizes too large for him and in urgent need of laundering. A colourful abundance of pens, pencils and rulers grew out of his breast pocket. He pointed through a window to their left. 'That was domestic in Chongwen District.' He was enjoying the chance to exercise his English. They saw a blouse stretched out on a paper-covered workbench. It was peppered with linear stab holes and tears, and stained with blood that was now dry and grey-brown. 'Husband come home and find her lying on floor of bedroom. Thirty-seven stab wound. At first we think she interrupt burglary. Turns out it is husband. He has other woman and wants rid of wife.' He grinned. 'I like this new Chinese crimewave. It make life ve-ery interesting.'

He swung his rear end at the security sensor on the door

of his lab. The magnetic identification card in the billfold in his back pocket activated the lock, and with a whirr and a dull clunk the door opened. He grinned again. 'Make life easy when hands full. Welcome to my lab.' Margaret, Li, Qian and Sang followed him in, all garbed in the white lab coats they had donned in the ante-chamber at the entrance to the suite. Feet had been scraped on grilles and wiped on mats, to prevent dirt and dust from the outside world tracking in on the spotlessly clean and shiny floors.

The comparison microscope sat on a table on its own. Its base was between two and three feet square. It supported two stages, each about six inches square, where the objects to be magnified and compared were placed beneath bright lamps that would illuminate them for the lenses. Above them, a maze of mirrors and lenses arranged on two turrets, fed the magnified images up to a couple of eyepieces where the examiner could scrutinise the images side by side. From a port beneath the eyepieces, a video signal was fed to a large colour monitor on a stand.

The sections of vertebrae cut from the necks of each of the victims stood in four formalin-filled jars on the lab table. Mr Qi's assistant removed each of them in turn and washed off the formalin so that the fumes would not make Mr Qi's nose burn and eyes water as he examined them under the microscope.

Mr Qi, meantime, clamped the bronze sword they had found in Birdie's apartment to a rolling stand that would hold it steady as the blade was placed on its stage for examination, a few centimetres at a time. It had already been subjected to minute forensic examination, revealing no fingerprints, no blood. All traces of its owner had been carefully and meticulously excised. But its blade had been sharpened on only one side, and so only one edge had been used for cutting.

Mr Qi dropped the blinds on the window to the corridor with a clatter and turned out the lights. The room was plunged into darkness except for the glow of the monitor and the lamps in the comparison microscope that illuminated the white coats of the little group of investigators that was gathered around it.

The assistant trimmed the first section of vertebrae with a jeweller's saw, and placed it on the left-hand stage. Mr Qi arranged the blade of the sword so that a section about two-thirds of the way along its length rested on the right-hand stage, approximately in the area of the 'sweet spot' that Margaret had spoken about at the autopsy. He peered down into the eyepieces and began adjusting his focus. For the moment the image on the monitor was blurred, and the detectives shuffled impatiently. Margaret knew that the process would take time.

Centimetre by centimetre, Mr Qi moved the stage upon which the blade rested, by means of a series of small cranks and gears, focusing on the tiny nicks and striations shown up under magnification, and comparing them with the microscopic scores left on the cartilage of the first piece of neck.

'Aha!' he said suddenly, and they all jumped. 'We have a match.' And he refocused the lenses so that the image on the monitor slipped into sharp focus. Side by side, the hugely magnified images of the neck cartilage and the blade revealed an identical and matching pattern of vertical scores of varying heights and widths. Mr Qi grinned at them triumphantly. 'This sword cut off this head.' And he took a red, felt-tipped pen from his pocket and carefully marked the section of blade that matched the piece of neck and annotated it with the specimen number. 'Next,' he said happily.

One by one, Mr Qi matched up sections of the blade to the other three neck specimens. The first three sections overlapped at either the left or right margins. The fourth was about an inch away, nearer the handle end. Mr Qi marked each match with a different coloured pen.

With practised expertise, Yuan Tao had hit the sweet spot of his blade with unnerving accuracy. His own killer had not achieved the same degree of precision. But beyond any shadow of a doubt, this was the murder weapon. Li stared at the red, yellow, green and blue markings on its blade with a brooding intensity.

Sang was gleeful. 'Still think Birdie isn't our man, boss?'

CHAPTER ELEVEN

I

Up here felt like that magical world beyond the clouds. Nothing down there could touch you. You could see it all, but were above it all. On the steps up, Margaret had passed the last straggling tourists on the way down as the light began to fade in Jingshan Park. Now she sat all alone on the warm marble steps of the pavilion on the top of Prospect Hill, with Beijing spread out at her feet, the vast empty spaces of the Gobi Desert stretching away to the north, the huge crimson orb of the sun sinking slowly beyond the purple mountains in the west. The scent of pine rose on the warm air with the evensong of birds before sleep.

Three months ago, Li had brought her here for the first time. It was a place, he had said, that he liked to come and think. Where he could be alone in a city of eleven million people and yet still be at its very heart.

She had come here to think now, to try to put her life into some kind of perspective, and make definitive decisions about her future. Less than a week ago she thought she had done just that. But the world had turned, and events since had changed her thinking and her life, possibly for ever. She had met Michael. Earnest, sensitive, intelligent Michael who had asked her to marry him. If he was here now, he would no doubt tell her how this very hill upon which she sat was artificially created with the earth dug out of the vast moat surrounding the Forbidden City below. She smiled at the thought, and then wondered what it was that she really felt about him.

It was not, she knew, the fiery and intense passion she had felt for Li. That had been born out of extraordinary circumstances: fear, hate, love, a cauldron of passions that had forged an extraordinary relationship. But it was Li himself who had extinguished its flame. Snuffed it out between finger and thumb, burning himself in the process, the pain of it a constant reminder of his own regret.

Michael was so different. For a start they spoke the same language, shared the same culture. There were no cross-cultural misunderstandings, no political gulfs to be bridged, no requirement to defend or criticise one country over another, capitalism over communism.

Margaret knew that however much she had grown to love this country and these people, her future could not be here. She could only go home. But home was just a word for a place where everything was familiar and you could be comfortable with the people you loved. And in reality she had no home. Home was a distant memory of a happy childhood, or of the years spent sharing the same space and bed with a man who was now dead. She was thirty-one years old. In ten years she would be into her forties. Forty-year-old Margaret Campbell, fifty-year-old Margaret Campbell. It all seemed too close and too real. Life could just pass you by.

Down there, in the world below the clouds, Li was confronting a shell of a man with the murder weapon that had been used to take the lives of four men. Other people were going about their everyday lives, returning home after work, preparing evening meals, making love, giving birth, growing old, dying. Red taillights stretched off into the distance like visible time. Sometimes it crawled by. Other times it whizzed past. Either way, the journey always ended too soon.

She felt the hopelessness of her life well up inside her.

As the sun slipped lower behind the mountains, it washed the city red, and she looked up, suddenly startled by a flash of lightning and a crack of thunder. Great crimson-edged purple clouds were rolling across the plains from the east. She smelled rain in the breath of it that reached her ahead of the storm, and she knew it was time to go.

II

The sword lay on the table between Li and Sang on one side, and Birdie on the other. He gazed at it uncomprehendingly.

'It's not mine,' he said.

'Oh, we know whose it is,' Sang told him. 'What we want to know is what it was doing in your apartment.'

Birdie shook his head. 'No, not in my apartment.'

'It was in your wardrobe. We went to your apartment this afternoon and found it there.'

Birdie dragged his eyes away from the blade and looked up at Li, and for a moment Li was shocked by the appeal he saw in them, as if somehow Birdie recognised in him the doubt, and the possibility of an ally. 'No,' Birdie said. And, very directly to Li, 'I want to go home, please. My birds need to be fed. There is no one to feed my birds.'

And Li saw again the apartment filled with chattering birds in myriad cages, the stink of their shit, the sacks of seed that stood in the corner of the living room. He wondered what would happen to them if they detained Birdie further, if they sent him to Section Seven to be grilled by the professional inquisitors. Perhaps he should detail a couple of officers to clear the apartment and take all the birds down to the market at Guanyuan.

'I'm afraid that's not possible,' he told Birdie.

Sang was determined not to be sidetracked. He stood up and lifted the sword. 'This is the weapon that Cat used to chop off the heads of Monkey and Zero and Pigsy. And then you used it to chop off the head of Cat.'

'No!'

'What's the point in denying it, Birdie? We know it's true. We know you went to his apartment and found this under the floorboards. We know that you drugged him and tied him up and then cut his head off. We know you did it because you hid the sword in your own bedroom. Why don't you confess? Get it off your chest. We know you feel guilty about Teacher

Yuan. You've carried that guilt with you for thirty-three years. You don't want to have the guilt of Cat on your head for the rest of your life, do you? You want a clear conscience. It's so much easier when you don't have all that weight of guilt to carry around. And maybe you could tell the judge it was self-defence. After all, we know Yuan was going to kill you.' He lay the sword back on the table and leaned across so that his face was inches from Birdie's. He almost whispered, 'Confess, Birdie. Just tell us all about it. You know you'll feel better.'

Birdie's tears came again. But they were silent this time. He gazed off into the middle distance, right through and beyond Sang, to some half-remembered past. *It's party policy to be lenient with those who confess their crimes, and severe with those who refuse*, they had said to him, and when he refused to confess, kicked and punched and beat him until he was almost senseless. *Do you really think all we know how to do is feed our faces? Speak up!* 'The revolutionary masses express their devotion to Chairman Mao in every imaginable way because of their profound feelings for their leader,' he said to Sang, and the rookie detective looked back at him with astonishment.

'What are you talking about, Birdie?'

'You are treacherous and slippery, like the prick of an oily dog,' Birdie shouted, and both Li and Sang were startled. And then he covered his face with his hands and began sobbing, and rocking backwards and forwards as he had done earlier.

Li stood up and drew Sang back from the table. 'Enough, son,' he said. He was not sure why, but he felt profoundly sad looking down on the weeping shambles of what had once been a man. He represented a whole generation who had lost their youth, in some cases their lives, in twelve, turbulent, horror-filled years of insanity. In Birdie's case, he had lost his soul and was consumed by emptiness. He was both perpetrator and victim.

Xinxin sat on Li's desk in the ring of light cast by the angle-poise lamp and sifted through the pieces of her jigsaw. In her left hand she clutched a half-empty carton of orange juice. The detectives had spoiled her, feeding her all sorts of sweet things and soft drinks, playing cards and helping her with her jigsaw. Now, as most of them drifted home in the early evening darkness, Li stood at the window and was only waiting for Margaret to return, so that they could take Xinxin back to Mei Yuan's. He had no idea where she had gone. She had been silent and subdued for most of the day after their visit to Beijing university. He knew she had lost interest in the case. And after they had confirmed the sword as the murder weapon she had told him she had things to do, but would be back later.

He didn't understand why, but somehow Xinxin had briefly built a bridge between them, a bridge that neither of them had had the chance to cross before he had smashed it down again by taking her to the university. He cursed the jealousy that had motivated his attempts to try to discredit Zimmerman. He had tried to justify it to himself as police procedure. But he knew that was just self-delusion. It was as if, in denying her to himself, he was determined to ensure than no other man could have her either. It was neither right nor fair. Was he really so weak? No wonder she had looked at him with such hatred this morning.

His mind wandered back to the pathetic figure of Birdie being led off to a holding cell in the basement. Li still found it impossible to believe that Birdie had possessed either the presence of mind or the intelligence to track Yuan down to his rented apartment, that he had been able replicate so closely the *modus operandi* of the previous murders, that he could so successfully have made it appear that Yuan was the fourth victim. And there were all the unanswered questions and inconsistencies: the bright blue vodka, the bottles of red wine, the blue-black ceramic dust, the wrong nickname.

And yet he had both motive and opportunity and, most damning of all, the murder weapon had been found in his apartment. Either, Li thought, Birdie was fooling them all with a stunningly convincing performance, or the real killer had planted the sword in his apartment. But that thought, too, was inconceivable. For the killer to do that, he would have had to have known that Birdie was the prime suspect. And outside of Section One no one knew that.

Lightning flickered briefly in the sky, followed by the distant rumble of thunder, and he turned to find Margaret standing silhouetted in the doorway watching him. Xinxin, engrossed in her jigsaw, had not seen her yet. For a moment, they stood looking at each other across the darkened room, and he sensed something painful in the silence that lay between them like an unbridgeable chasm. Then Xinxin saw her, screeched her delight and scrambled off the desk to rush to give her a hug. Margaret felt the warmth of her little body, the tremble of her excitement, and felt a pang of regret at the decision she had taken just an hour before. Xinxin jabbered at her incoherently.

Margaret looked to Li. 'What's she saying?'

'She wants you to help her finish the jigsaw.'

'Sure,' Margaret said and glanced at her watch. 'As long as it doesn't take too long.'

It took less than ten minutes to finish the jigsaw, and Xinxin was led, protesting, down to the Jeep, until Li told her they were going to Mei Yuan's, and then all was sweetness and light again.

The night had turned sticky hot as the clouds rolled in from the east, heavy and dark and prescient with rain. Traffic had thinned in the aftermath of rush hour, and taxis and private cars buzzed in and around lumbering buses and trolleys, like insects driven mad in anticipation of the coming storm. People everywhere knew that rain was on its way. Canopies and umbrellas were raised over smoking stoves and sidewalk braziers, and marketeers drew awnings over goods laid out on open stalls. Normally dilatory cyclists pedalled hard to get home before the heavens opened.

When Mei Yuan opened her door to them she lifted Xinxin into her arms and carried her to the table.

'This evening,' she told Li and Margaret, 'you will stay to eat. Xinxin and I cannot manage all the dumplings ourselves. So I will fry those that are left.'

As she busied herself at her tiny stove, Li and Margaret sat at the table, with Xinxin reading her story books to Margaret for the umpteenth time. Li stole a glance at her and saw that she was not really listening. Not just because she could not understand, but because she was miles away. There was a great distance in her eyes, and her spirit was subdued. But, still, she managed to smile for Xinxin and hide from the child whatever it was that disturbed her. She caught Li looking at her and her eyes flickered quickly away, back to the book, almost as if afraid that by meeting his eye he would be able to read her thoughts.

Mei Yuan served up the spicy dumplings, fried brown and sticky, and they shared a bowl of chilli soy to dip. The taste and texture of them took Margaret back to the eating place that Michael had taken her to in the Muslim quarter in Xi'an, and she was reminded again of the things she had decided on Prospect Hill.

Mei Yuan was aware of the atmosphere, although she did not understand it. She did her best to try to change the mood. 'So,' she said brightly to Margaret. 'I have given much thought to your riddle today, but I still have no answer.' She looked at Li. 'What about you, Li Yan?'

Li shook himself free from his thoughts and looked up. He had forgotten all about the riddle, and was about to say so when the answer came to him, quite out of the blue. He smiled and shook his head. 'I think I know,' he said. 'But only a stranger to Beijing could pose such a riddle.'

'What do you mean?' Margaret asked defensively.

'You wanted to know how I could walk from Xidamochang

Street to Beijing Railway Station during National Day without being seen,' he said. 'And the answer you are looking for is that I went down into the Underground City and followed the tunnels to the station.'

'What's wrong with that?'

Li looked at Mei Yuan. 'Do you want to tell her?'

Mei Yuan put a consoling hand over Margaret's and smiled. 'The tunnels do not lead to Beijing Railway Station,' she said.

'But I saw a sign,' Margaret protested. 'It said *To the Station*.'

'That's the old Beijing Railway Station,' Li said. 'It used to be on the south-east corner of Tiananmen Square at Qianmen before they built the new station a couple of miles further east.'

Margaret made a token protest. 'OK, so they moved the station. How am I supposed to know that?'

Li shrugged. 'Like I said, only a stranger to Beijing could pose such a riddle.'

In the difficult silence that followed, Mei Yuan asked if they wanted beer. But Margaret shook her head. It was time, she said, for her to go. Li said he would run her to her hotel. They all stood up. Xinxin's upturned face looked from one to the other, perplexed by the sudden abandonment of the dumplings. 'What is it?' she said.

'Margaret has to go,' Li told her.

Xinxin was crestfallen. 'Will I see her tomorrow?'

Li asked Margaret, and for a long time Margaret seemed lost in tormented thought before suddenly making a decision.

'Tell her,' she said, 'that I will come tomorrow morning and take her to the playpark beyond the bridge. To say goodbye.'

'*To say goodbye?*' Mei Yuan asked, taken aback.

Margaret looked at Li. 'I am leaving on Monday,' she said.

Outside, beyond the trees, a slight breeze ruffled the dark surface of Qianhai Lake, and the first fat drops of rain splashed on to the hood of Li's Jeep, making craters in the dust. Li caught Margaret's arm as she started for the passenger side. 'Why are you leaving so soon? The investigation is not yet over.'

This time she met his eyes with a steady gaze. 'It is for me.' she said. And the drops of rain, more frequent now, felt cool on the hot skin of her face. 'Everything's over, Li Yan. You, me, China.'

'And Zimmerman?'

But she wasn't angry with him any more. She smiled sadly. 'Michael has asked me to marry him.' And she saw the disbelief and pain in his eyes. 'I told him no. But the offer's still open. And I'm going to go home and think about it. Very seriously. Away from you. Away from him. Away from here. For ever.'

A flash of lightning and a crack of thunder immediately overhead, was a prelude to the heavens opening. Rain fell in sheets, and in a matter of seconds they were soaked through. But neither of them moved. He saw the outline of her breasts, wet cotton clinging to their contours. Her hair was stuck in wet curls to her face, a face pale and freckled and lovely. He could not be certain whether it was tears he saw spilling from her blue eyes, or just the rain. Her face shone wet and sad in the sheet lightning that lit up the sky. He knew this was the end. There was no way forward, no way back. She reached up on tiptoe and kissed him softly on the lips. He felt her fingers lightly trace the line of his jaw. And then she was off, running down the *hutong* into the night, swallowed by the dark and the rain. He knew he would never see her again, and that all those moments they had shared, the fear and the passion, their one physical consummation in an abandoned sleeper in northern China, would be lost for ever, like tears in rain.

From the bar of the Ritan Hotel, Michael saw Margaret step from a taxi, and he hurried across the vast expanse of shiny marbled foyer to intercept her at the door. She took one look at him and burst into tears, to his confusion and distress. He took her in his arms. She was wet and dishevelled, mascara tracks on her cheeks. 'For God's sake, Margaret, what's wrong?'

'Nothing's wrong,' she mumbled into his chest. 'Nothing's wrong, Michael. Just hold me.'

III

Margaret had her back to him. He saw Michael approach her. There was something in his hand, but he could not quite see what it was. Then she turned as he raised his arm, and the blade of a dagger glinted in the light as it arced through the air towards her. Li called out, but his voice would not sound.

He tried to move, but his hands were bound behind his back, and he became aware for the first time of a white placard hanging round his neck. He could read his own name on it, and realised it was upside down. Now he looked up and saw that it was not a dagger, but a sword, and it was not Michael who held it, but Margaret. She had the strangest smile on her face as she brought the blade slicing down on him.

His own scream brought him to consciousness, and he heard the distant echo of it reverberating in his dream. He was breathing hard and lathered in sweat, as if he had just run a race. Blood pulsed painfully at his temples. He looked at the digital display by his bedside and saw that it was only one o'clock. He had barely been asleep half an hour.

He swung his legs out of the bed and reached for his cigarettes. He had only just lit one when he was startled by a fist pounding on his door. 'Hello?' he heard a woman's voice shouting. 'Is there anyone there?'

He ran through the dark apartment and unlocked the door, throwing it open to reveal the middle-aged woman who lived across the landing. She was a fearsome creature with a big ugly face and whiskered chin, a very senior officer in the Ministry of State Security which shared its compound with the Ministry of Public Security. She wore a pink cotton dressing gown wrapped around her overample frame, and her face was covered with white cream.

Li stared at her in astonishment. 'What is it?'

'I heard someone screaming.'

He breathed a sigh of relief. Was that all? 'I was having a

bad dream,' he said, and noticed that her eyes had strayed down to his middle regions. With a shock he realised he was stark naked. 'Is there anything else?' he asked.

Reluctantly she dragged her eyes away from the focus of their interest and glared at him. 'You're disgusting!' she said. 'Exposing yourself to a helpless woman in the middle of the night.' But she didn't sound too disgusted. 'I've a good mind to report you.'

'What for?' he asked. 'Failing to get a hard-on? One look at you, comrade, and there isn't a court in the land that would convict me.' She flushed. 'Thank you for your concern.' And he shut the door on her indignant face.

He wandered through to get a beer from the refrigerator, but he had drunk it all. He pulled on a pair of jogpants and sat in the dark of the living room taking long pulls at his cigarette. Outside, he could see, the rain had stopped. But the leaves on the trees were still glistening wet in the light of the streetlamps, and dripping on the sidewalk below. He thought about Margaret, and immediately stopped himself. It was too easy. It was all he had done all night. He was damned if he was going to sit here and wallow in self-pity. He got up, walked out on to the balcony and forced his brain to work in other directions.

An image of Birdie in his holding cell floated into his mind, pathetic and sad and curled up like a foetus on the unyielding boards of his bunk bed. Another thought crowded in, an earlier thought that he had already dismissed. And an image that went with it, of a shadowy figure creeping through the dark of Birdie's apartment to hide a sword in the bottom of the wardrobe. He heard the birds, screeching, disturbed from their sleep, alarmed by the movement they could not see. And he suddenly remembered Qian fumbling with the padlock on the steel shutter. *The lock's burst*, he had said. *We didn't need the keys after all*. Li cursed himself. He had not even bothered to look at it. Had it been forced, or was it simply broken? He lit another cigarette and ran a hand back through the stubble of his hair. It had not even been an issue at the time. No one could have suspected then that someone might have broken into Birdie's apartment to plant the murder weapon. It was by no means certain now. Li checked the time. It was still only one thirty. He went back through to his bedroom, pulled on a tee shirt and slipped his feet into a pair of trainers. He did not have the patience to wait until the morning to ask Qian.

The air was filled with the smell of damp earth and wet leaves as he cycled north through the dark deserted streets, wondering if his determination to check out the lock on Birdie's apartment was simply a means of shutting Margaret out of his thoughts. He put his head down and pedalled harder, trying to free his mind from the burden of any conscious thought.

The duty officer at Section One retrieved Birdie's keys from the evidence room and handed them to Li. 'He asked for pen and ink and some paper a couple of hours ago,' he told Li. 'Haven't heard a cheep from him since.' He smiled at his own sad pun.

The alleyway leading off Dengshikou Street was deserted.

The windows of the apartment block stood in dark, silent rows, one upon the other. Li wheeled his bicycle into the courtyard, and startled a rat foraging among the pile of garbage on the steps. It scurried off into the night. He parked his bicycle under the lamp by the door and went inside. From somewhere in the depths of the building he heard the distant hum of something electrical. Otherwise, the building was deathly silent. The lift doors were shut, and the normally illuminated call button was dark. Li made his way to the foot of the stairs and took out the keys to unlock the stairgate. But the gate creaked away from his hand as he touched it. He took out a penlight from his back pocket and shone it on the lock. It was seized solid, and had obviously been that way for some time. So anyone could have gained access to the building anytime after ten o'clock when the lift was switched off. He began the long ascent.

By the time he reached the ninth floor he was seriously regretting not having given up cigarettes long ago – and his automatic response was to light one immediately and take a deep draw. A faint light from distant streetlamps washed in through the windows and illuminated the corridor. He made his way along it and turned left into the darkness of the hallway where his penlight picked out the number 905 above Birdie's door. The shutter was lying ajar, and Li felt a surge of anger at the carelessness of his officers for leaving it that way. He crouched down and lifted up the padlock on the end of its chain. The top loop slipped in and out of its hole, but failed to lock. Li focused his penlight on the keyhole and saw several fine scratches in the metal, shiny and freshly made. The lock had clearly been disabled. Recently. And by someone who knew what they were doing. He stood up and let it go and it clanked off the metal of the door. Someone had broken into Birdie's apartment and planted the sword there. Li stood still for a moment, shocked by the revelation, and puzzled. It hardly seemed possible.

He turned the handle of the inner door and pushed it open. He heard the beat of wings in the air, a screeching chorus of alarm, and something flew at him out of the darkness. Something big and dark that struck him violently in the chest. He staggered backwards, taken completely by surprise, and robbed totally of his ability to breathe. As the shape emerged from the deepest shadows, he saw that it was the figure of a man, quite a bit smaller than himself, lean and wiry. But he had only the vaguest glimpse of the silhouette before another foot struck him in the chest, and a small, iron-hard fist smashed into his face. His head struck the wall behind him with a sickening crack, and he slid down it to the floor, blood bubbling from his mouth and nose. His attacker leaped nimbly over his prostrate form and was gone in a blur, through the door and away down the corridor. Li heard the footfalls on concrete, the banging of a door, and then steps echoing in the stairwell as his assailant made good his escape.

Li sat for several minutes, leaning against the wall, gasping for breath. His chest hurt like hell, and he half-choked on the blood that ran back down his throat. He felt like a complete idiot.

*

Qian looked at the blood that had dried in streaks down the front of Li's white tee shirt and shook his head. Li's face was in quite a state. His bottom lip was split and swollen, and blood-soaked cotton wool trailed from each nostril where a medic had stuffed wads of it to stop the bleeding. 'Must have been a big guy to make that much mess of you, boss.'

Li shook his head grimly. 'Nothing to do with his size. He took me by surprise, that's all. I wasn't expecting there to be anyone in the apartment.' He was embarrassed.

The whole block was now a blaze of lights. With the arrival of the police, sirens wailing, residents had poured out on to landings and into the courtyard. Neighbouring blocks had also been roused, and there was a crowd of several hundred curious men and women in the street, some with sleepy children clutching parental hands and blinking blearily at the comings and goings of uniformed officers.

Qian had only just arrived, dragged reluctantly from his bed by a call from the Section One duty officer. His face was puffy with sleep. 'So what do you think he was doing in there?' He looked through the doorway at the uniformed officers who seemed to be dismantling the entire apartment. 'What are *they* doing in there?'

'Same thing as he was,' Li said. 'Looking for something. Only difference is, he knew what it was. We don't.'

Qian frowned and scratched his head. 'You've lost me, boss. You mean, you know who he is?'

'Sure. He's the guy who broke in and planted the murder weapon in Birdie's wardrobe.'

This was a new one on Qian. '*Planted* the murder weapon? You mean, you don't think Birdie did it after all?'

'I never did. And the only reason I can figure the guy came back is he left or lost something while he was here. Something he thought might be incriminating.'

'And do you think he found it before you disturbed him?'

Li shrugged and winced. The medic had strapped up his ribs, but they still hurt. 'Who knows. But if there's something there, I want to find it.'

It was almost five o'clock before Qian emerged from the apartment holding up a small, clear plastic evidence bag. Li was squatting in the corridor, small piles of ash and cigarette ends around him. The analgesics he had taken earlier were wearing off and he was starting to hurt again. He got painfully to his feet. 'What have you got?'

Qian shook his head despondently. 'Maybe something, maybe nothing.'

The first light was appearing in a sky washed clear by the previous night's rain. The clouds had all moved on. Li took the bag and examined its contents. It was a small diamond stud not much bigger than a match head on the end of a short, blunt pin. 'What the hell is it?'

'It's a stud earring,' Qian said. 'The kind of thing people wear in pierced ears to stop the hole healing up. I don't think it's Birdie's.'

Li looked at him with undisguised dismay and pointed at his own face. 'Are you telling me it was a woman that did this to me?'

Qian grinned, amused by the thought. 'Not very likely, boss. Lot of young men get their ears pierced these days. A nasty habit picked up from the West.'

Li looked beyond him, disappointed, towards the apartment. 'Nothing else?'

'Afraid not, boss. At least, nothing that would raise an eyebrow. We were lucky we found that in the mess in there. If it hadn't caught the light . . .' Qian went to take the bag from Li, but his boss hung on to it.

'Could be Dr Campbell's,' Li said. 'She was in the apartment yesterday. What room was it in?'

'The bedroom.'

Li nodded thoughtfully. To Qian his face was impassive, but inside his heart was pounding painfully against bruised ribs. He had a reason to see her. It was stupid and self-defeating, he knew, and it would probably only lead to more pain. But it was a valid reason.

'I'll get cleaned up,' he said, 'and go and ask her.'

The stalls of traders in furs and toys that lined the west sidewalk of Ritan Lu were shuttered and padlocked. In the park opposite, groups of men and women were gathering to dance the foxtrot or practise their *tai ch'i* or *wu shu*. Li could already hear the sound of scratchy music issuing from ghetto blasters mingling, among the trees, with the plaintive wail of a violin and the haunting voice of a woman singing a song from the Peking Opera. The first rays of watery yellow sunlight slanted and flickered among the leaves. The air was fresh in a way that it rarely was in Beijing these days.

Although it had barely gone six, the street was already thick with cyclists on their way to the park or factory or office block. A few vendors had established themselves at street corners selling freshly baked sweet potatoes hot from the coals of their braziers, or *jian bing* or roasted chestnuts. The smell of sweet things cooking for early breakfast drifted across the street in the smoke.

Li cycled slowly north. Each revolution of the pedals hurt his ribs. He had a splitting headache, and his lower lip throbbed painfully with the swelling. But he was almost unaware of these things as he looked up and saw the white-tile façade of the Ritan Hotel rising behind the trees. As he reached the gate he braked and slowly dismounted. A taxi honked its horn at him as it drove by, skirting a neatly arranged flowerbed and drawing up under the red painted framework of steel and glass that formed a canopy over the hotel entrance. Li was about to follow it through the gates when he saw a familiar figure hurrying out of the hotel and climbing into the taxi. It was Michael Zimmerman, looking happy and relaxed, and with a marked spring in his step. The sight of him leaving her hotel struck Li with more force than his assailant at Birdie's apartment. Zimmerman could afford to be pleased with himself, Li thought bitterly. He had Margaret.

Li immediately pulled back, withdrawing behind a car parked on the sidewalk, and watched as the taxi emerged from the driveway and headed off down the street.

Zimmerman did not notice him. Why would he? After all, Li was just another Chinese face in a city of eleven million Chinese faces. He caught sight of two security guards in brown uniform watching him with undisguised suspicion from where they stood smoking outside the gatehouse. He hesitated for a long time. He could not go in now. She would know he had seen Michael leave. He did not want to confront the reality of that. He never had.

Slowly he turned his bicycle round and remounted it. Later today he would send Sang to ask her about the stud earring. It was not something he had to do himself.

IV

As soon as he turned his bicycle into Beixinqiao Santiao, and saw a dozen uniformed officers standing smoking in the dappled shade of the trees, he knew that something was wrong. An ambulance stood half on the sidewalk at the side entrance to Section One. The officers turned and looked at him as he appeared, and the hubbub of lively conversation died away. He parked his bike and hurried inside.

There were more officers gathered at the far end of the corridor, at the top of the half-flight of stairs that led down to the holding cells. Li had a sick sensation in his stomach. He ran the length of the corridor, pushing past the officers, and down the steps two at a time.

Birdie's cell was full of plain-clothes and uniformed officers. Two medics were crouched over a prostrate form on the floor.

Bodies parted to let Li in. Birdie's head rested at a peculiar angle. His eyes were wide, and staring lifelessly at the wall. The tip of his tongue protruded through blue lips. A short length of dirty rope lay on the floor beside him, its weave still visible in a dry, golden-red abrasion furrow around his neck.

'He hanged himself, boss. Sometime during the night.' Li turned to find Wu at his shoulder.

'How the hell did he get the rope!' Li's shock was turning to anger.

Wu said, 'Seems he used it to hold up his pants. He wore his tunic out, so no one saw it.' He paused and added significantly. 'And no one checked.'

Anger was now turning to despair. Li let his head drop and squeezed his eyes with his thumb and forefinger. He released a long, slow exhalation of frustration and looked at Birdie again. Grotesque though his features were, contorted by strangulation, there was a strange peace in his eyes. He had escaped. After thirty-three years he was finally free of his guilt. Free, like the birds he had loved all his life.

'He left a confession, boss.' Wu was watching him carefully.

Li turned to him, frowning. 'A confession?'

Wu nodded. 'The chief's got it.'

Chen handed him the two flimsy sheets of paper, characters scrawled across them in a clumsy, childish hand. He said grimly, 'There's going to be hell to pay for this, Li Yan. The Ministry does not like prisoners killing themselves in police custody. There will be an investigation.'

Li nodded. He scanned Birdie's confession with a sinking heart.

'At least,' Chen said, 'we have his confession. The case has been cracked, so the political pressure will relax. You have no idea just how much pressure I've been protecting you people from.'

Li could imagine only too well. He shook his head. 'It is just a pity the "confession" does not stand up.'

Chen glared at him. 'What do you mean?'

Li waved the sheets of paper dismissively. 'All he's done, Chief, is repeat, almost word for word, the accusations that Sang levelled at him yesterday. Go and listen to the tape. He's just told us what we wanted to hear. It's like the kind of self-criticism they would have made him write in the Cultural Revolution. Confess, confess, confess. That's all they ever wanted. Whatever "crimes" they dreamed up, that's what they wanted you to confess to. And that's what he's done. Confession is the path of least resistance – even when you didn't do it.'

Chen glared at him angrily. 'Rubbish!' he said. 'He gave us a false alibi, he had the perfect motive, and we found the murder weapon in his apartment.'

'Motive isn't proof of guilt, Chief. You know that. He was confused about where he was last Monday night, that's all. And the murder weapon was planted in his apartment.'

'What proof do you have of that?'

Li pointed a finger at his face. 'What do you think this is?'

'You got a bloody nose when you interrupted a burglar at Ge Yan's apartment. What does that prove?'

For a moment Li was stumped. Of course, he knew he had no proof that the sword had been planted in Birdie's bedroom, no matter how certain he was of it. 'There are a dozen other inconsistencies, chief. The nickname, the wine—'

Chen cut him off. 'I don't want to hear it, Li. And I don't want you repeating it.'

'But, Chief—'

Chen's voice was low and threatening. 'As far as I am concerned, Deputy Section Chief, we have proven beyond doubt that Yuan Tao murdered the victims known as Monkey, Zero and Pigsy. It was an act of revenge for their victimisation of his father during the Cultural Revolution. We now have a confession from an individual who believed he was next on the list, that he murdered Yuan before Yuan could murder him. His confession is given credence by the fact that the murder weapon was found in his apartment. End of story. End of case.' He paused for a long time. 'Do you understand me?'

The two men glared at each other for several more long moments. Li was seething. He wanted to throw Birdie's confession in Chen's face and tell him what he could do with it. But the longer he restrained the urge, the more he realised just how futile a gesture it would be.

In the end, all he said was, 'Yes, Chief.'

CHAPTER TWELVE

I

Margaret stretched lazily on the bed, luxuriating in a sense of freedom. However painful it had been to make her decision, having made it she felt released from an enormous burden. She had lain for a long time in Michael's arms last night, simply curled into him for comfort, childlike and secure, and then they had made love and she had slept like a baby until becoming aware of him leaving shortly after six.

'Where are you going?' she had asked.

But he had simply smiled and kissed her forehead. 'Sunday is not a day of rest in China. And there is no rest for the wicked. I'm required on location. I'll see you later.'

Now she rolled over and looked at the time. She had promised to take Xinxin to the park. A tiny stab of pain, an echo from another life, came to her with the recollection. She regretted having made the promise. She had done so before confronting Li with her revelations about Michael and her decision to go home. Now all she wanted was a clean break. It could only be painful taking that one step back, even if it was for just an hour or so. But she had promised, and she could not let the little girl down. Too many people had done that already.

She showered and washed her hair, and as she blow-dried it, looking in the mirror, she thought she looked older, pinched, a little haggard. She had lost weight and could see the faint outline of her ribcage. She enjoyed being slim, but skinny was unattractive. She had seen women in their thirties, desperate to stay attractive, dieting to the point where they aged themselves prematurely. A little flesh on the bone kept you looking younger. All she wanted to do now was get home, and a little comfort eating would do her no harm at all.

As she went through the clothes in her wardrobe, she realised she would have to pack sometime today. But she didn't linger over the contents of the rack. There were clothes hanging there that carried too many memories. Clothes she had chosen to wear for Li on certain occasions. Clothes that would always make her think of him. Clothes that she would give to the Salvation Army back home. She pulled on a pair of jeans and tucked a fresh tee shirt into them, then rummaged through the shoes at the bottom of the wardrobe, looking for a pair of trainers. She picked out a white pair with pale pink piping, and froze as she saw a scattering of blue-black powder on the wooden base beneath them. For almost a full half-minute she remained motionless, the trainers in her hand, looking at the powder. She could hear her blood pulsing in her ears. Slowly she reached in and took a pinch of it between her fingers and looked at it closely. The texture and colour were the same as the sample Li had shown her. She turned over her trainers and saw the blue dust compacted in their treads. Without being aware of it, her breathing had turned rapid and shallow. She was trying to remember when she had last worn these trainers, where she could possibly have picked up this strange powdery residue. She retraced her life over the previous few days, and realised with a sudden shock that she had not worn these shoes since the day she had visited the Terracotta Warriors with Michael. Down there in the pits, with the dust and rubble of centuries, the smashed pottery of the warriors had deposited their crumbling ceramic dust, a fired clay that had turned blue-black in the searing heat of the kilns. And she had tramped it into the treads of her shoes.

But it made no sense. What possible connection could there be between the underground chambers in Xi'an where two-thousand-year-old ceramic warriors stood guard over their emperor, and a series of murders in Beijing? A series of murders which, to all intents and purposes, had already been solved.

And as quickly as she had let her imagination run riot, she stopped herself. She had no idea if this blue powder matched the other samples. But to her immediate regret, she realised that she wanted to find out. And she found herself suddenly, and quite unexpectedly, being drawn back into a world she had been trying very hard to escape. The force that drew her was irresistible, as was the curiosity which she recognised now was edged by just the faintest hint of apprehension.

Margaret's doubts about whether Mr Qi would be at work on a Sunday or not were quickly allayed. After all, criminals did not take weekends off, why should criminalists? He looked at the sample of powder she had brought him in a white hotel envelope and scratched his chin thoughtfully. Her shoes, in a plastic bag, lay on the table.

'It look ve-ery much like same dust,' he said. 'Most probably about seventy per cent composition fired clay. The rest organic, mineral, some artefact.' He looked at her. 'Where did you find this, Doctah Cambo?'

'I picked it up in the treads of my shoes at the pits of the Terracotta Warriors in Xi'an.'

'Aha!' Mr Qi's face positively glowed with illumination. 'Then this almost certainly same dust,' he said. 'We did analysis on mineral component of clay. Most commonly found in area of Shaanxi Province west of Xi'an City. If you find it in pits it must be clay they use to make Terracotta Warrior more than two thousand years ago.'

And Margaret remembered now reading in the forensic notes that the clay had originated in Shaanxi Province. But she had never made the connection with Xi'an. There had been no reason to, until now. 'How soon can you tell if it's the same as the other samples found in the Yuan Tao murders?'

'Oh,' he said cheerily, 'it quiet today. No problem. Couple hours, maybe. I can do low power analysis with stereo microscope, and maybe density gradient analysis. Even mineralogical profile if you want. You wanna wait?'

She glanced at her watch. 'I can't.' She thought for a

moment. 'Could you phone Deputy Section Chief Li with the results?'

'Sure,' he said. 'No problem.' He grinned. 'You clever lady, Doctah Cambo. You should come and work for Chinese police.'

She smiled. Not a chance in hell, she thought.

Her taxi dropped her at Silver Ingot Bridge. The corner grocery store was doing good business, and the paths that followed the contours of the lakes were dotted with couples and families out for a Sunday stroll. It was, at least, a day of rest for some. Margaret walked briskly along the south shore of Qianhai Lake, past decaying single-storey brick dwellings, and into the quieter leafy lanes that led to the Lotus Flower Market where Sunday crowds would already be gathering round food stands to buy plates of boiled pig's intestine garnished with coriander. But Margaret turned off before she got there, through an arched gateway that led into Mei Yuan's *siheyuan*. She had been entirely preoccupied with thoughts of the dust of aeons gathered in her shoes, found in a dead man's apartment, scraped from the clothing of a murder victim. If the samples matched, then the only thing that connected them was the clay used to mould the Eighth Wonder of the World – the thousands of pottery soldiers fired in 220 BC to guard the underground burial chambers of the First Emperor of China. It was baffling. Margaret could make no sense of it.

Xinxin shrieked and rushed out to greet her in her slippers. She had been standing waiting at the door ever since breakfast. Margaret gave her a big hug and took her hand and led her indoors where Mei Yuan greeted her with a wide smile. 'She is very impatient,' she said. 'I could hardly get her to sleep last night, she was so excited that you were going to take her to the playpark today.' Her smile faded. 'You are not really leaving Beijing?'

'I'm afraid so,' Margaret said, shrugging off her embarrassment.

'There is trouble between you and Li Yan, I think,' Mei Yuan said.

Margaret just nodded. She wasn't about to elaborate. And then she felt Xinxin tugging at her arm. She turned and found her staring up with wide, sparkling eyes, and chattering rapidly.

'She's asking you to hurry up,' Mei Yuan said with a grin. 'She says she's been waiting for hours.'

Margaret took Xinxin's hand. 'Come on, then,' she said.

'Just a minute.' Mei Yuan stopped them. 'She's still in her slippers. Her trainers are by the door. She needs help with the laces.'

'I'll do it,' Margaret said, and she squatted on a low stool by a collection of shoes that Mei Yuan kept to the right of the door. Xinxin's trainers were tiny, smaller than Margaret's hands, and Margaret thought how expensive it must be to keep her in shoes she was constantly outgrowing but never wearing out. As she lifted the left shoe, she saw the traces of blue dust on the floor, dark like a stain on the pale green lino, and she felt all the hairs on her neck and arms stand up.

Xinxin dumped herself on Margaret's knee, urging her to

hurry up, but Margaret was hardly aware of her. She turned the trainer over and saw the blue-black dust ingrained in the tread. The other shoe was the same. Confusion swept over her in waves. Now this really did not make sense. Xinxin had not been to Xi'an.

'What's wrong?' Mei Yuan looked at her, concerned.

Margaret said, 'When did Xinxin last wear these?'

Mei Yuan frowned, perplexed by the question. 'Yesterday,' she said. 'They're the same ones she was wearing when she was out with you and Li Yan.'

Margaret simply could not get her brain to function. It seemed to be adrift on a sea of extraneous thoughts. Where had they been? She looked at the soles of her own shoes. When she had found the residue in the treads of the trainers from Xi'an, she had put on the same shoes she had been wearing yesterday. But there was no trace of the blue dust. And then she remembered. Of course, there had been a downpour last night. She had run off from here through wet streets in search of a taxi. Whatever residue might have been trapped in her treads would have been washed away.

So, where *had* they been?

She tried to focus. They had been in the Jeep. At Section One. At the university . . .

'Jesus,' she said aloud. Xinxin and Mei Yuan were staring at her apprehensively. At the university they had been in the conservation lab, in that dirty, dusty room where they restored and preserved ancient artefacts. Professor Chang had apologised for the mess. *We've been restoring the ancient treasures of*

China in here for decades, he had said. *I guess it just never seemed all that important to clean up behind us.* Professor Yue had worked there too. And it was on his trousers and shoes that they had first found the residue of blue dust.

Margaret became aware of Xinxin pulling at her hand, her voice whining at her in disappointment. She dropped the tiny shoes, slipped Xinxin from her knee and stood up, her face flushed with confusion and excitement. 'I'm sorry. Mei Yuan. Apologise to Xinxin for me, but I can't take her now. I'll come back later. I have to go to the university.'

The stone lions guarding the west gate seemed to glower at Margaret as she slid from the back seat of her taxi. Of the three huge, studded doors between the columns of the gate, only the centre one remained open. The other two were firmly shut. The uniformed guard watched Margaret approach and she wondered how she was going to explain to him why he should let her in without a pass. But as she got closer she recognised him as the guard who had let them by yesterday. He recognised her, too. Perhaps he remembered that she had been accompanied by a senior police officer, for he waved her through. She smiled, and like Alice through the looking-glass, she slipped from one world into another.

The gardens and lakes and pathways of the campus were virtually deserted. Willows drooped along the water's edge in the breathless heat of the morning. The occasional student meandered by on his bicycle. She crossed a stone bridge over still water and saw the white-painted pavilion of the archaeology department shimmering beyond its lawns, partially obscured by trees. She was certain that the lab assistant had led them east to the Arts building, past the administration centre, around the edge of Lake Nameless, but there were so many paths she was not sure which one to take.

It was a full fifteen minutes before finally, close to despair, she found what she was looking for. All the paths and pavilions looked alike. But she had recognised the two dusty greybrick blocks immediately. The plaque by the door of the west building revealed it to be the College of Life Sciences, confirming that the building opposite was the Arts building, housing the archaeology labs. The courtyard, filled yesterday with bicycles and students, was quite empty and eerily quiet. The air was heavy with the hum of insects and she could hear birds singing in the trees beyond. Somewhere away in the distance she heard a girl call out a greeting, and even more distantly a boy returning it. The Life Sciences building seemed to be locked up. The Arts building, too, appeared deserted, its rust-red doors closed and forbidding.

Margaret climbed the three shallow steps to the entrance and pushed the right half of the door. It was firmly bolted. She pushed the other half and it swung in to a dark interior. Tentatively she stepped inside, moving slowly across the tiles until her eyes adjusted to the gloom. The corridor, which ran up the centre of the building, had no windows and was very dark. The distant sunlight that bled into it from the glass around the main door barely lit its length. But halfway up, a single slash of bright light fell across it from an open door, and as she approached it, Margaret saw that it was the door to the conservation lab where she and Li had interviewed Professor Chang.

'Hello,' she called out, and her voice seemed inordinately loud as it reverberated back at her along the corridor. But there was no response. She reached the conservation lab and pushed the door wider. It creaked open. Sunlight sliced through Venetian blinds in narrow strips that distorted uniformly across the contours of the room. 'Hello,' she called again. But there was no one here. The sword that Professor Chang had been restoring was still held tightly in the jaws of a vice on the big central workbench. The room was as dirty and cluttered as she remembered it. She took a small, clear plastic bag from her purse, then laid her purse on the table and crouched down to examine the dust on the floor. Here, there were wood shavings and a kind of sandy grime. She moved around the room to an open area of floor and saw that it was thick with the blue powdery dust. She crouched down again and ran a pinch of it through her fingers. It looked and felt like the same residue that had gathered in the treads of her shoes in Xi'an. She scooped as much as she could into the plastic bag and stood up again.

She had come round the far side of the central workbench, and saw now that it had been moved forward, towards the door, sliding on some kind of mechanism that was bolted to the floor. Beneath it, the lid of a large hatch in the floor stood open, and wooden stairs disappeared down into the lit interior of some kind of basement. For the first time, Margaret began to feel apprehensive. She edged closer to the opening and peered down. 'Hello,' she called. But there was no reply, just the smell of cold, damp air rising to greet her, like the musty, fetid stink of the tunnels of the Underground City.

She hesitated for a long moment before her curiosity got the better of her, and she slipped the plastic bag into her pocket and carefully tested her weight on the wooden stairs. They seemed pretty robust, and she tentatively went down into the large, square chamber below. The walls here were stippled with rough-cast and stained with damp. A single light bulb hung from the ceiling, and a cable fed off along the curved roof of a tunnel that was illuminated by a lamp every fifteen or twenty yards. A metal gate at the opening of the tunnel stood ajar. Again she called, and again there was no reply.

She was tempted simply to turn and climb the stairs back to the conservation lab and hurry out into the warmth and safety of the sunshine outside, when she noticed the brown, crusted smear on the floor. She crouched to look at it more closely. It was blood. Old blood, turning grey-brown. Several weeks old. She looked up and saw that there was a trail of it leading from the tunnel, as if a bleeding body had been dragged into or out of it. Now her apprehension was turning to fear. She felt the chill of the air in her bones. But she was drawn, inexorably, both by her fear and her curiosity, into the tunnel, to follow the trail of dried blood. She made her way carefully along it, keeping a hand always on the wall. It grew colder, her breath billowing in clouds around her. She could see no more than ten or fifteen feet ahead in the mist of dampness. She felt, for all the world, as if she were back in the tunnels of the Underground City, making her way towards the old Beijing Railway Station. As she went further, she saw that the blood had spilled more freely on the rough concrete floor, and she realised she was getting closer to the point of trauma.

Then, out of the mist, she saw that the tunnel opened out into a large, vaulted chamber. Her eyes were drawn to the blood on the floor. There was a huge pool of it there as she entered the chamber, and she recognised the distinctive cast-off patterns that had been flung from the sword delivering the fatal stroke. She looked up and let out a tiny cry of fright as she saw rows of figures standing watching her silently in the gloom. And then the lights went out and she was plunged into total darkness.

II

Li stood smoking by the window. His mind was numb, disabled, it seemed, by some kind of mental inertia. There was a part of him that simply did not want to think about any of it: Birdie's 'confession', the inconsistent evidence, the intruder who had attacked him at Birdie's apartment, Chen's instruction to close the case. Most of all, he did not want to think about Margaret: that she was leaving tomorrow for good, that she would even consider marrying Zimmerman. So he filled his head instead with smoke, and gazed emptily at the trees below obscuring the All China Federation of Returned Overseas Chinese.

Qian knocked and poked his head around the door. 'Boss, I've got someone downstairs in the interview room I think you should see.'

Li did not even bother turning to look. 'I'm not seeing anyone right now,' he said.

'I think you'll want to see this guy,' Qian persisted. 'It's Birdie's friend, Moon. The one who couldn't give him an alibi for Monday night.'

Moon was a shrunken little man with a completely bald head and a small round face. He wore a shabby grey suit over an open-necked white shirt with a collar frayed and ringed with grime. He sat, legs crossed, on the chair where Birdie had sat only yesterday pleading his innocence. A hand-rolled cigarette had burned down to nicotine-stained fingers. He was pale, and agitated.

'Well?' Li barked at him as he came into the interview room.

Moon glanced nervously at Qian who nodded and said, 'Just tell him what you told me.'

Moon looked apprehensive. He took a final draw on the stump of his cigarette, stood on it, and then started rolling another. It gave him something to look at rather than meet Li's eye. 'I heard what happened,' he said. 'I just wish I had come last night. Now it's too late.'

'Too late for what?'

'I screwed up. I don't know why. We always played checkers on a Tuesday night, me and Birdie. And we did move it to a Monday night one week because I had a cousin coming in from the country on the Tuesday. Only for some reason, I thought it was the week before last. I was sure it was.' He looked up, finally, at Li, his moist eyes appealing for under- standing. 'I don't know . . . I forget things these days. It wasn't until my cousin phoned yesterday that I realised. If I'd known it was so important . . .' His voice trailed away and he looked down again at his roll-up to hide his tears.

'What are you saying?' Li asked.

Moon lit his cigarette. 'It was last Monday we played, just like Birdie said. Down on the wall at Xidan. Till late. Then he came back to mine for a beer. Didn't leave till the early hours. So whatever it was you thought he did, it couldn't have been him. I swear on the grave of my ancestors.'

Qian chased after Li along the top corridor. 'What do you mean you're not going to do anything about it?'

'Chen doesn't want to know.'

'And that makes it right?'

'No it doesn't!' Li turned on Qian, annoyed that this cop, his senior by several years but his junior in rank, should think that Li was in any way happy about it. 'All Moon's alibi does is confirm what I already knew. Chen didn't want to know before, he's not going to want to know now.'

Qian looked at him and shook his head. 'Meantime, who- ever did it is still out there. And you're going to let them get away with it?'

Li gasped in frustration. He knew Qian was right. 'No,' he said despondently. There was no way his sense of justice would allow him to do that. But it would mean a fight, and right now he did not know if he had the heart for it.

'Li!' Chen's voice reached them down the corridor, and they turned to see the Section Chief hurrying towards them. 'Take a couple of officers and get out to the airport.'

'Chief,' Li said wearily, 'there's been a development on the Yuan Tao case.'

'Now, Li!' Chen said, as if he hadn't heard. 'We've got an emergency out there.'

Li glanced at Qian. 'I'm sorry, chief, I'm not going anywhere until we discuss the Yuan Tao case.' Chen was stopped in his tracks. There was no way he could ignore this direct challenge to his authority. Li went on quickly, 'There was a mix-up over Birdie's alibi. The guy he said he was playing checkers with? The one who said he wasn't? He got his weeks mixed up. He just came in to tell us he realised he was with Birdie that night after all. There's no way Birdie could have killed Yuan.'

In the presence of Qian, it was impossible for Chen to ignore this. He paused for a moment, looking dangerously at Li. At length, he made a decision. 'We'll talk about it when you get back from the airport.'

Li's frustration bubbled over. 'What the hell are we going to the airport for? That's the jurisdiction of the aviation police.'

Chen kept his temper in check. He said evenly, 'A large shipment of Terracotta Warriors, destined for a touring exhib-ition in the United States was being loaded into the hold of a cargo plane at the Capital Airport this morning. There was an accident with one of the forklifts. A packing case containing a warrior fell twenty feet on to the tarmac, breaking open and smashing the contents.'

Li frowned. 'I don't understand. What's that got to do with us?'

'There were two warriors in the packing case,' Chen said.

'So?' The penny still had not dropped.

Chen sighed. 'There was only supposed to be one.'

Li's counterpart in the aviation police based at Capital Airport was a man of medium height, hair swept back and plastered to his skull with some kind of scented hair oil. Deputy Section Chief Wei was perhaps thirty-five years old. He wore a white shirt with jeans and sneakers, sported three rings on each hand, and wore a chunky chain bracelet on his right wrist. He reeked of aftershave. He gave Li an oily smile and shook his hand and introduced him to his subordinate officers, one of whom was in uniform. Li, in turn, introduced Wu and Qian. Formalities over, Wei slid open the door of a Toyota people carrier that would take them out on to the tarmac.

It was a long drive across the apron to where the cargo plane sat shimmering in the heat. Behind them, the old and new terminal buildings had receded into the hazy distance. Ahead of them, a truck and a forklift were parked by the open hold of the aircraft. There were several police vehicles and at least two dozen uniformed officers and several other individuals in civilian clothes. The airplane had been completely ringed off by yellow and black striped tape that fluttered and bowed in the hot breeze that blew unfettered across the runway. The people carrier pulled in beside the aircraft, and the investigating officers from Beijing stepped out into the breeze, negotiating the tape and moving towards the centre of interest – which was a large wooden crate split open by the impact of its fall. Thick protective wadding, which had failed to protect the contents, had sprung free. The shattered remains were spread all around it. Shards of pottery warriors that had survived more than two thousand years only to end up smashed to pieces on the apron of a Beijing airport. Two heads were clearly visible, one of them split completely in half.

'Who's in charge of this stuff? Li asked.

A middle-aged man in a suit and wearing sunglasses stepped forward to shake Li's hand. 'Jin Gang,' he said. 'Head of security at the Terracotta Warriors Museum in Xi'an.'

'You supervise the packing?'

Jin nodded. 'There are five of us accompanying the exhibition. My deputy, an archaeologist and two researchers, all from the museum. We were all present when the warriors were packed.'

'And only one went into each case?'

'That's right.'

'So how come there are two in this one?'

Jin crouched by the broken crate and pulled away several strips of side planking. 'See for yourself,' he said. 'There's a false bottom. The second warrior was already inside when the crate was packed. We've checked the rest.' He nodded towards the stacks of crates half unloaded from the truck.

'They are all the same.' He paused. 'Two go out. Presumably just one comes back.'

Li squatted beside him, looking at the splintered packing case. He picked up a piece of broken pottery and frowned. 'Are they genuine?'

Jin glanced up at an elderly man who was leaning over and watching every move. The man nodded to Li. 'I am Yan Shu,' he said, extending his arm to shake Li's hand. 'The senior archaeologist at the Museum. They are all genuine Terracotta Warriors, Deputy Section Chief. There is no doubt about that.'

Li looked up at the faces ranged around him and looking down at him expectantly. 'Well, where the hell did they come from?'

No one said anything. The wind was increasing in strength, whistling around the undercarriage of the huge metal bird that loomed over them.

'Well, who made the crates, then?'

'A packing company in Beijing, in Haidan District,' Jin said, getting stiffly to his feet. 'But they were commissioned by the organisers of the exhibition, not by the museum.'

Li rose, too. 'So who are the organisers?'

'An American company. The Art of War, Inc. It's a dedicated company, set up by the Americans to organise the exhibition to go with the documentary series.'

'What documentary series?' Li felt like he was wading through a sea of ignorance, the answers to which, apparently, seemed obvious to everyone but him. He glanced at Qian, but he just shrugged.

'Michael Zimmerman's *The Art of War*,' Jin said. 'It starts screening in the United States next month.'

Li felt the skin on his face and neck tingling as it tightened, and in spite of the heat he shivered as if someone had just stepped on his grave. 'What's Michael Zimmerman got to do with this?'

Jin said, 'He's organising the exhibition. The Art of War, Inc. is his company.'

The twin towers of the China World Trade Centre, where Michael Zimmerman had his apartment on the twenty-second floor, towered over the east end of the city, reflecting the warm autumn sunlight. The head of residential security had carefully scrutinised the search warrant issued by the office of the Procurator General, before riding up in the elevator with Li, Wu, Qian and several uniformed officers. Service staff had confirmed that Michael had not spent the night in his apartment. But Li already knew that.

The security man unlocked the door and opened it on to a world of luxury beyond the experience, or even the wildest dreams, of most of Li's officers. There was a vast expanse of thick-piled wall-to-wall carpet, a luxurious white three-piece suite, a beautiful beechwood dining suite with matching coffee tables and bureau. A huge colour television stood on a white semi-circular stand with a video recorder on the shelf below. There were video tapes piled on the floor all around it. Fine, framed prints hung on cream walls, and wall-to-ceiling windows looked out on spectacular city views. The windows were draped with tastefully patterned curtains that could be drawn, when required, on a world where hundreds of feet below, whole families lived in single rooms. One door stood ajar, leading to a Western brand-name fitted kitchen with every possible appliance and convenience. Another led to a fitted bathroom with a circular sunken bath and a separate shower cabinet. The taps were gold-plated. A master bedroom with fitted wardrobe and king-size bed had an en-suite dressing room.

The detectives stood looking around for several moments in awe. It was hard to believe that such luxury could exist cheek by jowl with the comparative poverty of the people who lived all around it. Li wondered what must go through the minds of those who cleaned and serviced these apartments, returning at the end of the day to crumbling *siheyuan* homes, or tiny apartments in state-built blocks where communal heating was not turned on until mid-November, when the frost was already lying thick on the sidewalks.

He turned to the security man and told him he could wait outside. When they were on their own, Li said to his officers, 'We don't know what we're looking for, so we'll look at everything. But go carefully, we're on diplomatically sensitive turf here.'

A saxophone lay discarded on the bed. Rows of Italian suits and designer jeans hung in the wardrobe. There were more than a dozen pairs of shoes on the rail beneath them. Drawers were filled with name-labelled tee shirts and boxer shorts. The bathroom cabinet was well charged with brand-name soaps and shower gels: Yves St Laurent, Paco Rabane.

From the moment he had stepped into the apartment Li had been vaguely, almost subconsciously, aware of a low-pitched scent that hung in the air. It was very background, and it was not until he walked into the bathroom and it became stronger, rising above the scents of soaps and shampoos, that he became properly conscious of it. He tracked it down to a small, brown bottle with a screw cap that was squeezed into a corner of the bathroom cabinet. Li unscrewed the cap and sniffed the sweet, pungent smell of the essential oil it held. He looked at the label. Patchouli. He knew immediately it was what he had smelled in both of Yuan's apartments. Very faint, barely registering. And he realised now that the strange sense of something familiar that had always haunted him around Zimmerman was that same scent of Patchouli. Never strong, but always there, somewhere just beyond consciousness. He cursed himself for not being aware of it before. While it had promoted an uneasiness somewhere at the back of his mind, it had never made the leap to the front of it.

But now he knew that Zimmerman had been in Yuan's embassy apartment, and the one he had been renting secretly in Tuan Jie Hu Dongli. Probably on the night Yuan had been murdered. Something turned over inside him, and Li realised with a shock that there was a strong chance that Margaret could be in danger.

He went back into the main room as his officers sifted through Zimmerman's personal belongings. Wu, sunglasses pushed back on his head, was examining the piles of videos stacked on the floor around the TV cabinet. 'This guy must watch a hell of a lot of movies,' he said. Li took one of the boxes from him and read the label.

'They're rushes,' he said.

'What's that?' Wu looked at him uncomprehendingly.

'VHS copies of the stuff Zimmerman's been shooting out on location. Presumably he looks at it each day when he gets in at night.'

'*If* he gets in at night,' Wu said with a raised eyebrow.

In spite of the fact that none of his detectives knew about the relationship between Margaret and Zimmerman, Li felt himself blushing.

But Wu didn't notice. He was too concerned with trying to get one of the tapes to play. Finally he got a picture up on the screen of extras dressed as peasants, storming the square below the stele pavilion at Ding Ling, and Li recognised the setup he had witnessed out on location two days earlier. A big, red-bearded face beneath a baseball cap ballooned into shot. 'OK, cut,' said the face, and its owner ran a finger horizontally across his throat. The picture slewed haphazardly across the square before dropping to an out-of-focus shot of a piece of ground and then cutting to black.

Li didn't know what he hoped to find here. He had no idea what Zimmerman was involved in, or to what extent. But he did not have high expectations of something incriminating simply dropping into his lap. He crossed to the bureau. A micro-hifi sat on top of it, and there were a dozen or more CDs on the shelf. He flipped idly through them, curious about Zimmerman's taste in music. They were nearly all jazz, and a few classical collections. Verdi, Mozart, Bach. And, incongruously, one collection of sentimental love songs by Lionel Ritchie. He wondered what it was that had attracted Margaret to him. Li had taken an immediate and instinctive dislike to Zimmerman the first time they had met at the Sanwei tearoom. But then his view of him had been clouded by a jealousy he neither wanted nor could control. Now that Zimmerman was a suspect in both a murder investigation and an attempt to smuggle priceless artefacts out of the country, Li's feelings towards him were coldly professional.

'Hey, boss,' Wu said. 'Look at this.' And he held up a tape. Li crossed to have a look at it. 'Why do you think he's got a security tape from Beijing University? What's the Fourth Chamber?'

Li snatched the tape and examined it. It was a labelled tape from an internal video security system at the university. Written on it by hand were the words, *Fourth Chamber*, and it was dated *September 14th*. Li repeated the date aloud. 'September fourteenth . . . Should that date mean something to us?' Wu shrugged.

Qian said, 'We found Professor Yue's body on the fifteenth.' Li handed the tape back to Wu. 'Put it on,' he said.

Qian drew the curtain on the window behind them to stop sunlight reflecting off the screen, and all the officers gathered around to watch. The picture flickered and jumped as a fuzzy black and white image came into focus. The lighting was poor, and it was difficult to tell what they were looking at. There was no soundtrack. There appeared to be rows of dark figures standing still in the background. But then almost immediately a moving figure came into shot, emerging from the bottom of the screen, from below the camera. It was the hunched figure of a man, staggering as he was pushed forward by a more erect figure following behind. As they reached almost centre screen, the second man forced the first one to turn and then pushed him to his knees.

'Shit,' Wu said. 'That's Yue Shi, Professor Yue. Look, his hands are tied behind his back.'

And they saw, also, the placard hanging around his neck and could clearly read the name, *Monkey*, upside down and scored through, below the number 4. The professor seemed to be weeping. The other man, whose face they still could not clearly see, appeared to be talking to him and looking around. And then he turned, so that he was almost facing the camera. Li had known, from the moment the figures stumbled into shot, who they were. But it was still a shock to see Yuan Tao turning towards the camera, his face triumphant, almost gloating. The last time Li had seen him was on the autopsy table.

Yuan raised something from his side, and they saw that in his right hand was his executioner's sword, the bronze replica that he had commissioned from Mr Mao in Xi'an. The professor made a half-hearted attempt to get to his feet, but Yuan pushed him down again. He was easy to manipulate under the influence of the flunitrazepam. Yuan put his hand on the back of Yue's head and pushed it forward, then he stood back, adopting a position, legs astride, slightly behind his victim and to his left. He placed the blade of the sword briefly on the back of the professor's neck, and then in one swift and expert movement, he raised it high over his head and brought it down to send the professor's head spinning away across the floor.

In Zimmerman's apartment there was a collective intake of breath, six men watching in horror as the headless body of Yue Shi fell forwards and sideways, blood spurting from the severed carotid arteries. Yuan stepped back, took a rag from his pocket and drew it swiftly along the length of his sword, then seemed to look behind him again at the rows of silent witnesses.

Li said, 'No wonder they knew how to replicate the murders. They had the whole thing on tape.'

One of the uniformed officers made a dash for the bathroom, hand over his mouth.

'What's Yuan doing?' Wu asked in a hushed voice. 'What are those figures he's looking at in the background?'

Li picked up the remote control and pressed the *pause* button. The picture flickered momentarily, and then held in a perfect freeze-frame. Li leaned forward to try to make out what it was in the background. 'In the name of the sky,' he whispered. 'They're Terracotta Warriors.'

Margaret stood shivering among the silent figures. She was not certain if it was the cold or her fear that made her tremble so violently. In the momentary glow of the pinpoint of red light that flashed at regular intervals overhead, the faces of her companions took brief form in the dark and then plunged again into blackness. But their faces were cold as stone, lifeless eyes staring off towards an eternity into which they had been marching for two thousand, two hundred years. She did not know how many of them there were. Dozens perhaps. They stood in hushed rows, one behind the other in the cold and dreadful darkness of this underground chamber. They had had time to get used to it. Margaret had not.

At first, after the lights had gone out, there had been a distant clang of metal and she had called out, frantically hoping that someone would hear her. Terrified, she had felt her way back up the tunnel, inch by inch, one hand on the wall, one probing the darkness ahead of her. She could not remember ever having been so completely without light. The blackness seemed to take form and substance, enveloping her totally. It was frightening, disorientating. She had wondered if this was how it felt to be blind, and thought briefly of Pauper losing her sight slowly, first one eye, then the other. When she had told them her story of the sun rising red over the Yellow Sea and firing the town of Chongqing in the light of its crimson dawn, Margaret had been able to visualise it so clearly. Now she could see nothing, not even in her mind's eye.

Up ahead her hand had touched something cold and wet, and she recoiled with a little scream. After a moment she had reached out again, and realised that what she felt was the cold metal of the gate at the tunnel's entrance. Her relief was only momentary, as she realised that the gate was shut. And locked. Any illusions she may have harboured that she had been shut in here by accident had quickly vaporised. Her fear had turned to terror, and she had made her way quickly back to the chamber where the Terracotta Warriors stood waiting for her, as if it had been their destiny, and hers, to share the darkness of this awful place.

It was some time before she had realised that the winking red light which afforded her the briefest glimpses of her companions, was the light of a security camera mounted on the wall above the tunnel entrance. Was it an infrared camera? Was there someone, somewhere, at a monitor who could see her in the dark, who was watching her every movement? The thought made her feel sick.

Now she squeezed herself carefully among the warriors to crouch down and obscure herself from the camera and huddle, arms around her legs, for warmth and comfort. She wanted to cry. She did not know how long she had been here. But it seemed like a very, very long time.

III

Li slammed down the phone and shouted, 'Wu!'

Wu appeared quickly in the doorway. The office behind him was buzzing with activity.

'Boss?'

'Get down to the Procurator General's office and pick up that warrant for Zimmerman.'

'On my way.'

Qian took his place in the doorway as Wu left it. 'No one

seems to know where Zimmerman is, boss. He's not out on location, or at the production office. He's not at the American Embassy ...'

The phone on Li's desk rang. He snatched the receiver. 'Just a moment,' he barked into it and put a hand over the mouthpiece. He flicked his head at Qian. 'Try that bar where he said he was the night of Yuan's murder. The Mexican Wave. I think it's in Dongdaqiao Lu.' And into the phone, 'Deputy Section Chief Li.' He flicked open his file on the murders and a couple of sheets of paper fluttered to the floor. He leaned over to pick them up.

'It's Mr Qi here, Deputy Section Chief. At the Centre of Material Evidence Determination. Hope I didn't get you out bed.'

'What do you want?' Li was in no mood for Qi's levity. He laid the fallen sheets on his desk in front of him.

'I've got the results here that Dr Campbell asked for. She wanted me to phone you.'

Li frowned. 'What results?' His eyes were drawn by the printed sheets he had picked from the floor. They were in English, two of the pages from the print-out Margaret had made of the *North California Review of Japanese Sword Arts* after she had downloaded it from the Internet.

'The dark blue dust she brought in this morning. She wanted me to run a comparison with the samples you found on Professor Yue and at Yuan Tao's embassy apartment.'

Li was mystified. 'She brought you a sample? This morning?'

'Yes,' Qi said. 'It was a positive match.'

He now had Li's full attention. 'Did she tell you where she found it?'

'Sure,' said Qi. 'It was in the tread of her shoes from when she was in the pits of the Terracotta Warriors in Xi'an.'

But Li barely had time to register this information before a name leaped out at him from one of the sheets of paper on his desk. A name that came several paragraphs below Yuan's, in a list of winners in a minor Tameshi Giri competition in San Diego. It seemed extraordinary to him that they hadn't seen it before. But, then, they hadn't been looking. He felt sick.

'Hello . . . hello . . .' he heard Qi saying. 'Are you still there?'

'Sure.' Li's throat was thick. He knew now who had killed Yuan. 'Thank you, Mr Qi.' He hung up and sat for a moment. A thousand conflicting computations ran through his mind before one of them punched up an answer that sent a chill through him. He became aware that the sheet of paper in his hand was trembling.

He jumped up suddenly, lifting his jacket from the back of his chair, and headed for the door. In the detectives' office he called to Qian to give him the mobile phone. Qian threw it across the desk and he caught it deftly and clipped it on to his belt. 'Keep me in touch with any developments,' he said. 'I'm going to try to find Dr Campbell. I think she could be in danger.'

The playpark was almost deserted. A handful of toddlers played in a sandpit watched by their mothers, who sat nearby on toy cars, smoking and talking. A breeze that stirred the leaves of the surrounding trees rattled the empty climbing frames. A giant Donald Duck, facing a slightly smaller dinosaur, presided over motionless swings and roundabouts. Out on Lake Houhai, the warm wind sent tiny ripples racing across the surface of the water. Li looked around with an increasing sense of anxiety. Margaret and Xinxin should have been here by now. But there was no sign of them. There was a shop in a tiny pavilion on the waterfront selling soft drinks and cigarettes. The proprietress sat reading a magazine. She shook her head when Li asked if she had seen a *yangguizi* with a little Chinese girl. No, she said. She had been here all morning and would have noticed something so unusual.

Li hurried back through a small park, past a garden where a woman in a white coat administered a massage to a fat, middle-aged man lying face down on a table. A few old men sat on benches around a circular flowerbed, staring into space. There was barely a flicker of interest in their eyes as Li ran past them to the *hutong* where he had parked the Jeep. He backed up and drove to Mei Yuan's *siheyuan*.

She was surprised to see him, and he was relieved to see Xinxin. He looked around. 'Where's Margaret?' he asked, expecting that she would come through the door from the other room any moment.

'She wouldn't take me to the park,' Xinxin said petulantly. 'She promised.'

'She said she'd be back later,' Mei Yuan said to her. 'You know that.'

Xinxin folded her arms crossly. 'Fed up waiting,' she said.

'Well, do you know where she went?' Li asked impatiently.

Mei Yuan nodded towards Xinxin's trainers by the door. 'She got very excited when she found some dark blue powdery stuff on Xinxin's shoes.'

Li stooped immediately to look at them, and recognised the blue-black ceramic dust he had found on Professor Yue and in his killer's apartment. He frowned his confusion. This didn't make any sense. He looked up at Mei Yuan, but she just shrugged.

'She said she had to go to the university.'

IV

Margaret felt her fingers and joints stiffening. She had started to shiver uncontrollably, her lower lip trembling with every breath. It was, she recognised, the early stages of hypothermia. She had lost all sense of time now, and realised that soon she would start to become drowsy, comatose. If she allowed herself to drift off into sleep she knew it was a sleep from which she would never awaken.

Stiffly she got to her feet again and stamped them on the concrete floor. She swung her arms in circles around her body to try to get her circulation going and generate the heat that would keep her alive. For a long time she had been afraid of someone coming. But now she would have welcomed it. Anything would be better than dying down here in the cold and dark, simply slipping away without so much as a fight. They were insidious, intangible enemies, the cold and dark.

You could not fight them. Their patience was endless, and would far outlast her will to survive. It seemed ironic that just a few feet above her the sun was shining, warm and bright and full of life. But there was no way she could reach it, or it reach her. And not for the first time did she feel the urge to cry, but fought it back. Tears would be futile.

She had long ago stopped trying to make sense of anything. Her thoughts and her senses had been focused on the need to stay alive. Twice she had made her way back to the gate hoping that she might find some way to break it down or force the lock. But it was solid and unyielding.

She had carefully picked her way through the ranks of the warriors to the back of the chamber. There it narrowed, and two steps led down to the opening of another tunnel. Hope had flared briefly, only to be extinguished by the discovery of another gate, which was also locked.

One by one she had counted the warriors. There were sixty-seven of them, including eighteen kneeling archers. She had felt their features, as if she might find in their faces some expression of comfort. But their cold, hard bodies were icier to the touch than the dead she had dissected on her autopsy table. And now she felt physical and mental control slipping away from her. Fear of death was slowly giving way to acceptance of it. How long could you remain afraid? Fear, like pain, could not sustain itself indefinitely.

But it was fear that returned, like a knife plunged into the heart, as suddenly she found herself dazzled by light. They were the same feeble lamps as before, but their light now seemed blinding after the dark. She screwed up her eyes against the glare until her pupils shrank to bring the light into perspective, painfully restoring her sight. The chamber appeared smaller somehow than it had in the darkness of her imagination. The warriors stood mute and expressionless, unblinking in the sudden light, unmoved by her plight.

She heard the distant clang of the metal door and the scrape of it on the concrete floor. She eased herself back among the soldiers as if they might protect her. A soft footfall echoed along the corridor towards her. She strained in the mist and gloom to see who it was, fear almost robbing her of the ability to breathe. This is what she had wanted. This is what she had told herself would be preferable to dying of hypothermia alone in the cold and dark. Now she was not so sure.

The shadow of a man moved through a halo of light cast by the lamp in the tunnel just beyond the chamber, but it had no definition in the mist, insubstantial and wraithlike. She wanted to scream, but no sound would come. And then the figure stepped into the chamber and she saw Michael's sad, smiling face, and her legs nearly buckled under her with relief.

'Michael,' she gasped. And his eyes flickered among the serried ranks of the warriors until he picked out her face, pale and frightened, among the bold, bearded faces of her protectors. But her relief was momentary, and quickly replaced by a deep chill that had nothing to do with the cold in this place. 'Michael, what are you doing here?' And she was almost surprised by the calm of her own voice.

He shook his head, and his smile was laden with regret. 'I

should be asking you that.' He stepped towards her and she withdrew among the warriors.

'Don't come near me!'

'Jesus, Margaret, you don't think I'm going to harm you!' And there was hurt in his voice that she could believe him capable of such a thing. 'I love you.'

She looked at him and was shocked to see that he meant it. 'So what are we doing here, Michael?' she asked. 'I mean, this is where Professor Yue was killed, isn't it? Right where you're standing. Before you moved the body to his apartment.'

Michael looked down at the dried pool of blood at his feet. He nodded slowly.

'For God's sake, why?'

He looked up again, and there was a light in his eyes. 'It's the final part of the story,' he said. 'The only bit I can't tell. At least, not yet.'

Margaret found herself breathing rapidly, almost hyper-ventilating. Her fear and panic was mixed in equal parts with disillusion, frustration, even anger. 'What are you talking about?'

'Hu Bo's greatest achievement.' Michael sunk his hands in his pockets and moved across the chamber, head bowed as if deep in thought. Then he looked up and his face was alive and intense. 'The building above us,' he said. 'The Arts building. It was the home of the archaeology department during the Cultural Revolution. It's where Hu Bo and several of his colleagues sought refuge from the madness. Here, they could keep their heads down below the parapet and wait until it was all over. Then, in '74, they got word of an extraordinary find in Xi'an. Life-sized warriors fired in clay and buried underground to protect the tomb of the First Emperor. Some of them had been dug up and restored by the local cultural centre. But the authorities in Beijing did not yet know.' He drew his hands from his pockets and spread them out towards her, as if appealing to her imagination to picture what he was telling her. 'Imagine, Margaret, how they felt. What could turn out to be one of the most extraordinary finds of the century, discovered at a time when Red Guards were still roaming China, ransacking museums, destroying the country's relics and artefacts.'

And Margaret realised it was not really her he was addressing, but his audience. This was a story he had probably rehearsed in his mind a thousand times. She glanced up at the security camera and wondered if the performance was being recorded for posterity.

'Hu and two of his colleagues slipped out of Beijing and travelled to Xi'an to see for themselves.' Michael's absorption in his story was complete. 'It was true. They talked to the people at the cultural centre, the peasants who had dug the wells, and persuaded the head of department back in the capital that an exploratory dig was worthwhile. But they would make no big thing of it, for they did not want to attract unwelcome attention.

'And no one paid them any. A bunch of old men, with the aid of a few enlisted peasants, digging holes in the middle of nowhere.' His eyes sparkled and he clenched his fist in triumph. 'But those holes took them right down into what the official team later called the fourth chamber. And, just like the archaeologists who came so soon after, they found that it was empty. Filled with sand and silt.' He paused, eyes wide, breath billowing about him in haloes. 'Except for one antechamber that was crammed with warriors. Nearly a hundred and thirty of them. Perhaps they had simply been stored there, awaiting later deployment. Perhaps they were flawed in some way and had been discarded. We'll never know. But Hu and his colleagues understood the importance of their find. And they knew that it was only a matter of time before the authorities found out what they were up to.'

Michael moved about upon his stage, as if addressing himself to an audience of the very warriors he was talking about. But his eyes were fixed on Margaret, appealing to her to share his excitement, desperate to draw her into his story, to know how it was he felt, how this had all come about.

'The warriors they found had been badly damaged by the collapse of the roof and the walls,' he said. 'But Hu's greatest fear was that the Red Guards would come and destroy them for ever, denounce them as "old culture", proof of the crimes of the "imperialist royalists" of China's past. So they brought in a mechanical digger and simply dug out the whole antechamber, filling crate after crate with earth and pieces of the broken warriors. The crates were shipped back to Beijing by road and stored in a warehouse belonging to the university in Haidan. Then one by one they were transferred to the university itself and secreted down here in the bomb shelter that their predecessors had dug in the sixties.'

Michael let out a deep breath and smiled at Margaret. 'You

see, they thought they were saving them for posterity. But, then, to everyone's surprise, the authorities sanctioned an official excavation, and within a year the thousands of warriors in Pit No. 1 were being uncovered. Hu Bo and the others were trapped by their own good intentions. To admit that they had removed the warriors from the fourth chamber could leave them open to accusations of theft, or worse.

'So they made a pact. They spent the next twenty-five years restoring the warriors they had recovered from Xi'an, piece by tiny piece, down here in what they came to call their own fourth chamber, and upstairs in the conservation lab. Their existence, in fact the very existence of the bomb shelter, was known to only a few. The university authorities who had been here in the sixties had long since been purged. Officially, this place didn't exist. Still doesn't. It was the perfect hiding place for the warriors.'

In spite of herself, in spite of her situation and her fear and her anger, Margaret had been drawn into Michael's story. 'What was the pact?' she asked.

Michael knew now that he had her back again. 'They agreed that whichever of them outlived the others, would reveal the existence of the warriors before he died, so that they could be returned to the nation and their rightful place in the fourth chamber that they had been taken from.

'In 1998, Hu Bo, who by then was the last surviving member, was diagnosed with cancer. He had only weeks to live, and he confided the secret of the fourth chamber to his protégé here at the university.'

'Professor Yue,' Margaret said. Michael nodded. She said, 'Don't tell me, I can guess the rest. He got greedy, right? I mean, down here there's all these Terracotta Warriors that no one else knows about. If he can get them out of the country, boy, is he going to make a lot of money. How much would just one of these fetch in the West?'

Michael spread his hands. 'They're priceless, Margaret. We're talking millions. For the lot, tens of millions, maybe hundreds of millions. And not too many to flood the market and bring down the price. There are dozens of tycoons out there, men who have everything, men who will pay extraordinary amounts just to know that they have a genuine Terracotta Warrior standing in their library or in their study.'

'And so all that stuff about the wonders of history and the science of archaeology goes out the window because you see the chance to make a fast buck.' Margaret had moved now, out from the safety of her towering warriors. She remembered the night she had first met Michael at the ambassador's residence. *The truth is never dull*, he had told her. *That extraordinary mix of human passion and frailty, maybe darkness, that leads to the commission of the crime.* No, she thought now, it wasn't dull. Just sordid.

Michael seemed shocked by the sudden contempt in her voice. 'You don't understand,' he said. 'It wasn't like that. Yue Shi had no way to get them out of the country. When he confided in me I knew I was uniquely placed to do it. I'd organised exhibitions before, my high media profile gave me a lot of clout. But, I mean, it's not as if we were stealing them. No one knew about them anyway. And they'd be just as safe, if not safer, in the hands of private collectors. And the things I could do with the money, Margaret. The projects I could fund without having to go cap in hand to universities and charitable organisations and broadcasters back home. There are excavations all around the world that are just waiting for funding.'

'How noble,' Margaret said. 'And this money, these excavations . . . they're worth killing for, are they? Worth the lives of men?'

Michael shook his head and moved towards her, appealing for her understanding. 'For God's sake, Margaret, that's really not how it was.'

'Don't come near me!' she shouted. And he stopped in his tracks, startled by the fear in her voice and the hate in her eyes. He had lost her again.

He sighed. 'We'd installed a video security system,' he said, almost hopelessly. 'So that none of us who knew what was down here could cheat the others.'

'Whatever happened to honour among thieves?'

He shook his head, ignoring her barb. 'I got a phone call from the lab assistant upstairs. He and the professor had been organising the removal of the warriors, one by one, to a workshop we were renting in Haidan. He was in a hell of a state. Professor Yue had been murdered down here in the underground chamber. The whole thing was on tape. I hurried over and we found the body lying there, decapitated.' He looked down at the huge pool of dried, crusted blood. 'We knew we had to move it or risk the warriors being discovered. We wrapped him in blankets and polythene sheets and took the body to his apartment. It was a bloody affair. I've never seen so much blood.' He blanched at the thought, remembering the detached head, the strange form of the headless body. 'And then I looked at the tape and recognised Yuan Tao straight away. God knows why the professor brought him down here. Maybe he was trying to buy him off, buy his life back. Who knows? The thing was, Yuan had seen the warriors. He knew they were here. We were no longer safe.'

'So you used the tape to replicate his murder of Professor Yue, to try to make it look as if they had both been killed by the same person.'

Michael nodded grimly. 'We didn't know about the other murders until we confronted him at the apartment at Tuan Jie Hu Dongli. That's when we discovered that he'd already killed two other people.'

Margaret shook her head in disbelief. She had thought that she knew Michael. Never in her worst nightmare could she have dreamed him capable of this. 'And you had no qualms about any of it?'

'Of course I had qualms,' he protested. 'But you've got to understand, we had no choice. The smuggling of artefacts out of China is a capital offence. If the authorities caught us we would be executed. And we weren't about to start having a whole lot of sympathy for Yuan Tao. After all, he was a murderer. He'd just killed three people. When the cops eventually caught up with him, it'd be a bullet in the head in a football stadium somewhere.'

His logic was impeccable, but Margaret still found it impossible to empathise. She sublimated her fear beneath a strange professional detachment. 'How did you know that the fourth victim should be numbered with a three?'

He shook his head. 'We almost didn't. But in the apartment, along with the sword, we also found three lengths of silk cord, and three placards already numbered – one, two, three. We realised that he must have been counting down from six.'

'And the drugs?'

'They were there under the floorboards with the rest of the stash.'

'And how did you force him to take them?'

Michael shrugged. 'It was strange. I think he realised that there was not going to be any way out for him, and he almost seemed happy, as if we were relieving him of the responsibility of having to kill again. He suggested the vodka. He said the drug was more effective with alcohol.'

'And it didn't strike you as odd that it turned bright blue?'

Michael frowned at her. 'How did you know that?'

'It's my job, Michael,' Margaret said contemptuously. 'Didn't you think anyone would notice when they cut him open? Did you think he had duped his victims with a bright blue drink?' She almost laughed. 'He was leaving a message for us. A clue. And we had no idea.' She thought for a moment. 'And the nickname. Where did that come from?'

Michael looked perplexed. 'We'd seen the nickname around Yue's neck, and figured we should put one on Yuan's.'

'And you believed him when he told you it was Digger?'

'We had no reason not to.'

Margaret shook her head in frustration. 'We've been so fucking blind!' she gasped. What was it Li was forever quoting his Uncle Yifu as saying? *The answer is always in the detail.* 'Digger,' she said. 'That's you. The archaeologist. Another clue we were too damned stupid to see.' She looked at him. 'So who was it who did the dirty deed? Who was it who actually brought the sword down on that man's neck and cut his head off?'

'It wasn't me, Margaret. I could never have brought myself to do something like that.'

'No,' Margaret said. 'You'd take the money, but you wouldn't spill the blood.' She paused, her thoughts racing, then turned on him. 'And how did the murder weapon find its way into Birdie's apartment?'

He shuffled awkwardly and scuffed his foot on the floor. 'One way or another you kept me pretty well apprised of developments.' He shrugged but wouldn't meet her eye. 'Jesus, Margaret, you told me yourself he was the number one suspect.' He paused. 'And his address was right there among the stuff we took from Yuan's apartment . . .'

He glanced up to see the pain in her eyes. She turned away, tears filling them. Her disillusion was complete. She had trusted him totally. Just as she had trusted the other Michael in her life. And they had both betrayed her. She had never felt so utterly empty before. If she was to die now, then at least it would be an escape from her own extraordinary stupidity.

*

Li walked quickly, half running, through the shaded paths of the university campus. It was deserted in the afternoon heat, the first withered leaves beginning to drift from the trees on the edge of a warm autumn breeze. The guard at the gate had remembered Margaret arriving. But that had been this morning, and he had not seen her since, he said.

Li had first tried the archaeology department, but the pavilion was locked and deserted. Now he was following Margaret's footsteps of several hours earlier, in search of the Arts building.

The afternoon sun slanted across the courtyard in front of the greybrick block, shadows lengthening as the sun slipped progressively lower in the sky. One half of the door stood ajar, and as Li climbed the steps, a young man emerged and almost bumped into him. It was Wang Jiahong, the surly lab assistant who had brought them here yesterday. He was startled, and his face coloured beneath his shock of black hair. He ran the back of a dirty hand across his forehead to wipe away a fine film of perspiration. 'What the hell are you doing here?' he asked. His voice carried more confidence than his frightened rabbit eyes.

'The American lady I was with yesterday,' Li said. 'Have you seen her?'

Wang shook his head. 'Here?' he asked.

'No, in fucking Shanghai!' Li barked. 'Of course, here!'

'No,' Wang said. And there was more than a hint of truculence in his tone.

'Are you sure?'

'Of course I'm sure. There's nobody here but me. And I've been around all day. I'm just about to lock up. You can look around if you want.'

Li glanced at his watch. If she had been here at all, she must be long gone by now. 'No,' he said. 'That's all right.'

Wang stood watching Li out of sight as he retraced his steps towards the west gate. The reflections of weeping willows shimmered on Lake Nameless as the breeze ruffled the surface of the water. A bird swooped low across it, calling as it went, before veering off and rising skyward beyond the treetops. Li felt curiously deflated, and apprehensive. Where had Margaret gone? She had been on campus, certainly, but perhaps she had left by another gate. He took a small notebook from his back pocket, checked a telephone number and then unclipped the mobile from his belt. He dialled Mei Yuan's neighbour and asked her to check if the *yangguizi* had come back yet. After a long wait Mei Yuan came to the phone to say that there was no sign of Margaret. Li sighed and made his way back to the west gate. He asked the guard again if he was certain that he had not seen Margaret leave. If she had left, the guard assured him, it must have been by one of the other gates.

Li was about to turn away in search of his Jeep when he caught sight of a familiar vehicle parked across the road, a vehicle he had seen just two days ago parked outside CID headquarters downtown. The red *shi* character on the registration plate filled him with a sudden sense of dread. And he knew that Margaret must still be here, and that her life was in grave danger.

By the time he reached the Arts building again he was breathless and sweating. The door was still ajar. Wang had not locked it as he said he was going to. Li made his way cautiously inside, down the darkened corridor to where light still fell out across the floor from the open door to the conservation lab. As he moved towards it, he heard a rustle of clothes and a shadow filled the light that came from the doorway. He had no time to move before Wang was upon him, pushing him back against the wall. A pain like a vice encircled his bruised ribs and he gasped, momentarily disabled. Wang sensed the moment, and took off like a sprinter from the blocks, his sneakers squeaking on the tiled floor as he hurtled down the corridor and turned out of the door. For a moment, as Li caught his breath, he contemplated going after him. Then he saw, through the open door, Margaret's purse lying on the workbench in the conservation lab.

Margaret's face was streaked with tears. 'All those lies,' she said. 'All those lines you fed me. And I swallowed them all. What a fool I've been!' She heard her own voice echoing back at her through the mist, like a voice of reprimand. And she began to feel her control dissolving.

He took her by the shoulders and shook her. She was beyond resistance. Almost beyond caring any more what happened to her. 'It's not true,' he said. 'I meant every word. Margaret, you must believe me. I love you. I want you to marry me.'

She broke free and looked at him with disgust. 'Don't insult me, Michael. Don't make me a bigger fool than I already am.'

His despair was patent. 'Margaret, none of this has to end badly. It really doesn't. Nearly half the warriors are already on their way out of the country. We could be rich, you and I. Beyond our wildest dreams.'

She almost spat in his face. 'You make me sick, you know that? You proved to me that I didn't know you at all. And you really don't know me any better, do you?' He stepped towards her and she backed off. 'I told you, stay away from me!'

'What do you think I'm going to do, kill you?'

'No. No doubt it'll be one of your friends who'll do that.' Her tone was acid and filled with contempt.

He shook his head in despair. 'I'm not going to let anyone hurt you.' He held out his hand to her. 'Come with me now. We'll get on a plane and just go. I don't care about the rest of these.' He waved his hand towards the warriors. 'Only about you.'

'Is that right?' she said, and she retreated further, backing into the ranks of Qin's underground warriors. She reached out and pushed with all her strength at the heavily armoured figure of a general. The ancient warrior tipped forward on his base, overbalancing and crashing to the ground at Michael's feet.

Michael winced, almost as if in pain. 'Jesus, Margaret! What are you doing? These things are priceless!'

'I thought you didn't care.' And she pushed again with all her might, and a standing archer followed the fate of his general, great shards of splintering pottery scattering across the floor.

Michael tried to grab her, but she retreated further among the silent figures. 'Don't, Margaret. Please. These things have survived more than two thousand years. They are part of an historical record of the achievements of mankind. Don't harm them.'

And in his sincerity, she saw again that part of him which had first drawn her to him. But she knew it had been corrupted by greed and murder, by that human passion and frailty and darkness that he had talked about the night they had met. His sin had been weakness. And the flaw ran too deep. Redemption was impossible.

'I'll abandon the filming. We'll go to America. When we get there I'll tell the world about what happened here, about the warriors of the fourth chamber. It doesn't matter if they're in a museum or some rich man's study. But we must preserve them. At all costs.' He looked in abject dismay at the shattered pieces of the two warriors lying all around him.

'Very touching.' The voice came out of the mist and startled them both. Michael spun around as Sophie emerged from the shadows of the tunnel holding a gun. Her face was pale and grim.

'How long have you been there?' Michael asked quickly.

'Long enough,' said Sophie. 'Wang called me right after he called you. So I've been treated to the greater part of your little performance.' She turned towards Margaret with a superior smile that carried with it more than a hint of bitterness. 'Good, isn't he?' Margaret stared back at her filled with conflicting emotions of fear and dismay. 'Only, he's not good at all,' Sophie said. 'He got me involved in this. It was he who came running to me for help. I'd have done anything for him, and he knew it.' She laughed at her own stupidity.

'*You* killed Yuan,' Margaret realised.

Sophie flashed her a look. 'Not bad for someone who looks like they ought to be in the second grade.' Her smile was sour. 'Ironic really. I even took part in the same Tameshi Giri competition as him in California one time. He didn't remember me, of course. I wasn't in the same class as him. But I still managed to cut his head off. I did all Michael's dirty work. Even planted the sword for him.' She paused. 'You think you're the fool? Well, I'm the biggest fool of all. Because I thought I could make him love me the way I've always loved him. I even introduced him to you, so that when I suggested to Dakers that you do the autopsy, we could still keep track of things.' She swung her gun in Michael's direction and raised it at arm's length. 'Only the stupid bastard went and fell in love with you. And now he wants you to take his hand and skip the country, leaving me to face all the shit.' Tears filled her eyes. 'Well, no fucking way!' And she fired a single shot that struck him in the throat.

The sound of it crashed deafeningly around Hu Bo's secret fourth chamber as Michael toppled backwards, sending several of his beloved warriors tumbling to the ground with him. Margaret screamed, and her hand shot to her mouth in horror as she saw the blood bubble around Michael's lips, gurgling from his throat where the bullet had severed one of his carotid arteries and smashed through his windpipe. His eyes flickered in panic as the life ebbed from him, his hand clutching hopelessly at his shattered throat. His mouth opened, as if he would speak, but no sound came out of it.

Margaret saw Sophie's shooting arm swing towards her, and caught the light glinting on the tears in her eyes. It was almost certainly those tears, blurring vision, that caused Sophie's first shot to miss. The head of the warrior next to Margaret shattered, and razor-sharp needles of it slashed her cheek. She turned and fled towards the dark interior of the chamber, toppling pottery figures as she went. Another shot sounded, and Margaret heard a warrior explode into the ceramic dust of two millennia somewhere off to her left. Then she slipped on the slimy surface of the floor and crashed down heavily on her elbow. She gasped in pain, and turned to see Sophie looming over her.

Then suddenly, bizarrely, there came the electronic trill of a telephone ringing. There was a moment of confusion in Sophie's face as she turned. Li was about ten feet away. In his right hand he held the sword that Professor Chang had been restoring. His left hand was fumbling to switch off the mobile phone on his belt. But it was all too late. Sophie's face lit up in a savage smile. She fired, and Li spun away to his left, tumbling among the debris of the warriors.

Margaret screamed and staggered to her feet, clutching her arm, almost blinded now by her tears, and numb with terror. She stumbled towards the tunnel entrance at the rear. But she knew it was hopeless. She knew the gate there was locked. And even if it hadn't been, how far would she have got before Sophie caught up with her? She waited for the bullet in her back, almost praying for it to release her from this hell. But it didn't come. She reached the gate and shook it, as if perhaps she rattled it hard enough she could somehow make it open. Then she turned, her back to the bars, and saw Sophie walking slowly towards her. There was a strange, mad, fixed smile on Sophie's face, like the face of a deranged child. She reached Margaret and looked into her eyes for a very long time before hitting her hard across the face with the barrel of her gun.

Margaret was almost blinded by the pain, and the light that seemed to fill her eyes. She felt her legs buckle, and she slid to the floor. She sensed the shadow of Sophie's gun crossing her face, and she looked up to see the barrel of it staring back at her. 'Bitch!' Sophie said, and then her eyes and mouth opened wide, as if in great surprise. And she and Margaret both looked to see the long blade of a bronze sword projecting from her chest. She hung, as if suspended on it, for several moments, before the blade suddenly withdrew and she collapsed like a house of cards to reveal Li on his knees behind her, supporting himself on the sword, his white shirt soaked red with his own blood.

Margaret howled and scrambled towards him on her knees, in time to catch him as he fell. She fell with him, cushioning him against her breast. She managed to pull herself up into a half-sitting position, his head in her lap. Quickly, efficiently, she tore away his shirt, folding it into a thick wad and pressing it hard into the wound high on his chest. Her tears ran freely as she rocked him back and forth. 'I'm so sorry,' she whispered. 'Oh, Li Yan, I'm so, so sorry. I made such a mistake.'

His eyes flickered open and he looked up at her, shaking his head, almost imperceptibly. 'My fault,' he said. 'I was stupid and did not follow my heart. Next time ...' He coughed and flinched from the pain and screwed his eyes shut.

She glanced back through the shadows of the warriors, and saw Michael lying dead in the debris. Poor, stupid Michael. And she knew what it was that had corrupted him most. It had been his innocence, his belief that somehow, like one of his stories, everything could be as simple as he wanted it to be. That stealing what no one knew existed wasn't theft. That killing a man who had killed others wasn't murder. That love could be secured with a ring and a proposal. Her own words came back to her from the night they had shared in the Muslim Quarter in Xi'an. She had said to him, *None of us would ever embark on the journey if we thought too much about where it was going to end.* Neither of them could have dreamed then that he would become the tragic end to his own story of Hu Bo, lying lifeless among the shattered remnants of the warriors of the fourth chamber.

She looked down at Li lying in her arms, his breathing shallow and erratic. She had always loved him. And all she had ever wanted him to do was love her back. 'You know what this means?' she said still sobbing.

He opened his eyes again. 'No. What does it mean?'

'It means I'm going to have to cancel another flight for you.'

He smiled. 'You don't have to cancel a flight just to come to my funeral.'

She laughed through her tears. 'You stupid baby,' she said. 'You're not going to die. I'm not going to let you die. But if I'm not around, who's going to bring you your food in the hospital?'

ACKNOWLEDGEMENTS

There are many people whose help has been invaluable in researching *The Fourth Sacrifice*. In particular, I'd like to express my heartfelt thanks to Dr Richard H. Ward, Professor of Criminology and Dean of the College of Criminal Justice at Sam Houston State University, Texas; Steven C. Campman, MD, the Armed Forces Institute of Pathology, Washington, DC; Professor Dai Yisheng, former Director of the Fourth Chinese Institute for the Formulation of Police Policy, Beijing; Police Commissioner Wu He Ping, Ministry of Public Security, Beijing; Professor Yu Hongsheng, General Secretary of the Commission of Legality Literature, Beijing; Professor He Jiahong, Doctor of Juridical Science and Professor of Law, People's University of China School of Law; Professor Yijun Pi, Vice-Director of the Institute of Legal Sociology and Juvenile Delinquency, China University of Political Science and Law; Ms Chai Rui, Department of Archaeology, Beijing University; Stanley J. Harsha, Cultural Affairs Office, US Embassy, Beijing; Ms Zhang Qian, Xi'an Foreign Language University, Xi'an; Mr Qiang, Director of the Terracotta Warriors Museum, Lintong County, Shaanxi Province; Zhao Yi for her wonderful Mongolian hotpot; and Shimei Jiang and her family in Beijing for their friendship and hospitality.

COMING SOON

THE KILLING ROOM

Peter May

CHINA THRILLER 3

Li Yan and Margaret Campbell travel to Shanghai:
where a new ally, and a new enemy, await.

AVAILABLE IN PAPERBACK
17 NOVEMBER 2016.

www.riverrunbooks.co.uk

COMING SOON

CAST IRON

Peter May

THE ENZO FILES: BOOK 6

The red-hot finale to the cold-case series featuring
Enzo Macleod – from the bestselling author of
The Blackhouse and *Coffin Road*.

AVAILABLE IN HARDBACK AND
EBOOK 12 JANUARY 2017.

www.riverrunbooks.co.uk